May the [...] you
ride in life be
full of adventure.
Best Wishes,
    Peggy Farrell

MAUI SNOW

PEGGY FARRELL

IUNIVERSE INC
NEW YORK BLOOMINGTON

Maui Snow

This is a work of fiction. All of the characters, names, incidents, organizations, and dialogue in this novel are either the products of the author's imagination or are used fictitiously.

iUniverse books may be ordered through booksellers or by contacting:

iUniverse
1663 Liberty Drive
Bloomington, IN 47403
www.iuniverse.com
1-800-Authors (1-800-288-4677)

ISBN: 978-1-4502-4830-3 (sc)
ISBN: 978-1-4502-4813-6 (dj)
ISBN: 978-1-4502-4807-5 (ebk)

Library of Congress Control Number: 2010911102

Printed in the United States of America

iUniverse rev. date: 10/12/2010

With love for Jack and Sally Farrell

PROLOGUE

Liat's Story
Waikiki, Honolulu – 1993

Seven year old Liat (Lee-ott) Kawa scooped a fresh handful of wet sand from the bucket at her feet, dropped it inside the rook of the castle she'd been building for the last two hours, and with careful fingers cemented the final layer into place. Finished, she sat back on her heels and with the steady gaze of a Tibetan monk, surveyed each curve of the circular monument.

It would have to do. Still, Liat was worried about the center tower where her plastic doll, hair twined in tight braids, lay imprisoned.

"Too high," she scolded herself out loud. With a hand cupped over her brown eyes to shield them from the sun she walked around the castle, carefully eyeing the three and a half foot column in the center. "If the tower's too high the king won't be able to save her."

"I'll save the princess!" Boomed a familiar voice from behind her back.

Startled, she turned just in time to see the Seedaso boy standing a short distance away.

He'd been at the resort for nearly two weeks now and it had taken Liat all of about five minutes to see that he was trouble. In her mind she crowned him "The Waikiki Beach Bully" although she didn't dare call him that out loud. At eleven, the boy towered over Liat.

He was in the sand now, just a few feet away. Suddenly the warm patch of sweat that had been trickling down the back of Liat's neck chilled over, making the tiny hairs beneath her ponytail rise. But the warning came too late. With a smirk, Benny pumped his pudgy eleven-year old legs and ran straight at her.

"No!" Liat cried, ducking low in the sand and raising her arms to shield her face. Seconds later Benny sailed his chubby body over her head with his arms spread out like superman and his thick glasses glued to his nose with a glob of sand and suntan lotion. More sand from his belly and feet rained down on Liat as she peeked through her arms and watched, horrified, as he landed a perfect belly flop into the left side of her castle.

"Oooops! My bad," Benny said, dissolving into a fit of satisfied giggles.

"Don't worry. I can fix it." He rolled around the castle then, waving his arms and legs as if he were making snow angels and destroyed Liat's creation beyond repair.

Liat lifted her head only to find Benny's oafish feet dangling in her face. Staring at the destruction laid out in front of her Liat's fear evaporated and her eyes narrowed. Enraged at the unfairness of his actions she retaliated with all of the logic and resources of an angry seven year old. She clamped onto his big toes and started pinching and twisting with all of her might.

"Ooooouch," he cried, squirming under her grip, yet still laughing at what he'd done.

"Sttopppit." Benny couldn't help himself. He let out a fresh round of pain filled giggles.

Liat didn't realize it but her attempt to get back at the bully was actually making the game better for him. More interesting. Because Benny knew what most bullies know. That breaking stuff is fun. Pissing little kids off, pushing them to the brink? Well, that was even more fun. Fighting back was okay too, as long as the victim was small enough. Bullies love tears of defeat. Liat didn't seem to have a clue about that. What she did have though was a really good grip and at the moment *she* was the one pinching the crap out of Benny.

"Cccut it out Liat," he cried, his high-pitched giggles dropping into a growl as the pain intensified.

"Sttoppit! Sttoppit right now or I'll make you sorry. You know I will."

Liat paid no attention. Her castle was in ruins. She had a tight grip on Benny's fat toes and she kept on squeezing. But her hands were little and in the end she didn't really stand a chance against him.

***

At the ripe old age of eleven, Benny was a seasoned bully. To that end he'd chosen his victim well.

For starters he'd spent most of the last two weeks alone at the Outrigger Reef resort, while his mother, Angela, went after husband number four. Benny was supposed to be keeping an eye on his nine-year old half sister January. Instead, he spent most of his time watching Liat. Benny felt confident that for a good part of the day Liat was alone too.

Every morning a dark haired woman dressed in a hotel uniform kissed the girl on the head and then left her at the beach. A few hours later, the same woman returned with lunch. For days the bully had been watching as the woman and the girl ate their packed lunches, talking together and laughing. When they were finished the woman would get up, kiss Liat on the head, and go back into the hotel. Again with the kisses, he thought to himself by the third day. The woman always came back by four o'clock. Happy and smiling and calling the girl's name. Liat, Liat…she would call. Liat…what a stupid name.

Once she was left alone though Benny noticed that Liat spent hours building stuff in the sand. Occasionally she'd walk up to the resort's pool area to get a drink or to talk to one of the adults who handed out the towels or worked the bar. They all seemed to know her. But that was just for little bits at a time. Mostly she stayed on the beach where she would get her bucket, drag it back and forth to the ocean for water, and then make stuff. All kinds of stuff, like fishes and dolphins and sea turtles. One day he even watched her make an entire house. It had bricks and windows on the outside and Liat made a big tree with a snowman that went in front. It reminded Benny of the real snowman he and Jan made once when they visited a place called Massachusetts. He was eight then and his real dad was still alive. Anyway, he had to admit that her stuff was pretty good for a little kid. For some reason that bothered him too. He had no idea why. Maybe it was because the house she made reminded him of a better time or maybe it was because she was too small to be that good at something. Benny didn't know why it bothered him. But it did. And as the building stuff and the laughing and the lunches wore on it bothered him more and more. With lumps of time thrust into his hands like too many sugar cubes, Benny chewed thoughtfully over what he should do about that. Then Liat built that stupid castle.

***

"Give it up kid," he warned, pawing through the sand with his right hand in search of the plastic doll he'd watched Liat stow in one of the big towers she'd built.

When he found it Benny gripped the blond headed doll and raised his arm in the air swinging her triumphantly by a matted braid.

"Let go of me you savage little toothpick," he growled. "Let go of me or I'll rip your little princess to shreds and throw her pukey body into the ocean."

Liat dropped Benny's feet and ran, circling the ruined castle. All that remained of it now was one thick wall of sand about three feet high, flanked on either end by two crumbling rooks.

Liat crouched behind the wall and tried to think. She was determined to get her princess back. She could see the doll above the wall swinging back and forth in Benny's hand. Fuming, she sprang to her feet, reached over, and tried to snatch it back to safety. But Benny was waiting for her. He dropped the doll in the sand and then pulling himself up onto his knees, he grabbed at her wrist. He missed.

"Give her back," Liat demanded from her side of the wall. "Give her back to me and go home!"

"Here she is," Benny taunted, waving the doll over the wall and then pulling her back the second Liat reached out.

"Leave her alone!" Somewhere near the edge of the water an old man yelled a warning at the bully.

Benny heard the man and became angry. He hadn't made Liat cry yet.

"You want it? Take it," he dared, crushing through the wall with his fist and making a giant hole through the center. He bobbed the doll in and out of the hole baiting Liat to grab at it.

Liat crouched in the sand and waited for the doll to come out far enough for her to take a chance. When she did, Benny went for broke. He snatched the doll out of her reach and crashed his head through the hole in the sand, scaring Liat half to death. Baring his teeth he snarled at her like a rabid pit bull and then did his best to bite at her outstretched hand.

Liat yelped, snatching her hand out of harm's way. Benny stuffed his head in farther and tried to snag the bottom of her tee shirt before she could get away. What he got instead was a nasty surprise—one that would stick with him for the rest of his life.

This time Liat didn't run. Something swelled within her. Deliberately, she lowered her tiny frame in the sand until she was nose to nose with the sweaty, barking, bully. An uncommon energy deep and magnetic roiled within her belly. Gaining momentum it spread to her brain, igniting a wealth of neurons previously untapped in the seven year old. Reaching out with both hands she grasped the bully by the ears and resting her palms against his chubby cheeks she locked onto his eyes with a terrifying gaze.

"Pau…Go HOME," she ordered.

Benny's body went numb with the sudden impact of Liat's brown eyes boring through the panes of his thick glasses. He blinked in a desperate effort to break away from her stare. He couldn't. Trapped, Benny's blue eyes began to burn under the energy of Liat's gaze. Her pupils grew large expanding like some strange new universe; the gold flecks in her young eyes pulsing like baby suns, glaring with truth. Truth that was now boring unwanted comprehension into Benny's brain. The kind of truth that bullies, like Benny, rarely choose to face. At light speed Liat shot streams of fear, pity, pain, and power past his thick glasses, past the cool blue of his eyes until it settled deep into the core of his brain.

Unable to blink Benny absorbed Liat's gift. He squirmed as chunks of pain, both his and hers, and that of a thousand others, ricocheted in his head and slammed together, sticking like tiny new planets to the walls of his damaged eleven-year old soul.

The girl's stare was pure torture. The worst of it came as Liat's head shifted and her tears, heavy with both hope and despair, spilled from her eyes and pelted the rim of his glasses. They splashed onto his eyebrows and then dribbled down his nose toward the corners of his eyes. With little choice in the matter Benny absorbed what she offered, his blue eyes growing dark with the effort. When it was over she let go of his face. Dazed and disoriented the bully summoned what was left of his strength. He stood for a moment and stared down at her as if trying to sort it all out. Trying to make some kind of decision. Then he tore off his glasses, dropped them in the sand at Liat's feet, and ran to the water's edge as if the devil himself were chasing him. He waded through the shallow surf then dove headlong into the ocean and swam toward deeper waters.

"Have mercy. Liat girl, you okay? What dat boy do to you?" Asked Toby, the hotel amenities manager.

Liat didn't answer. She was standing now and facing the ocean. With a hand resting above her brows she sheltered her eyes from the sun and watched as Benny threw himself into the surf, her doll still clutched in his fist. Liat sighed. The princess was still in trouble. More would have to be done.

Toby eyed Liat for a moment to make sure she was fine. Then the two stood together and stared out at the ocean. They watched as the boy who'd been pestering her dove beneath the waves. With awkward strokes he swam away from the beach and past the edge of the pier where pairs of red paddleboats were tied to a small dock.

"Dat boy hurt you?"

"I'm okay Toby. You can go now."

"I'd a been 'ere faster but ohhhh dat woman," he said, clutching at his gray head with one hand and motioning with the other toward a bony woman wearing a cream colored beach hat. "She keep me busy, tellin' me da beach mat's too small, and it's too much sun, and no enough ice in her drink." Toby rolled his eyes and circled a finger at his temple. "I tink there's no enough sun in her head, dats what I tink."

Liat shot her old friend a grin of acknowledgement. With life at a resort, complaints were part of the package. At her tender age, even Liat understood that. Some people in this world were infected with the dreaded whine disease and not even a paradise as potent as Hawaii was an adequate vaccine.

"Why no one else step up ta stop that lil' menace, well, I dunno," said Toby, glancing with disapproval at the collection of lotion slathered bodies nearby. At 73, Toby was an old time Hawaiian who expected people to have good sense. To help a child in need.

Toby and Liat stood watching.

"You wan I go git him? Let security haul him off?" Toby asked, even though they could both tell that wasn't a good idea. Doing so might risk Bridget Kawa's job and it was a good job. That wasn't the way to solve the problem.

"I'm okay Toby. The bully's gone. He won't bother me like that anymore." She picked up the old man's hand and gave it a reassuring pat.

"You can go back to work, now," she said, smiling up at her friend. "And you don't need to tell my Mom. She'll worry."

Toby stood by Liat for a moment longer and watched Benny dipping himself head first in and out of the water.

"You sure okay, little peanut?" He asked one more time.

Liat didn't hear him. She was humming a tune now, and playing in the sand. On her knees she plied the old walls of her castle, working the golden soil between her fingers, forming them into a new and foreboding structure.

The old Hawaiian's eyes were…well…they were old. Too dim for the poor man to see what Liat was making. Toby smiled down at Liat's shiny dark head as she worked the sand. A few moments later he shuffled back to his post.

As if in a trance Liat plied the sand through her fingers patting away the old rooks and smoothing it down into a large muscular mound. She added water from her bucket to make the sand hard and with deliberate fingers she fashioned a sharp tail that curved out toward the sea. Then straightening her hand and tilting it sideways she chopped two neat rows of ridges into either side of its body to make a perfect set of gills. She added a fin. Then she added more sand and more water to make the shark's head, propping open its mouth, and fashioning two distinct rows of pointy edged teeth both top and bottom.

Liat worked inside the shark's empty jaws, which faced the hotel where her mother was. She deposited a fresh mound of sand into the shark's open mouth, the sun beating down on her arms and legs as she struggled to get the new lump just so, making the torso plump enough, carefully inching out the right bit of empty space that belongs in the crook of an elbow, mindful not to ruin the shark's teeth she'd just molded as she laid the arm out over them. Liat diligently shaped the fingers of the right hand ever so tightly around the braids of her sand princess. And the head, she worked tirelessly on the head, getting the boy's dark curls just right, carefully fashioning the eyes and nose. When she was finished with the shark, when she had the boy with the doll hanging out over its jaws at just the right angle, Liat sat back in the sand and stopped humming. As she did, her hand fell onto something hot and hard. Benny Seedaso's glasses. Without thinking she slipped them onto his new sand sculptured nose.

Minutes later at 3:10 on that sunny island afternoon a piercing round of screams rang out from the ocean. A shark had been spotted in the water near the resort with a young boy trapped in its teeth.

Unaware of the growing commotion Liat picked up the worn green bucket she'd been using and walked toward the edge of the water. People were gathering there now, standing on the beach, hands covering their mouths, shocked, horrified. There were moans and shouts and pale suggestions as to what should be done, all of course, from the safety of the beach.

Liat walked right past them toward the lifeguard stand as her mother had taught her to do and waded into the ocean up to her knees. She dipped the green bucket into the water and filled it without looking down, staring instead at the endless sea in front of her. When it felt heavy enough she turned back toward the beach, dragging the bucket with her along the bottom of the ocean.

By now the lifeguards were frantically blowing their whistles at the guests and waving them out of the water. Lulled by the gentle waves many of the vacationers had let themselves drift a good quarter of a mile out into the clear Waikiki waters.

Panic saturated the beach. People who'd been peacefully sleeping under the late afternoon sun were jarred awake. Soon nearly everyone was at the water's edge scanning for shark fins and watching frantic swimmers climb out of the ocean. Eventually, a few brave souls waded in to help the struggling find their way out.

It took Liat both hands to drag her bucket back up the beach. She never noticed the salty red water sloshing at her feet. No one else noticed either. They were too busy watching the rescue boats race through the inlet in search of the missing boy.

Lifeguards from the next beach down arrived to lend a hand and the hotel's pool staff made their way to the water's edge, pushing onlookers back to make room for the ambulance now screaming across the beach.

A few feet from the sculpture Liat put the bucket down. She picked up the matching green shovel and used it to dig a round groove out of the sand underneath the outstretched hand of the boy holding her doll in the sand sculpture. When she was finished, she dumped the contents of the bucket into the shallow pool, splashing some of the bloody concoction up onto the sculpture. She stood back, eyes staring blankly. After a moment she went to the bucket, stuck her hand inside and fished around, checking for something. All she came up with though was some wet sand and a few broken shells. Liat picked the bucket up and headed back toward the ocean.

Meanwhile the back doors of the ambulance opened and two medics jumped out and started unpacking supplies. In rapid succession they laid out a stretcher, an I.V. and other equipment. When they were finished, they removed a large chest of ice from the ambulance and placed it in the sand. Then they waited.

Onlookers crowded in as close to the ambulance as they were allowed to get, gawking at the equipment, edging in front of each other to get a better view.

Liat headed back to the ocean ready to dip her bucket in one more time. When she got to the lifeguard stand a blonde haired girl of about nine was already standing there. Liat watched her bend down and pick something up out of the rolling surf. The girl paid little attention to the object, letting it hang limp at her side as she cupped her empty hand over her eyes and stared out into the ocean.

Without a word Liat walked up behind the girl and took the princess out of her hand. There were splotches of blood on the doll and its hair was now a watery shade of strawberry red. Liat didn't seem to notice. Distracted, she fussed absently over a black stone that seemed to be imbedded in her princess' hand. She tried to pry the shiny gem loose but it wouldn't budge.

"Hey! Give it back. That's my brother's," the blonde girl argued. "I saw him drop it. Now it's mine!"

Liat wasn't listening. She'd taken the doll and was heading back toward the sand sculpture.

"Don't walk away from me you little pipsqueak. Get back here!"

Before she could get ten steps away from the bigger girl Liat was snatched under the arms and lifted clear out of the sand.

Jolted by the sudden movement, Liat blinked hard. She was completely disoriented. Frightened, she squirmed, kicking her legs to get free. Then she twisted her neck, glancing over her shoulder to get a better look at who had a hold of her.

"Mommy?"

"Shhhh...it's me baby...are you alright?" Bridget Kawa asked as she headed up the beach toward the hotel.

"Were you in the water? What happened?"

Bridget stopped cold in her tracks when she caught sight of the splotches of blood all over her daughter's shins and feet. She set the girl down and took inventory, searching Liat head to toe for wounds. There were no injuries. Just watery blood stains across her lower limbs. She quizzed the seven year old again.

"Honey, were you in the water? Did you see a shark?"

"Bring that kid back here," demanded the blonde-haired girl in a shrill voice.

"She stole my doll."

Bridget looked down at the plastic doll her daughter was carrying and despite the doll's bloody new hairdo she recognized it immediately. She'd bought it for the girl just two days ago. Besides, Liat's necklace, the one her father had given to her, was wound tightly around its neck.

Bridget picked Liat up again and turned around.

"I'm sorry, honey. You must be mistaken," she told the girl. "This one is Liat's."

The blonde opened her mouth to complain and then stopped. Tilting her head sideways the bully's sister pointed at something in the sand.

"What the heck is that?"

With her lips pressed against Liat's forehead, her arms wrapped safely around the little girl, Bridget Kawa looked in the direction the blonde was pointing and saw the sand sculpture.

"JesusMaryandJoseph," she breathed.

The shark, swishing this way and that, its sinewy lines raised life-like out of flat sand, had its jaws opened wide with a not-quite-all-of-the-way swallowed boy hanging out of it, with his left arm, just above the elbow, dangling between rows of jagged teeth.

Bridget spotted the eyeglasses perched on the sand boy's nose and almost threw up. A boy was missing and those glasses were real. She lowered her eyes, wanting to drag herself away from the awful thing, but instead she caught sight of the sand boy's hand. His pudgy fingers so accurately carved and dripping with watery blood were clutching something that looked a lot like Liat's doll.

Her brain raced. Liat was always carving things in the sand. And she was good. Very good. But nothing like this. Nothing so—there were no words. Bridget stared at it. The shark was remarkably accurate. Way above anything Liat had ever done.

By now the crowd had drifted closer to the lifeguard stand where the bloody water had begun washing ashore in a steady stream.

"Liat, did you see a shark in the water?" Bridget had to ask. "The boy. Did you see him? Honey, do you know who it is they're looking for?"

Then, almost afraid of the answer, Liat's mother pointed at the thing in the sand and asked, "sweetheart, did you see who built...that?"

Liat followed her mother's gaze and looked at the sculpture, half-surprised to see it. As if it might be the first time she laid eyes on it. And yet, knowing...

...something.

She looked back at her mother but didn't answer.

"I wish your father was still alive," Bridget whispered out loud as she set Liat down in the sand.

"Me too," Liat finally spoke as she wandered toward the boy in the sand sculpture and reached out to touch his curls. They crumbled and fell away from his head. "In my dream last night he was so sad."

Liat could see her father flying past the cliff in her dream. His legs and arms spread out into the wind, with all of those tiny black rocks glinting in the sun above his head.

"Daddy said he wants me to look for a Maui snowball. Then he opened his hand and showed me one that was black and shiny. He's so silly, Mommy," Liat giggled as she stuck a finger out and poked at the shark's teeth. "Everybody knows that snowballs are white."

Bridget's knees began to buckle.

"Oh, and Mom? What's a soooonami?"

The wind rushed out of her lungs and she collapsed in the sand next to her daughter. With an effort Bridget Kawa reached past the gruesome sculpture and clamped a tight hand over Liat's mouth.

Hours passed and bit by bit people trudged away from the scene, spreading snatches of the story as they drifted through the hotel lobby, in and out of cabs, around the city, chatting over shrimp and mai tais, discussing details while trading traveler's checks for tee shirts and gift mugs. A missing child they gossiped, a boy...no a girl. Drowned? No bitten unspeakable by a shark. Twins? No, no, it was two great white sharks. Why? You heard twins? Yep. Boy and a girl. Only one survived. Heard the lifeguard say chunks of his arm and nose washed up on the beach. What a shame, heard it was his birthday too. Just turned three. Yeah, can you believe that? Some pervert snatched him just like that. You could hear his poor mother wailing his name up and down the beach. Unspeakable. For days the rumors rolled in and out like that, as relentless as the crashing waves.

CHAPTER ONE

Maui
January 2010

His hand was much paler than I remembered. A side effect, no doubt, of the coma ward's harsh fluorescent lighting and sterile gray walls.

I wanted so badly to lift him up. To grab his hand, drag him out of there. Past the walls. Past the nurses. Outside and into the warm Hawaiian sun. I wanted to run until our feet hit the edge of the surf and we could launch our boards into the Pacific. We'd fight the tide. At least I would. He never needed to. We'd paddle out, laughing, swallowing bits of the sea as it washed over our heads and then we'd fly down blue walls of water. At the end of the day we would let the tide carry us in and drop exhausted into the warm Oahu sand.

I remembered the way he was when I first met him, all kind and mischievous. Not like this. Slack bodied. Eyes closed. Frustration stabbed at my insides, clogging my throat, and I had a sudden urge to pick up one of those stupid pillows stacked neatly at the bottom of the bed and thwack him in the head with it. I pictured him waking up, smiling all lopsided and groggy. So happy to see me.

I squelched the urge. Concentrating instead on his forehead, on that wisp of hair that always seemed to land in his eyes, I did my best to ignore the hum of machinery and the heavy tangle of wires that disappeared inside the bed sheets.

It couldn't end like this. Could it? Not after everything we'd gone through. Liat, Mak, January, Nick, and Kai, we'd all seen so much. Done so much. I couldn't stop what happened. Couldn't change what *I'd* done. Strange that it all seems so clear to me now, that I can feel everything, hear everything. Thoughts as loud as words, details, once frayed and obscure speed through my brain at will now. I see things about all of us. Understand them in a way that was just not possible… before.

I felt a touch on my shoulder.

"You should go home, Willow. There's nothing more you can do here."

CHAPTER TWO

December 2009
Philadelphia, PA

"This better be good Harry," I grouched into the cell phone as I hurried past the corner of 8ᵗʰ and Walnut.

"It's only been two weeks since my escape from the loony bin, and so far, not having such a good day."

I could actually hear him wincing through the phone.

"Keep your voice down. Good Lord, Willow, why do you keep doing that? Saying stuff out loud where people can hear you. You know, Angela went to a boatload of trouble to keep your situation quiet and for some reason instead of thanking her for saving your career you seem bent on ruining it."

"You're right Harry. In fact I should send her a note. But I hear she changed addresses last night. You wouldn't happen to have her new one would ya?"

5,4,3…I waited for the words to sink in. I loved Harry, really I did, and to be fair he was just looking out for me, for my career. But he was so fretful lately that it was getting on my last nerve. He had to have read the front page this morning. He's an editor at the *Philly Chronicle* where we both work. You see, Harry's always up at the crack of dawn making sure he's prettier than everyone else so I know that he had plenty of time to read my story about what happened last night…2…

"Oh geeze, Willow, I'm sorry. That's why I called you in the first place. Shit–Angela and Bill Priest shot dead? You right there on the scene afterwards? It's unreal. Gotta be the last thing you need right now. Tell me, Wil, are you...okay?"

There it was again. That stupid pause. The one Harry keeps throwing into all of our conversations these days. That slight but intense, full-of-crap pause. As if that extended blip of silence was somehow going to magically bloom the truth. Answer his constant question: Is she really herself again? Or is she still crazy.

"Knock it off Harry," I quipped, aggravation getting the better of me. "I'm fine."

"Right, right, Wil, 'course you are. It's just that walking in on a thing like that well...it could be hard on anybody. Especially a friend as good as Angela and so I...I just wanted to make sure that you're alri–"

"God Harry," I interrupted. "You're worse than a damned building inspector." This time *I* paused for effect. "Stop...checking me...for cracks."

Honestly, it was maddening.

"Not to worry," I added, jiggling the crowd of prescription bottles buried at the bottom of my pocketbook. "I've got plenty of meds. Oh, and those swell guys in the white lab coats? Yeah, well, they spackled the hell out of all those cracks in my banged up psyche, just before I booked it out of nuthouse central. Yep, Harry. Packed up those holes real good. Three to five years, guaranteed. So stop worrying." Then, after a moment, and in the most sincere voice I could muster, I added, "I promise not to crumble to pieces in front of you."

"It was not the nuthouse Willow, it was a private...ranch. Really it was more like a spa for overworked individ–

"It was a nuthouse, Harry."

"Shhhhh, Willow, please," he sighed. "It's not...I don't...I'm not trying to drive you cra –bug you," he caught himself and let out an oversized sigh. "I'm just trying to help."

I laughed. I'm not sure why. It just suddenly struck me as funny. Harry; my clear, concise, never at a loss for words editor had been reduced to sounding like Elmer Fudd when dealing with me. It was more than I could take. Especially before coffee. It was either laugh or run screaming. Run screaming was probably the saner choice.

"Go ahead, make fun. I'm just trying to look out for you," Harry responded, his voice petulant. "When I left work last night the front page was a picture of the Ben Franklin Bridge and a headline about some boring traffic study. I wake up this morning sit down to my stack of pancakes and see: **Couple gunned down in Society Hill home.** It was bad enough when I read that it was Angela and Bill but I nearly had a coronary when I saw your byline."

"You sure it wasn't the pancakes Harry? I've tried to warn you about all that butter you slap between every layer. And don't even get me started on the syrup."

Truth? Harry is thin, blonde, and seriously good looking. A regular Calvin Klein model despite the fact that he's within spitting distance of fifty. The pancakes were probably whole grain and thinner than my patience.

"Stop with the jokes, Wil." I could hear the exasperation creeping into his voice.

"Just tell me how you wound up in the middle of a domestic dispute between Angela and Bill Priest."

"That was no domestic dispute," I said quietly. "And I didn't wind up in the middle of anything. By the time I showed up it was way too late. Bill was dead and Angela was barely hanging on. Geeze Harry, did you even bother to read the article?"

"Of course I read it. Then I called a friend of mine down at the precinct this morning to get the latest information, smarty-pants. Turns out they don't think much of your theory about some unidentified person lurking around on the second floor. In fact they're leaning pretty hard in the direction of domestic dispute."

"Well then the detective in charge needs a compass," I grouched. "What about forensics?"

"Not back yet. The preliminary investigation suggests that Bill shot Angela first. They tried to get specifics from her but all Angela did was confirm that it was her fault."

Harry paused.

"You're holding back Finnegan."

It was all business now. Harry only uses my last name when he starts digging around a story.

"Did you purposely leave information out of your article? Come on, we're talking about Angela here. If she gave a statement to the cops before she died then I know she told you more. So why didn't I read it this morning?"

"You didn't read anything else because I don't know anything else. Yet. If Angela knows…knew," I caught myself. "If she knew anything well she was in no mood to share."

My tone was defensive. I couldn't help it. Angela *was* protecting someone. That much I was sure of. The thing is–the reason I was so edgy this morning–what I wasn't telling Harry–is that I was scared to death she was protecting me. You see some of last night's details are a bit too fuzzy.

It's because I get these flashbacks. To Iraq. Stuff that happened while I was on assignment over there. Stuff I don't want to think about. Ever. Besides what I do remember, what Angela *was* rambling about last night didn't make any sense.

"Come on Wils. My guy at the precinct says Angela admitted it was her fault. It's hard to believe she'd keep the details from you. And even if she did that doesn't explain why you left the short version out of your article. It's a direct quote. A deathbed admission for cripes sake. You must've had a reason."

I didn't respond.

"Look, I know what Angela did for you. What she meant to you. Hell, I'm probably the only other person on the planet who understands what a brilliantly twisted heart of gold that old broad had. But she was in the spotlight all the time. Truth is, if she did it, if she admitted shooting Bill, then she would've expected you to print that."

"Really Harry? Would she? I guess she would have expected me to bolt out of there too, with my jeans still drenched in her blood. I suppose she wouldn't mind that I plopped myself in front of the computer to bang out the gory details fast enough to make the deadline. Ahead of everyone else of course. After all, front page is great but an exclusive? Even better. Yep, I'm sure that's what she expected. What are friends for, right?"

"That's the job Willow," Harry said quietly. "In fact that's the very career Angela went way out on a limb to protect for you just a short time ago. Don't underestimate what Angela would've expected. The lady had both feet firmly planted in reality. She would never hold that against you. Hell she would've been glad it was you Willow."

Harry was right about that. It didn't make me feel any better though and I was tired of talking. My mind was a mess with the blood and details. At least the ones I could remember. The thing is, Angela's admission of guilt wasn't the only thing I'd left out of my article. For starters, her four-carat diamond ring was weighing down my ring finger. I twirled it unconsciously with my thumb as I turned the corner toward Chestnut Street.

"Is there anything else Harry? It's almost nine and I really need to get some coffee."

Harry groaned. "Good grief. You're loose on the streets before coffee? Who'll protect those poor unsuspecting souls trying to get a little warmth on top of the steam grates," he tsked loudly. "I just hope to god you're not wearing stilettos."

For an instant I let myself smile. That was my Harry. Wild, outrageous, inappropriate. Hands down one of the best editor's in the business, and the kind of friend who would never miss a chance to make fun of my coffee addiction.

Friends are good. New friends can be really interesti –

There it was again. That odd voice. Echoing in my head. All of a sudden I felt nauseous.

"Hey Harry?"

My head…it was pounding something awful.

"Harry," I forced myself to continue. "Your friend at the precinct. What else did he tell you?"

"Just that Angela must have already had the other pistol in her hand when she was shot. Oh, and Angela's shot? Dead on. Bullet hit Bill about an eighth of an inch above his right eye and blasted straight through his brain. It's crazy isn't it? You think rich people have it all. I guess having a pair of diamond studded pistols worth more than the average house stashed away in your antique end tables isn't all it's cracked up to be, huh?"

"Watch it Harry." I squeezed the sides of my forehead.

"I'm just sayin'. You never really know with rich people."

"You never know with anybody, Harry."

I flipped the phone shut before he could say anything else.

CHAPTER THREE

I'm not claustrophobic. But as I stepped out of the cold December air, away from the comfortable swim of Philadelphians darting toward their gravel-gray caves in search of Friday paychecks, and into the Tenth Street Starbucks, *my Starbucks*, I was struck by a wave of pre-Christmas cheer so warm I thought my lungs would collapse.

It was that time of year again. Those dreaded weeks before the holidays when suburban revelers felt it their duty to converge on the city to go shopping, do lunch, and maybe catch a show. Really, it was barely nine o'clock. Way too early for a working stiff's coffee shop like this one to be crowded with shoppers agonizing over lattes versus espresso. Even worse, they were stopping to chat with each other before actually ordering, clamoring on about the round of upcoming parties that were just not to be missed.

I listened in, annoyed but amazed, as one woman proceeded to quiz the overworked coffee jockey for tips on which flavored syrup would cause the least amount of damage to her hips and butt. She giggled at the Starbucks guy, who, by the way, was young enough to be her grandson. She even made it a point to pat the tight stretch of denim spanning her rear end. He flashed her the mandatory company smile, but his skin turned slightly green and I suspected he might be in need of a bucket. He politely suggested caramel.

It was all I could do to keep myself from shouting from the doorway: Lady, get a grip! That kid is like seventeen. Besides, there's not a syrup on the planet that could rescue those granny jeans.

It was mean and judgmental, I know. Especially considering that my own favorite jeans were rolled into a bloody ball and stuffed into the corner of my closet, right next to the vintage surfboard that I took from Angela's house last night.

Normally I'm not that judgmental. Although psychologically speaking, I suppose the team of shrinks who treated me after I came back from Iraq would have considered my response a step up on the recovery ladder. Truth is before Angela got me to spill my guts about what happened over there (aside from the broken ribs and smooshed left leg) I didn't have much of an opinion about anything.

But Angela is dead. And I can't picture myself sharing that gem of a story with anyone else. Not Harry. Not my large, close knit, Irish family (seven sisters, four brothers). In fact, before I clammed up, they all got the same basic details as the army medics who followed me from Iraq to Germany to the fancy secluded gardens of Nuthouse Central in the Pocono Mountains. As far as they knew, I was embedded with the 186th for seven months. We were behind a tank. Tank hit an IED. People died. No mention was ever made about the Iraqi boy wearing my Led Zeppelin shirt. Or about what happened to my friend Matt.

Angela had dragged it out of me though, and with such sketchy methods too. As my injuries started to heal and my lack of appetite and friendly chatter became more apparent, Angela was the one who very quietly enlisted the headshrinkers. Strong doses of painkillers; that was the excuse they used to explain my lack of communication. Considering my injuries it was a reasonable explanation. Friends and colleagues were respectful.

My family didn't buy it though. They came in numbers and they came often. They pestered the doctors for answers. They did everything they could to coax me back from the brink. When that went on too long, when no progress was being made, Angela convinced them that I needed a new set of doctors and a change of scenery. She promised results. At that point I think they were willing to try anything. So Angela had me whisked off to a remote facility in the Pocono Mountains, complete with windows and a fancy garden. That's where she began her own daily routine of therapy.

Don't get me wrong. She brought in plenty of high priced headshrinkers to analyze me. But every day Angela came to see me first.

9

And I do mean every day. She would come and sit by my bed, always bringing two cups of fresh hot coffee with her. Dancing it under my nose. And she'd talk. All about the coffee. What kind of beans, what part of the world they were grown in, what type of roast, what kind of cream...on and on and on. When I wouldn't talk back she'd drink them both. After Angela finished the coffee she'd talk about Iraq. Insisting that I buck up, tell her what happened. That she'd help me deal. When I didn't respond she'd make up her own awful scenarios. Every day it was the same thing. When that didn't work she had a small coffee roaster and an espresso machine brought to my room...and she stepped up the one-sided conversations. It was cruel, but effective. Way more effective than anything the shrinks tried. What are friends for, right?

Anyhow, you know that saying? The mind is willing but the body is weak? Well it turns out that coffee is stronger than body and mind. Way stronger than mine, anyway. One day I sat up, grabbed the coffee out of her hands, and told her if she would just shut up long enough to let me drink it in silence I would tell her what happened. And to my surprise I did. I started off easy. Telling her all about Matt. How close we'd grown while I was in Iraq gathering information for my articles. Conditions were rough and there was a lot of fear over there but with Matt I always felt protected, slightly outside of any real danger. That is until...well, anyway, he was like a big brother to me. Strong, stoic, but with a funny side too. To keep things light, Matt and I would talk about our hometowns. We spent hours trading stories about the people we cared about. His were mostly about the love of his life, a girl named Bonnie Jean. Of course, stories about Bonnie Jean aren't exactly what landed me, mute, in the nuthouse. Well, not entirely.

After the niceties though, Angela began to push. So I told her about the young Iraqi boy we rescued. About the months Matt and I spent with him. Telling him stories, teaching him 'go fish' and English and math. How to cook. How to hide. Holding him tight when his sister died. I told Angela how Matt and I plotted ways to get the kid out of Iraq.

Actually that was all I planned to tell. Really. But day after day she plied me with coffee. On days when that didn't work Angela tried long hikes through the empty snow capped mountains. It was so quiet up there, almost desolate. Even the deer and bear kept to themselves.

In fact, except for some paw prints and the occasional yawn of a tree branch too heavy with snow, there were almost no signs of life out there at all. It was desolate but peaceful. A far cry from the constant rumbling of humvees, the clack of rifles being loaded and stacked, the thunder of orders, barked and obeyed. There were no broken buildings and no clouds of dirt along those white-mountain walks. No flesh. No blood. Still, Angela *was* persistent. Eventually I caved.

She didn't cringe, not even once, when I finally spilled the gory details about what happened to Matt and me. To the boy. Details that were permanently etched into my retinas and could now replay themselves at will despite the massive effort I was expending to keep them at bay. When I finished she held me until I slept. Then she came the next day and the day after that, coffee in hand. Always with the coffee. Coffee and zero judgment. Angela had that way about her. Me? I can't quite seem to get there. But then again, Angela certainly wasn't your average socialite. I knew that from the second we met.

It was eleven years ago. Not long after I started at the newspaper. I was walking away from an ATM machine, cash in hand, when someone grabbed me from behind. He took the money and my pocketbook then bolted down the street. Angela, with her fresh wet nails splayed in front of her, came waltzing out of the salon. The thief was about four feet away, bearing down on her. Angela stuck out her bright green, four inch heeled Jimmy Choo, and the Purse Snatcher went flying onto the pavement. People crowded around to keep him there. They say she leaned down and whispered something in his ear. I have no idea what she said. Angela never did tell. It must've been good though because when she straightened up, the thief stood up next to her and didn't move. They waited for me. I was running like a loon down the street in their direction. When I caught up to them, the thief, who was really just a stupid kid headed down the wrong road in life, apologized to me. He handed over the money and my pocketbook. Someone started to call the police. Angela stopped them. Then she wrote something on a piece of paper, handed it to the kid, and sent him on his way. As for me? She marched me back into the nail salon with her, sat me in a chair with a cup of coffee, and had me wait while they fixed her nails. I waited. I don't know why exactly, but I waited. Afterwards we went to lunch and became fast friends. It was clear from the get go that she wasn't anything like the rest of Philadelphia's high society. I mean sure, they all do charity work. But Angela was different. She had a habit of getting personally involved. Over the years I watched her very quietly help people that the rest of us don't even notice. I asked her about it a few times but her answer was always a smile. In a way, I guess I was always trying to discover what made her tick. It took a gunshot to the stomach before she finally told me. I felt bad about that. Angela had done so much for me.

I thought about what she said the day before I checked out of her 'garden of enchantment.' It seemed curious to me at the time. She told me, "Willow, stop looking for rocks to stand on, to hold you up. There are no rocks. Just big clumps of earth packed in tight and waiting on an ocean or hurricane or hell even a mist to roll in and change them. Loosen your feet. Learn how to live in the sand, Willow. You'll be safer there. Happier too."

At the time I had no clue what she was talking about. I was just trying to keep the anger and the blood soaked images in check. But her words, the idea, somehow it got stuck in my head. And for whatever reason, it eased the memories. Tuned down the flashbacks to a dull roar so I could get a grip. Learn to keep them at bay.

Of course now they were all gone. Angela, Private Matthew Edwards, the Iraqi boy. They were part of the past, along with my breakdown. I was better now. Really. For sure. Almost as good as new. Unfortunately, there was this one little thought that had been nagging at my brain all morning. If I wanted to *stay* all bright and shiny and good as new again I was probably going to have to figure out what really happened at Bill and Angela's house last night.

No problem, I told myself. After all, most of the night's memories were quite sharp. Most of them. As I shifted from one foot to the other, I felt the prescription bottles rolling sideways across the bottom of my purse. Yep, my brain nagged, I would have to remember every last fuzzy detail.

In my opinion the police department's domestic violence theory was simplistic and sloppy at best. I know what Angela told them. That it was her fault. But she never actually came out and said that she shot Bill. Or that he shot her. I know that because I remember asking her. Frantically. At least a dozen times. I remember she kept staring at me with that funny expression on her face. Telling me, "it's okay, it doesn't matter anymore Willow. My fault…please…not Bill. My fault…don't worry Willow…all my fault."

But it wasn't her fault. I could feel it in my bones, and as near as I could tell, it wasn't Bill's fault either. The guy was a teddy bear and would never in a million years have hurt Angela. He would have been lost without her. I tried to tell the police that. Tried to tell them that someone else had been in the house that night. I heard…I saw… someone.

Someone?

A foot…I saw a foot climbing up the stairs. I heard noises…someone running through the second floor. Just before Angela moaned. Just before I looked down on the floor and saw her there with a spigot of blood squirting out of her side and Bill leaning dead up against the dining room wall. When I thought hard about it, that's what I could remember. That mixed up with dirt and blood and flying limbs from Iraq.

I tried not to worry. Forensics was bound to turn up evidence. Fingerprints. Something. They had to. I just hoped to God it didn't have anything to do with me. Or that old surfboard. I didn't want to take it. Felt in the pit of my stomach that I should have put it back. Shoved it into the back of that closet and left it there to rot. But Angela insisted. And after Iraq, after what happened with Matt…I couldn't let down another friend. Another dying friend.

I was having second thoughts about not telling the police though. I should have told them. It was a mistake not to.

Laughter rang out from the front of the line and I watched as the horny grandma coffee hog finally picked up her caramel latte and moved on. Only six more people to go. I inched forward and let my eyes wander toward the fake fireplace lined with red stockings. I did my best to focus on the white fuzzy parts at the top where the names of the employees were scripted in glitter. Jason, Brooke, David, Sayesha, but it was no use. My thoughts kept wandering back to the night before. Plodding over the bloody details, poking at the scene in my head for answers. It wasn't supposed to be like this. Last night was supposed to be fun.

CHAPTER FOUR

Low key. Girl's night at Angela's house. That's all. Some cheese steaks and a couple of chick flicks. About the only kind of fun I was up for since checking out of the funny farm. Bill was supposed to be at the Union League for dinner, smoking cigars and drinking brandy with some of his architect buddies. Angie and I planned to watch *Ghost* in their home theatre while she spilled the latest in society gossip. Of course I couldn't care less what the high-throned ladies of Philadelphia were whispering about behind their tennis rackets. Angela knew that. That's why she was willing to spill. She considered it harmless fun. Angela was determined to keep my feet planted in normal.

As for me, I had every intention of bolting long before the serious chatting started. Somewhere after the last bite of cheese steak and before Whoopi Goldberg handed that big check over to the nuns. I didn't want to chat. I knew Angela too well, which meant that I knew where the conversation would eventually go. To her other favorite subject. Dating. Angie was always trying to fix me up with one of Bill's uber rich cohorts. Not that I didn't adore Bill, but his friends were a bit long in the tooth. Enduring the torture of a blind date is one thing but having the old fart's 'enhancement' prescription fly off the dashboard and into my lap while he peels out of the restaurant parking lot in his awesome new Jag is altogether something else.

Oddly enough though, as I strolled up the cobblestones to Angela's Society Hill home I remember thinking that with my current life stats I should probably reconsider her constant fix-up offers. Not that I'm ugly or anything. Well, at least I don't go breaking out into hives at the face staring back at me when I brush my teeth in the morning. Okay, so maybe my hair is a bit flashy. I like to think of it as strawberry blonde but the emphasis is pretty much on the strawberry. The problem is it's curly. Long and curly. After the hair it's pretty much average. Average height, average weight. Well, kinda slim actually, but with some assets. Oh yeah, and a pair of wide green eyes. Looks were not the problem. Heck I couldn't even blame my lack of a love life on my recent bout of crazy since nobody actually knew about it. The thing is, at 34, I was a divorced workaholic. Boring. I hadn't quite reached the more-cats-than-furniture-lady stage yet, but you get the picture. In my defense, I did have a dog for a while. He was a good dog too, a cute black lab named Bear. But I gave him up. The thing is I was leaving him alone a lot and it made me feel bad. Since Iraq I had enough things making me feel bad and I just couldn't take Bear's sad old puppy dog eyes following me every time I walked out the door.

Anyway, that's what I was thinking last night as I headed for Angela's front door. She lived at 2nd and Pine. A nice address if you can afford it, and trust me, Bill Priest could. His money, along with his Philadelphia blue blood, flowed all the way back to the days of Ben Franklin and Billy Penn.

Bill was fifty-two when he married Angela. He was a lonely widower and she was a good twenty years younger. Angie's own marital condition before Bill was, well, it was busy to say the least. Despite those facts his high-minded relatives caved and gave their approval. Angela had that effect on people. Yeah, she was a bit too blonde for their tastes but it was impossible to ignore how genuinely happy she made Bill. So his relatives applied a good dose of Chanel, a proper salon, and some family jewelry to disguise the rest. That was sixteen years ago.

Last night the front door was open a few inches when I got there. At least that's what I remember. It's hard to say since I'm not exactly sure when the flashback started. But the door. I remember that the door was open. I pushed it in a few more inches and called out Angela's name. What happened next is mixed up with bits and pieces from Iraq. Time kept sliding in and out. I could feel the dirt, the blood, and I could hear Matt's voice in my ear. The next second, at least it felt like a second, there I was, in Angela's living room with a diamond studded gun sitting in my hand. And Angela's blood all over me.

No, wait. That's not right. Moaning. I heard moaning. Yeah, that's it. The front door was open a few inches and then I heard moaning.

I found Angela first. She was lying on the floor in front of her very spiffy, Italian fourteenth century couch. She was doubled up and holding her stomach. When I touched her, when I moved her hands away, I could see what amounted to a spigot of blood spilling out of her side. The hardwood floor underneath of her was soaked with blood.

I covered the hole in her stomach and started pounding her with questions. What happened? Who did this? Where's Bill? She was semi-conscious and mumbling his name. She pushed my hands away from her wound and pointed toward the dining room.

I found Bill with his back against the dining room wall. He was in a sitting position with one knee pulled into his chest and the other splayed out in front of him as though his legs had suddenly given out and he'd slid to the floor. His arms were limp at his sides. When I moved his right hand I found another diamond-studded pistol underneath of it. Oh yeah, and there was a bullet hole above his right eye. I slipped my fingers under his neck to check his carotid artery and couldn't find a pulse. Just in case I was wrong, I stuck my hand under his nose. That's how my sisters had taught me to check for their babies' breathing whenever I sat for them. I left it there as long as I could stand it, my fingers dripping splatters of black blood from Angela's liver, all over the collar of his shirt. I waited but that warm rhythmic puff of air that's supposed to brush across your knuckles? It never came. Bill was dead, his blue eyes trapped wide with surprise.

I winced. Bill was such a nice guy. Life should have ended differently for him. It was awful to see that expression of surprise in his eyes. Honestly. Resignation, hate, love, even fear, any one of those seemed fairer, a more prepared way to meet your maker than flat out surprise. I closed his lids and ran back to Angela, trying to sort out what happened. Bill had a gun under his hand. Angela was bleeding like a stuck pig and yet, in the years since I'd known them I couldn't recall so much as an ugly stare or a cross word passing between them.

I looked down at Angela. The bleeding was getting worse. I covered the bullet hole with my one hand and punched 911 into my cell phone with the other. The thing is, reality kept crashing in and out. My stomach lurched, as memories of Iraq surged through me at will. Time drifted out of focus.

When the next lucid moment swung through my brain I did what Angela had taught me. I grabbed onto it for dear life and opened my eyes.

What I saw was bad. Bill was dead and Angela looked like she was headed there fast. I swallowed hard and struggled to stuff the images back, careful to add the haunted look in Angela's eyes to the mix of memories I would need to squelch later on.

She wasn't going to make it and she knew it. Time was closing down on her the way it does on those few short weeks of honeysuckle that bloom in the summertime. Exquisite and highly abundant one day. Then bam. Out of nowhere the scent evaporates. Leaving behind those nasty, cloistering, whiffs of bad plant breath. The realization of it glared through Angela's tears and stung me in the face. Then her eyes fell shut.

"Angela no!"

"Wait!" I shouted. "Don't die! Please don't die. You have to tell me what happened. Who was it?" I cried. "Who did this to you?"

Angela opened her eyes wide then, and suddenly stared up at me. I couldn't think what to do. Blood was everywhere and my head? It was pounding something awful. I felt so confused.

That's when I heard it.

Over the pounding in my head, I heard it. Then I heard it again. Footsteps. I turned away from Angela's frightened eyes and cocked my head sideways. Yep, there it was again. The sound was unmistakable this time. Someone else was in the house. I could hear the floorboards creaking on the second floor. Of course, I told myself. Angela and Bill could not–would not–have done this to each other. Someone else was responsible. It was the only *logical* explanation. It was someone else, and judging by the sound of it, that someone else was still upstairs.

"Angela, quick," I whispered. "Tell me. Who's up there? Do you know? Do you know who did this to you and Bill?"

More footsteps. I listened harder. A window. Someone was opening up a window on the second floor. I could swear I heard a window being opened.

"Hurry!" I shouted at the 911 Operator. People are dying here! I think whoever did it might still be in the house!"

I wanted to get up, wanted to run up those stairs at full speed, to throw open every door until I caught the rotten coward. But I was afraid to leave Angela. Afraid what might happen to her if I let go of the hole in her stomach.

"Angie, please," I begged, tapping her cheek to keep her awake. "Please talk to me."

"I'm sorry," she said, groaning in pain. "I'm so sorry...not supposed to turn out like this. Bill... he tried to warn me. Poor Bill...not his fault."

"Warn you about who? Angela, please. Who else is in the house?"

She looked directly up at me. As if she were surprised at the question.

"Just us," she answered.

I kept the pressure on her wound. I stared back at her, willing her to stay awake, but again she closed her eyes. I waited, tears swelling away the vision in my own.

Moments later Angela came to. I have to admit, this time it was me who was surprised. She looked different. The expression on her face was calmer, and her voice was full of purpose.

"This is my doing Willow," she stated with authority. "I did this. To all of us. You understand?" She practically glared at me. "My fault...but that's not what concerns me now. You need to listen to me Willow. Are you with me? Stay in the present Willow. Please. I need *you*, Willow. I need *you* to stay in the present."

"What? Why would you say that? You can't take the blame, Angela. I know you, this is not...someone else did this, right? Tell me. Please. Tell me who."

My head was still pounding. The blood...the bullets...the tank...the explosion. The dirt in my mouth...Matt covering my back....Angela... oh god Angela...bleeding on the floor beneath me.

She's protecting someone. That's it I thought. She's protecting someone.

Hhhmmmm...wonder who?

My heart rocked so hard against my chest it made me nauseous. That voice again. I looked down. Angela's wound was gushing. I forced myself to be still. To quiet my racing thoughts so I could listen better. But the footsteps were definitely gone now. Whoever was up there, well, I couldn't hear them anymore.

The blood flowing across my knuckles was dark. Had to be from her liver. Twenty minutes was the most she would last. Angela was fading in and out now. Spit, tinged with blood, dribbled down her chin as she struggled to speak.

"That's it Willow. Stay in the present," she whispered. Then she looked at me so sadly. "I can't die yet Willow…can't. Not yet. There are things…unfinished. Important…all that matters now."

"You are not going to die," I barked at her. "I refuse to let that happen."

"But you have to help me, Angie. Please. I need to know…you have to tell me. What happened?"

She flashed me a brilliant smile.

"Doesn't matter, cupcake. Stupid guns, though. I really should've known better. Remember when I found them at that little antique shop in Lambertville? It was a gloriously sunny day. You tried to talk me out of buying them. Remember that day, Willow?" She sighed. "You took them out of my hand and gave them back to the dealer. Told me no one *needs* guns, let alone ones that are studded in diamonds. But as soon as you walked away I went back and bought them. I just had to have them. They looked so cute."

I remembered it clearly. Now, though, I looked over at the lamp sprawled on the floor. Up at the end table with the drawer pulled open. On the floor next to my knees, next to Angie, was one of the pistols. Bill had the other one. Both of them shot. Why? Why couldn't I remember five minutes ago?

"It's okay, Willow," she said. "What's done is done. Something… more important to take care of now. It was my responsibility. I was supposed to do it…but I was afraid to go back to Hawaii. I put the surfboard in a closet and forgot about it. I was selfish. I had Bill. He was so good to me and I just wanted to forget everything else. So I did. I left Hawaii. I forgot about that damned black rock. Threw the surfboard in a closet and now, people are going to die. Your job now, Willow. We both know you owe it…you owe me."

Angela tried to sit up. "I'm here!" she shouted.

Angela was staring past me now and I had the distinct impression that she was looking at someone over my shoulder. I whipped my head around and scanned the room. No one was there. I shuddered. Then checked the room again. Still empty. I tried to shake off that creepy, unhinged feeling. The one I used to get when I first entered the hospital up in the Pocono Mountains. It didn't work.

"Any minute, Angela. The ambulance will be here any minute. I pushed her back gently against the floor. "Save your strength."

Gently?

"Can't. Have to tell you everything…so you can fix it."

"Okay Angie. Whatever you want. Just stay with me."

So I listened. Listened to the story she spun in labored breaths about a life she'd lived years ago in Hawaii. I kept my hands pressed against the ugly hole in her side and listened.

Angie told me that by the time she was twenty-eight she'd been divorced three times. She had a modest house on Maui but spent most of her time at a resort in Waikiki. "I was busy coaxing number four to the altar," she explained. Turns out that was Bill.

But she wasn't alone. My tough cookie friend, the one I thought I knew so well? Apparently Angie had a couple of kids stashed in her past. Kids, she admitted, with as much regret pouring out of her now as blood, that she had largely ignored.

She had a son, Benny, and a daughter named January. Unfortunately, while she was closing in on Bill, a shark closed in on her eleven year old son. A number of people on the beach that day remembered seeing the boy splashing about in the surf just before the large dorsal fin of the shark appeared above the surface in the shallow Waikiki waters. It was hours before Angela even had a clue that the boy everyone in the hotel was chattering about might be her son.

Tears streamed down her face while she admitted that she wasn't even at the beach during the commotion. That Bill and the bartender were the only two people she'd spoken to that day. Despite a massive effort, her son Benny was never found. The only thing the ocean coughed up that day was an unhealthy cloud of blood on the sand. Days later Angela flew out of the islands with Bill. Oh yeah, and she left her nine-year old daughter, January, behind.

Angela struggled for air and looked up at me. I looked back, hoping she could see the sadness I felt for her and not the judgment.

"Not...exactly...Mother of the Year, huh?"

"Sshhhhhhh, save your strength Angie. It's okay you don't have to tell me anymore."

"I took January to her father's...and left her there. I was a mess, Willow. No excuse but I was." Angela whispered. "Left her there. Told her I'd be back. Then hopped on a plane to Philadelphia. It was six years before I had the guts to pick up the phone. But it was too late," she cried. Tears of regret slid from the corners of her eyes and melted into the brassy blond hair at her temples.

"You know, I dragged her to Philadelphia once. When she was about sixteen. She hated it. Hated me. First chance she got the kid stole my credit card and flew straight back to Hawaii. Swore she'd never come back."

"It's okay Angela. Don't feel bad don't worry. I get it," I told her, even though I didn't mean it. I come from a big Irish family where there's always room for one more at the dinner table or on the rec-room couch if needed. Leaving your kids was not an option.

Pale and dying, she called me on it.

"Liar," she said, cracking what was left of her smile.

"Angie, please. The ambulance will be here any minute. You need to save your strength."

"No. I need to use it. There's more to tell you...more you need to do."

I looked down at my cell phone lying open on the floor next to us. I leaned toward it and shouted, afraid, to let go of Angie's side.

"Hurry! What the hell is taking you people so long?"

It felt like an hour but I was guessing it had only been a couple of minutes since I'd called them. The 911 Operator answered me in soothing tones but the phone was too far away for me to make out what she was saying. By now, even the tops of my hands were warm and sticky. She was losing too much blood. How did this happen?

How indeed?

"It's bad Wil. We both know I'm not going to make it. You owe me now, so listen. I need you to go to Hawaii...I need you to fix something. Before more people die."

"The ambulance it's...coming."

Angela raised herself up, propping her weight on her elbows as best she could. It didn't last. She fell back into my lap and what little color she had left, drained right out of her. Her eyes fell shut and I thought she was finally gone. Out of nowhere though, she reached for my shoulder. She missed and her hand fell into my hair, her bloody fingers snagging hard about half way down the thick mass of curls that reach to my waist. Not that that's important. Hell, for me, having hair that long wasn't so much a fashion statement as it was common sense. After years of Ronald McDonald haircuts and massive amounts of teasing, I discovered that the sheer weight of letting it grow to my waist was the best way to keep such a tightly wound mess of curls from causing me trouble. Angela closed her fingers around them and yanked me down, closer to her.

"Cut the crap...and listen. Closet near the stairs," her voice cracked. "There's a surfboard...way in the back. Go get it. Now!"

"Are you crazy? I'm not letting go of you. If I do you'll bleed to death."

"Let go Willow."

That's what she said. I was sure of it.

Yep, that's what you heard—let go Willow. Let go, let go, let gooooooo!

"There's a diamond. It's called the Maui Snow," Angela continued, her hand still snagged in my hair. "It's big, 43 carats big. It's as black as a night ocean and even bigger trouble. The surfboard...it's key...only way to find the diamond. Sam made it that way on purpose. Find it. Take the board back to Hawaii. You hear me, Willow? Take it back. Find the Maui Snow. It's pilikia, that black diamond. It's pilikia. I'm sorry Willow. But you owe me now. So sorry."

Why is she still talking? "I'm sorry Willow, please Willow, please. I'm so sorry Willow." Yellllk.

"Should've listened to Sam," Angela wailed. "It's on you now Willow. Have to find it...put the Maui Snow back. Don't tell...anyone. Do this for me Willow. Do it and the demons in your head, the craziness, it will go away. It will all go away."

Angela promised me. "You'll be well again," I heard her say it. "Well and complete."

Right Willygirl. That's right...it was Angela who told you that.

But I knew that didn't make sense. Why would Angela want me to let go of her wound like that? And why would she make promises about me getting better? I *was* better. Angela knew that. She was the one who'd gotten me there. She was the one who convinced me to cast aside the awful questions plaguing me since Iraq. Cast them aside in favor of fresh air. And pajamas that don't tie your arms to the sides of the bed. And coffee. Fresh, hot, coffee.

"Go!" She shouted. "Get the surfboard out of the closet…hurry…

I tried to stay in the moment, to cover her wound, and somehow stave off the flood of memories. The flashback. But Angela, she…must have pushed my hands away. Right? She must have. But reality…the memories…everything kept shifting in and out of focus. And that voice. That damned voice.

Find the surfboard Willow. Find it fast…before the paramedics get here!

I remember…

Kneeling over her

No…standing…running. And there it was. Buried in the back left corner of the closet. Next to an old Miller Lite Box jammed with beach stuff; flip-flops, sun tan lotion, a couple of shells. Part of me was surprised to find it there. Part of me was convinced that Angela was delirious from the gunshot. Surfboard, black diamonds, kids? I couldn't remember her ever mentioning any kids. I thought the blood loss was fogging her brain. Creating stories that couldn't be true.

But the surfboard was real. It was old and there were pictures, writing, etched into it. I took it outside and threw it in my jeep. When I came back Angela was smiling at me. I could tell she was relieved. Next, she wiggled the square cut, four and a half carat, diamond engagement ring she got from Bill, over her knuckle, and then she pressed it into my palm. At least I think she did.

"Please," Angela wailed. "Just give the ring to January. Please Willow? I'm not asking much. I'm dying and I need her to have it so… so she'll know that I gave a damn."

"Not that much? Are you kidding me Angie? Of all things. Another diamond ring? Why? Why would you ask me to deliver another diamond ring?"

Sirens. I could hear the sirens. Loud. Screeching in the distance. My head...the pounding...the images...Matt...the bullets...the blood...the diamond. I felt so fuzzy...so confused.

So...hurry! They're coming. Better hurry.

"Wil, the Maui Snow, the surfboard. Don't let Jan know. Pilikia. It's pilikia. She won't be safe if she knows about it. Do what's right Willow, please. She's my daughter."

Angela...still talking...why? Why is she still talk—

I looked up. The front door was wide open.

"Shhhh...it's okay. I have the board now...it's okay."

I *tried* to soothe her. I remember that part. I remember trying to soothe her. It was just so hard and the sirens...they were getting louder. Closer. Tires screeching. Car doors banging.

I looked it up online later that night. After I made my statement to the police. After I wrote the article. After I peeled off my favorite Seven for all Mankind jeans and took a shower. Pilikia. It means trouble in Hawaiian. I don't know what made me look it up. I guess I was hoping it meant something else. Something better like good luck charm, or maybe stamp. Yeah, stamp. That would've been good. Bubble wrap that odd vintage surfboard. Slap on a nice big pilikia and woooosshhh send it airmail from Philly straight into the good old Pacific. Just like Angela wanted. Job done. Fresh start for me. Maybe I could do that. Forget everything. Forget Iraq. Forget what happened to Bill and Angela. Forget all that blood. Forget the diamonds. But pilikia doesn't mean stamp. It means trouble.

Besides, even if I did manage to shove back all the horror, I couldn't ignore the diamonds. They were real. And a bit ironic. Most women dream about the diamonds they want in their lives. How big, what cut, the perfect man who will present it on bended knee. Me? I couldn't seem to get away from them. Right now I had three. My own round shaped carat from my ex, Shane. The perfect half-carat that Private Matthew Edwards had planned on giving to his girl, Bonnie Jean, and now Angela's four and a half carat square monster. Not to mention this Maui Snow thing. According to Angie, a 43 carat black behemoth, shot straight from the stars, and apparently worth mega millions. Seriously, the last thing I needed in my life right now was another diamond.

Hhmmmmmmm...guess we'll see about that.

"Shhhh…it's okay, now," I soothed. "Save your strength…that's right…shhhhh quiet…stay quiet…they're almost here. They're almost… Angie?"

Good

The EMT's arrived first and pretty much shoved me aside. I watched them check her eyes and tap her cheek with no response. They slipped a blood pressure cuff on one arm and tried to insert an IV in the other while a third EMT assessed her wound. Fast and efficient, they just about had her loaded onto the stretcher by the time the police got there.

They took one look at me, eyes wide, covered in blood, and started firing off questions. Who are you? What are you doing here? What happened? Did you touch anything?

"My name is Willow Finnegan, I'm a reporter for the *Philly Chronicle*," I answered, professional mode kicking in. "Angela Priest and I are friends. We were supposed to grab a couple of cheese steaks tonight and watch a movie. Jeezuz, Bill wasn't even supposed to be here," I added, looking down at all the blood on the floor. "The door was open when I got here. I saw Angela…the hole in her side, all that blood." I stopped talking and leaned against the couch for support. The lead detective eyed me suspiciously.

"Then what?"

"She was crawling toward the kitchen, calling for Bill. I found him in the dining room. He looked dead, felt dead, so I ran back to Angela. I tried to help her. I called 911. You know, I think that someone might have still been upstairs when I got here."

"Did you see them? Did anyone run past you?"

"No, but I heard things. I heard something," I tried to clarify.

He looked over his shoulder and motioned for a couple of officers to check upstairs.

"Did you touch anything?"

"What? Yeah. Sure. I touched everything. Angela, Bill, the guns. What the hell took you people so long?"

"Thirteen minutes, Ma'am," said one of the EMT's as he lifted the bars on the side of the stretcher and locked them into place. "Not our best. But given the city, the traffic patterns, it's about average these days."

25

"What's that in your hand?" Asked the detective.

I didn't answer right away. I looked down at my closed fist and tried to remember, but like I said, the details were fuzzy. Plus, I was trying to place the officer. He was big. At least six three with a large head, square jaw, and suspicious eyes. Unfortunately, I didn't recognize him. Not that I knew every detective in the city but I've been a reporter for the *Philly Chronicle* for twelve years now and I knew a lot of them.

He reached out grabbed my wrist and pried open my fingers. Angela's diamond ring sparkled in my palm. He took one glance at Angela's empty left hand and shot me a look hot enough to wilt cactus.

"Where do you think you're going with that?"

I opened my mouth to speak but nothing came out. He was still holding my wrist when Angela's hand fell through the bars of the stretcher and landed on his sleeve. I nearly jumped out of my skin when she opened her eyes. She yanked at the blue cotton fabric of his shirt and whispered,

"Hawaii…right Wils? To give to my daughter."

The detective pointed at the center of my forehead. "You! Don't move!" He dropped his arm and turned toward Angela but then thought better of it and pointed at me once again. "And that ring stays here. It's evidence."

"Ma'am can you tell me what happened? Who did this to you?"

"Not dead yet," she croaked at the detective.

"Ring…not evidence. Nothing to do with this. Still mine…I choose who owns it next. Right now that's Willow."

She looked straight at me then, her eyes clear and blue. "Hawaii. First thing. You give that to Jan…for me. She needs it more than–

The ring was still in my hand. I stared at it horrified…wondering.

"Officer we need to go," said the lead EMT. He pointed to the pool of blood they'd just lifted her from and said, "gunshot to the liver. She's in bad shape."

"Ma'am, what happened? Your husband–

"All my fault. My doing. Poor Bill…he didn't mean to…couldn't believe that he…and then I reacted…I just pulled the trigger… I just wanted to stop it. Stop it all from happening."

Angela's arm drifted from his sleeve and fell slack against the stretcher. Once again the EMTs jumped into action with two of them wheeling her down the walkway while the third straddled the stretcher and went to work. But that was it. That was the last thing Angela said before she died a few minutes later in the ambulance.

Detective Wilson followed them outside, shouting questions at Angie all the way down the sidewalk and into the ambulance.

I must've put Angie's ring in my pocket. I really don't remember. But I must have.

"Miss, can I help you? Miss?"

Someone touched me from behind, nudging me slightly forward. I looked up and saw a good six feet of empty space between me and the front counter at the coffee shop.

"What can I get for you today?"

A few minutes later the Starbucks guy handed me a Venti with a half an inch of non-fat milk on the bottom followed by the daily strong brew and topped off with a thick pile of whipped cream. I lifted it off the counter and my cell phone rang again. It was Mitch Barrens, the editor I'd filed my story with the night before.

I dropped the phone in my pocket and ignored the call in favor of a large swig of dark creamy sanity.

Too bad it didn't last. A few sips later and a measly two blocks from the *Chronicle* some bozo in a bigger hurry than me rounded a corner and nicked my arm. It was just enough to knock the cup out of my hand. Of course the lid came off mid-air and hot coffee flew in every direction. Without a word people in the general vicinity dispersed outward in unison and then continued on their way, including the man who caused the accident. I have to admit it was impressive, like they were all operating on the same wavelength or something, expanding effortlessly to avoid the hot trouble and then bam right back into their own forward moving lanes. Meanwhile I was struggling just to keep the road in sight.

"Jerk!" I turned my head and yelled after him. Then I turned back in the direction of the *Chronicle* and walked right into another man's chest.

"Willow?"

I stepped back from his cream colored jacket and noticed that I'd left a perfect pink lip gloss mark there. You're gonna have some 'splainin to do if there's a Lucy, I thought with a laugh. Then it hit me. The man had called me by name. I looked up.

"Shane?"

Ex-husband Shane Galveston. Gorgeous. Curly brown hair, lovable blue eyes, and oh yeah he was my best friend since seventh grade. Did I mention world champion Triathlete? He started out as a runner. Even won the Boston Marathon once. After that he set his sights on the Ironman Triathlon. Nothing like swimming for miles, then biking for miles, then running what's left of your butt off. Shane likes to keep busy. In fact I hadn't seen him for a year and a half. We've been divorced for three. I heard he finally gave up his apartment in the city, which is probably why I hadn't seen him for so long. Still, he's a Philly boy at heart and I was surprised I hadn't run into him sooner. Part of me was always expecting to. Waiting for it actually. Except for today. Not today. Nope. Nada. Cannot handle this today.

I smiled wide flashing him more pretty whites than a stage full of Osmonds and then carefully launched myself into performance mode.

"Hey, long time no see. Sooooo...how ya doin'?

"Good," he answered, glancing sideways at the coffee massacre on my coat and shoes. "What happened to you?"

"Nothing. Really, it's nothing. Just some jerk. He banged into me and knocked the coffee right out of my hand and...hey where's my briefcase," I wondered out loud, then bent down to retrieve it.

Shane got there first picking up both my briefcase and the morning edition that had fallen out of it. I folded it over covering the front page as Shane handed it back to me.

"Too late," he said. "I already read it. I was glad to see your byline again. Heck of a come back though. Sounds like you had quite a night last night."

I stood there trying to think of something to say but nothing came out. The thing is that on any given day Shane is never too far from my thoughts. But seeing him standing there, listening to him comment about my work almost as if our last conversation had been ten minutes ago and not a year and a half was a bit of a shock to my system. A system that had taken too many hits already.

When I didn't answer right away he took me by the elbow and led me toward a nearby bench.

"Are you okay?"

"I'm fine. Except for the fact that I'm wearing my coffee instead of drinking it. I'm just surprised to see you," I added, holding back the 'I can't believe you never called me when I came home from Iraq' part that I wanted to blurt out.

"So, are you in town for an event?"

"Hang on a sec," he said, then left me there and jogged into the next block. I watched, curious, as he stopped at a hot dog vendor who was setting up shop for the day. Half a minute later he jogged back with two steaming cups of coffee.

"Okay, so you've got a hot dog vendor who stashes coffee for you. Impressive. Especially considering that you don't live here anymore."

"Who? Bob? We go way back. When I was training he used to keep Gatorade under there for me too. Jealous?" He teased.

"Kind of," I admitted, taking the lid off the cup and swallowing a decent gulp. The coffee wasn't bad and it was blended with just the right amount of cream. He remembered.

"So, how's the mega-athlete thing going?" I heard you won another marathon."

"Yeah, it was a great race, kinda smooth. I was near the lead for most of it."

"I heard about your Pulitzer," he countered. "Congratulations." Then he added, "I kept up with your articles while you were traveling with the troops in Iraq. Impressive stuff. Eerie but impressive."

He was sitting right next to me on the bench and his hand strayed to my forearm, I think without his even realizing it. A second later he was squeezing my wrist. "I'm glad you're home, though. Sounds like it was rough over there. I heard you got banged up a bit. Considering the circumstances, I guess you were lucky, huh?"

"Yeah," I replied. "Lucky."

"You did it though, didn't you? You got your Pulitzer. That's great."

He sounded genuinely happy for me. Not a trace of bitterness left. Considering what an obstacle work was in our marriage, mine for him and his for me, it was a surprise.

"Guess all things considered, it was worth a few broken ribs."

"Yeah," I replied, careful to look down into the coffee and not into his uncomplicated blue eyes.

"All things considered."

"So what else have you been working on lately? This morning's article is the first one I've read in awhile."

"New subject," I said abruptly.

Shane looked at me funny. One thing we'd always been good at was conversation. Pick a subject any subject and we could talk for hours. Okay so sometimes the discussions turned into arguments but that was half the fun. I drank more of the coffee and waited. Shane didn't know that I'd basically wound up in the nuthouse after Iraq, and I didn't want him to know. Not yet anyway. Maybe some day. When we were back together.

"Okay, then how about Mom and Pop Finnegan? How are they?"

"Good. They're good. How about yours? No more heart attacks from your Dad I hope."

"Nope, he's fine. Retired in June. Spent the summer dragging Mom to the Grand Canyon in an RV."

I laughed.

"How 'bout the rest of the Finnegan crowd? Still expanding?"

"You know it. Pru finally had a baby girl last year and Aggie has twins. The total on nieces and nephews is around eighteen or nineteen now. You'd have to ask my Mom though she's the family scorekeeper."

"Wish them all Merry Christmas for me and tell them I miss them. You're lucky Willow. They're a great bunch."

"I gave Bear to Jake as an early Christmas present," I blurted.

Blurting. What a sucky little habit. There oughta be a law.

Surprise lit his eyes. Judgment quickly followed.

"You gave away Bear? Why?"

My cell phone rang. I looked down, mostly to avoid Shane's eyes, and saw that it was Harry. I held up a finger and answered it.

"You should have called me," Shane said, his tone wounded. "I would have taken him."

"Not now, Harry," I whispered into the phone struggling to keep my voice even.

"What's taking you so long, Willow? That meeting about the G-8 Conference in Europe is almost over and they want to know where you are."

"Not now Harry." I closed the phone.

Bear was our cute little monster of a black lab. He had thick paws and a playful personality. We raised him for about a year and a half before the break-up. When I gave him away it seemed like the right thing to do. Now it seemed stupid. Just like our break-up.

Okay, colossally stupid. We broke up not long after Shane's first cycling event in France. I came over for the race and we had an amazing time. He finished third and despite the fact that he was an American the crowd was enthusiastic. Cycling politics aside, people tend to like Shane.

We spent the next two days lounging in the South of France. Until I got a call and had to head over to Ireland to cover a car bombing in Belfast that killed a couple of grade schoolers. When I got back to Philadelphia, Shane had a surprise waiting for me. A house. A huge Victorian house in Yardley. Outside the City. Way outside the City. In my defense I was jetlagged. I was cranky and hungry. But Shane was on a mission. He whisked me through room after room babbling about couches and barbeque grills and baby furniture. Baby furniture!

By then Shane had won two Triathlons and placed in a bunch of smaller marathons and cycling events. I was just getting started. Besides, even wealthy athletes shouldn't buy houses without talking to their spouse. You wanna surprise me? Bring me a Big Mac and some fries. Not a house. Somehow a small fight turned into a giant fight. Clothes were tossed out of the apartment. Suggestions were made that he should go live there by himself. He did. Pride turned into stupidity. Stupidity into divorce. Divorce into regret.

"I don't understand," Shane was saying, his tone now slightly less condemning than his eyes. "Why would you give Bear away? You loved that dog. I loved that dog."

"I was away...too much. Bear was always with Jake anyway and Christmas was coming and I don't know. It just seemed like the right thing to do. For Bear and for Jake."

After a minute Shane put his hand over mine and gave it a squeeze.

31

"I'm sorry."

"Me too."

I missed him. From the look in his eyes he missed me too. Suddenly I was keenly aware that lack of love was not the reason we'd ended.

"Hey," I said, breaking the spell. "Aggie's having a party tomorrow night. Why don't you come and see everybody. It'll be fun. I'll even call Jake. Make sure he brings Bear. He got so big you won't even recognize him."

"Shane! Shane!"

A leggy blonde in a pink cashmere coat rushed across the street. She was heading straight for us.

"Shane, what's the name of those cookies your Mom loves?"

"Hamentashen. Cherry or Poppy only. No lemon." Shane and I answered at the same time. Then we looked at each other and laughed. Shane's mother hated lemon. It felt good to laugh. But the blonde was still standing in front of us.

"Okay, that was weird," she said, her lips parting into a white chicklet smile that *seemed* friendly and more genuine than I wanted to admit.

"Hi. I'm Cathy Tanglewood."

I stood up from the bench although it didn't seem to matter much. At five foot three I was still looking way up. The young blonde—and I do mean young—stood at least six inches taller than me.

"Hi Cathy. I'm Willow Galveston."

Why that came out of my mouth I'll never know. Even when Shane and I were married I used Finnegan, my maiden name.

"Okay, I get it," she laughed. "That explains the whole cookie routine. You're Shane's ex, right? Nice to meet you," she said, putting out her hand. "Love your articles. We never miss one."

Young, confident, and she can even read. Just peachy.

"I hate to interrupt but I need to get back in line at the bakery. There's this sweet little grandma holding my place. The cookies," she said, "hominwhat?"

"Hamentashen," we said in unison again.

"Right. Cherry, poppy, but no lemon," she repeated. "Be back in a jif."

She was adorable. Good-natured. Well mannered. Still, as soon as she crossed the street I couldn't help myself.

"What is she fourteen?"

"No. She's not fourteen." But a blush stained his cheeks anyway.

"Fifteen?"

"Okay, maybe sixteen," I kept at it, refusing to let up on him. "I have to admit though she at least looks *tall* enough to drive."

"Go ahead, get it all out. But I remember not so long after our divorce seeing your picture splashed all over the paper with what's-his-name," he snapped his fingers trying to remember, "something-tattoo-rocker-boy."

"Are you talking about Eddie Gaeton, the drummer for the Blue Skunks? For starters that was a charity auction. And at least he was old enough to buy us drinks. You can't even compare the two."

"Compare what?" Cathy asked. She was back—and faster than a Philly minute. Maybe not so confident after all.

"Compare the last two Triathlons. Willow was asking me about my last win."

"I'm more interested in your next," she grinned as she linked arms with *my* husband.

"Shane has real talent. I think he should take it as far as he can."

I bit the inside of my lip to keep from responding.

She stretched out her right arm, dangling a white bakery bag in front of me.

"Cookie?" She offered.

"No thanks. So where are you from?" When I'm uncomfortable and can dive into reporter mode, I do.

"Starter, Michigan. It's just outside of—

"Deerborn," I interrupted, the air in my lungs deflating.

"You know it?" She sounded surprised. "Starter is a such a small town."

"If you say so," I answered, trying to keep my voice from going all hollow. "A friend of mine from Iraq used to live there. Maybe you knew him. Matt Edwards."

She looked at me, and I saw the smile on her face begin to fade as his name fell into place in her brain. Too bad Cathy's name didn't fall into place in *my* brain. If it had, God only knows what might've come out of my mouth. Right then and there, standing next to Shane on that street. But the night before had been rough. I'd barely slept, and didn't have near enough coffee in me yet to function. Yeah, I guess there's no telling how differently things might have played out if her name had clicked with me sooner. Considering her connection to Matt it really should have. Who knows what I would have said. Or done. Right there on the street.

"Yeah, I uhhm, knew Matt," Cathy stammered.

I saw a hint of guilt cross her face. But it melted fast.

"What an awful shame. I still can't believe it. Matt and I, we... uhhh...she paused, glancing sideways at Shane for half a second. "We went to school together."

"Really? Do you know his girlfriend? Is there any chance you're headed home soon?"

Cathy's name didn't click with me but what did was the possibility that I could palm off a rather sticky obligation. One I had been avoiding since Iraq. You see I still had Bonnie Jean's engagement ring. The one Matt was planning to give her when he came home. Meeting Matt's girl, handing her his ring, I was still in no condition for that. In fact, I wasn't sure I would ever be ready to face it. Besides, the idea of this little hottie going back to her hometown—pronto—well it felt kind of right.

"I think her name's Bonnie Jean," I said. "Bonnie Jean Copansky."

"Bonnie Jean? No. I'm pretty sure she and Matt were over. Yeah," she added confidently. That ended long before he went to Iraq. You remember Bonnie Jean, honey?" She asked Shane as she squeezed his arm again. "You met her when I took you to the Cup Ten Diner."

"Sure," Shane agreed, smiling back at her.

Those smiles. It was more than I could take this morning. Besides, there was something about the look in Cathy's eye when she spoke of Bonnie Jean. Something about her mention of that diner that set my teeth on edge.

"Soooo," I drawled. "Where did you two meet?"

"On the Wall."

"Where?"

"The Wall, Willow. You remember the Wall in Manayunk. The famous one that people fly in from all over the world to ride? They have

34

a race there every year. I've won it a few times. People lining the streets, lots of shops and bars and ice-cream stores, remember?"

"I remember," I answered defensively. "It just didn't register right away, that's all."

"Anyhow," Cathy interjected, sensing the tension between us, "that's where we met. About a year and a half ago, me, and a bunch of girlfriends from college were on this road trip. Actually Bonnie Jean was there. We were on our way to the big Apple and we sort of got lost. We ended up in Manayunk, at the Wall, and that's where Shane basically rescued us," she explained, squeezing his arm for like the tenth time.

"Lucky me, huh?"

"So, do you ride too?" I asked, deciding to keep my opinion about the state of her luck to myself.

"Just for fun. Shane's been a big help though always trying to improve my technique. Of course it'll be months before I can even think about getting back on a bike."

"Leg injury?" I asked, hoping that one of her perfect looking plastic doll limbs might be a little *less* than perfect.

"No," she laughed, "nothing like that. It's just that I have a tendency to fall off and with the baby due in March, I wouldn't want to chance it."

Giggling, she let the pink cashmere coat slip open and rubbed her hand over an unmistakable bump.

My heart absorbed the impact about as well as that tank did when it rolled over the IED in Iraq. Suddenly I feel it all again. In one massive unexpected second I feel the explosion. Arms. Organs. Steel and diamonds. All flying upward, outward, hanging there suspended in mid-air.

I push back against the thoughts. Fast. Before it's too late…before I can't. Breathe, I warn myself. In. Out. I focus on each puff of air and make the images fade. But the dread stays. Shane is having a baby. Not mine.

I look ahead, somewhere below their faces, and plant a weak smile on my face. That's when I see it. Third finger left hand. A perfect pink heart-shaped rock. Shining in the winter sun as she drums her pink fingertips on top of that clingy pink cashmere dress. It was such a cute dress. A perfect match to her cashmere coat. Just like she was

35

pretending to be the perfect match for Shane, with that perfect heart-shaped diamond on her finger to prove it. Why is it that something relatively commonplace, like a blue sweater, or a goldfish, or yes, a diamond ring, why does it go from being something you barely notice to something you suddenly see everywhere. Something you can't seem to get away from.

Hahaha! No matter how hard you try, right Willygirl?

My cell phone rang. Harry's timing was something else today.

"Are you trying to get fired?"

"Maybe," I replied weakly, my brain still smothered in pink cashmere.

"The G-8 meeting is underway and Mitch Barrens is looking for you. I've been stalling but...Willow? Are you still there?"

"Right Harry, sure...we should talk about that. I'll be there as soon as I can."

I closed the phone and looked up to find Shane flashing me the saddest smile I'd ever seen.

"Congratulations," I managed to spit out. "Both of you. Really. That's great news. Just great. Well, that was Harry. Shane you remember Harry. Anyway, according to Harry, I'm late for a meeting. So. Shane. Be sure and tell your parents I said hello. It was good to see you. And so nice to meet you, Cathy," I managed.

"Good luck with the ahhh...

I couldn't say it. I pointed in the general direction of her belly...of that flashy diamond ring.

"Nice meeting you too," she responded. Then, generous conqueror that she was, added, "Shane honey, I'm starved. I think I'm gonna go grab a hot dog. You want one?"

No, he does not want a hot dog. He's a health nut. He eats wheat germ donuts. Not hot dogs.

"Sure babe, thanks," he said, letting out a sigh. "I'll catch up with you in a few."

I put up a hand in her direction. The gesture was more defensive as in 'please no more' than it was a wave. She returned it with a confident smile and headed for the vendor.

"I'm sorry," he said as soon as she was gone. "I should have called. I didn't mean for you to find out like this."

"It's okay Shane," I said letting him off whatever hook there was left. "We're divorced. It's not like you owe me an explanation."

"You have to understand."

No I don't. Not me…right Willygirl?

"This…it just happened so fast…and I didn't know what to say. And you…I heard you were in rough shape when you first came back from Iraq. Shit, I tried to come see you but every time I called I got the run around. Harry said you needed your space, that after the surgery on your leg you had all you could deal with with the rehab. You know, I actually got in the car one day to go see your parents. To get them to tell me where you were. My mother stopped me. She said I should let you be. Give you time to heal. That I should wait for you to call me."

Terrific. Just peachy. Words of wisdom from good old Mother Galveston. From the day I met her Harmony Galveston hated me. With the thick paw of a lioness she drew a line in the dirt in front of her cub and with saliva dripping from her fangs she dared me to cross it. Funny thing though. She eased up on me big time about ten months before Shane and I broke up. It was like she knew. That she'd somehow spotted the cracks we couldn't see. I looked down the block now at Cathy and couldn't help wondering how Harmony was taking this leggy new circumstance. Not much better than me I imagined. The thought brought a grim smile to my face.

"So I did," Shane continued. "I waited. After a while it just seemed like you dropped off the face of the earth. You know, I called your brother Ted a few times, left a couple of messages. I tried Aggie too but I never heard anything. I figured my mother was right. I figured you'd call me when you were ready."

I opened my mouth to speak but nothing came out. I could feel the anger gripping my stomach…invading my veins. That was another new thing. The anger. By nature, I was not an angry person. Far from it. Life's too short. Right? But that was before Iraq. These days it seemed to surge in out of nowhere.

"Look, this thing with Cathy, it just took off. And now, well, now there's the baby. You and me, Willow, we've been…friends…since forever. Really, I honestly thought that some day we'd figure this thing out."

"Me too," I admitted.

He reached out and pulled me into one of his great bear hugs. "I'm so sorry Willow. I wish it had gone differently. You know I always wanted it to be...

I broke away. I didn't want him to finish.

"Cathy seems terrific. Go...be happy."

I walked to the Chronicle in a daze. Without thinking I lifted the coffee to my lips and drank. It was cold and bitter. I found the nearest bin and trashed it.

CHAPTER FIVE

Byodo-In Temple in Oahu
December 2009

"It wasn't the cigarettes, Liat."
   "It was fear."
   Bridget Kawa was dying when she said that. The cancer was in her bones by then and the doctors didn't expect her to last out the week. She didn't. That was a year ago, today.
   Liat stood at the koi pond now, absently watching the fish swim and thought about their last real conversation, about her mother's fears. In the end Bridget had come to believe that passing those fears onto Liat was a grave mistake. Liat didn't think so. Not then. Not now. Yet here she was a year later, shivering, staring, as raindrops pelted the surface of the pond with tiny circles of water, and replaying that conversation.
   Bridget had asked Liat to bring her to the Valley of the Temples one last time. Located west of Honolulu and then north into the mountains, the Valley is a sacred place. The houses of worship that line its pastures include a variety of religions. Taking special care with her mother's frail frame, Liat had walked Bridget to the Byodo–In Temple, which is set near the rear of the Valley against a wall of ridiculously steep cliffs that rise straight out of the grass. The grounds leading up to the cliffs are simple and green, and include the temple, the meditation house, a koi pond that stretches across several acres, and a nearly three ton brass

Peace Bell that when touched rings in low, calming, waves. The day, like many on the island, had been sunny and a steady eighty-two degrees.

They spent time in the temple and the meditation house, although neither mother nor daughter had done more than lean in the direction of Buddhist teachings. It didn't matter. The place was peaceful.

As they exited the temple, Liat was drawn to the Peace Bell. She stood there for a few moments and without realizing it, synched her breathing to the bell's rhythmic tones. Bridget waited at her side, watching. Eventually, she pressed two cold fingers to Liat's elbow. Liat reached down and covered Bridget's hand with a warm one of her own. Then the two women made their way down to the pond.

As they sat down, a pack of cigarettes fell from Bridget's pocket. Liat reached down and picked them up, a stern look crossing her face.

"Mom, the cancer…you shouldn't be smoking."

"It wasn't the cigarettes, Liat."

"It was fear."

"What are you talking about?" Liat asked, studying her mother's green eyes. They were worn out, much older than her forty-seven years. Tears caught in Liat's throat.

"The fear," she sighed. "It ate away at me, honey. Did more damage than cancer ever could. Probably caused it. The worst part is I passed that fear onto you."

Bridget shook a cigarette out of the pack and then put the rest in her pocket. She raised it to her lips but when she caught sight of Liat's worried expression, she couldn't bring herself to light it.

"I'm sorry it took me so long to figure it out Liat, but it's true," she confirmed. "After what happened that day on the beach, I let fear take over my life. And yours."

Bridget never mentioned Benny's name. Or the sand sculpture of the shark Liat built that day. She didn't have to. They both knew what day at the beach she was talking about.

"Mom, no." Liat stammered. "That day…it was all my fault. Afterwards, ever since then, you've done nothing but protect me."

Again Bridget sighed. "It was a mistake Liat. You were special. I was afraid of it, afraid for you, and because of that I taught you to suppress it. Forced you to suppress it."

"You didn't force me Mom. You gave me options. Good options. You taught me to channel my energy in other directions. Because of you my paintings are…well…people like them Mom. And surfing? You took me to contests. Kept me focused. I make a living competing on the world tour now. That's what you gave me."

"Still, I was wrong. When you get this close to death, Liat, you see things differently. Life becomes much clearer. The way you looked at that boy…what you told me afterwards…I was so afraid for you that I couldn't see what an extraordinary gift it was. That maybe there was a higher purpose, a bigger reason for it. One that I was too short-sighted to see."

"It doesn't matter," Liat said quietly. "It's gone. I can't look at someone…can't do that anymore."

It was true. Liat's stare was still slightly hypnotic and people were drawn to her but what she'd done to Benny was no longer possible. There were a couple of times in grade school when she would lock gazes with a person and she could feel…*it*…start to happen. But Liat had struggled successfully to gain control, to hold it down. On occasion the urge was still there but the power of it, whatever that was, had all but lost its potency.

But that was only the half of it. Liat's stare may have lost its ooompf. Her art had not.

Liat kept the sculptures to herself. It happened so fast. Started so out of the blue. She hadn't been able to get a grip on it yet. She couldn't seem to stop. Keeping quiet about the sculptures was the only thing she could control. Besides, her mother had enough to deal with. She was already sick with cancer when the episodes started. The last thing Liat wanted to do was worry her mother.

"You need to own yourself Liat. Let go of the fear."

Bridget squeezed her daughter's hand.

"How's Makani? Have you seen him lately?"

"No Mom. Mak and I don't date anymore. Besides, he's in Australia, surfing on the tour."

"He still loves you, Liat."

"I'm with Nick. He loves me. He's–

"Safe," Bridget answered.

"I was going to say kind. But you know Mom, Nick does make me feel safe. Is that so terrible?"

Bridget lifted a weak and chilly finger up to Liat's chin then tilting it, stared her daughter square in the eyes.

"I think maybe it is Liat."

The rain began to fall harder now but Liat stayed by the edge of the pond. She watched as the fish dove downward and began to swim along the bottom, carefully avoiding the choppy waters at the surface. Liat thought about her mother and felt the hairs at the back of her neck go up.

Later that day she drove to her apartment near the University of Hawaii and pulled three fresh canvases out of the closet. Then she made her way to Manoa Falls, just a short distance from the campus. Tucked away from the buildings and highway, it was a spectacular waterfall that dropped nearly fifteen stories, straight down into a pool of water. Plants flanked the steep hills on both sides and the smell of fresh earth and tropical flowers spilled out over the falls with as much intensity as the water. And then there were the rainbows. After such a wet morning Liat knew they would be in abundance at the falls. Unfortunately, she was afraid that people would be too. The falls were a popular spot with the student body. Liat crossed her fingers and hoped the early rain was enough to keep them indoors for a bit longer. She wanted…needed… to paint in peace today.

Liat hiked up on the left side of the cliffs, dirt clogging her yellow work boots, and found her favorite nook about half way up. She looked up and spotted a few students picnicking near the top of the falls, then noticed a handful more swimming in the pool below. Deal-able Liat decided, then she dropped her backpack in the dirt, set up the first canvas, and began to paint.

It wasn't long before she reached for the third canvas. The first two were face down in the dirt. Liat was frustrated. Ever since the episodes with the sculptures had started, her paintings had suffered. They were lackluster. Boring. Today was no exception. The falls, the rainbows, they were dazzling, and yet Liat was bored to tears. She stared at them, at the light and the colors glancing off the water but her mind was still back at the koi pond. Thinking.

All of a sudden Liat got an idea. She reached for the paints and before long, had a good facsimile of the steep falls and the pool below it. Then she painted her mother's face inside the falls. Next she added in the raindrops she'd seen earlier at the koi pond, carefully edging in the ripples, the tiny pools each drop had created on the surface of the pond. She dipped her brush into the colors and filled the pools with tiny circular rainbows. Light, ethereal, barely skimming the surface, types of rainbows. Liat's hand moved fast and sure across the canvas. It was the first painting in nearly a year and half that she felt any good about. That's when the screams cut through the air.

"Stop! No! Let me go! Help!!" The girl shrieked.

Liat looked up and saw a girl hanging by her feet near the top of the waterfall. For a split second she froze. Then, stomach in knots, her eyes fell back to the painting. It was so serene. Waterfalls and rainbows…a far cry from the sculptures she couldn't seem to stop making. Again, the girl screamed. Liat glanced at her mother's face in the waterfall. With a sigh she dropped the paintbrush and headed up the cliff.

Two students, supposedly friends of the girl, had her by the ankles and were dipping her arms in and out of the water at the top of the falls. Stupid. Dangerous. Three or four more people from their group were standing around yelling just that at the perpetrators.

By the time Liat got closer, more people had a grip on the girl and were trying to reel her in, but the goofball holding her by the right ankle was not done having his fun. It was getting more dangerous by the second. Liat stepped in and tugged on his arm. He shrugged Liat off and then turned, laughing down at her.

They locked eyes. Liat held his gaze. For the first time in years she didn't look away. She glared at him. Hard. And then she felt it. Deep in her stomach she felt…it…gathering. Slight but intense. The man drew his head back and his eyes grew slightly wider. He loosened his grip on the girl's ankle and stumbled back a step. Then he reached out a beefy arm, pushed Liat down in the dirt, and planted a foot on either side of her ribs.

"Mind your own business," he barked down at her. Then he turned back toward the waterfall just in time to see the others set his victim back on her feet. In a state of agitation he glanced down at Liat and then stomped away.

43

Liat brushed off her shorts and hiked back down to gather her things. She took her backpack and battered canvases and threw them into the truck. Then she lifted the oil painting she'd been working on and hesitated. The circular rainbows flowed so nicely across the canvas. But they were unfinished. She tossed it on top of the others and then slammed the door shut.

Later on Liat paddled into the ocean and searched out the biggest wave she could find. With expert precision she guided her surfboard into the rising swell and stood. She could feel the wave roll at the back of her board then curl up, and over her, she could taste the salty spray flying off from the lip and for the first time all day Liat felt better. It had been a tough anniversary. Worse than she thought. But in the end Liat's mind was clear. Her mother had been right the first time. She had given Liat a normal life. Her failed attempt back at the waterfall today was proof. All Liat needed to do now was to figure out how to stop making the sculptures...stop the episodes. She'd done it before and she was only seven then. She would do it again. Once again, Liat inched her board forward, ahead of the giant wave curling at her back and smiled. She felt relieved. Then a cross wave smacked in unexpectedly and swept her from the board.

CHAPTER SIX

Philadelphia

Something floated over the wall and landed on my desk. Airline tickets to London. I looked up to see Harry hanging over my cubicle. I put the tickets aside. I was on the phone but that didn't stop Harry from coming around and plopping into the chair next to my desk. The newsroom seemed louder than usual this morning. Phones were ringing off the hook, CNN droned from the flatscreen hanging from the ceiling. Even the static from the police scanner was more jarring than I remembered.

"If there's a window seat I'll take it...great, thanks a lot," I said, un-cupping my right ear and hanging up the phone.

"Window seat? Where do you think you're going? I just dropped two tickets to London on your desk."

I opened my mouth to answer but Harry interrupted me.

"Wait, wait, wait. Before I let you give me chest pains over the plane tickets something was definitely up when I called you earlier. You were talking at me but making zero sense. Then click, you're gone. Was someone there?"

"Sort of. I ran into Shane."

"Shane? Delicious, curly headed, ex-hubby with the six-pack, Shane? Spill it sweetheart. I want details."

"Careful Harry, you're salivating. Wouldn't want you to ruin that Gucci tie you're wearing."

"A specimen as fine as Shane deserves a little drool."

"Yeah, well, not to worry. Pink'n preggers has that one covered."

"What?"

"It seems my ex is officially my ex. He's married or at least he's engaged. Anyway, her finger…that pink diamond…it was so fat I couldn't actually tell if there was a wedding band behind it."

"Okay honey I'm not getting you. Was her finger fat or was it the diamond?"

"Doesn't matter Harry. She's pregnant. She's tall and blonde and very young and pregnant. And oh god I can't believe I'm saying this out loud. She seemed so nice."

Harry scrunched his nose like there was bad fish underneath it. "Wills, I'm sorry." Then he got up from his chair leaned down and hugged me tight. "It's his loss. She'll never be as good as you."

"Thanks," I said, giving him a brief hug back before squirming away. My emotions on the subject had been neatly tucked under the proverbial carpet (along with all the other junk I had hiding there) well before I walked through the door to the newsroom. Exploring the lumps, even with Harry, seemed like a bad idea.

"Can we just skip this and move on?"

Harry looked like he was about to say something else but I didn't give him a chance.

"Take a look at this. I just tracked down Angela's daughter."

Harry sat back down.

"Kid's name is January Pokani. She's 25. Just got her Master's in Art and is teaching a freshman class at the University of Hawaii. And get this she's a world-class surfer. According to a feature article in the school's newspaper Angie's daughter is competing in the Triple Crown of Surfing. Bit of a looker too don't you think?"

I shifted the monitor on my computer so Harry could see the picture on the University's faculty website. She sort of looks like Angela. Don't you think?"

"Yeah. Nice," he agreed glancing away from the monitor and back at me. "What were you saying a minute ago on the phone? Something about a window seat? Remember, you're going to London. These tickets are for London," he said waving them in front of me. "The G-8 Conference is next week. You shouldn't have any problems with the funerals either

46

because from what I hear Bill's family is pushing for burial as soon as possible. I doubt that it'll interfere with your schedule."

"Yeah. I'm not going to the funerals. I'm going to Hawaii. Today." Hoping to graze right past that piece of news, I added, "how about that Angela having a kid stashed in her past?"

Harry cocked his head sideways and looked at me kind of funny. I squelched a sigh and tried not to take it personal.

"London. You're going to London. And are you telling me you didn't know Angela had a ki–

"Surfing," I said, cutting him off. "Tell me everything you know about surfing."

"I do not surf," Harry, replied, indignant. "I don't even swim."

"Oh come on Harry. You're talking to the reporter who just pulled a big old surfboard out of Angela Priest's closet last night. I'm pretty sure if I spend a few minutes poking around your drawers I can turn up at least one cherry red Speedo."

A deep blush spread across Harry's face inching all the way up to his white blonde temples. Despite his embarrassment, his eyes narrowed and the rest of what I said began to sink in. I crossed my arms and waited.

"Did I just hear you say that you pulled a surfboard out of Angela's closet?"

I nodded.

"Does it have something to do with what happened last night? I don't remember reading anything in your article about a surfboard."

"I'm not sure yet," I replied, turning my screen back and browsing the Internet. "I'm still looking for information."

"Well what did the police say? Do they have any theories?"

"Yeah. About that. It's gonna be kinda hard for them to come up with any theories about the surfboard."

"Willow. Please tell me you're kidding. Tell me that you did not take something from the Priests that might in any way shape or form be construed as evidence."

"Yeah, I can't tell you that."

"Willow! Are you crazy? You took a surfboard–a surfboard–from a crime scene?! Didn't it occur to you that the police might care?"

"I don't know Harry. Am I crazy?"

Harry's shoulders slumped.

"That's not what I mean and you know it," he said. "Come on Willow. The police are gonna find out. A loose key? Maybe. But a surfboard? Helloooo," he said wrapping his knuckles on the side of my head, "what about witnesses? Someone is bound to come forward. Seriously, what were you thinking?"

I didn't answer right away. I was busy printing an article I'd just found on the Internet about the diamond Angela had been rambling about before she died.

"Take a look at this, Harry. It's from a local Hawaiian newspaper dated October of 1993.

Rare gem stolen, suspect leaps to his death
By Elwin T. Anahola

A rare forty-three carat black diamond worth over eighty million dollars was stolen yesterday from the Bishop Museum in Honolulu. Nicknamed the Maui Snow, the diamond was donated to the museum by Queen Liliuokalani shortly before the Monarchy was overthrown in 1948. Vaulted for most of the year by the National Treasures Institute on Oahu, the diamond had just gone on display two days ago for the annual six-week run.

According to police the suspect, Sam Kawa, 34, had been prepping a display of vintage surfboards for the museum shortly before the gem went missing. Kawa is a local surfboard shaper and shop owner. Around 10:30 a.m. two security guards along with their dogs were found asleep on the floor. There was no hole cut into the display case and police are still trying to determine how the suspect avoided the facility's heat sensitive laser beams.

Kawa was spotted seven hours later near the Pools of Oheo where he jumped to his death. His body was recovered a short time later. The Maui Snow was not found at the scene.

"I'm stumped," said Ted Johnson, Curator for the museum. None of this makes sense. Sam was a good man and a respected member of the community. I can't understand why he would do this."

The Maui Snow was discovered back in 1835 in a cave near the Pools of Oheo, oddly, not far from where Kawa lept to his death. According to

Johnson, attendants of King Kamehameha III had taken shelter in the cave during a tropical storm. After chipping away at the strange rocks they found in the cave walls, they carried them back to the palace.

An alchemist at the palace experimented on the rocks and determined that they were diamonds. It was a rare find. Some scientists theorize that black diamonds were formed in space as the result of a supernova, the explosion of a star. According to a study in the Astrophysical Journal in 2006 by Jozsef Garai and Stephen Haggerty, along with researchers Sandeep Rekhi and Mark Chance, during the explosion, the amount of pressure created is so great that carbon and hydrogen are immediately compressed into diamonds with multiple aggregates rather than the singular crystals slowly formed in white diamonds on earth. The presence of hydrogen is also a telltale sign that the diamonds were formed in the vicinity of a supernova.

Rare black gems like the Maui Snow could have entered the earth's atmosphere by means of an asteroid, shattered into chunks, and were then embedded in the caves on Maui. After they were discovered in 1835 prospectors flocked to the caves and began digging. This went on for several years until a series of small earthquakes rumbled beneath the volcano Haleakala. At that point according to Johnson King Kamehameha III outlawed prospecting in the caves and also in and around Haleakala.

Yesterday, hours after the gem was stolen on Oahu, a pair of hikers from Michigan, Dale and Mitzy Bradford, watched as Kawa lept to his death amid a swirl of black diamonds.

"It was unreal," said Dale Bradford, 68. "We were sitting by one of the pools eating chicken sandwiches when we heard this screaching whistle. We thought it was a bird but then we looked up and there's this guy running at a major speed, like he was being chased by the devil himself. Poor fellow never even hesitated when he neared the edge. Just kept running. I'll never forget that—the way his legs kept going—one in front of the other even when there was only air underneath him."

"It's like he thought he could make it to the other side, only there weren't no other side," added Mitzy Bradford, 63. "Craziest thing I ever saw. He ran off that cliff and he was hanging up there in the air with his legs still running like I don't even know what. Then whooooosh, just like that he dropped into the pool. We swam in after him but it was too late. He was all smashed up on the bottom."

So far police have no other suspects. They are asking anyone who thinks they have information about the Maui Snow, or the two vintage surfboards Kawa was working on, to come forward and give a statement.

"We didn't see anyone else," said Dale Bradford, "but the man sure ran like he was being chased. I spent time in Korea and trust me that's how you run when you're being chased."

Police searched Kawa's surf shop, the Mau Loa, on Honolua Bay in Maui, as well as the apartment above the shop where he lived with his wife and daughter, but without results.

"I don't know what the police are looking for," said Dave Yamaro, a sales clerk at the shop. "I don't know how Sam was involved in this but he's no thief. The brah's a pure humanitarian. He's always got a hand stretched out to the people here. Besides, he doesn't need the money. His boards are the hottest stuff going this year. Surfers from all over the world have orders in with Sam."

Kawa was born in Hawaii. He was orphaned at age 8, while traveling with his family in India. His parents drowned in a boating accident and Kawa was raised at a local monastery. At age 20, he returned to Maui. Police expect to release his body the day after tomorrow. The family could not be reached for comment.

When Harry was finished he turned the pages over on the desk, looked up at me, and whistled.

"A diamond worth eighty million dollars? I admit, that's one helluva a motive to commit murder. But why so messy? Why shoot each other? Not to mention that Barry already had a boatload of money. Besides, from what I could see they actually liked each other."

"My point exactly," I agreed.

"Check this out," I added, turning the monitor around so that Harry could see it. I'd just found another article from the same Hawaiian newspaper. Only this one was dated twelve years later. Apparently one of the two boards shaped by Sam Kawa was found in the attic of an old surfer after he died. Turns out he was a friend of Kawa's. It says that the police investigated, but that was all they found. No diamond. There was some kind of drawings on the board, something about the Goddess Pele and some kind of poem. No one could figure it out. Eventually the board was put up for auction.

I turned the monitor back and searched further. I got a bit of a shock when the name of the man who bought it popped up. Alfred Pokani. Angela's daughter's name was Pokani. It was too unlikely to be a coincidence. I Googled him.

"So it was Angela's ex-husband who bought the other surfboard," I said to Harry. How about that?"

"Okay, maybe you have something here. Maybe there was more to it than domestic violence. Either way you need to take this info to the police, Willow. And bring the surfboard too. By the way, how did you know the surfboard was in Angela's closet in the first place?"

"Gotta go, Harry," I answered, ignoring his question. "My flight leaves for Hawaii in two hours."

Harry stood up too.

"Willow you can't. What about the G-8 conference? You're job?!"

"Cover for me willya Harry?"

"What about the funerals? Don't tell me you're really going to skip Angela's funeral. You can't do that. You owe her Willow."

I pulled Angela's diamond ring still crusted in blood out of my pocket and held it up to Harry.

"You want to know the last thing Angela asked me to do before they took her away? Before she died in that ambulance Harry? She asked me to fly to Hawaii and give this ring to her daughter. You're right. I owe her."

Harry stood there, stunned, staring at the ring.

"Do the police…

"Yes Harry. The police know I have her ring. Angela practically rose from the dead to make sure they didn't take it from me. Go ahead. Call and ask them if you want."

"But the funerals. Shouldn't you just wait? You can give Angela's daughter the ring then."

"She's not coming Harry. Angela knew she wouldn't. I think that's why she made me promise to take her the ring in the first place."

"Look this is the best flight I could get. I really have to go."

I took the article about the Maui Snow and put it in the computer bag with my laptop. Then I deleted it from the screen and shut down my office computer.

"What if the police call? What if they have more questions for you?"

"Tell them the truth. That I went to deliver Angela's ring. But don't mention the surfboard Harry. I need to time to figure that out. Angela told them the shootings were her fault. Maybe it's better the police think that for now. I probably shouldn't have told you anything yet. I don't know what possessed me. I should've waited until my leads were more solid. I just...I have a hunch Harry. I need to figure out what the deal is with this surfboard. What it means. Why Angela had it in the first place. If I do then maybe I can figure out what really happened to the Priests."

"You wanted my advice and I'm giving it to you. Going after a story is one thing but holding back evidence? Not good. They'll find out. And when they do, they're gonna have questions. Lots of 'em. Willow I get that you think there's a story to break here but taking evidence? That's crossing the line. The police might think you had something to do with...with what happened."

I reached out with both hands and ruffled Harry's perfect hair. Then I slung the computer bag over my shoulder, stepped away from my desk, and let out a deep laugh.

"Oh Harry–now *that's* crazy!"

CHAPTER SEVEN

Oahu
December 2009

It was four-forty in the morning by the time twenty-two year old Nick Porter spotted Liat Kawa walking on the deserted stretch of beach. A bare layer of light had just begun to chip away at the darkness. A steady flow of raindrops pelted the ocean and sand.

When Liat hadn't shown up for their date Nick tried not to worry. This was not the first time Liat had disappeared. He made the usual calls to their tight-knit group of friends on campus at the University of Hawaii but no one had seen her since ten that morning. He kept his tone light with each inquiry. After what they'd all been through a few days ago, searching three separate islands for Liat, the last thing he wanted to do was scare people. With the last phone call though panic crept into his bones. Nick couldn't think of anyone else to call. He got in his car and started to drive.

After hours of searching Nick finally spotted her blue pick-up near a Kamani Tree in the park next to Waikiki beach. He trudged through the sand with his cell phone open in front of him for light. The beach was dark but the light spread surprisingly far. Nick made his way toward the ocean and tried not to think the worst: that she might be hurt. Or, and he hated himself for thinking it, but the thought came anyway, that she might not be alone. It was surf season and Makani was back in town.

Nick let the thought die. He brushed at the rain on his face and continued to search the beach. He trusted Liat. More than he'd ever trusted anyone. He was in love. But Mak, well, Mak was another matter. The Triple Crown wasn't the only reason he'd come back to Hawaii. In fact, Mak had made that perfectly clear to Liat even though Nick had been standing right there with his girlfriend's tiny frame tucked inside of his arms.

Again, he pushed the thought away. Find Liat. Right now that was all that mattered. These disappearing acts were becoming more frequent and to be fair they had started way before Mak flew home to Hawaii.

Something about Liat was off lately. She was quieter than usual. Not that she'd ever been loud. But her presence, that serene hypnotic way Liat had about her had been disturbed. Usually people were drawn to Liat without even knowing why they wanted to be around her. But lately she seemed vague, distracted. There was a distance about her. Something had a grip on her and whatever it was Liat was intent on keeping it to herself. Nick was worried.

He covered the beach in both directions and was about to head back to their cars when he caught sight of Liat emerging from the ocean, carrying a large bucket in each hand. She was nearly back to her truck by the time he was close enough to shout.

"Liat! Liat…wait!"

She kept walking. Nick ran up the beach trying to close the gap between them.

"Liat, Liat!"

Still no response. Nick watched her load the buckets into the flatbed and then slip behind the wheel.

"Liat! Come on. Wait!"

Liat didn't seem to hear him. She didn't seem to notice his beat up Camry parked next to her truck either. Theirs were the only two cars parked along the deserted strip of grass.

By the time he fumbled his key into the ignition Liat was already pulling onto the highway. He followed her. After a while he realized she was heading toward the University of Hawaii and was relieved. Then she turned left, away from the campus apartments and drove down a narrow strip of roadway near the back of the University. Five minutes later she stopped at a building known as the Barn.

It was an old wooden building on the outskirts of the University that at one time had been used for Art classes. At the barn, students had worked on everything from wood, to metal, to glass blowing. After the new art wing opened a few years ago on the upper campus though the Barn was only used for storage. Nick couldn't imagine why Liat would go there at all, let alone in the middle of the night.

Liat took the full buckets out of the back of the truck and went inside.

Nick pulled into the parking space behind Liat's truck and sat there for a moment wondering what to do next. Maybe it was just an art project. Maybe he should let her be. Still she'd blown off their date. And it wasn't exactly safe to be wandering around beaches and hanging out in remote places on campus in the middle of the night. He had every right to be worried. He was trying to decide whether to stay or go when the smell hit him through the open window of his car. He looked up at the long row of windows on the outside of the building. Smoke was pouring out of the last one near the back of the building. Nick opened the car door and ran inside.

"Liat where are you?!"

No answer. No fire, either, from what he could see. But there was smoke. He headed for the back of the building.

"Liat?"

He could hear her moving around back there. As he got closer Nick could see that she was sliding something across the floor. It was a metal basin filled with mud. And Liat was dragging it toward a huge furnace near the back doors of the barn.

Nick was no art student but he knew that the furnace was used for glass blowing. A Journalism Major, he'd written an article when he was a freshman about one of the Art Professors and had watched a rather impressive demonstration. The professor took a small stick of glass, melted it, and then blew it into a fourteen-inch vase. Blowing glass was no job for sissies. Within four minutes the guy was sweating profusely. The veins in his neck were an inch thick and his face was deep red. Nick remembered finding out during the interview that the furnace was capable of reaching temperatures in the thousands.

He knew he should stop her. But something made Nick hold back. He wanted answers. Up until now Liat had refused to talk about what was troubling her. Nick had tried. It was starting to come between them. He took a good hard look at the furnace from where he was standing. It was hot but well contained. They were in a remote part of the campus. At some point though someone was bound to spot the smoke. Nick brushed the thought aside. He stood his ground and watched in silence.

It was the slow methodical way she was moving and the fact that she didn't seem to know anyone was there that held Nick's attention. Some kind of sleepwalking episode he decided. She hadn't answered him once yet. Not at the beach. Not when he called her name as he entered the building. He watched her lift a heavy looking black pot and place it on top of a black grill and then slide it into the fire. He had no idea what was in the pot.

He watched her walk to a stack of shelves opposite the windows and take down a work of art. It was a sculpture carved out of Styrofoam. It was in three separate pieces. Put together it was about three feet long and about four feet high and two or more thick. She brought it over to the basin of mud she'd left near the furnace and then dug a hole and put the bottom piece of the carving inside the mud. Then she brought one of the buckets of sand over to the basin. She reached in, took out handfuls of wet sand, and placed wads of it here and there into the Styrofoam. Afterwards she took shards of colored glass from the pocket of her sweatshirt and tucked them into already carved impressions. When she was finished she packed more mud around the entire piece and patted it lightly, smoothing it all into place. Next she took a long metal rod and hooked it onto the grill. She tugged on it pulling the grill away from the fire and when it was directly over the basin she hooked the rod onto the handle of the black pot and tipped it forward. Scalding liquid metal spilled out of the pot and flowed into the basin of mud.

Nick watched as Liat poured the metal into the basin, disintegrating the Styrofoam and filling the void left behind, the mud serving as a perfect mold. As she poured, Liat reached down and took another handful of sand, dry this time, and tossed it at the flowing metal. Twice more she did this. With no gloves, no glasses, no protective gear at all, she was splashing handfuls of sand at the molten metal. Nick wanted to shout at her to grab her by the shoulders and pull her backwards away from danger but he was more afraid of what might happen if he tried to stop her. So he stood there, dumbfounded, fascinated, and watched her work.

Then she started to hum. After a few bars Nick thought he recognized a Jack Johnson tune.

Liat turned the empty pot upright for the third time and settled it back onto the grill. She turned off the furnace and methodically began to clean up. When she was finished she walked back over to the basin. With a hand shovel she loosened the mud around the edges of the basin. She flipped the basin over onto the cement floor of the Barn and then gripping the handles was able to shake out the large clump of mud the way a baker shakes a cake from its pan. With both hands, she reached through the mud, clearing it away from the newest piece of her sculpture. When she was finished cleaning it, Liat laid the last piece alongside the others and smoothed it into place.

It was spectacular. Sand and metal all splashed together like nothing Nick had ever seen. It had the feel of a sand sculpture yet with the sturdy permanence of metal running through it. Liat had created a miniature open room. Even with his untrained eye Nick knew it wasn't finished. It needed fine-tuning. The edges were rough and would have to be welded together. Still it was haunting. With its intricate detailing, the piece was unlike any of Liat's other work.

In the center of Liat's sand and metal room was a bar. A figure, a man, wearing what looked like a tuxedo, stood near the bar with one hand clutched at his throat. Floating toward the man in the tux was another hand. It was wrapped around the stem of a martini glass. The arm was blunted off at the elbow in mid-air but it looked like a woman holding out the glass to the man. There was something dark inside the glass but Nick couldn't tell what it was. On the wall behind the bar, above what looked like a row of champagne bottles were four miniature paintings, the frames of which reached all the way to the edges of the sculpture. There was more to the sculpture but Liat was standing in front of it and Nick couldn't quite make it out.

When she was finished Liat got up and brushed off her knees. At the very back of the Barn on the opposite wall from the furnace was a door. Liat dug a key out of the pocket of her jeans went to the door and opened it, humming all the while.

CHAPTER EIGHT

Maui, Hawaii

The airplane banked left and began dropping altitude. Jostled from sleep by the unexpected motion I clicked the Jack Johnson tune off my I-pod and glanced out the window. Beneath the wing a blanket of white clouds stretched out for miles, a dark surprise rising at its center.

Haleakala poked through the ring of drifting clouds. Still. Majestic. Immense with power. It was mesmerizing. The airplane circled the giant volcano and you could almost feel its ancient energy seeping through the plane's flimsy windows.

Over the loudspeaker the pilot shared facts about the volcano. I was glad for the distraction.

He told us that the volcano was swelling through those clouds at a height of over 10,000 feet. After the appropriate oohs and aahhs from passengers he went on to explain how despite its grand peak only three percent of the volcano is visible. Most of it, a full 97 percent of the behemoth actually resides below sea level, entrenched in the cool blue waters of the Pacific. The last interesting fact he left us with was the most compelling. Hale-a-ka-la (house of the sun) makes up 77 percent of the island. While Maui is lush with flowers and greenery, steeped in waterfalls and rainbows, rimmed with amazing black and white beaches, when you first step away from the airplane all of that pales in comparison to what you feel—that 10,000 foot giant standing at your side. Add in the vast surrounding waters of the Pacific and suddenly you feel like a speck of pollen shifting in the breeze between two such massive forces. Hawaii is like no other place on earth.

It felt so good to be on the ground. Standing there swallowed by nature, eyes closed, mind quiet, my face tilted high under the warm tropical sun. For a few brief moments I let the peace invade my body.

Then thoughts of Shane and his new love surfaced once again. I'd spent most of the flight fighting back visions of the two of them. Shane and Cathy Whats-her-name. Shane and Cathy and their new baby.

I unclenched my fists and brushed away the tiny crescents of blood forming on my palms. Why? Why was I so angry? Sometimes I barely recognized the person who had returned from Iraq. I wanted the old uncomplicated me back. I looked up at the massive volcano and felt dizzy. Dazed by its ancient beauty. I took a deep breath of the sweet tropical air and for a second I was okay again. For a second. Until I heard it...that far away echo of a voice in my head. Whispery thoughts that crawled in and then quickly ebbed away.

So that's it? Just let it go? I can't let you do that Wils —not when there's unfinished business on the east coast. Come on Willygirl...think. Matt... Cathy...the diner. Cathy Tanglewood...the girl from the diner! It's all her fault Willow...her fault that Matt went to Iraq. That's where it all started... right? So what? She walks away? Matt's dead and now she gets to have a baby? With Shane?

I walked back toward the terminal and tugged on one of the glass doors. I tried hard to open it. But Hawaii's trade winds are fierce and there was a great deal of resistance.

Later, I found myself sitting inside the terminal on one of those blue cushioned chairs near the window. The name of Shane's new wife, Cathy Tang...Cathy, Cathy, Cathy...chugging through my head, like an unhinged freight train. Only I couldn't remember why. I rubbed at my forehead and tried to clear my thoughts. My hands were shaking. When I looked down at them, I saw something in my lap. It was an airplane ticket back to Philadelphia. Why? Why would I buy a ticket back to Philadelphia when I'd just gotten to Hawaii? I wracked my brain but all I could come up with was Cathy.

I stared at the ticket. Wondering how it got there. And then I looked up at the clock. Boarding time was in two hours. I didn't remember buying it. After a few more minutes of crazed speculation, I dug a hand into the bottom of my pocketbook and reached for the prescription bottles. Unscrewing the lids on two of them, I dumped a handful of pills into my palm and swallowed them without water. Maybe they would help. Couldn't hurt. Right? Out the window the sun glowed high above Haleakala.

I pushed open the doors and stumbled outside. Once again, the warmth of Hawaii settled across my face.

FOUR
LOST
DAYS
LATER

CHAPTER NINE

Oahu
December 13, 2009

Again, I looked out the window as the airplane banked and came in slow. Everything was different flying into Oahu. Everything.

An eight year-old sitting in front of me described it perfectly to his mom and I couldn't help grinning. "Hey Mom," he cried. "Look! New York City is on the beach."

The wing dipped toward Waikiki and suddenly the ocean was rushing toward us. Just past the water I could see a beautiful crescent shaped piece of beach lined with tall hotels. Even from the air it had a different feel than Maui. The plane suddenly dropped even lower and we could actually see people windsurfing and sunbathing.

***

"Please tell me you have a room," I said to the girl behind the counter. "And no, I don't have a reservation," I added, glancing back to keep an eye on the surfboard and luggage I'd left by the couch in the hotel lobby.

Without looking up from her computer, the check-in clerk, who was cradling the phone between her ear and shoulder, held up a finger and basically requested the one thing I was out of—patience.

I stole a second glance at the luggage that I'd been too tired to haul over to the desk. Then turned back to the clerk, closed my eyes, and waited. This was the fourth hotel I'd dragged my stuff into since landing.

"You're in luck. We had a cancellation about ten minutes ago. It's one of the nicer rooms though," the clerk said apologetically. "The cost is $535.00 a night."

Cringing, I handed over my American Express card. It could've been worse. The last hotel wanted $850.00 for the only suites they had left. It was peak season in Hawaii. I booked the room for a week and told her I might need it longer.

"Lady, how'd you get your hands on this ride?"

I turned to find a string bean of a bellhop with shoulder length brown hair and bits of a beard patched across his thirty-something face, holding my stuff. He had one of my bags slung over his shoulder and the cover over top of Angie's surfboard pulled halfway off.

"Hey, don't touch that!"

Too late. Before I knew it the cover was on the ground and the bellhop was nearly drooling as he ran his hands over every inch of the surfboard.

"It's a Sam Kawa. This is the missing Sam Kawa board," he stated. "It is, right? An original Sam Kawa? Awww snap, here it is, here's the poem with the clues." The man let out a sweet, low whistle and slipped his cell phone out of his back pocket. "Lady do you have any idea how long people have been looking for this?"

There were only a handful of guests scattered around the lobby but nearly all of them turned to see what the bellhop was squawking about. Next thing I know the camera on his cell phone is clicking away. I dropped the room key the desk clerk was trying to hand me and ran.

"Wait 'til old man Pokani sees this. Dude's gonna shit the golden brick!" The bellhop was getting more excited by the second. "It's official, right? I mean it looks like the real thing. Just like the one with Pele on it. You know, I've seen that board too," he boasted. "Got delivered to the hotel by mistake and the old man freaked out, wanted it sent home, wikiwiki. Told him we could use my van, store it under my board for the ride. I even helped him set it up in his private study."

"Are you talking about Alfred Pokani? Here, at this hotel?" I asked as I picked up the cover and pulled it back over the surfboard, trying to act nonchalant.

"Yep, he owns it. Owns three others on this strip and at least two hotels on the other side of the island. Plus he's got a handful on Maui, the big island, even a couple on Kaui."

"Hotels?" I mumbled, more to myself than to the bellhop. Jetlag. Of course Pokani owns hotels. How could I forget? I just did that research what, like a day ago? Had to be the jetlag wreaking havoc on my memory like that.

"Okay, so you know Pokani," I said, handing him my other bag and then carrying the surfboard with me as I headed back to the check in desk to get the key. "How about his daughter, January?"

"Jan? Sure, I know her, " he said, following me to the elevator. "Everybody around here knows Jan Pokani."

"Is she here? Do you know where I can find her?"

"Right this minute? No," he said, stepping onto the elevator with me and pushing number five. "But I know where you can find her tomorrow. She'll be at the beach. At the competition with the rest of us."

"Tomorrow? I thought her competition doesn't start for a few more days."

"It doesn't. Tomorrow she'll be watching. So will everybody else. Tomorrow's competition is a prelim to pick the wildcard entrants for part of the men's triple crown. It's huge. Lots of locals compete and some of them are the best big wave surfers in the world."

"I get it. It's a big deal."

I could tell from the expression on his face that no, I did not get it, and that yes, he was going to make it a point to educate me until I did.

"Lady, at the end of the day tomorrow two locals will get to join the 45 top ranked surfers in the world. The ranked surfers are the ones who get to travel around the world and compete on the pro circuit during the season. As wild cards, tomorrow's lucky winners get a chance to compete at Pipeline. Lady, Triple Crown is the biggest event of the year. It's three separate contests. Six if you're counting the women's competition. Heck, the prizes for Pipeline and Sunset Beach are worth better than a quarter of a million each. But it's not just the money. The best surfers get their share of that with endorsements from big names like Element and Roxy and Quicksilver. Like I said though, it's more than that. Winning a spot is about respect. Surfing at Pipeline isn't about the money. It's about the waves."

"Point taken," I offered with as much respect as I could muster considering my fatigue. To be honest I was surprised. I had no idea there was so much involved in pro surfing, let alone such big paychecks.

"What's your name?"

"Vince. Vince Gunther."

"Hi Vince, I'm Willow," I said, extending my hand. "So tell me, where and what time is this great event tomorrow?"

"It's not far. I can take you if you want."

"Sure, why not," I replied as we stepped off the elevator and headed down the hall to room 538. I opened the door and leaned the board against the wall. Vince followed me in and set my bags on the floor next to it.

"Great. That's great," he gushed. "You're gonna love it."

Vince seemed a little too jazzed. I rolled my eyes. This is not a date, I thought.

"I'll meet you in the lobby by eight o'clock," he added. "I'd get here earlier but I gotta drop my brother off at work, first. You see it gets crowded really fast and with all the camera crews and stuff it's tough to get a good spot if you don't get there early.

"Camera crews?"

"Sure. The surf mags all bring their own crews for both in and out of the water. Then there're the sports networks."

"Sounds like I need to do some research," I said, unzipping the bag with my computer. "By the way how's the room service menu? If I don't get something to eat soon I'm gonna pass out."

It wasn't intended to be an opening but Vince jumped on it anyway.

"I'm off in ten minutes. We could hit the Barefoot Café together. It's right on the beach just a couple of hotels down from here. Forget the computer. I'll teach you everything you need to know about the waves. Give you better info than you'll get outta that metal box. Waste less energy too."

I wasn't so sure about that.

"Come on. Pick a meal. I promise you, the Barefoot Café will make it better than anything you've ever tasted."

CHAPTER TEN

Mahi mahi drenched in lemon and white wine sauce along with a risotto cake and some steamed vegetables all delicately seasoned in nameless spices arrived at the table twenty minutes after we ordered. By the third bite I decided never to leave Hawaii. Vince dropped his cell phone next to his plate and dug into his coconut prawns and paradise fries with equal enthusiasm. They smelled so good it was a bit of a strain not to reach across the table and take one. I squelched the urge and contented myself with the fish on my own plate, and the warm tropical breeze blowing around us.

"Bring the lady a Blue Hawaiian," he told the waiter. "I'll have a shot and a beer." Then he pressed a conspiring hand on the waiter's shoulder. "And keep 'em comin," he added.

It was easy to see why he'd chosen the Barefoot Café. It was situated on the beach in the back of a large hotel, located in the middle of a strip of hotels along Waikiki Beach. There was a name scripted on the back wall of the hotel but fronds from the palm trees were blocking some of the letters and I couldn't quite make it out. Every table had an umbrella and the seats were white and very well padded. Indoor comfort but with the ability to squish your toes in the warm sand. It was the perfect tropical atmosphere. The night was pitch black and it was too dark to see the ocean, but the edge of the waves, those tiny white inches that roll into the sand, were illuminated by a line of tikki torches. The effect was incredible. The constant roll and crash of waves fading away into an endless black pool. I relaxed and took in the surrounding beauty while eating what was arguably the best meal of my life. Philadelphia felt like another planet, a distant rock that I'd sprung out from under, leaving behind all those bad memories. It felt good to be away. Healthier somehow. Well, except for the slight headache I couldn't seem to ditch. Oh yeah, and that nagging sense of curiosity about the last couple of days. Where I'd been. What I'd been doing. Here and there a scattered thought danced randomly in the back of my brain. But I could never quite catch hold of it.

Careful Willygirl. Let it go.

Halfway through the meal, just as I was getting my stamina back and was about to ask Vince some questions, a band from the hotel collected themselves in front of the tikki torches to play the requisite tropical tunes. A dozen or so hula dancers, male and female, joined them. The women danced first, skirts flowing, arms swaying with the breeze. The men followed, launching sticks of fire and guttural calls while the drumbeats grew louder and faster, eventually reaching a crescendo and then dropping down to one final beat. Silence hung in the air. It was deep and effective and gave rise to a collective emotion among the diners—we were right with the world—we were in paradise.

My stomach and senses were filled to the brim. There was no room for anything else. For the moment I let myself live in it. Then Vince dropped his fork on the plate, scooted back his chair, and hooted at one of the hula girls. The spell was broken.

"That's Lani," he informed me. "We used to surf together. Too cool she's workin' here, I had no idea," Vince chatted, amiably. "Hey, you think maybe she could get me a gig? I play drums pretty good," he added, picking up his fork and knife and banging them on the edge of the table.

I reached across the table, grabbed the utensils on the upbeat, and dropped them onto my plate.

"Okay, so I want to cover the whole surfing thing, I do. But let's talk about the Maui Snow first. For starters what can you tell me about Sam Kawa? The news article I read said that Kawa was responsible but it looks like they left out a few details. For instance any chance there was an accomplice? Seems like a big job for one person to take on. Alfred Pokani, maybe? Were Kawa and Pokani friends?"

"Woah, wahine, you sure take off in a hurry. A body could get hurt movin' that fast."

"Please, Vince. This is important."

"I thought you were here to sell the surfboard to Pokani."

"Maybe. But I want to know what I'm selling."

Vince studied me for a minute then continued.

"Well, Sam and Pokani knew each other. But any ideas you have that they were working together are way off. Old man Pokani hated Sam and I mean hated."

"Why?"

Before I could get Vince to answer, the waiter came by with a dessert cart. Vince picked up three different cakes and then put them back down. Exasperated, I picked a coconut brownie brulee from the top tray and asked for two spoons. Served in half of a coconut shell it was a warm dark chocolate brownie covered in a thick layer of crème brulee. The waiter sprinkled sugar and coconut on top and then toasted it with a flame pen that looked like a mini tikki torch. I smiled at Vince and dug in.

"Why?" I asked again between bites.

"Because Pokani was in the process of opening his third hotel and Sam Kawa was getting in his way. Pokani was strapped for cash. Don't get me wrong, the dude was well on his way to becoming a success but he wasn't exactly the mogul he is today."

"So how does Kawa enter the equation?"

"The hotel Pokani had just bought was down the block from Sam Kawa's surf shop. It was old and small. Pokani was planning on gutting the hotel and building a bigger, better one. He was planning on adding at least two hundred rooms. Folks in the area weren't too happy about it and Sam kind of led the revolt. Pokani thought he could use his stepfather's Hawaiian heritage to push past the controversy but folks weren't buying it. It was kind of a lame move considering that Alfred is the spitting image of his Norwegian mother. Not that color mattered. He could've been as green as the grass. Sam Kawa wasn't about to let him get away with it. He went to the city counsel and had the old hotel declared historic. Pokani was allowed to do some repairs but he had to keep as much of the old building intact as possible to stay in compliance.

He was furious, but lawsuits cost money and at the time he didn't have the kind of cash it took for a fight."

"I don't get it. Wouldn't a bigger, newer hotel bring in more business for Kawa's surf shop? Was there bad blood between them, some kind of family feud?"

"Malihini (tourists)," he said, shaking his head. "You don't understand."

"Why do I get the feeling I was just insulted?"

"Not insulted just uninformed. You automatically assume that bigger, that newer, is better. More hotels more money, right? Well look around," he said patiently. Vince pointed to the tikki torches, to the ocean. He picked up a handful of sand and let it slip through his fingers. "I know the islands are beautiful and I understand why people want to come. There's a feeling here a sense of well being that you can't find most places in this world. But it's delicate. There's only so much space. If we go too far, build up every square inch, then the reason you come here slips away. Sam Kawa understood that."

He had a point. Minutes before I was able to lose myself completely in the atmosphere. Considering the mess my brain was in when I left Philadelphia, it had taken surprisingly little effort to melt into this enchanted atmosphere. The tropical food the warm sand on my feet the salty smell of the ocean. It was a far cry from the straight jackets and jello cubes in Pennsylvania.

"It's a constant struggle here in the islands," Vince said. "There are those who want to develop and those who want to preserve. Sometimes the clash gets ugly."

"Where do you fit in?"

Vince smiled. "I'm a surfer not a politician. The only thing I want to fight for is a wave."

"Back to Pokani and Kawa."

"This thing with the hotel. It was just a few months before the Maui Snow was stolen. If Sam did have an accomplice there's not much chance it was Pokani."

"But Pokani built all these other hotels. Where did he get the money? You said he was strapped for cash."

"Can't answer that. But it's not because he stole the Maui Snow. The old man's been searchin' on it for years. That's legit. If you ask me nobody is ever gonna find it. Sure, rumors got outta hand after what happened last year but nothin' came of it. Nothin' ever does. The Maui Snow is just a legend now. Boss Man will get all excited when he sees the board you brought. He'll spend a couple of years tryin' to figure out the poem like he did on the first board, the one with Pele on it. Then he'll hang it up on the wall and wait. That's my guess."

I put my elbows on the table and leaned forward.

"What happened last year? What rumors?"

For the first time that night Vince looked uncomfortable, like he'd said more than he meant to.

"Look, Vince, if you know something I wish you'd tell me. It might be important."

Vince absently drummed the edge of the table with his fingers and then leaned forward.

"Sam Kawa's surfboard, you brought it here to sell to my boss right? You know Pokani will pay you good money for it."

"I'm sure he will. But a friend gave me the board just before she died and I have a few things to take care of for her before I go selling her stuff off to the highest bidder."

I sat back brushing my hand over the pocket of my jeans. I could feel the bump of Angela's ring inside.

"Trust me," Vince said, "Pokani's your highest bidder."

"What happened last year?" I asked again.

"You first. Where'd you get the board?"

I sat back in my chair and studied Vince for a minute. The carefree surfer boy wasn't so carefree.

"January's mother. Angela Priest."

Vince's eyebrows went up. He sat back in his chair and let out a low whistle.

"I was expecting the night to get interesting but...

He let the thought drop and replaced it with another whistle.

"Does Jan know? Shit, old man Pokani's gonna pop a vein when he finds out that Kawa's other board has been with Jan's mother this whole time. Brilliant on Kawa's part though. Pokani thought his ex-wife was a space cadet and barely gave her the time of day when they were married. He never would have suspected that she had it."

I shouldn't have told him where I got the board. It was a risk. I just hoped it wasn't going to make it harder to keep Jan out of the fray, like Angie wanted.

"Look, Vince, January doesn't know about the board yet. For the time being I need to keep it that way. I promised her mother."

"Sure. We can work that out," he smiled at me a bit too wide and long.

"Back to the diamond," I said trying to refocus him. "What happened a year ago?"

"Right. So, about a year and a half ago, a handful of students from the University were hiking on the Big Island of Hawaii, near the slopes of Mauna Loa."

"Mauna Loa…that's a volcano, right?"

"Yeah, the last major eruption was back in the eighties, though. Next to it is Mauna Kea. You can still watch the lava flowing into the ocean from there if you want. It's pretty spectacular. You should check it out while you're here. It's safe enough if you check in at the visitor's center. They keep a sharp eye on the seismic activity and if you pay attention to what they tell you, it's worth the trek."

"And the hikers?" I asked, a bit impatient.

"Right, so this group of college kids went hiking in a restricted zone. They got lost. They got bored. So they stopped near the hot springs and one of them gets the brilliant idea to go skinny-dipping. Three of them jumped in. The other two wandered off and later admitted that they were gettin' busy behind a rock while their friends went swimming. The kids in the spring notice an odd smell and a few seconds later they're all howling. Acid from a fissure spilled up into the pool. Shit like that happens. Some of those springs get spills on a regular basis. Kind of like old faithful. Thing is, the ones that do are well marked. Somehow the sign from that pool was missing. They tried to climb out but all three of them died."

"Gruesome story. What does it have to do with the Maui Snow?"

"Well, one of the rangers found two small black diamonds on the ground near their pile of clothes."

"So whose were they?"

"Dunno." He shrugged.

"What did the police say?"

"Nuthin. They don't know either. That's what's so weird about it."

"So you're saying it was just some random thing? A bunch of kids are dead and oh yeah by the way here's a couple of rare black diamonds laying nearby?"

"It's possible, I guess. Hey, did you know that black diamonds weren't even formed in the earth like regular diamonds. That they kinda stormed in from outer space?"

Here we go again, I thought.

"The theory is that they were formed in the nanoseconds after the explosion of dying stars, that they fell on the earth like a big black snowstorm. Cool, huh?"

"Cool," I agreed.

"So those kids. Chances are one of them had some pretty good info on those black diamonds. Maybe one of them knows where the Maui Snow is. Did you know them Vince? Can you give me their names?"

"I told you. They're dead."

"What about the make-out couple?"

"They don't know anything. Since they were still in their clothes, and since the diamonds were found near the dead kids' clothes, the police pretty much believed them."

"I still want to interview them. I'm a good listener. Maybe they have information and don't even know they have it."

Again Vince hesitated.

"Trust me," he finally answered. "It's a dead end. If Pokani couldn't find a connection to the Maui Snow, nobody can."

Only I didn't trust him. I could tell that Vince knew at least some of the hikers on Mauna Loa and didn't want to give me names. I smiled and let the subject drop. An incident like that would have been covered by the local papers and would be easy enough to find.

"You should talk to Pokani. He'll pay you for the board. Trust me, you'll never find the Maui Snow. Not even if you managed to get a hold of both boards. Sam would have made it impossible. Personally, I think it's long gone. I think it went over the cliff with Sam. Some smart park ranger probably found it and by now it's stuck in some billionaire prince's sock drawer. The surfboard though, Sam's board…that's art. It's worth something. And Pokani wants it."

"You keep calling him Sam? How well did you know him?

73

Vince sat back and stretched his legs out in the sand. With the change of subject his entire body seemed to relax.

"I was just a kid when the whole diamond thing happened but I knew Sam pretty well. I hung around his surf shop on Maui. He taught me how to surf. Taught most of us kids who lived nearby. There are some big waves in that area and it's important to figure out where the fun ends and trouble begins. When you're a punk ass kid like I was, you have a tendency to paddle out without a care. Next thing you know, you're caught up in a bad wave and chuggin' down ocean shots faster than, well," he said, throwing me a leering glance, "faster than if they was tequila shots lined up between some hot chick's bikini. One minute you're up with the surf, next minute you're a goner. Course, if a guy did drown like that," he grinned, "well, I suppose there are worse ways to go."

He leaned a shoulder into me to make sure that I got his drift. The movement was awkward though and the small table bounced pretty hard. I lifted an interested eyebrow as his cell phone slid toward the edge of the table. Vince took it as a good sign and tried to wink at me too but couldn't quite manage it. The waiter had been replacing his empty beer and shot glass with an astonishing level of efficiency during the meal and it was starting to show. Time to bail, I thought. Except that Vince was getting more talkative with every beer.

"Sam was the best," he added, all choked up. "Brah gave us skills. Man, he could shape a board too like….like…really good."

I dropped my napkin on the plate and started to push back my chair.

"Hey, here's somethin I betcha dint know," he slurred. "Sam and Pokani aren't the only ones dint like each other. Boss Man's daughter Jan? Great surfer. Really Great. Primo artist too. Sam's daughter Liat? Even better. Now, the women's contest that's comin' up? Stahaaaaand back. 'Cause those two wahine's? They are in it thick. And y'know what else," he said pointing a wobbly finger at me to help convey the importance of his beer infused knowledge, "waves aren't the only thing they're competin' for. Well, Jan anyways. Don'tgetmewrong though, I like her…like Jan a lot. She's somethin' else. It's just that Liat's kinda… low key…real smooth most the time, does her own thing. But with Jan, well, the thing is," Vince finally squinted one eye shut and shot his finger across the table. "The thing is, if Liat's got it? Well, then Jan wants it. Just pick a prize…art, surfing, even men. And she's catchin' up too. Jan won all that art stuff at the college last year. This year she even took the first leg of the Triple Crown. Scooped it right out from under Liat with one good wave at the end of the last heat."

"Good to know. Thanks, Vince," I said as I stood up from the table. "It's getting late and I really need to get some sleep if we're gonna hit the beach for that competition tomorrow."

"Nah, come on, it's early," he said as he reached for my hand and nearly fell out of his chair. He grabbed at the table for support. It was just enough to send the cell phone over the edge and into the sand. "Don't go yet."

I hesitated for a second and then sat down and asked him one more question.

"Vince, the other surfboard, any chance you can sneak me in so I can get a peek at it? Privately, without anybody knowing I was there?"

Vince dropped his hand down on the table and laughed.

"Not a chance. Pokani's shackasaurus? Man that hut is locked up tight. Anyway, the two boards look almost the same. Well, 'cept his has Pele carved in the top n' yours has Poliahu. She's the snow goddess," he said with a smile. "Now she is hot." He giggled and then added, "acshully she's cold—cause she's the snow goddess." He let loose another round of giggles.

I signaled the waiter, handed him some cash, and made my escape before Vince could negotiate his way out of the chair. Oh yeah, and I reached down and scooped his cell phone out of the sand too. I headed down to the ocean by the tikki torches and walked along the water, letting it ripple over my feet, as I strolled in the direction of the hotel. With a sigh I flipped open Vince's cell phone and played with it until I figured out where his pictures were stored. Sure enough there were two perfectly clear photos of the surfboard. One was a close up of the poem. I held the phone up under the light of one of tikki torches and was able to read every word.

If you've searched the volcano and can't find the gem
Here's one final clue to your hand I will lend

Search inside the sand and glass of life's tales
Aligned by time these secrets connected unveil

The island first shaped true by Poliahu's board
Her tipped wave now sings the Maui Snow restored.

I still had no clue what it meant. Somehow I would have to get my hands on the other surfboard. The one Pokani had. I stood at the edge of the water and threw my arm back, ready to toss Vince's cell phone into the ocean. But something stopped me. Something Vince had said earlier in the evening, about the beauty of the islands, the delicate balance. I looked at the phone. At my elbow, all cocked and ready for action. Thoughtless action. I felt a sudden wave of guilt and lowered the phone. I deleted the photos and headed for the hotel.

I was full and tired and what I wanted to do most was crawl under the covers and consider all of the other information Vince had provided during dinner. Instead I crossed through the lobby and with my sandals hanging from my index finger I fished my American Express card out of my pocket.

"Here," I said, handing it over to the desk clerk, "I can't stay. Oh, yeah, and I found this in the sand," I said, putting Vince's cell phone on the counter too.

"Listen, can you do me a favor and leave a message for Vince Gunther when he gets here tomorrow? Tell him I had an emergency. Tell him I had to fly back to Philadelphia. It's important that he gets the message. That I went back to Philadelphia. I'm supposed to meet him here in the lobby around eight tomorrow morning."

Twenty minutes and another seven hundred dollars later I slipped under the covers at the Outrigger Reef Hotel and dropped off to sleep with the ebb and flow of the Pacific thundering beneath my window.

CHAPTER ELEVEN

I stepped in way too far. The waves were loud, almost deafening. Massive too. Biggest things I'd ever seen. Walls and walls of thick blue water that poked out of the ocean and then raced forward with the speed of a rookie mailman being chased by angry Dobermans. A good twenty feet high they peaked then curled, eventually crashing straight down and striking the ocean floor so hard that it loosened up a mess of sand. Clumps of it flew up into the shallow waters churning into cloudy peaks several feet deep.

I watched, fascinated, as the waves sped toward me then dissolved down to about seven or eight inches before ripping at my calves and then rushing back out to repeat the process. This was not your average New Jersey beach. More like the tide pool at the bottom of Niagara Falls.

The next wave rolled in and crashed around my legs, digging my feet deeper into the sand. I barely noticed. The spectacle of rising water was so mesmerizing that it actually drowned out the dark thoughts that had been steadily rising in my head again. Bits and pieces of those lost four days after I first flew into Hawaii. Days that I still couldn't quite sort out.

A hand shook my shoulder. The touch sent shock waves to my gut, startling me away from the sense of relief the massive waves were providing. I turned to see who was there and was surprised to find my feet wedged so far into the sand that only my hips and shoulders moved.

"Excuse me Ma'am, you really shouldn't be out this far. I know it doesn't seem like you're in too deep but trust me, you are."

Despite the fact that my head was now twisted unnaturally toward the beach my aggravation morphed into grudging appreciation. The man tapping me on the shoulder was beautiful. Strong, carved, about five eleven, he stood behind me in wet green trunks. His skin was that tropical chocolate color, warmed to perfection by centuries of Hawaiian descendants. His eyes were the same tone as his skin but deeper; tiny pots of chocolate with deep flecks of caramel swirled in here and there. Staring at me now, his eyes managed to dish admonishment and warmth all in the same glance.

He shouted over the waves, once again calling me what no man in his right mind, unless he's wearing a military uniform, ought to call a woman in her ahhhmm, very early thirties.

"Ma'am!!"

He looked at me and pointed to a sign just a few feet away from us on the beach.

Caution
Dangerous Surf.
Heavy Waves and Riptides.
No Swimming. Surfers Beware.

I was standing not swimming I started to insist. But then the next wave barreled into my thighs and made a liar out of me. It knocked me flat on my back and into the speeding water. Within seconds I was dragged toward the beach then just as fast yanked violently in the other direction. Toward the rougher surf. Toward those bigger than anything I'd ever seen in my life waves. My arms and legs went flailing every which way as I tried to gain control.

I rolled over three times before I was able to poke my head above the current to get some air. I sucked in about half a lungful before a large cross-wave socked me in the head and filled my open mouth with salt water. The sudden lack of oxygen was jarring enough but the tug of the undertow dragging me away rushed through my veins with a feeling of what, I wasn't exactly sure. Relief? Panic? There was no time to figure it out. The next wave would surely take me farther. Out into the real waves. Those monstrous walls I'd been contemplating a few minutes before. Suddenly there were hands underneath my armpits. Tugging at me until the wave let go. A moment later I was in the sand.

He rolled me over then forced my knees into my chest and waited until I gave back my stash of the Pacific. When I was finished coughing he helped me sit up. I sat there dazed for a minute and then started laughing. The coffee cup I'd been holding as I stared at the waves a few minutes ago was still clutched tight in my hand. What was left of it that is. My thumb and two fingers were poked clear through the cup and the only thing at the bottom of it now was salt water and chunks of foam. I found it amusing that in the face of sudden death I'd tried to drag my brew into whatever afterlife was waiting for me.

"You okay?"

I answered with another round of racking coughs. After tossing up more of the sea I turned my head upward hoping that my savior was anyone other than the man who'd just tried to warn me. But of course it was the Hawaiian kneeling next to me, his hand still resting on my back. He offered a smile. To his credit there wasn't even a hint of 'I told you so' in his expression.

"You're okay. Just sit a minute."

"Is your stuff nearby? Do you have a towel?"

I coughed some more and pointed to an umbrella farther up on the beach. He helped me up and as we started walking I sensed that he was looking around for someone to claim me. By now a handful of photographers were setting up their tripods and a group of young surfers had gathered around them to chat. Other than that the beach was nearly empty.

"It's just me," I said, sinking onto the towel he spread out over the sand. Without asking he reached into my bag and drew out another towel to spread around my shoulders. I threw it over my lap instead. The bottoms of my royal blue tankini were twisted and filled with sand.

"Thanks," I mumbled, trying not to sound too ungrateful. What he'd done was nice but I knew how to swim. I can take care of myself I thought.

"Hi, I'm Kai. Kai Malulani." He eyed the big umbrella and the bagful of stuff somewhat doubtfully. "First time at a surfing event?"

Apparently an umbrella at the beach with too much stuff is a Jersey thing. "Gee, what gave it away?" I managed a smile. We both laughed. Then he turned back toward the ocean and pointed to the surf.

"You picked a good day to watch. The waves are looking high and thick and there'll be some real talent in the water. It's shaping up to be a good competition."

I reached into my bag and pulled out another coffee glad that I'd gotten more than one at the drive through.

"Want some?" I offered.

He caught sight of the logo on the side of the cup and made a face.

"I wouldn't call that coffee."

Hhhhmmm a coffee snob. The guy had potential. Still, I found myself on the defensive. In extreme circumstances, like maybe on a strange island six thousand miles from home, I happen to think that Burger Joint coffee holds up better than most.

"Okay, so it's not exactly Starbucks. But this isn't Philly. It's not like you guys have one on every corner. In fact I don't think I've seen one since I got here."

The handsome Hawaiian made another face. "If you're lucky, you won't. Look around. Do you know where you are?"

"Yes, caped crusader. We're at the beach," I replied, the sarcasm in my voice sounding weak against the backdrop of crashing waves.

"All I did was swallow a few ounces of sea water. It's not like I cracked my head open and developed a case of brain damage."

"No," he said, disconcerted at the way I'd taken his comment. "What I meant is that you're in Hawaii, home to some of the best coffee on the planet. Kona coffee."

"Oh that," I said, pushing some of the wet curls out of my eyes. "I've tried it. Not impressed."

It was rude. I know. The guy had just done his good deed for the day, dragging me out of the sea, and there I go insulting his home brew. It wasn't on purpose. It's just that the thought fell out of my mouth before it ever occurred to me I might want to stop it.

Something barely readable flashed across his face. His eyes were quick and intelligent. And if I had to take a stab at it I would say the look was disgust. Luckily, it was for the coffee.

"It must've been a blend," he explained. "One hundred percent Kona is hard to come by on the mainland and pretty expensive. A lot of places butcher it by mixing it with other blends to make money. It ruins the taste."

"Trust me," he added, "a good cup of Kona is worth the experience. And I know a place that makes the best."

"Is that an invitation?"

Maybe I *had* hit my head. Because once again the thought fell out of my mouth before I could stop it.

Red crept up his face and shined hotter than sunburn. I'd put him on the spot. My stomach lurched and for just a second, floating face down in the ocean seemed less painful.

"Sure, uhhmm…sure."

I looked around: plenty of sand but no shovel in sight to bury my head. Then he did something unexpected. With the warmest smile I'd ever seen, he dropped down next to me in the sand, cupped my chin, and locked gazes with me.

"I would be honored to share…some very, very, good coffee with you."

Seriously. He said it like that. All slow and polite. Normally that would have been my clue to shove my feet into some Reeboks and run the other way. My taste in men was more hot dogs and hockey sticks than chivalrous. But waterlog got the better of me. Plus I was pretty sure that if I hightailed it off the beach right then, that the pound of sand twisted up in my bathing suit would make the getaway all kinds of slow and awkward.

So I tried to think of something witty to say. Unfortunately before anything witty actually occurred to me, we were interrupted by a group of young surfers heading up the beach in our direction. Laughing and jostling each other they managed to raise the energy level at least ten notches with every step as they approached us.

A slight man in his twenties with black hair shaved to a near stubble on his nicely shaped head reached Kai first, body checking the bigger man and then dropping a light punch on his shoulder.

"Hey, Prof. Doin' a little fishin this morning?" He nodded in my direction. He had on one of those tight stretchy shirts that surfers wear and a pair of plain blue swim trunks with Billabong scripted at the lower right leg.

"Best lookin' thing you've caught in forever," chimed in a young sandy haired man dressed in a similar fashion.

"That's because Professor Malulani hasn't figure out the right place to drop his bait," quipped a ridiculously stacked girl. I couldn't see much of her face with the hat she was wearing. Just a few wisps of blonde hair and a red bikini that left little to the imagination.

The small crowd laughed. Except for the girl standing next to red bikini. She looked embarrassed. A few inches shorter and not as obviously endowed as her friend, the girl had on a modest suit with a towel wrapped around her waist. Her hair was short and a pretty shade of brown and her eyes were kind and hazel. She was better looking in a much more natural way than the other girl but she didn't seem to know it. Not the way she stood at the other one's side with her surfboard tilted in front of her like a shield. It was as if the taller girl had sucked all the confidence out of the air around them.

I glanced at Kai, expecting another blush at the comment. None came. Obviously it wasn't the first suggestive comment he'd fielded from red bikini girl.

"So, you're a professor?" I asked diverting the conversation. "Any chance you teach at the University of Hawaii? I'm trying to locate the daughter of a friend of mine who teaches art there."

"Yes, but I teach Astronomy," he answered, happy for the change of subject. "And these bozos here are my students."

"Not all of us," corrected the blonde girl. "At least not anymore."

"Seriously, Prof. Who's the little mermaid?" Asked the man who'd punched him on the shoulder. He had the same tropical brown skin as Kai although a shade or so lighter. Despite his joking tone, he seemed more intense than the professor. That being said, I couldn't exactly blame him for the mermaid crack. After all, I was sitting on the beach, legs swaddled in a towel, with wet red curls dangling past my hips into the sand.

"Hi, I'm Makani Pau o'le. Friends call me Mak. And you are?"

"Amazed," I said, indicating the rising waves in front of us.

I found out later that his first name, Makani, means wind and that his last name, Pau o'le means never ending. The idea still haunts me. It kind of makes you wonder. About names I mean, about the strength of their meanings. Do they really carry any weight in this life? Are they surface titles or a life sentence? Is it possible some have stronger effects than others? I wonder. Maybe some names can never be outrun.

"Please. Tell me. How does anyone work up the nerve to go play in stuff like that?" I asked Mak as I pointed toward the waves that had somehow grown higher since Kai dragged me to the beach. "How about you guys? Do any of you compete?"

They laughed.

"All of us," Mak answered as if it were the most natural thing in the world. "Well, most of us anyway," he added, staring pointedly at the sandy haired man to my left. He was about the same height as Mak but with bigger shoulders. His eyes were green and curious and his sandy colored hair fell over his neck in relaxed layers.

"Don't let the waves scare you. It just takes skill. And a little nerve," Mak added directing the last comment once again to the sandy haired man.

The tension between them was obvious but to his credit the young man smiled and refused to take the bait. Mak turned back to me and asked,

"So, should I stick with the mermaid thing or do you actually have a name?"

"While the mermaid gig does sound interesting, I already have a job. I'm a reporter. My name–

"You're Willow Finnegan! Ohmygod you are! Aren't you?"

Everybody, including me, turned to stare at the blonde surfer who'd just gushed like a five year old meeting his favorite Power Ranger. He didn't seem to notice. He was too busy staring at me.

"You are Willow Finnegan. The one who writes for the *Philadelphia Chronicle*? I read your articles all the time. Diaries from Iraq. Oh man. The stuff you wrote, the daily ins and outs made me feel like I was there. Like I knew those people. There was that one guy you used to write about all the time. That kid from Michigan whats-his-name? Mark? I couldn't believe the story you told about how he ended up joining the service in the first place. All because of a piece of stupid pie. Man, some girl trouble, pie and blammo poor joe's in the middle of a war. I even wrote a paper on it once for English class. Got an A."

By now the eyes had shifted back to me. I was still staring at the shaggy haired kid leaning on his surfboard. I didn't know what to say. It's not like people recognize me every day. Not this far outside of Philadelphia.

"Not Mark. Matt," I answered, careful to keep my emotions under wrap. "The soldier's name was Matt."

Who was this kid anyway? And just how much did he know about me? In the two weeks since departing the nuthouse I'd been pretty successful at convincing myself that not everybody I made eye contact with could tell where I'd been. That they didn't automatically know my last 'vacation' was spent warding off electroshock burns and not Waikiki sunrays. But this kid, wham, out of the blue he just happens to read the *Philly Chronicle*? What are the chances? I took a breath and fought back the edges of a headache. No. No. No. Chill out I warned myself. Do not go there.

That's right Willygirl. No one knows about us. Not even yo—

"Wow! This is too awesome!" The young surfer stepped forward and put out his hand. Behind him the rest of the crowd looked at each other, and as if on cue, mimicked their friend in high pitched voices.

"Wow! Awesome! OMG!" Then they broke up in a fit of laughter.

The shaggy blonde stood unfazed.

"Hi, I'm Nick Porter. I'm the Managing Editor for the University's newspaper. I read your work all the time. It's great to meet you."

"Thanks Nick. Nice to meet you too."

"So, what are you doing here? In the islands, I mean. Are you working on a story? I'd love to help. I could show you around. Maybe do some research?" I'm originally from Kansas but I'm a senior so I've been in the islands for four years now and I know my way around pretty good. Seriously whatever you need," he rambled on. "And if you don't need anything well, then, maybe I could just shadow you? Pick up some tips from the expert?"

I had to admire the kid. And not just because he was a fan and my ego needed the boost. It was because his friends were standing behind him laughing and he knew it. He just didn't care.

"Slow down frat boy," drawled Mak. "Did it ever occur to you that the lady might just be on vacation and that she's trying to get a break from groupies like you?"

It was one remark too many. Nick's right hand clenched and he took a step in Mak's direction. Mak looked pleased. Nick read the look and rather than be goaded by it he backed off. With a tight smile at Mak he unclenched his hand and turned his attention back to me.

"Sorry, Ms. Finnegan. I didn't mean to intrude on your time."

"Sorry for what? You saw an opportunity and you took it. If you're going to make it in this field you have to be willing to put yourself out there."

"Besides," I added, taking a pad and pen out of my bag. "Help sounds good. I'm doing an article on surfing and this isn't exactly familiar territory. For starters, can you give me some details on today's competition? Who are the people to watch?"

"Perfect timing, Kansas," Mak laughed. "Go ahead. Drop your surfboard and lick that pen. Looks like the mermaid here just offered you a way out."

Nick looked pissed. As if Mak were wearing on his last nerve.

The girl in the red bikini dropped a cautionary hand on Nick's shoulder and stepped between the two men. Professor Malulani stepped closer too.

"Lay off Mak. That's enough."

A beach brawl was the last thing on my agenda. I was here to find Angela's daughter.

"Professor, could you give me a hand?" I interrupted.

He reached down and pulled me to my feet, lingering just a bit before he let go of my hand.

"I should get to work. Maybe you can answer some questions too Professor? Help out a waterlogged newbie?"

"Absolutely," he said. But he was staring more at the two men than me. Then he turned back and smiled. "Oh, and the name is Kai," he added in a softer tone. "Please, call me Kai."

The beach was filling up fast. By now there were a couple of dozen tripods, all with expensive equipment lined up at the edge of the water. Several men loaded equipment onto the back of jet skis and were moving them into the water. Far off to our left a section marked 'judging' was coming to life and bleachers were being set up along the back of the beach.

Nick stepped forward and held out his hand. "It was great to meet you, Ms. Finnegan. I meant what I said about working with you. It'll be great. But right now I have to go check in. I'm competing for a spot in the Rip Curl Cup at Sunset Beach. That's leg two of the Triple Crown. Make a note. Because when I get to Sunset, I'll be taking this guy down," Nick smirked at Mak.

Before Mak could respond Nick picked up his board and headed toward the judges' area. On his way to the table a petite Hawaiian girl with long dark hair stopped him. Judging by their movements, it looked as though another argument was brewing. She put the flowered surfboard she was carrying down in the sand in front of him. It was too far away to hear them but her intent seemed obvious. She didn't want him to check in. Whatever the conversation, it was short-lived. Nick moved the surfboard out of his way and politely moved past the girl.

I picked up my pen, and turned back to the surfers, ready now with a dozen questions. But the drama wasn't quite over.

"This is all your fault, Mak," swore red bikini girl. "You goaded him into this. Nick's not ready for waves like those. We all know it. Hell, even he knows it. You're always poking at him. That's the only reason he's going out there."

"Hey don't put this on me. Kansas Boy's the one talkin' stink and tryin' to hang with the big boys. He thinks he can take me down? Let him try."

"You wish it were about the waves, don't you Mak? But it's really about Liat. What you're really hoping is that Nick goes in there and doesn't come out."

"Not true," Mak stated quietly. But the tone in his voice had dropped a few notches and he shot red bikini girl a look of warning. Apparently the subject of Liat was off limits.

"Don't make this about me," he added. "You see me pointing a gun? Forcin' Kansas into the ocean? No. But if you look out on top of those waves, what you will see is pretty boy's ego blowin' kisses at him and singin' come on brah, come n git me. That's the call Nick's answerin'. Got nothin' to do with me."

"'Course," he admitted with a grin, "I'm not above takin' a front row seat to the punishment those waves are about to dish out."

"Don't get your hopes up too high," the girl answered. "Even if something happens to Nick, it won't help you. Not with Liat. The two of you are over. She made that clear as rain the other day. In front of everyone."

Mak ignored her. He turned toward the ocean, dropped his board flat on the beach, and sat down next to it. He picked up a handful of sand and let it sift absently through his fingers. A moment later he looked up at the girl in the red bikini with sadness in his gray eyes. "You don't get it," he told her. "I'm not sure you ever will. Whether or not Nick ends up twisted on coral at the bottom of the ocean has nothing to do with Liat and me. Never did. The two of us, we're…." he struggled for the right words.

"Finished," red bikini provided. "If you had half a brain you'd move on. You can do better than her," she sighed. "But since you won't let it go, the least you could do is let me help you."

"Familiar, we're connected," he finished, trying to explain the unexplainable.

"Why? Because once upon a time you two slept together? So what. Nick's got that job now. You're kidding yourself if you think otherwise. You might have more talent in the ocean Mak but from what I hear, when it comes to riding things in the sand, Nick–

"That's enough." Kai stepped toward the girl. "If you're going to talk like that about somebody, have the nerve to do it in front of them."

Red Bikini shot Kai a look and then turned back to Mak.

"If anything happens to Nick today," she whined. "It's on you. And don't expect Liat to come crying on your shoulder. We both know she's not the type."

"Is that respect I hear in your voice," Mak teased.

"Just a cold observation." She added, "and here's another one. You're right. Liat and Nick don't belong together. If you would drop the attitude and work with me we could change that. Without Nick posing as shark bate."

Mak brushed the sand from his palm and eyed Red Bikini from head to toe before shaking his head to the negative.

"You think I don't have a chance with Liat? Watching you throw your tart arsenal at Nick has been downright painful."

The girl's face went red and she leveled a withering stare at the young surfer. Mak was unfazed.

"Sorry sistah, but it's true. Despite your...uhhmm...obvious talents, my money's on the sharks."

I was standing there, listening, mildly amused by the childish argument when all of a sudden something about the tone of their voices, the speed of their exchange, hit me funny. I closed my eyes to ward off the flashback but the arguing voices melted into staccato pelts of gunfire before I could do anything to stop them.

I was back in Iraq. Lying in the dirt on the side of the road with Matt's broken body covering mine. I could see the tank riding ahead of us burning now in the middle of the road. Shredded and burning, with those ungodly moans wailing somewhere inside the flames. A second explosion came and I could feel the ground shake. Could hear the moans suddenly end. "Going home, going home, 18 days in 18 days in 18 days I'm going home," Matt cried, his right arm tight across my broken ribs.

I squeezed my eyes tight and tried to bring back Waikiki beach but when I turned my head to the side, instead of sand, my cheek slammed against the Iraqi roadside and my mouth filled with bloody dirt. I opened my eyes and saw Matt's left leg first. Torn off below the knee it lay thirty yards away near the tank. I could feel myself trying to crawl out from under him, looking up into the road, past the leg...I breathed hard, swallowing the dirt and blood in search of air. Fighting, fighting, fighting for air, fighting against where the vision would take me next...up into the middle of that road. Past the burning tank. Past his left arm. Oh God his arm...hanging in the air up there like that. Glinting in the sunlight all jagged and bloody and bent at the elbow his palm up...*nooooo.*

"It's okay. Take your time. Let it out."

I was sitting in the sand again, Kai's hands on my shoulder and back as I spat out the last few teaspoons of sea that had been rolling around in my stomach.

The rest of the surfers were gathered behind Kai, staring with concern.

"Okay," I coughed in hoarse tones. "I'm okay."

"Guess you swallowed more than I thought," Kai said. "Maybe you should skip the contest and go see a doctor."

"No, no. I'm fine."

The concern in his face was genuine. It wasn't that 'hey is there a straight jacket nearby' expression I'd gotten used to from the lab coat guys in the Poconos. Suddenly I was grateful for the near drowning incident. Kai and the others were gathered around me, concerned, but even more important, completely unaware that I'd just had a flashback.

"Besides," I added, getting to my feet. It looks like they're getting ready to start."

The bleachers were full and the beach was crowded with only small gaps in the sand between groups of spectators. The noise level had risen too. There were shouts and whistles for favorite surfers erupting at random from the gathering crowds. A couple of loud horn blasts rang out from the judges' section as they tested the equipment to start and end the heats.

I scanned the crowd, mentally trying to match up the headshot on the Internet of Angela's daughter to one of the faces on the beach.

"Are you waiting for someone?" Kai asked.

"Not waiting, looking," I answered. "Remember I told you that a friend of mine has a daughter who teaches art at the University? Well she's a surfer too and I was told she might be here today. Her name is January. January Pokani. Do you know her?"

"Cool, are you here to do a story on her?" Asked the brown haired girl who until now had been silent.

"Maybe," I answered, the question catching me off guard. "I need to talk to her first."

I was surprised when Red Bikini girl stepped in front of her friend and stretched her hand out toward me.

"Hi. I'm Jan Pokani," she smiled. "You said you were a friend of my father's?"

"No, not your father," I said taking the hand she offered and studying the face under the hat more closely. It didn't look at all like the sedate faculty photo I had printed from the Internet.

"I'm a friend of your mother's. She asked me to come see you."

Her smile soured. She opened her hand and tossed mine away as if she'd been bitten.

"So you're not here to do a story on me. You're here to do a story on my mother. How did you even find me?"

"That's not it. Your mother, she was a good friend of mine. I came here because she wanted me to—

"You know what, I don't care," January cut me off. "Hele aku (go away from me)." The girl was agitated.

"You say my mother was your friend? Well good for you because she wasn't mine. She's dead now so what does it matter. I'll tell you what—it doesn't."

Only it did. Angela's daughter was in pain. A great deal of it. Most of it old and buried, considering the way she was acting. I understood. But there was little I could do to change it. Angela had been a terrible mother.

"She hasn't bothered with me since the day she left these islands. I have nothing to say. Pau (finished). Go. You should go. You have no business here. This is over."

Kai and the brown haired girl closed in around January and tried to console her. Even Mak moved toward her, his body language shifting completely. A minute ago he'd been arguing with Angela's daughter. Now, an air of protectiveness invaded his stance. The message he sent was loud and clear. I was the outsider.

It didn't matter. I had come this far and wasn't about to back out now. I made a promise to a dying friend and I was going to keep it. Besides, I had a creepy feeling that my sanity depended on it. I stepped forward.

"Look January, it sucks. You had a crappy, crappy mother. You know it, and Angela knew it too. In fact, she told me as much the night she died. I wanted her to…

be quiet

…save her strength. But she wanted to talk. All she wanted to do was talk about you and your brother. How much she loved you. What a lousy mother she was, and January, she was a lousy mother. I can't even begin to pretend otherwise. But you need to know that she had good in her too."

"Stop. I don't want to hear this," January growled, pacing in the sand.

I kept on anyway.

"She helped a lot of people out of bad places in their lives. She helped me. Your mother had a knack for spotting people in trouble. She used whatever she had, including her own pain, to rescue the next guy from his. I'm here because I made her a promise."

I rummaged through the beach bag and brought out Angela's ring. It was clean and brilliant now, not a trace of blood left behind to mar its beauty.

"Your mother wanted you to have this. It's not enough. She knew that. But it was the only way she had left to say she was sorry."

I pressed the ring into her palm.

The tan drained out of January's face and her expression was grim. Kai looked concerned. The brown haired girl was gaping at the large square diamond. Mak's expression was intense and unreadable.

"You think I care if she was sorry? I was a kid. I lost my brother. Two seconds later my mother was out the door without so much as a look in my direction. I haven't seen her since. Never. Not once. So don't expect me to feel bad now because she picked the wrong jerk and got herself shot."

She threw the ring in the sand.

"My father is the only parent I want or need."

I picked up the ring and pressed it back into her hand.

"Then trade it in and give the money to a local soup kitchen. Donate it in your father's name if you want. I don't really care. But I'm not leaving here until you take it."

"Bitch," she mumbled, glancing down at the ring.

I'm not sure if she was referring to me, or Angela. Probably both. Either way the ring had caught her eye and there was no denying its value. Four and a half carats of flawless sparkle. Every spectator within earshot of our conversation was now straining in the sand to get a closer peek.

Somewhere across the beach a loud horn blast sounded and we all turned. A stocky, dark haired man at the judge's table stepped up to a microphone then and welcomed the crowd.

"Surfers," he said, "You'll have twenty minutes to get your waves. When the horn blows, bring it in."

"Heat one," he bellowed into the microphone. "Sammy Aidda, Craig Nickels, Nick Porter, and A.J. Miller. Be careful and good luck."

There was another horn blast and like Pavlov's dogs we all turned to watch the four men toss their boards and paddle into the ocean. The discussion was over. Out of the corner of my eye though I saw January slip the ring onto her index finger and I couldn't help wondering. Something the girl had said was bugging me. She said that her mother walked out and that she hadn't seen her since. Before she died Angela told me she'd brought the girl to Philadelphia when she turned sixteen. The discrepancy probably didn't mean a thing. Just a rant. An angry exaggeration on January's part. Still there was something about the way she'd said it.

The police didn't believe Angela when she told them that it wasn't Bill's fault. In domestic violence cases wives protect the men they love with alarming regularity. But domestic violence was still a long shot in my mind. Something or someone else had to be at the root of what happened that night. Besides, Bill was not the only person she loved and might want to protect. What if the person I heard rummaging around on the second floor was January? Could she have been involved? Maybe she was responsible for what happened.

That's one explanation.

Yep, I told myself with conviction. Angela would have protected Bill. But she would have protected her daughter too.

As I watched the first surfer break away from the others and catch one of those giant waves I made a mental note to check the flights from Hawaii to Philadelphia on the days preceding the murders.

The second surfer was close behind. He took off on the very next wave. I couldn't help cringing when the board flew out from under his feet. The crowd aawwwwwdd sympathetically as he curled into a ball and disappeared into the rolling beast.

CHAPTER TWELVE

Nick sliced through the water, choking back cheerios and fear as he maneuvered into the lineup. He paddled far left to avoid the main thrust of the crushing waves. Too far left. He was behind. Odd man out. The other surfers were lining up fast and one by one they jockeyed for waves.

Sammy Aidda was the first to find a wall. It was a respectable ride but the lip curled fast and there wasn't much time for him to make it look good, just enough to put up some points. Far to his right Nick watched as the next set swelled. Thicker and taller than the ones before, A.J. paddled in and rode his wave as it continued to rise out of the ocean. With a slight shift of his body he angled the board up towards the right and the crowd aahhhhhd appreciatively as the wave reached its crest and A.J. splashed through it. With a razor sharp twist he flipped the board and headed downward. Using slight fluid movements he steered the board forward, struggling against the angle of the wall. The beach was silent, with praise and oxygen held tight in people's throats as A.J. slid down the wave. He made it about a third of the way before gravity flicked the board out from under him and plunged him feet first toward the base of the wave. Off to the left Nick watched as the surfer pulled his knees to his chest and made a feeble attempt to cover his head before striking the water. The beach exhaled with a collective ooowwwwwch.

The wave swept by and a tense minute passed before Nick saw A.J.'s head pop through the white surf. A rescue unit jet skied in and tried

93

to pluck him out but another wave rolled in and they had to move out of the way or get crushed. Again the crowd held its breath as all eyes strained for a glimpse of the surfer.

Nick heard none of it. But he watched just the same as A.J. took a second pounding before eventually struggling his way to the beach. The crowd clapped and hooted. The rescue units moved into deeper waters. And waited.

Craig Nickels waited for a smaller wave a few minutes later and managed to score a few points of his own.

Nick pumped his arms half-heartedly through the water and pretended to head for the lineup, all the while questioning his sanity. He was out of his league. No doubt about it. Of course he'd known that before he accepted the invitation to compete for a spot in a Triple Crown event. The local competition he'd won to get out here was a fluke. He'd done the best surfing of his life that day and those waves hadn't come close to the size and thickness out here today. And this was just a warm up. Haleiwa? Pipe? Surfing that was insane. Of course there was no real need to worry about that. With only one respectable way back to the beach, he didn't expect to be alive long enough to worry about Pipe. Whatever the outcome though, he deserved it. He was out here because he'd let Mak goad him into it. Nick was usually so grounded. Always knew his own mind. Except where Mak was concerned. Mak made him feel uneasy about Liat. So when he was offered a chance to compete, to prove himself he put sanity aside and jumped at it.

It was the opposite of how he normally operated. Nick was all about goals. Figure out what you want. Work hard. Make it happen. He'd already found the most incredible girl on the planet. After college he planned to become a journalist and marry Liat. They were right for each other. Good together in ways that people rarely find in life.

Then along comes Makani. The guy was a myth when Nick first met Liat. Nothing more than a character in the surf stories that got exaggerated along with the number of beers being passed around the bonfire. A world class surfer, sure. But that was out there. Away. France, Australia, Africa, racking up prizes on the world surfing tour and only occasionally bouncing in and out of Hawaii. Until recently Nick and Mak had barely even crossed paths. Liat's doing no doubt.

Lately Mak was everywhere. And his obsession with Liat was beginning to irritate the hell out of Nick. It wasn't the fact that they'd dated for two years. That was over. Nick trusted Liat. It was something else. It was the nature of their connection. They had this thing...this low level beneath the surface intensity. Nick knew that it wasn't about sex—at least not for Liat. Again, he trusted her. But whatever it was, whenever Liat and Mak were in the same vicinity, it was there. She wasn't right... she wasn't herself when Mak was around. The guy bugged him. So now here he was. Paddling furiously against the current just to stay in place and wondering how in creation he was going to get back to the beach in one un-shamed piece.

"You're too far left."

Sammy had paddled up behind him. He was no stranger to Hawaii's large waves. At 31, he was the most experienced of the four men in the heat and was favored to win one of the wildcard spots. In fact with his big wave experience Sammy probably could have qualified for a position on the world surfing tour. But qualifying is one thing. Actually winning top prize money on a regular basis is something else. Sammy had a family to feed. Three kids and a wife he loved were reason enough to skip the suitcase life of the world tour and shoot once a year for a little respect at Pipe.

"Look kid, you're out here. Somehow you scrounged up the balls to paddle out so you might as well get it over with. Go for it," he chuckled. "Drop in on a wave and stand up. Simple as that. Before you know it you'll be crawlin' up the beach, spittin' corral outta your nose and chewin sand. And even if you never do it again, I promise, it'll still be the best moment of your life."

"If you say so," Nick answered flashing a half sick grin.

Sammy laughed. "Piece a cake. But remember, if you find yourself goin' down? Just suck in a big old lungful of air and stick with, now I lay me down to sleep. Fastest prayer on the planet, brah."

Sammy looked out at the ocean as another set of waves began to form.

"Awwww, now look at those beauties. I'm gonna take the second one. If you hurry, maybe you can catch the third."

He was gone.

Sammy fit himself into the wave and took off. Refusing to let another thought run through his own head, Nick followed.

He focused hard on the rising wave paddling, calculating, then turning his board he stroked into the thickest swell he'd ever been near. Flat on the board he leaned into the ocean stroking harder, faster, faster, down to that last life altering second…duck or go.

Nick committed to the wave and the heavy wall of water lifted him into the air far above the rest of the ocean. He gripped the sides of his board and popped his feet into place. The slope was fast and straight. Straighter than anything he'd ever ridden. Nick strained every muscle in both his calves and thighs just to stay in place. But the wave wasn't just straight. It was higher too. There was room to play. That is if he could just keep his balance long enough and control the board. Crouching low, knees bent, arms outstretched and wobbling Nick curved his board to the right. Squelching the rising panic in his throat he directed the board across the rapid water, willing himself to find a sweet spot and to stay one beat ahead of the massive curling wall crashing behind him.

Turning. Twisting. In then out shifting his board back into the wave forcing it back up the wall then jerking it downward and then once again back to the right until the wall above him curled nearly in half and Nick disappeared from sight.

Inside the curl a fine mist sprayed at Nick from every angle igniting both fear and excitement. He reached out and ran his fingers along the inside of the powerful wave while his calves and knees absorbed the shock of each new bump. He crouched down, bouncing along the bottom shelf, summoning all the speed his meager skills would allow. He willed the board forward, toward the hole, toward the sunlight, before the massive giant ended its thundering white roll and tried to suck him under. He flew out of the hole and rode the edge of the crumbling wall as far as he dared, aware that it was churning rapidly at his heels. Nick didn't care. He used every skill he had to play with the final lifts of the wave and then stepped off the board with a giant grin.

The crowd on the beach went wild.

Nick never heard them. The clock was ticking. He ducked under the nearest wave and paddled out as fast as he could. Pumped up and ready to risk it all again.

He caught two more waves before he got crushed. Half way down the wall on his fourth ride the board left his feet and Nick looked up to see the heavy lip of a Hawaiian North Shore wave curling above him.

"Ohhhh shhhhiiiiittt!"

It was a waste of precious oxygen but there was no stopping the scream he let out. His feet hit the water. He ducked his face into his hands. And went under.

Fear sucked hard at the air that was still left in his lungs. He struggled to keep his mouth shut as the wave pressed him toward the ocean floor. His board disappeared into one of the currents. Another ripped hard at his arms and legs, throwing him in different directions, rolling him sideways then head over heels. The massive weight of the wave pressed him down, farther and farther, pushing him toward the jagged branches of coral resting below.

He kicked hard to avoid the coral but the wave would not let up. His right leg and side hit first slicing open about five inches of skin between his knee and ankle. The wound wasn't bad but a thin trickle of blood seeped into the ocean. Jarred by the impact, Nick's mouth fell open. Salt water and panic rushed in.

He had to get a grip. If he didn't Nick knew he wasn't going to make it. Clamping his mouth shut he swallowed hard and forced down the salt water. His lungs took a beating and his nose burned but he managed to send most of the water to his stomach. Ignoring the pain, he focused on the water above him. Stretching his arms past his head he tried once again to swim to the surface. Once again he felt his body being yanked apart. A glimpse of Liat flashed in his brain. *Think!* He shouted to himself, willing his way past her long dark hair and big brown eyes. *Think*

And then it was over.

The pressure above his body disappeared. The wet grave was gone. Tanked to the brim with fear, Nick's legs propelled him straight to the surface. Popping his head into the foamy aftermath of the wave he choked in as much air as his battered lungs would take. Bleary eyed he spotted two red jet skis screaming toward him, along with another wave. Coughing, he sucked in a second feeble breath and ducked back under. The jet skis were fast. The wave, he knew, would be faster.

Hands stretched out in front of him Nick ducked under the surface and was about to descend. Then just below him something caught his eye. Long and gray it swam by fast. Shark!! Screamed his overtaxed brain. Whatever it was it disappeared before he could catch a better look.

Ten seconds later Nick felt a rough tug just above his right elbow. There wasn't much pain. Less than the cut on his leg from the coral, he thought. His lungs deflated and whatever air had been left in them bubbled to the surface.

Nick's body jerked clear of the water. With a loud grunt the rescue worker slung him by the arms onto the back of the ski and shouted for the driver to take off. The driver revved the motor, turning nearly sideways into the rising wave before speeding out of its reach, careful to avoid A.J. Miller as he broke through the lip. Miller hung in the air for the barest of seconds before flipping his board to the left and woooshing down the wall.

The crowd on the beach went wild for both the ride and the rescue. Miller scored solid points on the wave but not enough to pass Nick. The combined scores for his waves had put him in second place in the heat just behind Sammy Aidda. Not bad Nick thought as one medic tended to his cut while another one placed an ice pack under the small of his back. At least he could hold his head up (providing the swelling in his neck went down). The heat was over. At least it was for him.

What Nick didn't know was that after they dragged him up the beach and just before the horn sounded Sammy took off on another wave. It wasn't even that high. Just a bit thick. When the lip curled earlier than he expected, it clipped the end of Sammy's board and ejected him into the air like a pop tart out of the toaster. He smacked the water flat and broke his ankle and three toes. Nick won the heat and was advanced into the next round. Before the ice pack under his back had a chance to melt he was back in the water.

Two hours later Nick stood next to a surfer named Rick Kahali, the two of them grinning from ear to ear as their names were announced as the wild card entrants for stop two on the world's Triple Crown of Surfing, the Rip Curl Cup. Held at Sunset Beach, the waves are half a mile out to sea. They surge in twenty feet thick and up to four stories high. The pot for this leg of the contest is $250,000 dollars in prize money. That would be nice, Nick thought, but what mattered most was the look he hoped to see in Liat's eyes. Well, that, and the rush of coming out of the ocean alive and in one piece.

***

Leftover seaweed was still poking around at the lining of my stomach by the time the final horn of the competition sounded. It was the only side effect that I was willing to acknowledge from my bout with the ocean. Energy from the crowd and from the competition made that easy. I couldn't wait to get to work. Never mind that I wasn't a sports writer. Or, that I knew next to nothing about surfing. The *Philly Chronicle* was about to get a first rate in depth story. It felt good to be that jazzed. With a smile I shouldered my way into the sea of bodies now jockeying for position near the winners.

Working my way to the inner circle, I interviewed fans on either side of me as I squeezed closer to Nick Porter and Rick Kahali. Twenty minutes later I had enough material for a decent article. Not to mention the photos. January was in almost every one. Smacking herself up against Nick, it was impossible to get a clean shot of the winner without her. I felt a twinge of guilt as I snapped another picture of my friend's daughter. Angela had begged me to protect the girl and I wanted to, but for now January was the local angle the newspaper would need in order to run the story. Tomorrow morning, before the good people of Philadelphia slipped into their boots and trudged their way through eight and a half inches of dirty snow, they could sink for a minute into the life of their favorite socialite's long lost daughter. The story would buy me time. Time to find the truth.

As I lowered the camera I spotted Vince and a tall white haired gentleman making their way toward January. Vince tapped her on the arm. She immediately brushed past him and gave the elder man an enthusiastic hug. In turn he gripped Jan by the shoulders and set her back a step looking over her head as she talked. Alfred Pokani I assumed, but I didn't want to get close enough to confirm it. I took one more picture and then melted into the outer crowd.

I was about to head back to the hotel when I saw Mak make his way over to Rick Kahali to congratulate him. A new round of flashes exploded and I heard another reporter ask,

"Hey, Mak, as one of the front runners, tell us what you think of your newest competition. Did your chances of sweeping the Triple Crown just get easier or harder?"

The crowd laughed.

"A bit of both," Mak answered. "Rick is a real menace when it comes to the North Shore. When it comes to the big waves I would never count him out."

"What about Nick Porter? That was a heckuva showing for a newcomer. Does he pose a threat?"

Mak's smile went grim.

"Nah. Just a grommet that's wandered onto the wrong playground."

A collective ooooooohhh rippled through the crowd.

Mak turned around and tossed his next comment directly at Nick.

"Enjoy the moment, Kansas. I'm sure after those waves start crashing in your dreams tonight you'll wake up screaming and realize your mistake. If not. If you really are foolish enough to play in the next round then for god's sake take it easy on the rescue squad. Quality guys like that are hard to come by."

Another, louder, oooooooohhhhhh.

Nick stepped up. Chin squared, he stared hard at Mak and for the first time held his own against the tightly built Hawaiian.

"You wanna talk nightmares tough guy? Cause I got yours. When I lay my head down on the pillow tonight it'll be next to Liat. There's not a wave in the world you can put up against that. So you go ahead, *brah* and sleep on that. If you still wanna talk it over in the morning. I'll be right here."

All eyes turned to focus on the petite woman with the waist length black hair who just happened to be standing behind, and two screaming fans to the left, of Nick.

Nick felt the stare. Without turning he knew she was there.

"Awwww crap. Liat, I didn't know you were standing there."

"Shoulda quit while you were ahead," someone shouted from the crowd. With a look, Liat agreed.

"I'm sorry Liat. But I've had about as much of his crap as I'm gonna take today."

Rather than take a swing at Nick which is what Mak had been itching to do all morning, he backed away. Ignoring Nick completely he flashed a strange knowing smile directly at Liat.

Liat caught Mak's stare and flashed him a look of sadness before dropping her eyes. Then she stepped forward, reaching for Nick's shoulders, and pressed herself into his back.

Nick caught the look that passed between them and responded. "Not only will I take you on in the next round. I'll send you limping home."

There was another oooooooohh from the crowd and a fresh round of flashes from the photogs. With drama like this these articles were going to write themselves. Move over Gidget, I thought. Nothing goes better with limb-risking competition like bitter rivalry and girl stealing.

Before the exchange could go any further, Rick Kahali stepped between the two men and wrapped a tight arm around each of them.

"Ease up guys. No reason to get so tense. Cause I'm gonna toss both of you before you can get anywhere near the final heat."

Rick's good-natured approach diffused the situation and before there was a chance for anyone to stir it up again Mak ducked beneath Rick's arm and headed towards the ocean, taking a sizeable chunk of photographers and reporters with him.

Keeping a careful eye on Alfred Pokani, I strode quietly in the opposite direction. A few minutes later I saw Kai waving at me from the judge's station with a stack of papers in his hand.

"Thought you might want these," he said after making his way over to me. "It's a list of the surfers and their standings on the world tour. Thought it might help with your article."

"Thanks, I appreciate the help," I said, taking the papers and glancing down at them. Across the type written page was a number scrawled in yellow highlighter.

"What's this?"

"Oh, that's my cell number," he grinned. "You know, in case you need me to explain anything," he paused then said, "for your article."

"The point system they use is kinda tricky," he added sheepishly."

"What about that mind boggling coffee you mentioned earlier? Let's grab a cup and maybe you can explain it real slow. You know, so I can grasp it," I teased. "For the sake of the article of course."

Kai blushed at first. But then, with a grin, he took the game a step further.

"I read a lot of surfing articles. You know who writes the best ones? Surfers. Yep, people who've actually surfed. Don't get me wrong, though. Coffee's good. I could tell you what I know over coffee. But if we chat out there," he motioned toward the waves. "You'll understand things a whole lot better. For the sake of the article of course," he said with a grin.

I grinned back. For the first time since Iraq, I could feel something inside of my chest loosen. Just the slightest bit.

"What? You need another hero fix? Dragging me out of the ocean once today wasn't enough?"

"Don't worry. I was only teasing about taking you out there," he pointed to the waves again. When he dropped his hand this time he reached in and took hold of one of mine, grasping it as if we were old friends.

"There's a beach not too far from here and the waves are just the right size. I'll have you up on a board and surfing in no time. Come on, what do you say?"

Kai's eyes were warm and playful. I was beginning to like this Astronomy professor. But the thought was scary. I hadn't felt this way about anyone since my break up with Shane, and my feelings for my ex were still raw and confused. I was in no condition to start a love affair. Although I had a hunch it was long overdo. Who knows? Maybe if I had jumped into the game sooner....

Shoulda...coulda...woulda

"Kai! Hey, Kai! Willow! Wait up," Nick was waving a hand and running toward us.

I cast another glance into the crowd but could no longer find Vince and Alfred Pokani.

"There's someone I want you to meet."

Nick sprinted toward us tugging at his girlfriend's hand from behind. A few seconds later, he stopped short in front of us.

"Liat, this is the famous reporter I told you about. Willow Finnegan this is Liat Kawa."

At first, a warm genuine smile appeared to be forming at the edge of the young woman's lips as she raised her hand up to greet me. The girl was a knockout, young and very exotic. No wonder the men were fighting over her, I thought. She had that quality, you know, that X factor thing, that rare pheromone certain people are born with. They attract others to them like salt to a pretzel.

Geeze, no wonder January Pokani had issues with the girl. I dropped Kai's hand, took a step in her direction, and extended my hand to Liat.

As I turned to face her full on, our eyes connected. Immediately her hand dropped away from mine and fell, shaking, back by her side. The warm brown color drained from her face. Her smile evaporated and was replaced with a look of pure terror. Recognition. And terror.

I dropped my own hand as if she'd stung it. Had we met? I ransacked my brain but came up with nothing. Still, she knew me. I was sure of that. She knew me, and she looked scared to death.

"It's you." Barely a whisper, but the words fell out of her mouth just the same.

"Have we met?" I asked.

"No, no…uhhmmm…of course not. It's just that…Nick…he's so excited that he met you. He told me all about it."

It was a lousy recovery. Funny, watching her a few minutes ago, I would never have pegged her as a liar. Quite the opposite. My instincts are usually good about stuff like that. It's a reporter thing. Cops and judges have it to. Despite my recent circumstances, that was one thing Iraq hadn't deadened. If anything my instincts were stronger. Liat, for reasons I couldn't fathom yet, was lying.

Pushing ahead with her lousy attempt to cover her feelings Liat leaned forward and lifted her hand back up to mine. We shook. Again, I tried to place her. Nothing. Her fingers were ice cold and trembling.

"Glad to meet you," she offered.

A dead lie. Nick must have sensed it too. He slipped an arm around her shoulders and tossed her a look before turning back to me and trying to smooth things over.

"So, about that following you around thing? I can start whenever you need me."

"Good," I replied. "There's another story I've been working on and I think you might be able to help. Let me get your number. After I get this article to my editor I'll give you a call."

I took out my cell phone and handed it over so that he could punch in his number.

"Could you put Liat's number in there too?" I asked him before turning back to lock gazes with her once again.

"I'd love to interview you. About the women's title, I mean. I hear you've got a pretty good chance."

Kai raised an eyebrow at my sudden display of surfing knowledge.

"I didn't come here completely stupid," I said, answering his look with a laugh.

"There are other girls," Liat stammered, "Laney Kahu, Trish Jensen, Jan Pokani, really it's anybody's game. You should interview them."

"No, you should definitely interview Liat," Nick said proudly. "Trust me, Willow, she's being way too modest. This is your girl. She's gonna run away with the title, no doubt."

"Done," he added, handing back my phone. "Both numbers."

Liat flinched.

"We could get this over with now, if you like," I said, pulling a fresh notebook out of my bag. "Just a few questions. I promise."

"Can't. I really have to go," she said, carefully ducking out of Nick's reach. He took a few steps and caught her by the hand before she could walk away from us completely.

"Liat? What's going on?"

"Canvases," she answered. "There are two more left on campus and I have to bring them over to the Gallery. I have to get them set up. The art gala is Saturday night and I promised the director I'd get them in place. And my dress. I still need to get a dress. I'm sorry. There's just a lot to do."

"Art Gala," I asked?

Kai answered.

"It's for Keona Kuleana. About ten years ago he got caught in some heavy surf at Sunset Beach and drowned. So we throw a benefit for the community every year in his honor. You'll find some of the best art in the islands there, all in one night. Silent auction. Good food. Good people."

"Drowned, huh? What was that you said about baby waves?"

"Different beach completely," Kai swore. "Besides, I would never tempt the sharks on your first lesson. Second, maybe," he joked.

"Hhhmmm," I said, shaking my head no. "Maybe I should skip the sharks and check out the art."

"Chicken."

The easy banter between us didn't go unnoticed. It was Nick who raised an eyebrow this time but I got the sense he approved. Liat's expression was much more guarded.

"You should come Willow," Nick decided. "All the local surfers will be there. It's in one of the ballrooms over at the Outrigger Reef and a lot of the money we raise goes toward protecting the ocean, preserving the reefs. It's a big deal around here."

"Sounds good, I'm in," I said.

"There's still room at our table, right?" Nick asked Kai. "You still have tickets?"

"I'm sure Ms. Finnegan and I can figure something out."

"Nick, I really have to go," Liat interrupted, extracting her hand from his.

"Nice meeting you," she said, keeping her hands tucked behind her back. "I'm sorry about the interview."

I stepped forward and put my hand out anyway. She took it reluctantly. "Willow," I said, "my friends call me Willow."

"Listen, about that interview. Maybe we can kill two birds with one stone. Didn't I hear you say something about shopping for a dress?" I turned my head and smiled at Kai. "Because it looks like I'm going to need something spectacular to wear."

"How 'bout I tag along with you. I have no clue where to shop. You can help me find a dress and I'll ask you a few questions. I promise. It won't even feel like an interview."

Nick was grinning ear to ear. "Man what a great day. First, I make it into the biggest surfing contest in the world. Next week you are gonna take the second leg of the women's contest, Liat, and in the meantime you get to be interviewed by one of the best journalists in the world."

I smiled. This time so did Liat. She flashed Nick a small grin. She cared about him. That much was obvious.

"I have to drop the paintings off by four thirty. If you want I can meet you in front of the Outrigger right after," she told me.

"Perfect," Kai chimed in. "That leaves you plenty of time for your first surfing lesson."

CHAPTER THIRTEEN

The black Volvo SUV came out of nowhere. I was sure that I looked both ways before my heel left the curb in front of the Outrigger Reef hotel. But I nearly got creamed. There was that one brief moment of sweet peaceful air. The next—a black Volvo freight train came screaming right at me.

Liat pulled me back.

"Unf***ingbelievable!" She yelled.

Her left arm was strapped tight across my chest and I could feel her heart thumping wildly as she dragged both of us back up onto the sidewalk. Away from that tight woooosh of pressured air that slammed into my face as the car sped by.

"Are you alright?" She asked, not letting go of me until all four of our feet were firmly planted on the pavement.

"Are you?" I asked, unable to stifle the giggle in my throat.

For the second time that day her brown eyes were big and scared. And all I could do was laugh. I tried to stop myself but I couldn't. Of all the people I'd met since touching down in the islands, Liat was the last one I expected to let out a whopping curse like that one.

Liat shot me another, sharper, look. The kind Harry had thrown at me just before I left for Hawaii. The laughter died in my throat.

"Look, I'm sorry," I said, plopping down on the low white cement wall bearing the hotel's name as I tried to catch my breath. Liat leaned up against it and took in some air of her own.

"I didn't mean to laugh. It's just that, well, when that giant curse fell out of your mouth I wasn't expecting it. And well—it was funny."

We looked at each other and then Liat let out a laugh too.

"Not my usual choice of words," she explained, "but I wasn't exactly expecting you to walk into traffic either. How did you not see that SUV? You looked right at it….and then…

"Never saw it coming," I corrected evenly. "Sun was in my eyes. Then all of a sudden that black monster came screaming right at me. Crazy driver. Good thing you were behind me."

Liat shot me a longer, more probing look.

"I guess so. Traffic can be tough. People tend to get distracted when they come here. But you…I really thought you saw that car. Are you sure you're okay?"

Her concern was genuine. Interesting, considering her earlier reaction to me.

"I'm fine, I promise."

Without thinking I dropped an arm around her small shoulders and gave them a reassuring squeeze. The girl was more shook up than I realized.

"Thanks for dragging me out of harm's way. Now let's drop the whole thing and go shopping because I want to look good. Kai's the first man I've been interested in for a long time. I'd really like the chance to get to know him better."

As the thought left my mouth I realized how true it was. The idea that I liked Kai, more than a little, was scary. Much worse than getting run over by an SUV. As for Liat, the expression on her face eased for the first time since I'd met her.

"You genuinely like him," she said, her words more of an observation than anything else.

I stood up and headed for the corner again. I didn't want to answer.

"We should get going. I still have an article to write."

"Wait up," she said catching me before I got too close to the street again. "There're a couple of great shops in the hotel's lobby. Let's start there."

Liat was still leery of me. I wasn't sure what to make of her either. Angela had begged me to come here. To find a rare gem that Liat's father had stolen. It was *his* surfboard that Angela had given to me. I couldn't help wondering what Liat knew about the Maui Snow.

She held open the glass door to the hotel lobby and we made our way to the boutique.

We went our separate ways inside the small shop and before long we had amassed every decent dress they had and then lined them up on a couch outside the three stalls that made up the dressing room. I was glad to see the mood ease a bit as we slid in and out of a dozen gauzy island confections. I kept the conversation light, peppering her with easy questions about the upcoming competition. I was just about to deepen the interview to make it a bit more personal when Liat beat me to the punch.

"So what's the deal with you and Kai? Word on the beach is that the two of you hit it off hard and fast."

"We just met," I reminded her.

"He took you surfing. Invited you for coffee. Two things Kai never does lightly. You should know that about him."

"Noted. But why so much interest on the beach over a surfing lesson? Isn't that standard practice in Hawaii?"

"Like I said, not with Kai. He's a great guy and we're kind of tight knit around here. We look out for each other."

She hesitated for a second and when I didn't say anything she added, "he hasn't dated much since his wife died a few years ago. Not that he hasn't been asked. A lot."

"More useful information." I raised an eyebrow.

"So how'd you like it?" she asked. "The surfing, I mean. Are you any good?"

"Since the question is coming from a world class surfer, I'd have to say no. Then again, it was like an hour before Kai let me out of the sand and into the water."

Liat laughed. "Sounds like Kai."

I picked up a green dress then ducked inside a stall and went back to the interview.

"Tell me about your first surfboard."

I came out of the stall to find Liat standing on her tiptoes in front of the mirror. The evening gown was the vibrant yellowy orange of a fresh cut mango and it came straight across the top with no straps or sleeves.

She fingered the edges of the wide sash, smoothing it around her waist as she thought about the board.

"It was a white long board. I remember my Dad painted a blue wave at the bottom and a big yellow sun with long wavy rays near the top.

Perfect.

"Tell me about him. Is he the one who taught you to surf?"

"Yeah, when I was four. We used to live above his surf shop and I would bug him every day until he would close up shop and take me down to the beach. By the time I was nine I was winning competitions pretty regularly."

"He must have been proud watching you."

Sadness crushed her face and I felt bad.

"He never saw me compete. He died when I was seven. I was just a kid. Surfing was the best way I knew to stay close to him."

I hesitated. I was anxious to keep her talking but at the same time I wanted to come clean. I wanted to tell her about the surfboard up in my closet. The real reason I was in the islands.

Again, she beat me to it.

"Why did you come here?"

Liat turned away from the mirror and stood facing me.

"I know that you had a run-in with Jan Pokani today and that you knew her mother. Now you're interested in my father. Why?"

"It's just background information for the articles, that's all."

"Don't lie to me."

There was a look on her face that was hard to read. Fear? Maybe.

My questions about her family were well within normal limits for the article. Still, I could see that there was no point in arguing. She knew something.

What? What does she know?

"Okay, you're right. I am interested in your father. I take it you're familiar with the Maui Snow?"

Liat's face clouded over. "You're a treasure hunter? I thought you were a journalist. Nick said you were a journalist."

"I am. But I'm also looking for the Maui Snow. At least I think I am. What I'm really after is the truth. A couple of my friends died recently, Jan's mother and her husband. I think what happened to them has something to do with that diamond. I'd like to find out what. And, well, since your father's death is tied up with the Maui Snow it occurred to me you might want some answers yourself. Maybe I can help you. Maybe we can help each other."

"I was seven when my father died," she stammered, a definite edge to her voice. "I couldn't help you if I wanted to. Just like I've told the thousand other people who've asked me since then."

"Okay. Skip the Maui Snow. Let's try a different truth. Tell me why you were so upset when Nick introduced us. You know me. I'm not sure how, but you do. When we were introduced you recognized me and for some reason that I can't fathom, it scared the daylights out of you. Why?"

Liat hesitated.

"Please," I said, tossing her words back at her, "don't lie."

"Yes, I recognized you."

Then the words tumbled out. Before I could think. Before I could censor myself.

"You were there weren't you? In Philadelphia. The night the Priests were shot I heard someone up on the second floor. That's how you know me, isn't it? Tell me what happened!"

"What??! No!"

"No!" she shouted again.

But I saw it. That unmistakeable flash of guilt on her face.

"Oh my god, you *were* there. I knew it. I knew someone else had to be in the house that night. Why did you…how did you? The pistols. Tell me about the pistols! What happened, why did Bill and Angela take out their pistols? They must have caught you trying to steal the surfboard. That's it, isn't it! You were after the surfboard. Tell me what happened!"

I was on my feet by now grasping her by the shoulders. Liat went dead calm. She looked me straight in the eyes and in a quiet voice stated,

"I was not in Angela Priest's house. Not that night. Not ever. That's not how I recognized you."

Her doe shaped eyes, they were… I stood there. Staring at them. Her words. They slipped into my head. My messy, cluttered, head. An instant later she blinked and then turned away. I dropped my hands from her shoulders and stepped back.

"Okay," I stammered, struggling to regain my senses. Struggling to collect my thoughts. After a minute though, I spotted the messy eraser marks on her perfect denial.

"But you did recognize me," I murmured. "We both know it. And don't tell me it's because of my work. Aside from a couple of hardcore newshounds like your boyfriend Nick, nobody out here in middle of the Pacific knows who I am."

Liat looked more uncomfortable than ever.

"It's complicated," she said.

"I went to college. Try me."

"I can't," she answered. "If I told you, you'd think I was crazy."

I let out a laugh. "Kiddo, I've got a Masters Degree in crazy. Spill it."

She looked at me, mind closed, lips pressed tight. Whatever her secrets, the young Hawaiian had no intention of sharing. So she deflected instead.

"You asked about the Maui Snow. Like I said, I can't help you. I was a kid when it happened. All I remember is that they tore up our apartment. They destroyed my father's shop. My mother cried and couldn't stop. Back when it happened? The authorities searched every square inch of these islands. You know what they came up with? Nothing. No Maui Snow. When I was a kid I used to think the menehune took it."

"The mena-what?"

"The menehune. You're Irish, right? Finnegan?"

"Yeah...

"The menehune are sort of the Hawaiian version of leprechauns. Except that our elves work. They build things when no one is looking. Good things like fishing holes and grottos. But they have a wicked sense of humor too. Sometimes they take things."

"So you're joking. My friends are dead and you think this is funny."

"None of this is funny," she replied. "Don't you get it? There's nothing I can say that will help you."

I took a deep breath and considered my options. But then once again I let my mouth get ahead of my head.

"Okay, how about I share first? Who knows, maybe it'll help you remember something that will help me."

She shrugged her shoulders. It was meant to be noncommittal, like she couldn't care less, but Liat looked way too tense for that to be true.

"What I tell you stays between us. I especially don't want Jan Pokani to know. Since you two are rivals, I assume I don't have to worry about you swapping stories with her over beers at the bonfire."

"We're not rivals. Just competitors," Liat said evenly.

"Might want to re-think that," I suggested. "Jan's obviously got an eye for your boyfriend and she's not shy about it."

"Okay, so we're not BFF's. Doesn't matter. She's still one of us."

"Fine," I agreed, "Just keep this info to yourself. Jan's mom didn't want her mixed up with the Maui Snow."

"What about it? It's a stupid diamond. What makes you think it has anything to do with that house in Philadelphia?"

"Because your father was friends with Angela Priest when she lived here in Hawaii."

"So?"

"So, the other vintage surfboard? He gave it to Angela."

Liat's face was taut. Beyond that I couldn't read her expression.

"Angela took it with her to Philadelphia and stuffed it in a closet. Then one night I walked into her house and found her bleeding to death on the living room floor. Oh and she had one thing on her mind. Wanna take a guess what that was?"

The color in Liat's face drained when I described what happened at Angela's.

"What?"

"Your father's surfboard. Angela begged me to bring it back here to Hawaii so that I could find the Maui Snow. Put it back where it belongs. She told me that she promised your father."

"What's on it?" Liat demanded. "The surfboard. Is there a green hut at the top?" She tried to keep her voice even but the note of panic in her tone was unmistakable.

"Yeah. I guess you could call it a hut."

"Not just a hut," she insisted. A snow covered hut on top of a wave. With a picture of Poli'ahu on the roof and an inscription on the door."

"Yes, it says Maui Hau on the front door. It means Maui Snow, right?"

Liat looked shaky. She untied the sash to the Mango colored dress and shimmied out of it. She grabbed her jeans and tee shirt and hurried into them.

"How do you know what's on the surfboard? You told me yourself you were only seven when the Maui Snow was stolen. That surfboard has been stashed in a Philly closet for years." Again I asked, "Liat were you there that night?"

"No," she swore, looking at me with those eyes.

"But you know something. If you didn't see the surfboard at Angela's then how do you know what was on it?"

"I was there when my father carved it."

She was lying.

"You were seven. You're telling me you can remember the design that well? With that much detail? I looked at it this morning and I couldn't remember that the hut was green or that it had snow on it. That's odd," I told her.

"You're odd," she retorted, pretty much like a seven year old.

It was childish but effective. After all, I couldn't exactly argue with her assessment. I'd been struggling for weeks to keep 'odd' at a safe distance.

"If you say so," I retorted. "But that doesn't change the fact that you're hiding something. And you're scared. Why are you so scared?"

Liat wasn't listening. She was looking for her sandals.

"Tell me," I offered. "Let me help."

Completely dressed now Liat turned and locked eyes with mine once again. She was tiny but daunting.

"You're hiding something, too."

I stood there. Mute.

She broke the gaze and said, "You should go back to Philadelphia. Take the board with you. Bury it in another closet," she advised. Then she handed me a hangar and the mango dress. She stepped past me, through the doorway, and back into the shop.

"Get rid of it," she called over her shoulder. "Before you get hurt."

"Is that some kind of threat?"

But Liat was already gone. I dropped the mango dress on the floor and bolted through the shop but by the time I was able to catch a glimpse of her she was already through the glass doors of the hotel. I watched as she sprinted across the parking lot and disappeared into the highway traffic. So much for the slower paced island life. I couldn't have caught her if I tried. So I did the next best thing. I went back inside and shopped.

I felt this odd sense of exhilaration. My head was racing. I didn't know how yet but Liat was as thick in this thing as Angela was a few days ago.

I should have been tired. Exhausted, considering all of the sun, the surfing, the traveling, not to mention whatever energy I'd expended during those lost four days. The thing is, I really should have been dead tired. But I felt strong. Bursting with energy. It was a good thing too I decided because ideas were exploding in my head like popcorn in a microwave and I have to admit I was afraid to waste even a single one.

I hurried through the shop, mulling over ideas and trying on dresses. Within minutes I bought ten dresses without even looking at the tags. Then I bought at least as many bathing suits. I figured some for me and some for Liat. I liked the Mango dress on her but hey sometimes a girl needs choices.

Choices. Hhmmmm.

I felt a rush as I put the battered credit card down on the counter and skipped past anything inside of me resembling a limit. Everything was popping at once, the shopping, Kai, Liat, not to mention a wealth of new ideas, all of it, zipping through at warp speed. Until the sales clerk read the name on my credit card and brought me to a screeching halt. She reached under the counter, took out three items, and put them in front of me.

"I found these in the dressing room," she insisted. "They must have fallen out of your purse."

The first item looked familiar. It was a prescription bottle with my name on it. I pushed it aside and reached for the eraser. It was an old chalkboard eraser, you know, the kind that has a wooden top? I tilted it toward me and saw the words, St. Martha's Grade School, stamped in black across the wood. Huh. St. Martha's. When we were fifteen, Shane and I did summer stock at St. Martha's. Well, Shane's parents signed him up and I sort of tagged along. I thought it was fun. Shane hated it. All he wanted was to be outside. He gave the director and the rest of the cast such a hard time that when I finally suggested a clever way for the director to kill off his character in the first scene, everyone happily agreed. Well, Shane's Mom wasn't too thrilled on opening night, but we certainly had a blast that summer. I shook my head and put the eraser down next to the pill bottle. That was the only clear memory I had of St. Martha's. I was genuinely curious about the last item. It was a pink suede pouch just bigger than the palm of my hand, and it was cinched closed at the top with bakery string. Well, that is I was curious, until I saw the initials painted on the pouch in what looked like shiny pink nail polish. Funny, it wasn't even the initials, W.F., that made the hairs on the back of my neck go up. Nope, it was the pink bubblegum colored nail polish that bothered me. Something about it looked so familiar. I rolled the pouch between my fingers. There was something rigid in there something really...hard...inside. I reached for the string and started tugging at the knot. The thing is, whatever it was, I knew it wasn't mine. None of this stuff was. Okay, well, maybe the pill bottle, but the sales clerk had insisted that all three items had fallen out of my pocketbook and that didn't make any sense to me. I had the pocketbook with me the entire time I was in the dressing room. I hadn't dropped it. I hadn't spilled it over, either, and like I said, the stuff wasn't mine, so it couldn't have fallen out anyway. And the only other person in the dressing room had been Liat. Liat? Once again, my brain was motoring, racing with possibilities. Somehow, all of them, none of them, made sense as I fumbled with the knot. But before I could get a grip and straighten out my thoughts, the sales clerk pushed a pen and the receipt for a ridiculous number of purchases in front of me and smiled expectantly. I picked up the pen and then, I don't know, like I said, my brain was racing, so I sort of blew past the last few minutes like they never happened. I scribbled my name and exchanged receipts with the clerk. Then I opened my pocketbook and swept everything inside, my receipt, the credit card, the pill bottle, the eraser, the pouch, and I shook it all to the bottom. Later, I thought. I'll deal with it later.

With shopping bags layered to my elbows I headed for the elevators. Tapping my foot against the floor I waited for the doors to open. When they didn't, I dug the phone out of my white capris and started dialing.

"Harry? It's Willow. I need you to do me a favor."

"What? Jeez, Harry, slow down. I'm fine. I swear, Harry, I'm fine."

I avoided his next question, jiggling the still full bottles of pills at the bottom of my purse. They made me slow and fuzzy. Considering my very hazy recollection of the last few days, I decided it was safer to skip them. Besides, I didn't need pills before Iraq. I could do without them now."

I pulled the phone away from my ear. Harry's voice was at top volume.

"Damn it, Willow, you had me worried sick. I've been calling you for five days. Five days, Willow. Where the hell have you been?"

Five days? Was it really that long since I'd talked to Harry? I thought back to the airport. About that first night when I flew into Maui. About that ticket back to Philadelphia I found in my hands. Oh yeah, and the pills I took. Come to think of it, where was that ticket?

"What the hell have you been up to? Why haven't you called me?"

"Cripes, Harry, take it easy. I unplugged for a few days. Crept onto a nice quiet beach in Maui and soaked up the sun."

The words sounded so reasonable. In fact, they fell out of my mouth so easily I was hoping they were actually true. Harry let out a grandiose sigh on the other end of the phone.

"Well next time stay in touch. So, how is it in paradise? How are you, really?"

"Sitting on the beach, watching the tikki torches burn blah, blah, blah, Harry stop! I need you to focus. In about twenty minutes I'm going to e-mail you a surfing story. Walk it over to sports and talk Milo Yorty into printing it tomorrow. Tell him not to worry, there's a local angle–Angela Priest's daughter. Tell him it's the first in a series that will end with the Pipeline Masters. It's a good story Harry. Give me a call after you read it. Thanks, you're the best."

I hadn't actually written it yet but the story would be good. In my current state, I was sure of it.

"Okay Wil, fine. But listen to me for a minute. I've got news about the Priest investigation. You know, I've been trying to call you for five days about this. You were right. The shootings weren't so simple after all. My friend at the precinct, he–

"Gotta go Harry. Work to do. Call me after I send you the article. We can talk then. Promise."

I snapped the phone shut before he could get another word in. I looked up, still no elevator. More foot tapping and more ideas. I opened the phone and dialed again.

"Nick? It's Willow Finnegan. Got an hour? There's a research project I think you'd be great for. I have to warn you though it's a touchy subject. You might not want any part of it once I explain."

Nick was enthusiastic. I assumed that meant he hadn't talked to Liat yet. Whatever had her such a mess, well, she was in no hurry to share it with her boyfriend.

"Great. I'm in room 310 at the Outrigger."

"I'll be there in half an hour," he responded. "By the way, is Liat still with you?"

"No. Why?"

"Oh." There was deep concern in his pause. "It's just that her cell phone keeps going straight to voice message. No big deal. I'll be right over."

Apparently I wasn't the only one with questions about Liat. The floor lights above the elevator flashed at thirteen. Time for one more call.

"Hey, it's Willow Finnegan. Any chance you're free tonight?"

"I'm free every night. How'd you get my number?"

"In a fortune cookie," I quipped. "Does it matter?"

He laughed.

"I noticed something about you at the beach today and I think we should talk. If I'm right," I added, "then there's something I need to show you."

"Not that I wouldn't love to get a peek, but what about Kai?"

I groaned. "Not that kind of something. What I want to show you is way more interesting," then added, "much as I hate to admit that."

"I doubt it," Mak laughed. "But count me in anyway. When?"

"Let's make it nine thirty. I've got some work to do."

"Nine thirty it is. Meet you in the lobby?"

"Room 310. It'll be easier."

CHAPTER FOURTEEN

I tossed Angela's surfboard into the brown shag carpet between the king sized bed and the open doors of the lanai. Plopping down flat on top of it I practiced squatting into place to catch a wave the way Kai had taught me. I struggled to slow my thoughts as I practiced the motions. Tried to put myself earlier into the day, back on the beach with Kai. With slow breaths I returned to his surfboard, Kai sitting behind me, the clear power of the ocean rolling past our calves as they dangled over the edge of the board. I could feel Kai's hands resting carefully on my waist, waiting for just the right wave.

Pills, pills, pills.

Practice. Grip. Pop into place. Balance. Grip, pop, balance. Grip, pop, balance. Balance, balance, balance. I placed myself back inside the salt air and the waves. Back with Kai.

Kai...the oldest of four boys...his family lives on the Big Island. I learned that he's been an Astronomy Professor for the past eleven years and that the universe sways him as much as the ocean. He told me that when he was ten he stood some ten thousand feet in the air up on Mauna Loa, staring at the stars while another professor explained to him that when two hydrogen protons fuse together to form helium, a photon of sunlight is emitted into the air. "Sunlight," he said. "I was hooked."

"And the ocean?" I asked. Kai just smiled and sent me off into that first bubbly wave, the expression on his face a combination of satisfaction and mischief. The wave. His face. There wasn't a pill on the planet that could compete with that. I practiced the movements he taught me and once again—I popped into place.

When Kai asked about me I told him about my big Irish family. What a great way it was to grow up. I told him about work, how words were my version of the stars, just as vast and full of promise. When he asked about my time in Iraq I gave him the sanitized version and turned the conversation to other places I'd been. When he rubbed the third finger of my left hand I told him a little about Shane. I never mentioned Cathy Tanglewood. Or the baby.

I rode small waves and fell. Kai held out a hand and waited while I climbed back up on the board and tried it again and again. And we laughed. Good fun-in-the-moment laughter. I felt wholesome again and full of life. The dry choking chaos of Iraq was gone. The pristine chill of the mountains melted away. There was a sense of wonder inside those waves. And I wanted to stay there.

At the end of the lesson Kai steered his board a bit farther into the ocean. He wrapped his arms around my body and waited until a wave bigger than I was ready for rolled in and lifted the board. Gathering me to him Kai lifted us up in one smooth motion popping our legs into place and syncing our bodies for the ride. We sped forward, the board rocking hard on either side as Kai gracefully unfolded our arms into the salty breeze. We flew. Air and ocean speeding by us as our knees bent soft against the impact of the rising water. Deftly he navigated the board absorbing each new shock until in one flawless fluid motion he sent us sliding down the front of that wave, flying, fingers spread apart, brushing the rolling wall of ocean, dancing the board forward, straining hard to stay one step ahead of the onrushing tide.

Knock Knock.

Knock, knock, knock. Someone was at the door. Crushing away my smile. With a sigh I lifted the board out of the carpet and slid it back into the closet.

CHAPTER FIFTEEN

Before I could reach the door my cell vibrated new demands from the top of the dresser.

"Just a minute," I shouted while flipping open the phone. It was an urgent text from Harry. Whose calls I'd been ignoring.

Witness came forward. Nghbor saw u at Priests' house nght of shootngs. Cops hav ?s for u. Case re-opned. Worried. Please call.

Y r u worried? Cops kno I was there. I called 911 remember?

Nghbor saw u 15 mins earlier than 911 call. Time looks solid. Somthng bout a rcpt. for good n plenty's at market dwn the blok. Plus somthng big is up wth Shane. Pink n Preggers went missng. Serch undrwy. Shane frntic. Calld newsrm 5x's lookng for u.

With shaking hands I pulled four prescription bottles from the bottom of my pocketbook. I pushed right past the eraser and that suede pouch to get at the pills. Actually, I'd already completely forgotten that the salesgirl had given them to me…that those items even existed at all. Then I picked up the phone and texted Harry again.

Good n Plenty's???

Witness is old guy but very very sharp. Knows DOB, current events, even worked on Obama campaign. Call Shane. Call me now!

The knocking on the hotel room door was becoming more insistent as I set the bottles on the counter and opened them up. I stood in front of the toilet and lifted the lid. In one hand I held my cell phone, nimbly texting Harry with my left thumb. I gripped the prescription bottles with the other. For a long moment I held both hands over the water and stared at the objects resting in my palms. I held a steady stream of bad news in one hand. Pain free lapses in the other. One of them had to go.

More knocks rattled at the door. I hit the send button. Turned over a wrist. And flushed the toilet.

Sort it out 2morrow. Sorry Harry. Gotta go.

CHAPTER SIXTEEN

It was Nick at the door. He sat on the edge of my bed wearing a slightly dazed expression. The kind you see when a guy has just taken a hard left to the jaw. Actually, what I'd clobbered him with was an ugly idea about his girlfriend. From the look on his face it was clear he would have preferred the fist.

"I'm not trying to hurt Liat, Nick. I'm just trying to get at the truth."

I opened the bathroom door and slid my bare arms into one of the hotel's cozy terry cloth robes. The room was getting cold.

"Look, you're way off," Nick said. "I'm sorry about what happened to Jan's mother but that has nothing to do with Liat. She didn't even know those people."

"She's connected to them Nick. More than you think. And what about her little X files episodes?"

Nick looked at me, eyes wide.

"Don't look so surprised. I've checked around."

"You saw her this afternoon," Nick returned. "What'd she tell you?"

"Not enough. Of course I didn't know about her disappearing act then or you can bet I would've asked her. You know what she did tell me though? She gave me a rather uncanny description of a surfboard that's been stuck in the back of a closet in Philadelphia for the last fifteen years."

"So what. I know Liat. She wouldn't dream of hurting anybody much less shoot them."

"You sure about that? Have you even talked to her since she bolted from the dress shop?"

Nick stiffened.

"I've been trying to call her but–

"Let me guess," I interrupted. "You can't find her."

"Doesn't matter. You're still wrong," Nick said, defiantly.

"You know me better than that. Well, at least you know my work better than that," I corrected. "I did the research Nick. The dates match up. The day before the Priests were shot Liat went missing. She stayed missing for a good forty plus hours. In fact, you were so worried that you had half the student body at UH organized in a search that spanned four islands. In all that time no one saw her. Not one person."

I paused to let the words sink in.

"The only thing I haven't confirmed yet is what flight she took to Philadelphia."

"And you won't," he retorted, "because Liat never went to Philadelphia."

"Forty hours Nick. She was found wandering around the parking lot of the Kahului airport. You have no idea how she got there. Forty hours. It only takes thirteen to get to Philadelphia."

Sitting on the side of the bed Nick had his right toe pressed into the carpet and was absentmindedly bouncing the hell out of his leg. The way people do when they're either freezing cold or nervous.

"Here," I said, taking another one of the hotel robes off the bathroom hook and tossing it in his direction.

Nick caught it. Then, in one of those ridiculously quick movements innate in athletes, he jerked it back at me. One sudden movement. Fast. Completely unexpected.

"No thanks."

Almost instantly his voice sounded hollow. Far away. It was such a silly thing. A giant wad of terry cloth. So soft it couldn't hurt a fly. But that didn't matter. The robe hit me in the chest. By the time it bounced off and hit the floor I was drifting away.

Blood…flying limbs. My feet. My feet…still rooted in the brown shag carpet of a hotel room in Hawaii. I fought to keep them there. But my mouth…I could feel the dirt in my mouth. I could taste the dirt taste the blood. Gunfire…pelting the ground near my head… stuccato cracks of gunfire.

"Doesn't matter what you think. I don't care if she was gone for forty hours or forty days. Liat didn't hurt your friends. You don't know her like I do."

Nick was talking. Through the haze in my brain I spotted him, heard him talking. But the bullets were there too…whizzing past my ears.

Breathe…no…no…*flying limbs*, no dirt, no *Bullets!!* No…*blood*… not real. Not real.

But, oh that grenade, Willygirl. We both know that's…

Notttttttttttt real.

"Couldn't do something like that," I heard Nick argue. "She's just not capable."

"Oh she's capable," I responded in a voice so steady and reasonable it surprised me. "She's human."

Slowly and very very quietly I forced air in and out of my lungs. No dirt, no limbs, no gushing blood. Just a relentless banging against my chest. The tunnels of my heart were pumping non-stop and screaming for more oxygen much faster than I would allow it in. Slowly I let the breaths in and out of my nose, disregarding the tiny beads of sweat forming at the edges of my forehead. Beads of sweat not…

blood.

Just sweat.

"Are you okay Willow?"

"Sure," I answered. "Just a little cold." I crossed my arms and let out a small shiver as I chased back the last of the unwanted images. "These hotel rooms are like a freezer."

I forced myself to focus on Nick's face as I spoke.

"Okay, I get it. Liat's perfect. So then let's prove it. Work with me Nick. Help me untangle the facts. For starters, whoever killed my friends was searching for something extremely valuable."

At first, Nick didn't say anything. He got up from the bed and made his way over to the doors that led to the lanai. He held back the curtains, revealing a spectacular view. When I gazed past his shoulder, I could see that sunlight had nearly disappeared. Squelched down by the night sky, all that was left of the day was a bright fuzz of yellows and pinks and oranges simmering just above the ocean. After a minute Nick dropped the curtain and turned to face me. I smiled. If Nick had any reluctance left at all, well, it was tucked deep behind those green eyes.

"Okay, where do we start?"

"First things first. I've got a friend at the FAA who owes me a favor. I already put in a call. If he finds Liat's name on a flight list I promise you'll be the first to know, Nick. If he doesn't," I paused, then added, "I still think we need to find out where she was all that time. And who she was with."

Nick winced at the suggestion.

"What do you want me to do?"

"First of all, I need you to help me with January Pokani. She has access to something we need and she seems to like you. See if you can get a hold of it without her knowing why."

"What is it?"

"I take it you've heard of the Maui Snow?"

He hesitated, concern deepening his brow again.

"Monster diamond worth a bunch of money," he finally answered. "If you're asking me about it then I guess you know that Liat's father was accused of stealing it. People bug Liat about it all the time. Ask her all sorts of dopey questions. I don't plan on being one of them."

"Not Liat. January," I replied. "Her father has a rare surfboard with an image of Pele and a poem etched into it. I need to get a look at it if we're going to track down the Maui Snow."

Nick dropped into a chair by the doors to the lanai and burst out laughing.

"You're kidding me, right?"

"Serious as a heart attack," I answered, my breathing finally perfectly even. I bent down to the floor, picked up the robe, and tossed it onto the bed.

"Tell me," he said, still trying to contain his laughter, "what does the Maui Snow have to do with your friends in Philadelphia?"

"Everything. I'm convinced that whoever was in that house in Philadelphia was looking for the Maui Snow."

"Wow. How'd you come up with that theory?"

"Because Angela Priest had a pretty big clue how to find it."

Nick sat up and leaned forward. He wasn't laughing anymore.

"And you know this because…?"

I walked over to the closet door and slid it open.

"Because Angela gave me this," I said pointing to the surfboard now leaning up against the ironing board near the back of the closet.

Nick came up next to me. He peeked into the closet and looked back at me, eyes wide with shock. He ran his hands over the board, as if to prove it was real.

"It's beautiful," he finally spoke.

"Is this really it? Is this the other board? People have been…hell… Jan's father has been scouring the islands for this thing for years and you—

"Found it in a closet in Philadelphia," I finished. When he was done staring I slipped the board back into the closet and shut the mirrored doors.

"Just think," I told Nick. "If we put those two boards together I bet we can figure out where Liat's father hid the Maui Snow."

"Sure, no problem," Nick responded sarcastically. "We'll just match 'em up and blam, there it is, the mega-million diamond people have been hunting for for years. Let's get real, Willow. Even if we manage to get our hands on both boards it doesn't mean we'll be able to figure out the poems."

"Come on," I cajoled. Piece a cake."

Of course deciphering the poems turned out to be anything but. You see it wasn't just the information in the poems that mattered. The key to it all was a bit more personal than that.

"How hard can it be? Solve a few puzzles and, what did you say? Blam!"

Nick shook his head at me as if he were making the biggest mistake of his life.

"Piece a cake, huh," he repeated. "You talking Angel's food or devil's food?"

I flashed him my best Mona Lisa grin.

"Let's just call it coffee cake for now and let it go at that."

"Oh, and by the way," I added, taking a sheet of paper from the top of the dresser and handing it to him. "Check into this for me, will you?"

It was a list of three names.

"These are the students who died after swimming in that hot spring up on Mauna Kea about a year ago. The authorities found two small black diamonds on the ground near their pile of clothes. Check around campus. Find out everything you can about them. Look for connections, between them and to them. I'm talking hobbies, classes, girlfriends, boyfriends, pretty much anything you can think of that might connect them to the diamonds or at least shed some light on the subject. Oh, and I was told that there were two more kids with them that day. Another couple that were making out behind a rock while their friends were getting fried in acid. For some reason their names have been left out of the papers and there's no mention of them in the police report either. Still, I have it from a decent source that says two more people were on that hiking trip. I want their names."

Nick looked at the names and for a split second I saw his expression tighten. Then he folded the paper, stuffed it in his pocket, and headed for the door. He opened it, then hesitated and turned back to me.

"I'll talk to Jan and see if I can work something out about getting us in to see Mr. Pokani's board. The competitions at Sunset Beach are coming up though so it might take a few days."

"Just make sure January doesn't find out about the other surfboard," I warned Nick. "I don't want her to know about this just yet."

After he left I pulled open the closet and stared at the surfboard, trying once again to make some sense of the poem written below the hut with Poliahu on it.

If you've searched the volcano and can't find the gem
Here's one final clue to your hand I will lend
Search inside the sand and glass of life's tales
Aligned by time these secrets connected unveil

Before I could even read through it once, I was interrupted by a knock at the door. It was Mak. I slid the closet door closed, smiled at him, and then stepped back so he could enter.

"Hi Benny. What's new?" I asked in a light tone as he brushed past me.

Mak stopped dead in his tracks and threw me a sharp look with those magnificent steel gray eyes of his. Then I noticed him unconsciously slide a hand up onto his left arm just below the elbow.

"That is your real name, right? Benny Pokani. You are Angela's son."

He stared at me for half a beat, ready to deny it. Then changed his mind.

"How did you know?"

"You don't look a thing like Angela but you have about a million of your mother's mannerisms. You also share the same birthmark on the palm of your left hand. It kinda looks like a tiny wave, don't you think?"

Mak didn't say anything. He just glanced at the birthmark and then closed his fist.

"I'm also willing to bet that if you lift the sleeve on that shirt you're gripping so tight I'll find a nasty scar on your arm, compliments of a shark, right? When you were what, about eleven years old?"

"The scar's from a car accident," he replied automatically. It was the same lie he routinely gave to anyone who asked.

"Let me get this straight. The shark was driving a car when he 'accidentally' bit you on the arm. Really? Cool. Was it a Corvette or a Porche? A limo maybe? Yeah, must've been one of those stretch limos, you know, with sharks being so big and all."

Mak rolled his eyes and the edge of his lip shifted upwards in a slight grin. I had him and he knew it.

He let out a sigh. "My name's not Pokani though. It never was. Jan and I are only half sister and brother. My biological father was a full-blooded Hawaiian. He died when I was eight."

"But you are Angela's son. And that day on the beach? The day you were attacked by the shark? Everybody thought you died. Including Angela. There was so much blood in the water and there was no trace of you at all. They assumed you were dead. The truth is a fisherman found you floating in the ocean. He pulled you into his boat and took you back to Molokai. He carried you to a local doctor who nurtured you back to health—and then kept you. Is that about right, Benny?"

He looked at me and I saw the truth.

"My name is Makani."

"My father…the doctor who raised me…he's a good man. He gave me a good life. That's the only truth that matters to me. How he found me, the fact that he kept me illegally means nothing. After what happened I wanted to stay there. I don't know why you're dredging this up now but I won't allow him to get hurt."

"It's okay. You're mother…Angela…she knew."

The shock in his eyes deepened, and I felt bad. I wasn't trying to hurt him. I just needed him to know the truth.

"I found letters. In a closet after your mother died. Apparently you were in a coma for several months after you were rescued. When you started to come out of it you mumbled your name. Eventually the doctor checked into it and discovered that a boy had gone missing after a shark was sighted in the waters near Waikiki. He tracked your mother down in Philadelphia. They came to an agreement, a very silent agreement. Your mother didn't want anyone to know. She wasn't a bad person, Mak. She just wasn't a very good mother. By the time you woke up I guess she knew that. I honestly believe she thought you were better off with the doctor who saved you. I assume he never told you because he didn't want to hurt you."

"So why are *you* telling me?" He asked, still a bit dumbstruck.

"Because there's something I want to give you. But first, I have to ask. Does anyone else know? Who you are, I mean."

"No one knows."

He answered too fast. I stared at him for a second and right away it hit me. I couldn't help grinning.

"It's Kai. Kai knows."

Mak smiled but didn't answer.

"What I don't get," I added, "is why you haven't told your own sister? From what I can tell Jan has no idea who you are."

"And if you and I are going to be friends," Mak stated, "that's how it's going to stay. It's my business. When I want her to know I'll tell Jan myself."

Mak sighed. "Look, Willow, it's complicated. Jan…she's not as tough as you think. Our Mom, well, that was rough enough. But the relationship she has with her dad is even more complicated. She's vulnerable. Trust me."

"Fair enough," I said, opening up the closet door.

"There's something in here I want you to hold onto for me. For your mother."

I watched his reaction. Makani was as surprised as Nick to see the old surfboard made of koa wood. And just as curious about the poem. It was obvious he'd never seen it before. I doubted that he'd ever been to Philadelphia either although I would make sure to check the flights for his name just in case. Still, I was pretty sure that Mak had nothing to do with the Priests' death. Call it a hunch. His sister Jan, well, she was another matter. And then there was Liat. I still couldn't get over the way Liat had described her father's surfboard in detail.

CHAPTER SEVENTEEN

"Hungry?" Mak asked as he slipped the covered surfboard between several others he had atop the roof of his red Suburu station wagon. When it was well hidden, he tightened the ropes to make sure they were secure.

"Starved," I answered. "You sure this is smart?"

"In plain sight little mermaid, in plain sight. Trust me, it's the last place anybody will ever look. Besides, people here have my back. Anyone who goes sniffing around my boards won't get far. Face it," he said, giving my curls a friendly tug. "It's better than keeping it in your hotel room. I know old man Pokani pretty well. If Vince told him about this, he'll track you down. It won't be long before he figures out that you never went back to Philadelphia."

"You're right. Alfred Pokani is the last person I want to talk to right now. I'll deal with him later."

"Did it ever occur to you that maybe he's your man? Wouldn't be the first time an ex-husband showed up for a chat with his wife and it got out of hand. Especially if the subject of the discussion is a giant diamond."

"Already checked into it. Pokani's got a very public alibi. During the time Angela and Bill were getting shot in Philadelphia, he was on a golf course with the Governor and about a dozen others. Waiters, caddies, even the clerk at the pro shop can place him on the grounds at different points throughout the day. It wasn't Pokani."

"He could've sent someone."

"I know. He's got two airplanes. I checked the flight status on both. One was in a hangar on Oahu, the other was stashed at a private estate on Kuai."

"How about the Kolohe Kamali'i wahine? Did you check that one?"

"The koho-what?"

"The Rascal princess. It's a refurbished 727. It's got a couple of private suites plus it seats twenty regulars. Pokani leased it a few months ago for Jan. It's in her name."

"I had no idea. Thanks, I'll check that out. Now, about this whole starving thing. Did you ask me if I was hungry out of curiosity or are you planning on feeding me?"

Mak grinned. "Ever try poi?"

I groaned. He was at least the tenth person to suggest poi since I'd landed in the islands. Made from tarot root, its sort of like Hawaii's version of tofu. I love Hawaii, honestly, almost everything about the place is spectacular, but poi? Really? At least when you come to Philly the locals plop a nice chubby cheesesteak on your paper plate. Maybe even a hot soft pretzel.

"How about a big sloppy burger?" I whined. "With some fried onions and maybe some provolone cheese." In my defense, I hadn't eaten all day and my stomach was really starting to growl. "And french fries, god, I could really go for some good cheese fries."

"Come on," Mak grinned. "I know just the place."

I went back upstairs and changed into a pair of jeans and a white t-shirt. Forty minutes later we pulled up to a house with a backyard that sits on the beach near Haliewa. The house itself wasn't much to look at. In fact it was little more than an old-fashioned beach hut. Tiny, but charming, it also had a wrap-around porch that took up almost as much space as the house itself. It seemed a perfect match to the casual lifestyle of the North Shore. I was surprised when I found out it was Kai's.

"Here," Mak said, throwing a sweatshirt over the hood of his car to me. "You'll need that. The wind has a real bite to it once the sun is down."

The sweatshirt was green. Eco green. There was a logo on one sleeve that said Mission Playground and it was set underneath the silhouette of a child swinging on a swing. Mak told me that it was made with some recycled materials and that some of the proceeds went to preserving the planet. As I pulled the sweatshirt over my head and flipped my bulky curls free of the collar I couldn't help thinking. Another cause? Angela's son was getting more interesting by the minute.

As I came around the front of the car Mak was suddenly at my side, grinning down at me.

"Go with me on this," he said.

Before I could form another thought he wrapped his arms around me, pulling me in close, as he steered us around the side of the house and down toward the beach where a crowd of about forty people were laughing and drinking and throwing sticks into a roaring bonfire. He was walking so fast and holding me so close that when he stopped short in front of Kai and Jan, I had to clutch onto his rib cage just to keep from falling.

"Hey Prof? Look what I found. Didn't even have to go in the ocean. Little mermaid just jumped right out at me. It's a real shame, you losing such a treasure," he said, shifting me in front of him and making it a point to rest his chin on the top of my head.

"You see," he said, whispering near my ear but loud enough for everyone else to hear, "that's the thing with old guys. They fish a mermaid as fine as you out of the water and then hhmmmm…forget to feed you." He shook his head and tskked. "It's sad, really. The Prof here used to be such a worthy opponent. First it was the knees. Then his eyesight went. Poor brah can hardly drop into a wave these days. I'm sorry he forgot to feed you but I guess we should just be glad he still remembers his own name. So, Willow, what can I getcha? Some barbequed prawns? Hamburger? How 'bout some buffalo wings?"

"You can skip the wings," I said, grounding my heel into his toes and twisting out of his grasp. "I've had enough bull for one day."

Kai stepped forward, took my hand, and we laughed. January looked annoyed. Near the edge of the crowd a good twenty feet away I spotted Liat. She was staring at Mak and she was visibly upset. When I leaned over toward Mak, Liat's eyes shifted in my direction, but only for a second. As soon as our eyes met she turned away and melted herself into the crowd.

"Nice try grommet. Let's see how tough you're talking after round two at Sunset when I walk away with your crown," Kai declared, his grin as sweet as pie.

"Empty threats old man, empty threats," Mak teased back.

"What? You're competing?" I asked, dropping Kai's hand and staring at the two men.

"Not just competing. Winning," Kai answered, his grin unwavering.

"Competing in the Triple Crown. How? Are you some kind of wild card, like Nick?"

"Not just for the Triple Crown series. Me and the Mouth here are right up against it for the World Title. The points are close right now but that's just 'cause I've been playing with him, letting him think he stands a chance."

"But I thought you were..."

"Too old?" Mak teased.

"No," I suddenly glared at Mak. "An Astronomy Professor. You're head of the department, right? To compete for the world title don't you have to travel around the world? Africa, Australia, France? What about your classes?"

Kai looked embarrassed. He opened his mouth to say something then closed it without uttering a word.

Mak jumped to explain. "This is Hawaii, Willow. Everybody makes time to surf."

"Really," I said, my voice dripping with sarcasm. "So Everybody in Hawaii travels the planet and surfs professionally."

Why was I so upset?

Was it because the image I had of Kai, the wise and grounded professor, was starting to disintegrate? The truth is I didn't really know him that well. Then again, maybe it wasn't Kai I was worried about. Maybe it was myself. After all, this was just one more example that my own sense of judgment was off, that I wasn't getting all the facts straight.

"No," Mak conceded. "Not everyone here surfs professionally. But we're not as laid back as you might think. "I, myself, make a mean pizza," he teased. "The Prof here, well, he can't cook but I hear in his free time he strings up a real pretty lei. Jan and Liat? Well you know they both paint."

"Alright, alright, I get it. Maybe I am overreacting. But I'm just trying to figure out how you do it. I mean, don't the women have less events? Only six a year is what I read. The men have twice as many, right? Seriously, I'm curious. How do you manage classes with all the traveling?"

Kai looked at me and once again the color in his cheeks started to rise.

"My schedule at the University is pretty flexible. Most of my classes are arranged so that I can fly out on Thursdays for the competitions."

"Man, you are way too humble," Mak said with a laugh.

"The Professor has one other slight, ahhhmm, advantage. His talent. Much to my annoyance he doesn't need to surf every event on the pro circuit to stay competitive. Kai has an uncanny knack for taking first or second in the events he surfs. Which means the old man has actually racked up enough points early in the season that now he's right on my tail. There's even," Mak said as he squinted his eye and put his thumb and forefinger close together, "a slight chance that he could take the world title."

"Slight my a–

"It's okay though," Mak interrupted, "because after I annihilate him in the next round, the Prof here will be just like all the other poor slobs on the circuit –cryin' in his beer 'til next year. Isn't that right, Oldi-wan?" Mak queried as he bowed in mock solemnity to his more seasoned rival.

Kai laughed but then struck a defensive pose, arms stretched out in front of him, knowing that Mak would come up from his bow swinging. Mak was always in motion. He really did remind me of Angela; so full of life, full of adventure.

"Speaking of beer. Why don't you go grab one and give that mouth of yours a rest?" Kai suggested.

I watched Mak make his way into the crowd. He bounced as he went; laughing and joking with just about everyone he came in contact with. I threw a sideways glance at Kai. He smiled as he watched the younger man go. Then his gaze drifted toward the ocean. He was so still, seemed so comfortable in his own skin. I watched him for a moment and still felt uneasy. Kai was a world-class surfer. Not exactly the nerdy professor I imagined myself falling for. In fact, he was another athlete. Just like Shane. Shane. The thought was unsettling. Since coming to Oahu I'd convinced myself that I was moving in a new direction. Leaving the messes in my life behind me. Getting healthy. Making progress—that's what I wanted to believe. But was I? Kai drags me out of the ocean, smiles at me, and right away I decide who he is. That I know him? But I don't. Not really. Then again, how much can you know about anyone?

"Hungry?" Kai asked, turning back to me.

"You never told me you were competing."

Kai looked bewildered.

"Sure I did. I even gave you the list of competitors. Remember? I wrote my phone number at the top of the list. Wrote it right next to my name, then told you to call me if you had any questions."

"Oh right. Yeah," I hesitated. "I guess you did."

Only I didn't remember. I could not remember Kai ever telling me that he was a champion surfer. What I did remember was faxing that list to Harry. Along with my first article since the one I'd written about Angela and Bill. I faxed the list without bothering to look at it. Not exactly thorough. Suddenly I had doubts about the story I'd sent to Harry. A few hours ago I thought it was the best thing since sliced bread. But was it? I wrote it and faxed it. From first to last, I never glanced at a word twice. Only, that's not how I work. I always re-write. It's unconscious with me, like…

What? Putting meat in the freezer? Throwing a grenade? Pouring a second cup of coffee?

"Hungry?" Kai asked again.

I should call Harry. Maybe I wasn't ready to go back to work. A couple of weeks ago I was sitting in a chair and staring through a window at the garden outside of Angela's swanky nut retreat in the mountains. The most taxing thing on my brain then was whether to put half and half or two percent in my cup. Angela was alive then. I hadn't run into Shane yet. Or his pink and preggers girl/wife, whatever she was. Two short weeks ago. Or was it longer? Harry had said I was out of touch for what? Five days? And I could only remember one of them. It just… it hadn't felt that long. But I was resting, that's all, resting. Right?

Hmmmmmmm…

The thing is, you can lose track of yourself when you're sitting at the beach and the pill bottles are open and your eyes are closed. One day can fade into another and then another. It doesn't mean anything.

Maybe…maybe not

I started counting back the days in my head, trying to remember details…like…I remembered landing in Maui. The black dome of Haleakala peaking through the clouds. I tried hard to pick out other details…what I had for breakfast…whether or not it had rained…did I buy a t-shirt in Maui? I must've bought a t-shirt. For the life of me though, I could not retrace my movements from that first day when I landed on Maui. It was all too fuzzy. Again, that's time at the beach for you. Right? One moment blurs into the next and then the next. Pen and paper I finally decided. When I got back to the hotel I would sit down with pen and paper and retrace my steps. Once I put my mind to it, everything would fall into place. Yep, my mind. That was the key.

Getting warmer.

"Willow?"

Kai snapped his fingers and waved a hand in front of me.

"Starved," I finally answered. "Let's eat."

"Hey Kai," I added, grabbing his arm before he turned away in search of food. "How about some of that coffee you keep raving about? I could really use a cup."

Thirty minutes later Kai and I were sitting around the fire. Fed and feeling better I searched the crowd once again for Liat. She was doing a good job of avoiding me. Every time I spotted her she seemed to sense it and would slip away. Now she was near the edge of the ocean with Nick. They looked like they were arguing. A minute later she glanced in my direction, and then, leaving Nick, she stalked away and headed down the beach. Away from the crowd. Away from the bonfire.

Turns out I wasn't the only one watching Liat. As Nick blended into the crowd near the bonfire I caught sight of Mak. He was manning the grill. When Liat took off, he dropped the burger he was flipping and went after her. Two houses away, he swerved toward a line of rocks that began near the sand dunes. The rocks cut straight across the beach and led into the sea. Mak climbed over the giant rocks near the center, a good forty feet ahead of Liat, who was walking near the surf where the line of rocks was much smaller. I don't think Liat saw him. A minute or so later she crossed over the smaller rocks at the edge of the water. Frustrated, I watched her silhouette slip away in the dark.

"Bathroom?"

Kai pointed to the line of beer drinkers hovering near the back door of the house and grimaced. "It's through the kitchen and to the left. Good luck with that."

I made my way toward the house. But as soon as Kai's head was turned I took off for the rocks.

Away from the fire and the light of the house the beach got darker so much faster than I expected. The rocks were farther away too. When I got there I climbed the smallest one I could find near where Mak went over them. I wedged myself safely in between two rocks and then peeked down over the edge to make sure they hadn't seen me. I nearly had a heart attack when I realized how close I was too them. They were directly below me. It didn't matter though because Mak was pacing in the sand and shouting. Turns out they were way too busy arguing with each other to look up and notice me.

"You walk around here like a ghost, Liat." Mak was yelling. "Your surfing is off. Your paintings are off. Something's wrong, something's going on with you." His voice softened. "Whatever it is just tell me. Let me help."

Liat said nothing. Mak paced harder and once again his anger floated to the surface.

"You break up with me for no reason. I figure okay, you need space. So I give you some space. Next thing I know you pick up with that… that lightweight frat boy. That was bad enough, but now? Now you look scared all the time. Liat I can't take it. How am I supposed to help you if I don't know what's wrong?"

Mak's voice was raw.

Liat put a hand up, as if to stop the pain that was flowing in her direction, and then turned to walk away. Before she could Mak reached out and took hold of her hand.

"Is it Nick? Is he hurting you?"

"No! God no! Nick would never hurt me. It's not like that. Please Mak, let's not do this. Not tonight. Just go back to the party. Let it go. You have to…let me go."

Mak dropped her hand. But he didn't let go of her. Instead, he placed his fingers under her chin and tilted her eyes to his.

"Is that really what you want?"

She looked up but wouldn't meet his eyes.

"Come on Liat, we belong together. Face it kiddo—we were fused. Ever since that first day on the beach."

"You mean the day you bullied me. The day I…." Liat hesitated for a second and then finished, "the day that shark nearly killed you?"

Mak brushed her chin with his thumb. "Forget about the shark. Compared to the effect you had on me, the shark was an afterthought."

Liat pushed the sleeve away from his t-shirt and ran her fingers over the jagged fleshy scars that circled his upper arm; teeth marks so deep they nearly touched the bone.

"You call this an afterthought?"

"I changed that day Liat. In ways," he tapped his heart. "In ways I can't begin to explain. You did that. So yeah, compared to you, the shark is forgettable."

"Don't be stupid!" Liat exploded, almost as if he'd hit her. "Don't forget what happened Mak because…it could happen again. You never know. It could happen again."

"So what," Mak answered. "Can't be any worse than watching you with Nick. We were connected that day Liat. When I grew up I knew I'd find you. The second I laid eyes on you again I felt it. We felt it. Hell, we spent the next three years joined at the hip. Now, all of a sudden you want to pretend that didn't happen. That we don't matter?"

Liat shifted in the sand. Dropping her head she brushed tears from her cheek and turned away. Mak didn't reach for her this time. His hands remained clenched at his side.

"At least tell me why." His voice was hoarse with resignation. "You owe me that."

"What if I can't give you a reason? Not one that makes sense anyway. Oh and that shark, Mak? I can't just forget about that. I thought you were dead. For years…I thought that I–

"Thought what?"

"Liat, please." He took her by the shoulders and turned her to face him.

"Tell me what's wrong so I can fix it."

Liat sighed. "There's nothing to fix. We're over."

"That's a decision," Mak's voice was calmer now. "Not an explanation. If you expect me to let go then give me a reason. Give me the real reason, and I'm gone. But don't tell me it's because you don't love me. I know better. As far as Nick goes, maybe you do have feelings for him. So what. You care about him. You don't look at him the way you used to look at me. Trust me, if you did, if I saw that, I wouldn't be standing here right now."

Mak hit a nerve. And he knew it.

"Why?" He reached out a hand to brush a tear from Liat's cheek.

"Please Liat. You have to tell me. I'm gonna fall apart without the truth."

"I…it's a …I had a…a vision," she finally stammered settling on a word inadequate to describe what she'd been going through.

"You remember what happened to us that day on the beach? How we, how everything suddenly changed? I…well. There's another…event. I don't know what else to call it. It's different this time. That day on the beach things just happened. You had my doll. I wanted my doll… needed my doll back…and then it was over. This time…now…I can't explain it but there's an event, something big Mak. It's coming. I can feel it."

Liat looked hard at him.

"I'm afraid Mak. Afraid for both of us. The only thing I can think of is to stay away from each other. Maybe it doesn't have to be like last time. If I stay away from you maybe it won't happen. Maybe I can stop it."

Mak took a step back from her and let that day on the beach flood his memory. Liat's eyes boring into his, stirring him, and changing him forever. He'd been helpless to stop all that had poured out of her and entered him. But afterwards, well, afterwards he had to choose. He remembered bobbing in the ocean like a grain of sand. Free. Free of the ugly path he'd been headed down. Then that shark came along.

"Maybe you're not supposed to stop it. Look at me Liat. I'm still here."

That wasn't enough to convince her. She couldn't forget the sand sculpture of the shark, or the fear in her mother's eyes when she grabbed Liat away from it.

"Mak, there's something I've been wanting to ask you. Please. Just hear me out." Liat took a deep breath.

"I want you...I need you to sit out the competition at Pipe. If you don't surf, if you stay away from the crown this year, then maybe whatever this is...maybe it will pass. These visions," she struggled with the word again. "Maybe they'll just go away. Maybe nothing bad will happen."

"Oh please!" He spat, incredulous. "Is that what this is about? Pipe? The crown?" Mak paced in the sand again, getting more wired with every step.

"This is about Nick isn't it?" Mak laughed, only there was no humor in his tone.

"You don't seriously think your little boyfriend stands a chance of winning, do you? Because that boy won't survive the first heat whether I'm in the competition or not. Not with those swells. Nick is way out of his league. That's just a fact."

"I know." Liat's voice was quiet. "It's not him I'm worried about, although I don't want him to compete either. Just in case."

"In case what?"

"I told you. It's like what happened with the shark. Only worse. Something's going to happen. I...I know it. But if you just stay away from me...stay out of the water for awhile...maybe we can stop it."

Mak stopped pacing. He could see she was serious. She honestly believed something bad was going to happen. He stood in front of Liat then and took both of her hands in his, staring hard at her.

"I don't want to stop it. Whatever it is, bring it on. I belong in the water. As far as you and I go? You, ho aloha, you're like a freight train with all the bells and whistles. Stop worrying. Forget the baggage and please, just keep on rolling my way."

Liat squeezed his hands.

"What's coming is someone else, Mak. Another woman. She's waiting for you. I saw it. I *saw* her."

Mak dropped her hands and stepped back.

"Who?" He finally asked. "The journalist? Willow? Is that why you acted so weird when you met her?" He let out a low, knowing whistle. "You were jealous. You got some goofy premonition vibe thing about the two of us and you were jealous. Well don't be. I mean Willow's hot and all, at least for a wahine in her thirties, but she's with Kai. I would never step in on that."

It's not some goofy vibe, Mak. The way I looked at you…what happened afterwards. There've been times over the years, before I knew that you were alive, when I…when I'd stare at someone else… and I could feel something start to hap…but I squelched it Mak. I made it go away. My mother, she knew it. She would step in and I could see that look in her eyes…and I could stop it but now…" Liat sighed.

"Your mother was wrong Liat. What you did to me…for me…I'm glad you didn't stop it."

Liat looked at Mak as if she had more to say. More to explain. But in the end she didn't say another word. Instead, Liat moved into him, she hooked her arms around his neck, pressed her body to his and hugged him tight. Then just as fast she let go, rushing back toward the edge of the ocean. With her feet rustling in the foamy surf, I could hear more than see her as she ran up the beach and back toward the bonfire.

I hunkered down hoping Mak wouldn't spot me as he scaled the bigger rock two down from the pair I was scrunched between. Spying on them, especially in such a private moment was a crappy thing to do. I felt compelled to do it but I didn't feel good about it. Okay, so maybe I didn't mind the part where Mak said I was a hot wahine. Either way, my moral dilemma went unnoticed. With both eyes steadily trained on Liat, Mak never even glanced my way.

I waited a good ten minutes trying to sort out what I'd heard. So Liat was there on the beach the day that Angela's son went missing. Strange, but was it relevant? Angela had talked a lot about Mak and January the night she died. She talked about the Maui Snow. But she never mentioned Liat.

Now those visions, Liat's visions, they were another matter altogether. There was an interesting aura about the girl for sure, but visions? That concept was out there. Oddly enough the idea made me feel better, less alone somehow. Like maybe I wasn't the only one with issues.

Issues? That's so cute. You have a nickname for me.

Not that I believed Liat was actually having visions of the future. But I did like the idea. You know, that there was something sort of extra about her. Yeah that was it. That the possibility that there was something extra, something other wordly going on, not just with Liat but maybe with me too. For the first time since Angela's death, since I'd left the nuthouse, I felt a glimmer of hope brewing inside of me. Maybe I wasn't...

Dangerous?

...confused. I pushed against the sides of my head, pushed myself hard to think about the night Angela died. How she tried to talk. At first the image came a bit clearer. Angela. Staring. And that look in her eyes. So scared. So betrayed. But then the images curled at the edges of my brain and faded away. It was so frustrating. It was all because of those stupid flashbacks. That was the reason I couldn't remember things properly. It had to be.

Hahaha...good one

Since that night I'd been working hard to keep them at bay. But I needed to work harder. I needed to concentrate and rid myself of those flashbacks. Had to if I was ever going to live a normal life again. I wanted that badly. Maybe even with Kai. Damn those images. Swirling near the edges of my brain. Rolling in and out like ripples in the ocean. They were too small, too fast for me to grasp. Liat didn't seem to have that problem. Her visions were clear to her. She seemed to know exactly what she wanted from Mak.

I stood there on the rock breathing deep for a moment. I couldn't see the ocean but I could hear the dark brew rolling every which way out there in front of me. A fresh spray of salty air blew in off the waves and played havoc with my waist-length curls. Part of me could have stood there forever, letting my curls fly wild, letting my mind drift inside that vast black expanse. Then I thought of Kai. Waiting for me back at the bonfire. And something eased deep within me.

I walked toward the ocean. As I crossed over the rocks I could feel the manic energy I'd been living in since the traffic incident near the Outrigger, drain from my body, leaving me achy and exhausted. Legs heavy, I stepped off the last rock down by the water's edge and crushed my feet into the prints Liat had left in the wet sand moments before. Despite the wind I combed a hand through my hair and made an effort to push the impossible red strands away from my eyes. With slow steps I moved up the beach toward the glow.

CHAPTER EIGHTEEN

As the days passed I grew stronger, more confident.

Harry sent me a few more texts. The article was good. The sports editor published it in the Sunday edition and gave the go ahead to follow Jan's progress for the rest of the series. He mentioned Shane and his lost wife a couple of times. Wanted to know if I'd talked to him yet. I mailed Harry coffee and pineapples and ignored his questions about Shane. The article was good and I still had a job. I thought it wise to concentrate on the positive.

Kai came for me in the mornings. Just as the sun would inch its way above the Pacific, casting barely enough light for us to make out the boards in front of us, we would toss them into the sea and paddle out.

My skills were improving.

After a week I was able to stand up and ride small waves nearly all the way to the beach. Granted they were smooth and predictable. No sharp flips of the lip. No rude undercurrents sloshing in from six thousand miles away. Still I was getting the hang of it. And I was falling in love. As near as I could tell Kai was falling with me.

My life felt like it was in remission. The diseased thoughts choking the life out of me since Iraq appeared to be loosening their grip. The pills were gone. Replaced with a surfboard and the ocean I didn't miss them at all. Before Iraq, before Angela's doctors, I'd never swallowed more than an aspirin. Altogether my thoughts were clearer. There were no flashbacks. No headaches. In fact, for the first time since my split with Shane, I was genuinely happy. Maybe too happy.

I was concentrating on sand and swells more than the investigation. Nick was on it though. He was researching the Maui Snow along with events that happened the day Liat's father stole it from the museum. So far he hadn't found much that was new. He was working on Jan too. They were getting chummier by the day and he was making himself a regular at the mansion. But when he finally managed to wander his way into Alfred Pokani's study Jan got mad and yanked him back outside to the pool. Nick pushed it. He brought up the surfboard. Boasted that if she let him have it for a week he could figure the thing out. Jan laughed. Told him the idea was ridiculous and then she dropped the subject and made a pass at him. Nick politely refused. After that he went back to researching Liat's father.

Mak did his part too. He wasn't able to decipher the clues on the surfboard but he kept trying. He got curious about the image of Poliahu and did some research. He showed me a story, Pele and the Snow Goddess by W.D. Westervelt, Paradise of the Pacific, January 1910.

Basically, the gist of the Hawaiian legend is that Poliahu is a beautiful snow goddess who sometimes has issues with Pele, the goddess of fire. On one such occasion, Pele hid her identity and showed up at a sledding contest being held on the slopes of Mauna Kea by Poliahu. The two goddesses raced down the hill. When Pele lost, she got angry and spewed fiery lava in Poliahu's direction. Poliahu sped to the top of slopes and escaped the flames by freezing everything in her path and causing snow to fall across Mauna Kea. To this day the northern slopes are covered in snow and still considered Poliahu's home. It was a good story, but it didn't help us to decipher the poem.

I should have told Kai. Should have asked his advice. But I couldn't make myself do it. What I had with Kai was good. It was kind and clean and growing into something that felt so right. I was afraid. I didn't want anything bad to intrude on what we were building. Figuring out what happened to Angela was necessary. Deep down I knew that. Knew that I wouldn't be a hundred percent again until I remembered what happened. But Kai was necessary too. In fact, he was rapidly becoming more necessary.

Liat was the key. Her father had carved the surfboard. He wrote the clues. We needed her input but she was avoiding me like the plague. I even went to Sandy Beach and tracked her down. It was a waste of time.

As soon as Liat spotted me, she took her surfboard and headed straight for the big waves. Funny thing, after that Mak and Nick were in total agreement. Don't press Liat. I didn't like it but I had to give Nick some credit. He was right about one thing. Liat wasn't listed on any of the flights to Philadelphia in the days before Angela's death. It seemed like the investigation was at an impasse.

What I didn't know as I coasted through the waves with Kai that morning was that by the end of the day two more people would be dead. And Liat's forty hours of missing time would be accounted for in striking detail.

CHAPTER NINETEEN

The walls of the ballroom were alive with art. Oils, charcoals, and stunning originals hung side by side along with college student nods to Van Gough's Starry Night. There were life-sized sculptures made of plaster, steel, and even what looked like a mango tree fashioned from painted cookie dough and an old floor lamp.

The room was crowded and there was so much to look at that people were actually bumping into one another. I had to scrunch against the bar to get away from a large man wearing a purple and red aloha shirt under his tux.

"Sorry darlin'," he apologized with a midwestern twang. "Whhew! Nothin' hotter'n a redhead in a green dress. Here, lemme getcha a drink."

He turned, shifting his body toward the bar and whistled at the closest bartender. When he did, he caught his arm on one of the cookie dough branches and took down the entire sculpture. Before he could right it, I slid around the back of his aloha shirt and made my way to the other end of the bar. Kai was there. Behind the bar serving drinks. He smiled and handed me a Cosmopolitan.

"Malihini's got a point 'bout that dress," Kai grinned. You look great."

"Translation?" I grinned back.

"Visitor," Kai stated kindly.

"If he's a visitor what does that make me?"

"Hot, ho aloha. Verrry hot."

I laughed. "You look pretty too." And he did. Black tux, white shirt, and those warm brown eyes.

"So, what's with the bar gig? Don't you have enough jobs?"

One more thing I didn't know about Kai?

"Just helping out a friend for a few minutes," he said, wiping his hands with a towel before stepping away from the bar.

"Now that you're here, paying attention to you is the only job I want tonight."

"Yelch," I said, opening my mouth and pointing a finger towards my throat. "That's a bit gooey for you. Where's the drill instructor with the surfboard? Him I can deal with."

"Must be that dress," he answered, taking me by the arm and swinging me onto the dance floor.

It was a night and a half. We danced. We ate. We drank. We perused the artwork, choosing our favorites and bidding on them during the silent auction.

Fun. But I did have an agenda. From the minute I walked through the door that night my goal was to pin down Liat. The ballroom was big but there was no way she could avoid me for the entire night. My chance came while I was writing down a bid on the broken tree sculpture. Out of the corner of my eye I spotted Liat making her way to the lady's room. I caught up to her just before she opened the door.

"Come on Liat. I'm not your enemy. We need your help."

Liat sighed but she said nothing.

"If you work with us there's a chance we could clear your father's name. Don't you want that?"

"Nick told me that you're trying to decipher the poem on my father's board. That you think you can actually find the Maui Snow. I can't believe you talked him into helping you. The thing is? If I could stop you I would. Willow, I get that you have your reasons. You even think they're good ones. They're not. Your being here is...trouble."

"Why? What kind of trouble."

Liat opened her mouth to speak and then closed it, the fear in her eyes evident.

"Hiding from the truth won't help," I griped, frustrated. "Trust me. It only makes things worse."

"Like I said. If I could stop you, I would."

She brushed past me and went back into the ballroom. I went back to the table looking for Kai and found Nick instead.

That's when all hell broke loose. There was a crowd forming near the bar and they were shouting for help.

"911 call 911!"

People all over the ballroom flipped open their cell phones and started dialing.

"Move people!" Bellowed a young woman in a short silver dress and matching platforms. "The guy is choking to death. He needs a fist to the abdomen not a hundred people on cell phones." She pushed her way to the center of the crowd. "Morons," she mumbled as people cleared out of the way to let her in.

I stood up from the table and strained my neck to see what was going on. I caught a glimpse of a man dressed in a tux with both hands clenched at his throat.

When I told Nick his face went white. "No way. No friggin' way!" He swore. Then he got up so fast he knocked over his chair.

"This can't be happening." Nick rushed toward the crowd knocking down a second chair on his way. I followed, still scanning the room for Kai. He was nowhere in sight.

By now the girl in the silver dress had both arms locked around the man's waist, her fist buried in the stiff white cotton shirt above his belly button. As skinny as she was she Heimlich-ed the heck out of the choking man. Thrust after thrust after thrust she kept at it. But the man had gone limp and the layer of gray on his skin was getting thicker by the second.

It was a disturbing scene and yet it was Nick who held my attention. He tapped a bystander in front of us on the shoulder so hard he almost knocked the poor guy over.

"What happened?" Nick's voice was edgy.

"You know that fella Mason something or other? The one with the beard and stringy hair who teaches art over at the college?

"Professor Henker?" Nick barked.

"Yeah, right that's him. Well, so, he's been tossing back martinis all night and the guy, he's pretty tanked up. He's got his hands in the air throwin' his arms all over the place, and ya know, he's doin' that old man dance, the one guys do when they're trying to pretend they're still twenty. So he's dancing and drinking and it aint too long before he's gettin' friendly and pawing at every girl who comes within arm's reach. The guy's a total train wreck. Very entertaining. The wife and I couldn't take our eyes off him."

"And?"

"Okay, so at one point there's this hot blonde. And I mean hot, hot blonde. Waaay too young for old Mason. Hell, even if he were still twenty he wouldn't stand a shot with a girl like her. I mean she was really someth–

"And?" Nick demanded, rolling his hands and trying to speed up the story.

"So one minute he's all friendly. Next minute hot blonde comes up holding a martini in front of her and old Mason here does a one eighty. He gets ugly. He starts bitchin' at her, saying she owes him money. Asks her if their little venture is ever gonna pay off. Then the blonde gets a sore look. She leans in to tell him something. He reaches out like he's gonna touch something, if ya know what I mean," the guy winks at Nick. Nick just glared.

"Okay, alright," the man continued. "So hot blonde jumps back and starts raising the martini glass towards him. I swear she was gonna toss the drink on him. But then he reaches in and snatches the martini right out of her hand. Downs it in a single gulp. Next thing you know dude's on the floor gaspin' for air."

The man looked at Nick and then nodded toward the activity at the center of the crowd.

"Poor bastard," he said compassionately.

Nick didn't say another word. He just stared past him, toward the man choking in the center of the crowd. Trust me though from the look on Nick's face you would've thought he was the one choking. I couldn't help wondering why. It seemed like a bad time to start asking questions so instead, like Nick and everybody else, I strained my neck to see what was going on with Mason.

Sweating and frustrated, the silver mini-skirted woman jammed her fist deep into the prone guy's stomach and let out a yell. Then Mason's head jerked forward and the people who'd leaned in close to watch, instinctively flinched backwards. Something flew out of his mouth, hit the edge of a table, and rolled underneath. Eventually it came to a stop near the feet of a girl who looked vaguely familiar. She bent down from her chair and picked the offending object up off the floor with a napkin.

"It's an olive!" she shouted, holding it up for the crowd to see. Then she brought her hand down and inspected it closer. Something had caught her eye.

The crowd chattered for a moment about the offending object being an olive and then turned back to Mason who was now flat on the ground and still not moving. The girl in the silver mini-skirt was on her knees ready to start CPR. One of the bartenders stepped in to assist her. But no matter how hard they pumped at his chest, the gray refused to part from Mason's cheeks.

For some reason my gaze shifted back to the girl who had the olive. I tried to place her in my mind. It took me a minute to remember. It was the quiet girl. The one standing with the group of surfers, board clutched in front of her, on the beach the day I'd met Kai. I'd seen her a few times since then but I couldn't remember her name. She was at the bonfire talking books with Kai and Nick. I saw her bringing January some wax for her surfboard at the beach too. The girl was always hovering even though January barely gave her the time of day. Jan was paying attention now though. I left Nick and moved closer to them so I could hear what was going on.

"Ewwww gross. Don't stand there looking at it. Throw it out." Jan reached for the napkin with the olive in it. "Here, I'll do it."

But the girl squeezed it in her fist and held back.

"We better save it. I think Mason might want it. You know…as a souvenir."

"That's ridiculous."

"I would," she defended timidly.

"Melanie, the only souvenir Mason's going to want after tonight is a new lung."

"What are you doing here, anyway? Don't you work nights at the hospital?"

"It only takes ten minutes to get there. Besides," she added, feeling a sudden need to justify her presence, "I only came so I could bid on one of your paintings."

151

"Now that's a classy move," Jan approved. "Keeping a regurgitated olive? Not so much."

Jan held out her hand and waited. But Melanie stood her ground. She stuffed the napkin in her pocketbook and zipped it shut.

"I think we should let Mason decide."

"Not likely," Jan said, pointing toward Mason. The paramedics had arrived and were busy shocking Mason's prone body for the third time. Moments later they whisked him out the door.

Melanie pulled her purse a little tighter. She looked over Jan's head and saw me staring. Jan looked up and saw me too.

"Whatever," Jan sighed. Then she turned and walked away.

By now the medics had parted the crowd and Nick and I were on opposite sides. He was heading for the bar. Heading for Liat. Before long, their heads were bowed together. Even from across the room, the conversation looked intense. I scanned the crowd again for Kai but he was still nowhere in sight. Seconds later Liat pulled away from Nick and bolted for the double doors that led to the lobby.

No way, I thought. She's not getting out of here that easy. I bolted for the doors myself, and got there first, blocking the entrance like a goalie guarding his net during a shoot-out. Liat looked sick when she saw there was no getting past me. She turned, contemplating her options, but Nick came up fast behind her. Liat let out a sigh of defeat. I had no idea why she was running but from the look on Nick's face I knew it couldn't be good.

"Willow, there's something we need to show you." He stood behind Liat, holding both her shoulders and looking serious. If Liat could have melted into the floor, I think she would have. Poor Nick.

Before I could ask what was up, a warm hand fell across my own shoulder.

"Sounds interesting. Where're we going?"

It was Mak. There was no mistaking the look on his face either. Something was clearly up, and Mak wasn't about to let Liat out of his sight.

"Not now Mak," Nick protested. "This is a private matter."

But it was Liat who stopped Nick. She turned in his arms and put a hand to his chest.

"Mak should come. If we're going to do this, then Mak should be there. This involves him too."

"Liat," Nick said sharply. "You don't know that for sure. It could be me. It could be Kai."

Liat's face was resolute.

"Look, whatever you want to show me, I'm in. But does it have to be this second?" I asked, jumping into the fray. "I don't want to leave without finding Kai. Plus," I added, "I gotta go upstairs and get changed. These heels are killing me."

"Sorry Willow," Mak said. "Kai left a few minutes ago. He had some kind of emergency. Said he'll call you as soon as he gets a chance. He asked me to tell you but then things got hectic."

"Thanks," I responded, careful to suck down the disappointment without reacting. "I still want to take a shower, make a few phone calls. How about I meet you guys in the parking lot, in say, an hour?"

One hour and fifty minutes later we pulled off a long dirt road next to a line of trees and entered a small parking lot. I texted Kai twice more but with no luck. Either his phone had no service or he was ignoring me. I wasn't a fan of either circumstance.

"Where are we?" I whispered to Mak.

"Behind the University, I think," he answered. Then he turned to Liat. "What are we doing here?"

Liat looked at Mak but ignored the question. She and Nick climbed out of the truck and made their way to the building. Mak and I shrugged shoulders at each other. Then followed them in.

It was an old barn that smelled of wet plaster and smoke. Shelves were backed up against wooden walls and there was an assortment of artwork resting on them. They were all shapes and sizes. Some were made of wood, some of metal, and even more fashioned out of plaster. There were a few paintings and charcoals resting up against one of the walls but for the most part there were sculptures. Some looked like they'd been resting on those shelves for years. We followed Nick and Liat farther into the barn and saw machinery too. Ban saws, sandblasters, even a welding station. Near the back of the barn off to the right was some sort of oven. They walked past it. Then they turned left and headed for the back door.

Liat took a key from her pocket and unlocked it. Turns out it wasn't the backdoor. It was a basement or maybe more accurately, a dungeon. At least that's what it felt like heading down those concrete stairs. The walls were a creepy shade of pinkish brown and very narrow. I could reach both sides just by stretching out my elbows. Oh, and the steps? There were over thirty of them. Suddenly Nick stopped short in front of us and I plowed straight into Mak's shoulders.

Ahead of us, Liat hit a light switch and the room was illuminated. I noticed two things as I stepped down off that last step. The room was big, and except for a handful of sculptures in the center of the room it looked empty. Even at first glance the pieces were spectacular, gruesome but spectacular. They were made of sand, glass, steel, and what looked like an assortment of fabrics and other used materials. I'd never seen anything like it.

"What are we doing here? Who made these?

My phone brrrrrnged with a text message. It was Kai. Finally.

Where r u? Sorry about earlier. Somthng came up. Explain when I see you. Call me.

"We have no choice," Nick urged Liat. "You have to tell them. After what happened tonight, you have to tell them."

I started to text Kai back. Then one of the art pieces caught my attention. I closed the cell phone on Kai's text and stared at it, trying to wrap my brain around what I was seeing.

"This is gonna sound nuts," Liat started.

Not to me, I thought. Considering the amount of crazy I'd been living with lately I didn't think anything could shock me. Still there was that one piece. Something about the back of the figure's body—that hair—I couldn't stop staring at it. Oh and the way the figure was kneeling. Her hands, were they? Pressing down? And that zigzag on the back of her jeans...was that? OMG...it was. The logo on the back of the jeans was the same as the one stitched into my jeans. The pair that were still balled up in the corner of my bathroom, all crusted with Angela's blood.

"I've been having visions. Blackouts." Liat started explaining. "Sometimes I wake up in strange places and I have materials gathered nearby. Mostly I wake up down here. Filthy. Exhausted. With one of these pieces finished in front of me."

"When they started coming true. I didn't know what to think, what to do."

Nick's phone buzzed. He stepped away and answered it.

"What do you mean when they started coming true?" I fired at her.

"These pieces," she stammered. "They're of real events. I sculpt them. Then later on they…happen."

"You mean you read about events and somehow they inspire you to do…this," I corrected.

Liat looked at me and sighed.

"No. I sculpt them first. I don't know why. "It's bizarre," she said, tears beginning to spill from her eyes. "I have these episodes. I get these visions. Then I'm here…and somehow they're finished." Liat's body was visibly shaking. "After that…later on…what's happening in the sculptures…it actually happens in real life. I don't want to make these pieces. I don't want to make these things happen. It's driving me crazy. I need to find a way to stop it. Before I…before I hurt somebody else."

Her pain was palpable. It made the nerve endings in my head sting and before I could stop myself I went to Liat and wrapped a reassuring arm around her shoulders. I understood. I knew what it felt like to be swallowed whole by circumstance.

"You didn't cause this Liat. You can't 'art' people to death. You're just confused," I soothed.

Mmmm…mmm…mmm…careful there Willygirl. Going soft, letting people in—bad things happen when you care too much.

"She's not confused Willow."

Mak was leaning over one of the pieces, inspecting something near the bottom. The sculpture looked like a pool of water. There were several figures in it. All of them twisted in pain. Two were trying to climb out, reaching toward clothing strewn just out of reach. Something about the piece seemed vaguely familiar.

"Look at the dates etched into the sculptures."

"I remember when this happened," Mak said. "Those students who went hiking on Mauna Loa. They took a dip in one of the hot springs. Acid seeped in underground and they were all fried. The date on this is at least three months before it happened."

That's why it was familiar. That waiter, Vince, he'd told me about it the night we went to dinner. He said they found two small black diamonds at the site. I looked over at Liat's sculpture. Two shiny black objects were positioned next to the clothes those twisted figures were reaching towards. I moved away from it and went back to the other, more familiar sculpture.

I knelt down, shoulder to shoulder with the figure of myself in Angela's living room and couldn't help shuddering when I saw it. A replica of Angela's three and a half carat diamond ring sculpted to my finger. And that wasn't all. The knocked over lamp was there, the gun, the surfboard, even the stairs. The surfboard. I looked closely at it. The hut with Poliahu was clearly indented in the piece. So were parts of the poem.

"So she etched in some bad dates," I remarked, trying to convince myself. "Big deal. That doesn't prove anything."

"You can't accuse her of putting false dates on this one," Nick pointed to the sculpture in front of him.

It was the ballroom at the Outrigger Reef. Complete with tiny works of art hanging on its walls. Certain things were featured: the doorway, one of the tables, and the bar. For some reason Liat had sculpted a wheel to one of the double doors instead of a knob. The table looked just like the one where we'd eaten salmon and asparagus a few hours ago. Except for the white tablecloth. Poking out from beneath the bottom of the tablecloth was what looked like a woman's arm, jaggedly cut off at the wrist and oozing what looked like blood. Something was at the center of the ooze, as if the missing hand had dropped it. An olive. With a dark, very shiny, pit sticking out of it.

Disturbing to say the least but that wasn't the half of it. The image in front of the bar was what really stood out. It was the art teacher. He was clutching at his throat and choking. Across from him, somehow suspended in the air, was the missing hand, cut jaggedly at the wrist, and holding a martini glass.

Nick was right. There was no way Liat could have done this after the art teacher choked. We were all together at the party tonight. Besides, I'm no art expert, but to make a piece like that would take some time. I glanced down at the bottom of the piece. The date etched into the floor of the ballroom was weeks ago.

"None of this makes sense," I said.

Suddenly there were footsteps on the stairs. We all turned to see who it was.

"What doesn't make sense?" Kai asked as he stepped into the room. He let out a slow whistle when he saw the sculptures.

"Holy...." It was the only phrase he could muster.

"I think you mean hellish," I corrected, surprised to see him standing there.

Liat visibly stiffened at my description of her work. Not my best moment. I was definitely having trouble with the whole tact/blurting thing lately.

"Sorry. It's not like they aren't...good," I tried.

"Now you see why I didn't tell anyone. Why I've been avoiding you."

"Not an option anymore," Nick replied.

"You obviously told Nick," Makani pointed out.

"I didn't tell anyone. Nick found me. Working on a piece."

"After what happened tonight," Nick added, wrapping a protective arm around Liat's shoulders, "we had to tell someone. Since it involves all of us," he said, nodding around the room. It seemed the logical place to start."

"Start what?" Kai asked. "What is all this?"

Nick filled him in on everything. First, about Liat and her art. Then he told Kai all that I'd been holding back. He told him about the surfboard I'd brought from Philadelphia. And how Mak, Nick, and I were searching for the Maui Snow.

My mind was working overtime trying to figure out what to say next. How to get past the look I saw on his face. When I tried, Kai politely brushed me off in favor of studying Liat's work.

"Clearly there's a connection between Liat's artwork and the Maui Snow," Nick said, pointing to the piece with me, and the surfboard in Angela's living room. Willow, it's no accident that you showed up here with that surfboard. It can't be. Not after all this."

"So if you knew about Liat's artwork, knew that I was featured in it, then why didn't you say something when we met?" I asked Nick.

"Actually, I didn't know it was you. In Liat's sculpture, I mean. She's the one who figured out that what happened that night was real, and not just some bad dream she turned into artwork. Liat is the one who recognized that it was you in Angela's living room."

I shook my head. That certainly explained Liat's reaction when she met me.

"I should have told you sooner," he agreed. "Should've told you the second you showed me the Poliahu surfboard in your hotel room. It's just...I was surprised. I didn't know what to think. Liat and I have tried to make sense out of all of this, but," Nick hesitated.

"Anyway," he added, "here we are. Obviously we have to do something. Let's face it– people are dying."

As usual, Kai was uber calm.

"Let's put them in date order," he suggested. "Are there any sculptures of events that haven't happened yet?"

Good god, what if...

"Good question," I mumbled, my voice a bit hollow.

"Just one," Liat answered. "It's over there." She pointed toward a sculpture covered in a sheet.

"Okay," Kai directed, "we'll line them up in date order and see if we can make any connections."

I couldn't help thinking, how can Kai be so unfazed? Okay, so he's got this Zen-surf master thing all locked up. Actually, that was one of his more attractive qualities. But he was *so* calm. *So* collected. Hell, just the idea that Liat could make stuff like this had the rest of us freaked out. Poor Nick nearly had a coronary right along with old Mason back at the ballroom earlier tonight. Mak, well, he couldn't stop staring at the pieces. And me? Rubbing shoulders with my sand and steel counterpart was beyond creepy. In fact, I was starting to feel homesick for Angela's nuthouse in the Pocono's.

At Liat's direction we dragged the pieces into place.

"Run us through them one at a time, Liat. When did all this start?" Kai asked.

Liat hesitated.

"Well, there is one more piece. The first one."

Behind us, against the wall, was a cedar chest I hadn't noticed. Liat walked over to it, opened it up, and took out a sculpture that was about two feet in diameter and about three feet high. At first glance it looked like a regular sand sculpture, something that could've come straight off the beach. But when she gripped it and carried it towards the line-up, it stayed together, not a single grain of sand fell away from it. Whatever substance she'd treated it with during her 'episode' looked permanent.

"I built one just like it on the beach," Liat explained. "When I was seven."

"We all stared. It was the sculpture of a large shark, it's dorsal fin tipped slightly, its tail curved as though it was speeding through the ocean. The details of the piece were something to behold. But it was the creature's large open mouth, the young boy clenched between its jagged teeth that really commanded attention.

Mak leaned down and looked at the date. December 19, 2007.

"Jesus, Liat. This is the day before you broke up with me." He rocked back on his heels and looked up at her. "You should have told me."

"Mak, I was scared. When I came to after this…this episode, when I realized what I'd made, I was so afraid. I was afraid this time you would die. I figured that if I stayed away from you, then maybe nothing would happen. Maybe it would just stop."

It was Nick's turn to look surprised. He stared at the piece in silence. Then back at Liat. In a quiet voice Liat tried to explain.

"I was at the beach one day. I met this boy and he made me mad. He was being so mean. Then I, I…made a sand sculpture like this one. He ran off. He was playing in the ocean and then the next thing you know, there was a shark, and blood, and people were screaming."

Tears streamed down Liat's face as she explained. Nick stepped towards her but Mak cut him off.

"There's more to it than that," Mak stated. "It was me on the beach that day. And Liat had good reason to be mad. She was a tiny little thing and I was a real bastard, even at eleven. She was just this happy little kid. So content. I couldn't take it so I broke her castle. I took her doll and she…Liat…she held my face, my eyes. She did something to me. Changed me. Completely. I can't explain it. Just like I can't explain why that shark came after me. Or why it let me go. What I do know is the effect you had on me Liat."

He stepped in close. "You didn't kill me, Liat. If anything you saved me." He fingered the jagged scar on his arm and grinned. "Handed me a life worth living."

159

"Wait a second. I thought those scars on your arm were from a car accident," Nick argued. "That's what you told everybody."

"Not everybody, Kansas."

Nick was about to say something else, must have thought better of it, and instead reached past Mak for Liat's hand.

"Let's move on. It's getting late."

"Right." Liat dropped Nick's hand and stepped toward the next piece.

Nick brushed it off but I could see that he was struggling not to take it personal.

The second piece was of the students who had died in the hot spring on Mauna Loa over a year ago. It was dated several months before the actual incident.

The third piece was the death scene in Angela's living room.

The fourth piece was the art teacher choking in the ballroom.

And then there was the last piece. The one that hadn't happened yet.

Liat was clearly edgy about it. Yet it seemed innocent enough. Actually it was quite beautiful. The focal point was a majestic wave. Between the curve of it and the torched patina that lent swirling shades of blue to the swell, the piece was a tribute to movement. Poking through the barely curving lip sat a surfboard and its rider. Knees bent, arms outstretched, a ring of leaves crowning the surfer's head. Aside from the slant of a tail and the tip of a shark's dorsal fin visible, near the very bottom of the wave, this piece wasn't gruesome like the other sculptures. There were a few other items floating inside the wave as well, but they weren't the least bit threatening. There was a baseball cap, an orange bug, a bell, and a few scattered flip-flops.

Kai stepped forward. "Okay, so, I think what we should do is try to figure out the connections. What's the significance of each event and is it somehow connected to any of the others. Liat what do you know about the second piece, the one of the kids who got caught in the acid pool. Have you ever been there?"

"No. I mean, yeah I've been to Mauna Loa. Lots of times. I even went with you, Kai. When I was in your Astronomy class. But I've never been to that hot spring. That's in the restricted zone and there's like a million warning signs near those pools."

She was right. I remember the conversation I had with Vince about the incident. He said the same thing. The signs were everywhere.

"Look at this," I said stepping towards the sculpture. "There's a hole carved here next to the water. You made the rest of the ground smooth, except for this rock. And then there's this empty hole. Maybe it's for the sign. Maybe someone pulled it out," I suggested. "Maybe it wasn't an accident. Maybe someone wanted those kids to die."

"Interesting thought," said Kai. "What else stands out?"

"Well," Nick said. "Those kids? They were all Astronomy majors. Oh yeah, and it was January who found them dead. Jan and her boy of the day. Jan was in your class, too, wasn't she Kai?"

We turned in unison to look at Kai. He looked back at us; surprised.

"Are you sure?" He asked.

"Did the research myself," Nick assured him. I came across it again when I was searching for connections to the Maui Snow.

"I was in that class too."

Like sheep being herded on a hillside, we turned and looked at Liat.

"I was in your class," Liat confirmed. "But I wasn't there the day they died."

An uncomfortable silence followed as each of us processed the information, trying to decide what it meant, if anything.

"If connections are what we're after, then let's jump to the obvious," Mak said.

"Haven't you people noticed that there are small black diamonds in every one of these sculptures?"

Starting with the first piece, Mak pointed them out.

"I'm hanging out of the shark's mouth in this first piece but look what's hanging out of my hand. Look at the doll. Look at the black stone in *her* hand."

"Here, in the second piece. There're two more black stones near the pile of clothes. Don't you guys remember what a big deal the press made about it at the time? For the next month, everybody and their brother were out near those acid pools searching for the Maui Snow."

"There's none in this piece," I stated, looking down at myself again. "Just Angela's ring. You know, your average four and a half-carat monster of an engagement ring. Clear white."

"Not there. Here," Mak pointed out, "right here, tucked beneath the lamp."

Sure enough, a small, shiny black object was tucked just beneath the lamp.

"That's not a diamond, it's a bullet," I corrected. "There was a whole box of bullets in the open drawer on the end table where the lamp came from. No diamond—just bullets. Trust me, if there was a black diamond there I would remember it."

Mak looked unconvinced. Turns out he was right.

"What about the next piece?" I asked, moving on.

"Right here," Mak answered, pointing to the table in the ballroom. It's inside that pool of blood, right near the stump of that woman's arm.

"That's the olive Mason choked on," said Nick. "It's just an olive."

"Look at the pit," Mak directed. "It's pointed, it's dark, and it's shiny. Just like all the other black stones. "And jeezuz look at Liat's last piece," he added. "Look at the surfer's right hand. The one that's nearly buried inside the lip of the wave."

Mak was right. In between the surfer's fingers was a stone. A large, black stone...bigger than all of the other stones put together.

"I think it's the Maui Snow," said Liat, her voice quiet. "But I don't even care about that. Look at the surfer. Can any of you tell who that is? That's what I really want to know."

I looked at the sculpture. The figure riding the wave appeared androgynous.

"You made it Liat. Don't you know?" I asked.

"No. It's not...clear."

"But you have a feeling, right?"

"The only thing I'm sure about is that it's a champion," she said pointing to the wreath on the figure's head. Whoever it is has either won, or is about to win, The Triple Crown."

"So, in this room we're talking either me or Kai," said Makani.

"You said it could be someone who is about to win it, right, Liat? So, it could be me," said Nick.

Mak let out a genuine laugh. He started to say something but then just laughed some more.

Nick postured as if he were about to take a swing at Mak. Kai put out a hand to stop him.

"What about the girls' competition," he redirected, hoping to take the sting out of Mak's laughter. "Jan has already taken the first round and Liat we all know you're a strong contender. It could be a girl up on that wave."

"Don't you get it?" Liat's tone was frustrated. "Skip the competition. Look!" She pointed at the bottom of the wave.

"That surfer is shark bait on a stick! And check out the scale of the wave. It's huge compared to the surfer. I have a bad feeling about it. That wall is unfathomable. I don't care about the competition. Just help me figure out how to stop that from happening."

For a moment we were all quiet. We were drawn to the surfer up on the wave. Mesmerized by the large black stone in the surfer's hand.

"It's the Maui Snow," I said. "Deny it all you want Liat. That diamond is at the root of things. We need to find it."

"No!" Liat answered. "That's exactly what I've been trying to avoid. Let it stay buried. Wherever it is—just let it be. Because I think that without that stupid diamond," she pointed to the surfer, "this can't happen."

"Not true," I argued. "From where I'm sitting the only way to stop it is to finish it. So far everything you've sculpted has come true, right? So this time we don't just let it happen. We get ahead of it. We take control."

"You just want the diamond," she accused. "Just like everybody else."

I sighed.

"This isn't about greed. It's about peace. Finding that diamond is the only way I'm going to get any. Judging by this gruesome little art fest, I don't see much of it in you're future either. Please Liat. Just take a look at your father's surfboard. It might help shed some light on your sculptures."

Liat looked around. Everyone nodded in agreement. She stared back refusing to budge.

"It's late. Why don't we get some sleep? Come back at this with fresh eyes," Kai suggested. "Bring the surfboard Willow. I'd like to see it."

The lack of warmth in his voice bothered me. What to do about it bothered me more.

Kai found a large tarp on the floor near the cedar chest and dragged it over to the sculptures but it was too short to cover all of the pieces. Together, Kai, Nick and Mak edged the pieces closer together, some of them nearly touching.

A few feet away Liat tilted her head and stared at the configuration of sculptures, a dim sense of recognition toying at the corners of her brain. She couldn't quite grasp it. Eventually the image would become crystal clear. Eventually. Sometime *after* we realized that the bloody arm, poking out from under the tablecloth in Liat's fourth sculpture, was more than just an artistic touch.

"You know," I told Liat as she continued to stare at the sculptures. "People have flashes…premonitions," I corrected myself. "It doesn't have to mean–

"Premonitions? She interrupted. "Is that what you call this?"

"Ok 3D premonitions. What I'm trying to say is that you're not responsible. You didn't kill anyone. You didn't push those kids into that acid pool and you were nowhere near that art teacher tonight when he choked on the olive." I felt bad for Liat and wanted to let her off the hook. She wasn't buying it.

"But he didn't choke on an olive now did he? It was a diamond." Liat shifted her gaze away from the sculptures and turned toward me.

"Willow, you have no idea what I'm capable of causing." She paused and let out a long breath of air. "Because at this point, I don't know."

Ha! She's got you there, Willygirl. Liat doesn't know. She's actually admitting it. I wonder who else here doesn't know what they are capable–

"Shut up!" I yelled, hands up, gripping the sides of my head. "Just…. shut…up!"

They all stopped and turned their heads. That look. It was only there for an instant. But I saw it.

"Holy shit, Willow. Your blood sugar running low or something?" Mak teased. "Need a candy bar?"

I let out a long breath of my own.

"Sorry," I mumbled. "Just tired I guess." I tried to think of something better to say. A better distraction from my odd behavior. And then it hit me. Out of nowhere the image of Melanie picking up the olive clicked in my head.

"Liat! You're right! Maybe Mason did choke on a diamond. Either way, I know how we can find out."

Careful there, Willygirl.

"How?!" Kai was the first to ask.

"You're friend, whats-her-name, the quiet one who's always reading on the beach—Melanie."

"What about her?" Liat asked.

"She's got the olive. I saw her pick it up after Mason spit it across the room. She thought he might want it as a memento after the incident. Judging from the way she stuffed it into her purse Melanie was determined to be the one to hand it over to him. Call her," I suggested. "She's working at the hospital tonight."

"Yeah, she works in the file room," Liat confirmed. "How'd you know that?"

"I don't know, I heard her tell someone. Uhhmm, Jan. Yeah I think it was Jan."

"Anyway, call her. See if she still has it," I suggested. "If she does let's go get it."

"Tomorrow," said Kai. "I need to get going. I have to catch a plane home to the Big Island in about forty minutes. Why don't we meet back here tomorrow? Around three?"

They all nodded in agreement.

It was frustrating. I seemed to be the only one eager to follow up. If Liat was right and there was a diamond in the olive then someone must have put it there. Who? My brain went into overdrive trying to figure it out.

"At least give her a call. It can't hurt to call her."

Mak and Kai were already halfway up the steps. Nick held out a hand to Liat and she took it.

"Come on," I prodded as I followed them up the steps.

Liat dialed and put the phone to her ear. After a minute she folded the phone and slipped it back into her pocket.

"Well?" I asked.

"No answer."

I gave a loud sigh. "Try again."

"Okay, okay. I'll call you if I hear from her. I promise."

Outside Kai was already in his green Subaru, turning the key.

"Need a lift?" Mak asked.

"No thanks," I answered curtly, then headed straight for Kai's car. He was pulling away. I sped up, then stepped right into the path of his shining headlights.

Relax. It was no big deal. The car was barely going two miles an hour. No reason to read into it. There was plenty of time to get out of the way. Kai stopped of course and rolled down his window to talk. I ignored the gesture and hopped into the passenger seat instead.

"Look, I know you're mad," I started. "But I can explain."

"I'm not mad. I'm in a hurry."

"Of course you're mad. I told everybody but you about the surfboard. About searching for the Maui Snow. If you did that to me I'd be pissed off."

"Okay I'm mad. But I'm still in a hurry. I can't give you a ride Willow. My father had a heart attack and there's no way I'm going to miss my flight to the Big Island."

"Oh man. Kai, I'm sorry." I laid a hand on his arm but he took little comfort from it. "I'm really sorry. About everything."

I opened the door and got out. The parking lot was empty. Everyone else had gone.

Kai sighed. "Get in. If I can't get you a cab from the airport I guess you'll just have to fly to Kona with me."

"Okay."

"I was kidding Willow. There'll be plenty of cabs at the airport."

"No, no. Think about it. It'll be good if I come with you." I squeezed his hand and flashed him a mischievous grin. "We'll talk. We'll clear the air." Then the grin faded and there was a crack in my voice. "I want that Kai. I hope you do too." He didn't say a word. He just squeezed my hand.

We didn't talk though. Not then anyway. As soon as the plane took off I dropped my head on Kai's shoulder and fell fast asleep.

CHAPTER TWENTY

Earlier that night

Melanie was busy re-filing a shopping cart full of x-rays in the radiology file room. Mel was a good worker and on an average night she filed away about eight shopping carts worth of x-rays, CT scans, and ultrasounds. Some of the patient files were heavy and shoving them back into place was physically taxing. Mel didn't mind though. Most days it was the only workout she got. Besides, it gave her time to daydream. Sometimes she imagined herself a world-class surfer like her friends, winning contests, doing interviews, even posing for a photo-shoot. But mostly it was about men. She longed to find the right one. Of course Makani was at the top of her wish list. He had no clue of course and Melanie wasn't about to tell him. She thought Mak was out of her league. But not here in the file room. As she emptied file after file out of those shopping carts Mak made regular appearances in her daydreams.

The files were stored alphabetically inside five moveable steel rows of over-packed shelves that reached from floor to ceiling. Depending on which row a person wanted to file in, say, A to F or maybe L to O the rows had to be moved apart to make room for the staff member to work. When Melanie first started at the hospital it was done manually. There was a large wheel attached to each row that had to be cranked either left or right depending on which end of the alphabet you were trying to access. But the antiquated system caused problems. Squishing problems. During the day when cranky radiologists were demanding files, and there were multiple staff members trying to keep up with that demand, invariably someone would shift two rows together before checking to see if a co-worker happened to be working down that aisle. A good blood-curdling scream as the walls closed in was the method generally used to stop the offending co-worker. That is until six months ago when the walls were computerized and a safety system was put in place. A touch pad had been inserted into the center of each wheel. Push a button and that wall moved. As a precaution, a second touch pad was placed on the cement wall at the end of each aisle so that if someone accidentally moved a wall via the wheel, the person working in the aisle could stop it from the other touch pad. It was a great system. Unless you were in the center of the aisle when the walls started closing in. That's when most of the staff reverted to the screaming bloody murder system.

Mel was busy daydreaming in V to Z when she heard the noise. She turned to see what it was and a curious but happy smile lit her face.

"Wow. Hi. What are *you* doing here?"

"Came to see you. Got a sec.?"

Mel took the hefty file in her hands and laid it in front of the Y's. "Hey, did you here about Mason?"

"I just heard. Sad, huh?"

"I checked on him as soon as I clocked in. Major heart attack. I can't believe he's really dead. I mean he choked. That's all. I figured he'd be fine once they got it out. I still can't believe it. Can you?"

"No. It's…crazy. Look, Mel, we all know you took the olive Mason choked on."

"Yeah," Mel drawled, wondering what this was about.

"If you don't mind, I'd like to take a look at it."

Melanie came out of the aisle.

"Okay I guess. Wait here." Melanie went to the front of the file room and unlocked a drawer next to the copy machine. The person followed her. Mel removed her purse, carefully dug out the olive that was still wrapped in the paper towel and handed it over.

"Here you go."

The person inspected the olive and then closed a hand around it.

"We're friends now, right?"

Melanie smiled broadly. "Sure."

"I need to hold onto this for a little while, and I think we should keep that between you and me. I mean, Mason's dead. So he won't care. As far as everybody else goes, well, like I said, let's just keep this between the two of us. Because we're friends, right?"

"Absolutely. I'd like that. "We're friends. Definitely. Yeah," Melanie thought with growing excitement. We can be really good friends. If you want, I mean." Embarrassed she quickly added, "I won't say a word. Promise."

Melanie opened the drawer to stuff her pocketbook back inside. But in her haste she caught it against the side of the drawer and spilled most of the contents onto the file room floor. Immediately she dropped to the floor and bent over the pile, trying to scoop everything back inside the pocketbook, trying to put *it* back inside. Fast. But it was too late.

The other person reached past her. Plucked something off the floor. Held it up.

"Where did you get this?!"

Melanie flushed red. Then stammered. "I...uhmm...I'm sorry...I'm so sorry. I didn't mean to take it. We were on the beach ...all of you were in the ocean surfing and I...I ran out of lotion so I went looking for some and...*that* was in your bag. I picked it up and I was looking at it, admiring it, and then all of a sudden you were right there coming towards me and I...I panicked. I shoved it under my towel. Before I knew it you picked up your stuff, threw your towel in the bag, and bam you were gone. But you know," Melanie added, in a petulant attempt to defend her own actions. "You never even said a word to me that day. Like I wasn't even sitting there. Afterwards," she stammered, "I...I just didn't know what to do. I couldn't figure out how to give it back to you without you thinking I stole it. I'm sorry. I really am sorry."

Completely embarrassed, Melanie shoved the drawer closed, ran back to the Y's and picked up her file.

The person followed her and stood at the edge of the aisle.

"Please don't be mad," Melanie begged. "Look, take the olive. Keep the diamond. I don't care. Just don't be mad, okay?"

The other person let out a deep sigh.

"You looked inside the olive?"

Again Melanie flushed. "Well, yeah. I was kinda curious. It's not everyday somebody chokes on an olive right in front of you."

169

"How'd you know it was a diamond?"

Melanie smiled. "I'm not that great a surfer but I am smart. I know stuff. All kinds of stuff actually. I read the news articles. Read what happened to those kids on Mauna Loa. There were pictures of the diamonds. Stuff like that sticks with me. When I saw what was inside the olive I recognized it right away. I kinda wanted to keep it. But I guess since you're the one who put it in the olive—you did didn't you?" Melanie did not like the look she was getting. "Okay, so I guess technically that makes it yours. Maybe you shouldn't keep it either though. I mean look at all the bad luck they bring. Maybe it's cursed. Bad luck of the black diamonds or something. I...I wouldn't want anything to happen to you," she blushed.

"What kind of stupid are you blabbering?"

Melanie stiffened at the rebuke. She was caught off guard. More than that, she was hurt.

"I told you. I'm not stupid. People don't pay much attention to me but I watch. I know stuff."

The person at the other end stiffened and took a step forward.

Melanie was instantly sorry. She liked the surfing crowd and all their friends. She liked hanging out with them even if it was mostly on the fringe. She liked having parties to go to. She wanted to be their friend. She just didn't like being called stupid.

"You don't have to worry," she said, "It's not like I'm gonna say anything. Like you said, this can be our secret. We're friends. Good friends, right?"

The person at the end of the aisle smiled back as Melanie continued to ramble, then reached for the button at the center of the steering wheel and pushed it toward the left. The wall started to move. Melanie dropped the file. Like a deer in headlights she stared, confused, at the person standing at the open end of the files. She tried to comprehend what was happening. The person at the other end must've hit the button by accident.

"Hey," she stammered. "Hit the button. You have to hit the button again so it'll stop."

The opening, plenty wide enough a minute ago, was rapidly narrowing. She spun her head in the other direction and stared toward the keypad on the cement wall.

Stuck nearly halfway between the two, Melanie made her choice. And ran.

CHAPTER TWENTY ONE

When we landed on the Big Island of Hawaii I was caught off guard. Once again, the feel of this island is completely different from that of Maui and Oahu. For starters, The Big Island sprawls. There's a feeling of openness, a bit more empty space compared to the other islands in the chain. Of course not all the land is empty. The islanders grow coffee and chocolate, among many other things. When you add in the dry weather and the paniolos (cowboys), in some spots it feels more like the Old West than the tropical South Pacific. In some spots. But once you run up against Kilauea, all bets are off. The volcano shoots visible pyrotechnics on a regular basis and through a series of pipes, sends waves of lava steaming into the sea. Hawaii feels a bit like the teenager of the islands. Rough, adventurous, full of growing pains.

It took us almost two hours to get to the small hospital. Kai's mother and brothers were in the waiting area when we arrived. At first I felt like maybe I shouldn't have come. Not that they weren't polite. They were. It's just that I could feel that tight-knit family relationship thing as soon as we entered. Kai donned it like a second skin. In a way they were a lot like my own big Irish family back in Philly. The family I'd been doing my best to keep at a distance since coming home from Iraq.

His mother was a large woman. Her skin and eyes were the same shade as Kai's and I could tell right away that the resemblance between them went deeper than looks. Her smile was reserved but friendly. Not at all like my ex's mother. When I first met Shane's mother, Melody, her smile bordered on frosty—and then plummeted from there. After just a few minutes though Kai's mother already seemed a lot more normal than Melody Galveston. His brothers were great too. Once they got over the initial shock that Kai had actually brought someone to the hospital with him they warmed quickly and began peppering me with all sorts of questions.

"Give Willow a break," he chided them. "How's dad doing? What did the doctor say?"

"He's fine Kai, he's restin'. Big scare. Notin' more," she said, the island lilt in her voice much stronger than Kai's. "Go in. He won' say it but he's been waitin on you, son."

Kai turned to me. "Go ahead. I'm fine," I shooed him. He looked around at his brothers, thought better of it and took my hand.

The hospital room was as cheerful as a hospital room can be. Flowers and cards covered the ledge under the windows. The man propped up in bed was quite a bit smaller than Kai's mother. He had brown and gray hair and an open, sunny smile.

"Kai! Why'd you come all this way? Don' worry 'bout me. You need be worryin' 'bout those big waves your set to ridin' in."

Kai went to the bed and gave his father a gentle hug.

"Pehea' oe?"

"Maika'I no au – I'm okay, son."

"Now, whose that wahine you got hidin' back there. Come mere honey, lemme get a look at you."

"This is my friend, Willow, Dad." Then added, "Be nice."

"Aloha," he said as he took my hand and covered it with his.

"Aloha," I replied. "I'm sorry about the circumstances but it's good to meet you."

He looked over my head at Kai and in a groggy voice added, "she has maka 'eleu."

The old man smiled at me and then his eyelids began to flutter. He was tired.

"We're gonna go now, Dad. You get some rest." He leaned down and kissed the old man's forehead.

On the way back to his family's coffee plantation I asked what his father had said about me. Kai chuckled.

"Maka 'eleu means lively eyes. Pretty accurate assessment for an old man who just had a heart attack."

"How's that?"

"I mean there's a lot going on behind those emerald windows," he answered. "You plan on letting me in sometime?"

I was thinking never. Not if I wanted him to stick around. In less than two hours that neat little plan would go straight to hell.

The rest of the ride was quiet. Instead of talking we soaked in the scenery. For Kai it was familiar trees and dirt roads and hearty local crops. For me it was an endless exotic landscape, crushed with a sky full of unfamiliar stars. Everyone talks about how beautiful the islands are—the trees, the volcanoes, the beaches. Don't get me wrong. They are. But for an east coaster like me, the Hawaiian sky, well, it was just straight out amazing. Tiny glimmers of light bend across the night sky, and reach so far down it looks like they almost touch the ground. Somehow those stars filled me with wonder every time I looked at them. Wonder and hope. They made the dark realities on earth seem so small by comparison. The feeling never wore off. Every night those stars were right there. Waiting. It was a comforting thought. Maybe one day the effect would be powerful enough, would stay with me long enough, to wipe away all of the blood and bad dreams.

I opened the car window and leaned out to get some fresh air. Earth and coffee beans. Mmmmmm. Then tilting my head upward and with eyes half closed, I watched the stars swirling about, drenching the night air as if they were tiny Hawaiian snowdrops storming across a sea of blackness.

CHAPTER TWENTY TWO

It was an accident this time. Straight up. No flashbacks. No stray side effects from medication. Not an inch of nutty involved. Unless you count the fact that Kai jumped in after me. Now that was crazy.

It happened after the grand tour of his family's plantation, which is situated on the outskirts of Kona. Picture acres and acres of coffee trees stretching out toward the cliffs, toward the ocean. At night, off into the distance, sparks of orange could be spotted in the dark. Lava flows, Kai told me. Lava flows constantly pouring into the ocean, creating new land every day. It was beautiful. Seriously, I've never seen anything like it. We stood there together, hand in hand, drinking it all in.

Kai stepped away just before it happened. His cell phone rang. He said hello and then turned and took a few steps toward the house. Funny thing is, it didn't feel like I was all that close to the edge. Yeah, I suppose I did lean forward a bit, but just so I could get a better look at the view. God it was spectacular. Honestly though, there was still a solid six inches of dirt laid out in front of me. Until it crumbled. Before I knew it, a thousand little balls of dirt were raining down into the ocean. Then me. Screaming and wailing at the top of my lungs, all the way down after them.

I hit the water and was stunned. A constant layer of white foam erupted around me. It was caused by the waves that were crashing violently against the cliffs and then bouncing backwards into the sea again, until the momentum of the ocean pushed them right back against the cliffs. Again. Over and over again.

At first I was spared. The sheer weight of the fall sent me straight to the bottom. When I came up, head popping through the foamy water, I had just enough time to grab a mouthful of wet air, close my eyes and turn my back to the chunk of earth I was speeding toward.

The impact wasn't as bad as I expected. What happened after I slammed against the cliff was definitely worse. Caught in a brutal undertow I was dragged below the surface. I tried to kick my way up but the force of the water was so great I could barely move my legs. All the while I could feel myself being pulled backwards, my arms all whooshed out in front of me as I clawed for the surface. But there was no use. Salt water filled my throat, nose, and ears as the undertow had its way.

Then it let me go. Just like that. I broke the surface and coughed. I struggled to tread water. That's when I realized that I was still moving. Still flowing backwards. I fought to keep my head above the surface and breathe. Then I worked my eyes to adjust to the dark.

I was in a cave. Floating deeper inside with each passing second. While I was busy trying to make sense out of where I was two peaceful minutes ago and the sudden new circumstance I found myself in, Kai's head broke through the surface about twenty feet away.

"Kai!?!"

"Oh my god Kai! You jumped in after me? Oh, thank you God!"

He shouted something but I could barely hear him over the water still throwing a fit near the mouth of the cave. Then he swam in close.

"What the devil, Willow? One second I'm on the phone the next second I turn around and you're flying through the air." Water splashed over his face and into his open mouth. The current, even inside the cave, was rough. He spit it out, barely seeming to notice, and stared hard in my direction.

"Did you fall?" He demanded. "Or jump?"

The look in his eyes made me cringe. I ducked my head under the surface and swam against the tide toward the mouth of the cave. It was harder than I thought.

His wrist went around my ankle and yanked me back into the cave. More salt water burned my nose and throat.

"Let me go!" I hollered. "I wanna get out of here."

"This way," he said, tugging on my hand. "There's a ledge at the back of the cave."

I followed. My lungs hurt and my stomach was too full of water to argue. At the back of the cave there was indeed a ledge. It was wide, at least six feet out from the back wall of the cave. I stepped up onto it and the sense of relief at having something under my feet was palpable. My legs wobbled as I tried to gain my footing against an ocean that was still pawing hard at my calves.

Kai bear hugged me. Then rubbed his hands up and down my arms and over my back for warmth.

"You okay? Bleeding? Any cuts?"

"No. No, I'm okay," I promised. How about you?"

"Fine, no blood," he replied.

"Okay," I said, trying to work out a game plan in my head. "So I guess we rest up for a few minutes and then get the heck out of here. Right?"

"It's not that simple Willow. We can't just swim our way out of this."

"Why not?"

"How can I put this," he said rubbing his chin in mock consideration. "Because the ocean is a massive, massive force of nature."

I laughed, despite the lack of spare oxygen in my lungs.

"Wow. Sarcasm from Professor calm, cool and collected. Who knew? A little dive off a cliff and bam—bye-bye Zen, hello snarky."

"You think this is amusing?"

"No, but...come on Kai. It's not like I planned to go skinny dip in the ocean tonight. It happened. We got tumbled around a bit but we're okay. We're both still breathing. There's no reason to make a federal case out of it. Let's just get out of here."

"Really? Is that what you think?" Kai shot back. "Because we have almost no chance of getting out of this alive." He looked hard at me then.

"I think you owe me the truth."

"It was an accident. Kai, I swear. The ground crumbled right out from under me. Besides, if this is as bad as you say, then why did you jump in after me? Maybe you're the one with the death wish."

Kai was still staring hard at me but I detected the slightest upward tug at the corner of his mouth.

"Our chances really do suck, Willow," he said, his tone softer. "I figure we've got about fifty minutes. So if you really want to know, I jumped in after you because I love you. There it is. I love you Willow Finnegan."

His words struck harder than the ocean.

"Really?"

"Really."

I considered the possibility.

"A second ago you thought I was crazy," I finally managed.

"You asked me if I jumped off that cliff on purpose. If that's what you thought…then why? Why would you turn around and say that you love me?"

"Because I do."

"Again," I threw my hands out, palms up, "why?"

"What do you want me to say? That you're special? You are."

"Yeah, I'm 'special' alright."

"Coordinated too," he laughed. Then more seriously he added, "look, Willow, I get that you're struggling with something. I see that. Despite that, there's a kind of strength about you, this sense of vitality. Whatever's going on in that head of yours it's not the surface stuff that consumes most people. What can I say? There's no explaining it. I just know I love you. Knew it from the first day we went surfing. It's an instinct thing."

"Yeah, well your instincts told you to jump off a cliff. Might want to have that checked out," I joked.

Kai was still looking at me, waiting. But I couldn't say it. I felt the same way about him. I just couldn't say it. So I kissed him instead. It wasn't even much of a kiss considering how weak my lungs were.

"Sooooo…how 'bout we make a swim for it? Discuss this some more. Up there," I nodded, "Over that fab family coffee you keep promising me."

"Again, not that simple," he replied. "Look at the water. Notice it rising?"

Kai was right. When I first stepped onto the ledge it was just above my knees. Now it was inching toward my thighs.

"In about forty five minutes this cave will reach the ceiling. That's when we swim for it. When we get to the mouth of the cave make a hard left where you'll see some rocks. If we can stay behind those rocks there's a chance we can work our way back up the other side of the cliff. If we're lucky we'll find some roots or shrubs above the water line that we can use for leverage."

"What about breathing? Won't that be a little tough if we wait for the cave to fill?"

"No. Not really. It's not that far to the opening. Besides, we have to wait. You remember that nasty spin cycle that swallowed you whole and tossed you in here?" He asked.

"Well, it's still out there. Get too close to the mouth of the cave now and one of three things will happen. The current will get a hold of you and spit you right back in here. Or, it'll throw you clear out into the ocean where another current will pick you up and drift you farther into the ocean. Or, you'll get caught up in that really tight little current that slams you repeatedly into the wall of the cliff."

"Nice options. How'd you become such an expert?"

"Because a bunch of people slip off rocks or get too close to the edge of cliffs here in the islands every year. Only a few survive. Most of those happen in the daytime, when somebody sees it go down and rescue gets called."

"Oh."

"Trust me. Our best chance is to wait for the cave to fill up. When it reaches the ceiling, the force of the flow is reduced and there'll be more of a buffer from the nightmare current that shot us in here. But make no mistake Willow. It's still out there. Just a bit farther out once the cave fills. We'll have to swim hard. If we can make that far left and get to that line of rocks we've got a chance. Once we get that far, the rocks there will buffer us a bit from the waves slamming into the cliffs behind us. But not much. There's still a lot of water swishing in behind those rocks. We could get squished into the cliffs. We could get washed away from each other too.

"Jeez Kai. Don't sugarcoat it on my account."

He wasn't. Kai wasn't the kind of guy to sugarcoat a problem that he could clearly see. The thing is, you can't see everything.

In fact, neither one of us happened to notice the dorsal fin that was raised just a hair above the choppy waters inside the mouth of the cave. Kind of surprising, considering the size of the shark.

"I just…I want you to stay with me Willow. You need to hold on tight. In fact, if you're wearing a belt why don't you take it off so I can tie us together."

I kissed him again. Harder this time, despite the pain in my lungs. Kai kissed me back but then he pulled away and looked at me, his gaze turning deep. He was searching. I read the look on his face and turned away. It was the determined one Angela used to wear when she brought me coffee.

"This might be the last half hour we spend together," he said. "So spill it."

"Spill what?" "Oh…I get it. Yes, Kai, I love you. There. I said it." I kind of surprised myself. Actually, that's not true. I would've said just about anything to wipe that look out of his eyes.

Kai scowled. "Not that. You already admitted that," he said, tracing my lips with his finger. Then his voice turned serious.

"You said tonight was an accident. I believe you. But that first day when I dragged you out of the ocean? That I'm not so sure about. And Liat told me about the traffic near the Outrigger Reef. Said you stepped right in front of a speeding car."

I looked down.

"It's complicated," I said, taking a page out of Liat's book. "Iraq was rough—it's not worth talking about."

"I think you need to, Willow. Nothing's going to change the way I feel about you. But it might change the way you feel about yourself."

"Maybe that's what I'm afraid of."

"Doesn't matter. You need to tell someone."

"Tell me."

I was freezing cold and full of salt water. My lungs hurt. My legs hurt. And we were most likely about to die. Which meant, I suddenly realized, that I had probably already swallowed my last cup of coffee. Now that was depressing. "Crap," I blurted.

"Be a little more specific," Kai retorted."

"Fine," I said defiantly. "You want to know? You really want to know what's eating at me? How about I'm afraid that I'm losing my mind? That the details of the night my friend Angela and her husband Bill got shot dead are a little too fuzzy for comfort. Maybe *I* had something to do with it, Kai. I've been wondering about that since I left Philadelphia. Did I kill my friend? Oh, wait, that's right—I can't remember."

I choked in a few breaths of the cave's wet air.

"I remember being on the walkway that night, Kai. Then, I don't know…I had a flashback. I was back in Iraq. All I know is that when I snapped out of it I was covered in blood and pushing down on Angela's stomach. And then…oh hell…and then I stopped pushing. I let go."

The water was above my waist now. Neither of us spoke. I looked up at Kai for a moment and then I pulled away from him.

"I need some real air." I dove off the ledge and swam for the mouth of the cave. I didn't know it but the shark, that big gray shark was just about four feet behind me.

The sharp tug on my ankle came almost immediately. Without warning I was sucked backward again. Funny… except for some water up my nose, I barely even felt it.

Kai dragged me back up onto the ledge. Just above the shark. It was so close I could've reached down and touched it. But I didn't even know it was there. Not then, anyway.

"It's not time yet," he said, "and you're not done talking."

"What? Finding out your new girlfriend is borderline crazy, and who knows, that maybe she even killed a couple of her friends. What, that's not enough information to ponder before we make a mad dash for the cliffs?"

"You didn't kill anybody Willow. You don't have it in you. But you are avoiding something. Tell me about Iraq."

"You sound so sure of me Kai. Why?"

"Iraq," he said, raising an eyebrow, his hands locking my shoulders in place. "What happened?"

I raised an eyebrow back. Kai stared, unwavering.

Something cold brushed by my right leg. I looked down but saw nothing in the waters below. The cave was too dark. Looking back up at Kai I was struck by his face. There was such strength in him. Such integrity.

"Whatever happened over there, Willow, you need to trust someone with it."

Without warning tears stung my eyes, spilling warmth down my freezing cheeks.

"I tried that once. Told Angela. Didn't work out so well for her."

If at first you don't succeed…

"If you want to know that bad," I added, sarcasm creeping into my voice, "let's just wait 'til we drown and then you can ask Angela in person."

"Or you could man-up and tell me yourself," Kai goaded.

…try, try, again.

The man knew me well.

"Okay," I relented. "Short, ugly version." But then I looked at him and hesitated. Telling him might change everything.

"You do realize we could be making out right now?"

"Afterwards," he promised.

It got quiet then. The water continued to rise. There was no space left for triviality.

I told him about Private Matthew Edwards. Explained how, after eight months embedded with his unit in Iraq, that Matt was like an older brother to me. I told him how Matt was different than most of the other soldiers. Not as stoic. He let things in. Oh, he was good at his job. Soldiers in the unit were always glad when Matt had their back. But he took things hard. He couldn't separate himself from the people, from the innocents. He felt for them. For their families, their jobs, their homes. If the other soldiers went the extra mile, Matt went three. Shortly after I got there, Matt and two others were headed to a housing area on the outskirts of Fallujah. I went with them. So we were riding along and there's this kid, he's like nine. Skinny as a rail, dirty, distraught, kneeling on the side of the road. Matt assesses the situation and stops. A big no no but that's Matt. He stops. Turns out, the kid was trying to get help for his older sister.

"Kai, that girl…" I stopped and took a breath. I was desperate to keep myself in the present, in that wet cave in Hawaii and not on a dirt road in Iraq.

"It was ugly. There's no other word to describe it. I've never seen wounds like that. The girl had been brutalized…she was more dead than alive. And that look in her eyes." I shivered. Kai rubbed my arms. And waited.

"So Matt picks her up. He drives her to a M.A.S.H. unit for help and talks them into looking at the girl. I kept her kid brother company.

Gave him the Led Zeppelin tee shirt I was wearing over my tank top because his shirt was soaked with his sister's blood. Matt scrounged up a soccer ball, marked some lines in the dirt for goal posts, and the three of us played for a couple of hours while the medics did what they could for his sister. We didn't know his name and he wouldn't talk so Matt looks at the tee shirt and nicknames him Del. Anyhow, Matt and I, we teach him the game, make sure he scores a couple of times. When he did man...the kid...that smile you can't even imagine. Pure happiness. Momentary. But pure. Like when you find a puppy under the tree at Christmas."

"Willow..."

"Did I tell you we spent months with Del, after that? Teaching him how to build things, how to cook, even how to do some math and English. We brought him clothes and shoes. Food. Books. The English though, that was kind of brutal. He didn't talk much, but the more he told us, the harder it was to hear. What we learned about the rest of his family was just awful. After a while Matt and I started hatching plans. We were convinced that we could figure out a way to get the kid out of the country. Smuggle him out if we had to. Kid only weighed about forty-five pounds.

Kai cleared his throat. "What happened, Willow?"

"Right. So Matt's got 18 days to go. 18 days and he's out. Home free. But he's edgy. Then again everybody gets edgy near the end of a tour. I know I was. Anyhow, one night, Matt and I, we're hanging out with our army issue collapsible cups of coffee and we're rehashing what happened to Del and his sister. Trying to come up with a plan. Trying to hold onto a little of the joy in that kid's smile. Somehow though we end up wondering out loud how things get so awful in the world in the first place. But I can see how torn up Matt gets, so I change the subject. I asked him what possessed a guy like him to sign up for a job like that in the first place. He looks at me and lets out the saddest laugh. Says, to me "Willygirl..." Matt always called me that. "Willygirl, it all boils down to snow and a goddamn piece of cherry pie."

"Snow and cherry pie?"

"Yep. So he tells me how he was getting ready to propose to his sweetheart, Bonnie Jean Copansky. That it was a cold October night. He had an hour and a half before he was supposed to pick Bonnie Jean up from her job at Walmart. His buddies came by for a pickup game of football. Then it started to snow.

I stopped for a second and let myself remember Matt for a second. Then I did my best imitation. 'Nothin' beats football in the snow, Willygirl and that's a true fact. By the time I left the game I was ten minutes late. Made a big mistake then, Willygirl. Biiiig mistake.'

You see, Matt knew Bonnie Jean would be mad so he decided to stop at the town diner to pick up a piece of her favorite pie. Figured it'd sweeten the deal. He had it all set. He was going to propose. He wanted kids. He wanted to buy some ground and grow some corn. But when he got to the diner, something unexpected happened. He ran into his old girlfriend. Matt shook his head and said to me, "I go in the diner and there's Cathy Tanglewood. Cath and I dated for two years before me and Bonnie Jean. I guess she never really took to the idea of me and Bonnie Jean getting married. Cathy was a funny one. Always had to be top dog. Better than the other girls. Always had to be first."

"Willow," Kai shook me gently, trying to keep me on track.

"You wanted the story," I answered sharply. "Well this is important. It's part of why I went cr…it matters."

Yes it is Willygirl. Most definitely important.

"So Matt goes into the diner to get the pie. He runs into old girlfriend Cathy, orders the pie, and then shows her the diamond ring. Cathy smiles, tells him it's lovely and that there's fresh pie in the back. She wraps him up a big slice and wishes him luck. Matt gets back in his truck and heads for the Walmart. It takes him longer than he expected to get there because of the snow and now it's forty-five minutes since Bonnie Jean clocked out.

Bonnie Jean gets in the truck, furious. Matt gives her the ring, thinking the diamond will fix everything. But it doesn't work. Bonnie Jean tells him he's too irresponsible to get married. But the ring is pretty. Matt can tell she's softening. So he brings out one more little surprise. The pie. Bonnie Jean opens the box. Only it isn't her favorite. It isn't the apple pie he ordered from Cathy. It's Matt's favorite. Cherry pie with whipped cream and peanut M&M's on top. Bonnie Jean's allergic to peanuts. She tosses the ring, the pie, and the relationship. Matt was distraught. He never stopped to think. The next day he went and enlisted."

"So?"

When I answered Kai I told him the truth. Really I did. At least everything that had to do with Iraq. I did leave out that one small part. How that stupid waitress from the diner, Cathy Tanglewood didn't just stop at the wrong pie. Nope. I left out the part about Cathy and Shane. And that pink heart-shaped diamond on her finger. It didn't seem important just then. Besides, it had nothing to do with Iraq, right? Nothing at all.

"So?" Kai asked again.

"So, one of the gentlest souls I've ever met ends up with grenades, and tanks, and semi-automatic weapons in a foreign country that needs pretty much everything. Everything except grenades, tanks, and weapons. And why? Because of some snow and a stupid piece of cherry pie? It makes no sense."

"His choice," said Kai. "It was never in your control."

"You're right. But did he really understand that choice? Does anybody? I went as a journalist. An observer. I was so sure about my purpose. My reason for being there. But I didn't get it, Kai. I didn't understand war. Not really."

"Look, I don't know what happened Willow, but don't underestimate why you went there. The world needs to hear those stories. They need to see. That's what brings about change. You have to explain what's happening."

"I used to believe that Kai. But there has to be a better way. Besides, the things I saw? How do you explain the inexplicable?"

Kai sighed. "You said Matt went out of his way to help the people. That the two of you helped that little kid and his sister. Hold onto that Willow. Hold onto whatever good you were able to find."

I pressed a palm to my forehead.

"That's just it Kai. In war even the noblest moves can get blurred. It's the daily details, the ugly circumstances that take front and center. Unfiltered violence. Not just countries but people...people committing unspeakable acts against each other. War, what you see, what you do—it changes the fabric of a human being. It...it can warp the good in you."

"It doesn't have to. Don't let it. You can't erase what you've experienced. But you can make peace with it."

"You know the funny thing Kai? I still believe in the good of the human race. Somewhere. Deep inside. I know that it outstretches the bad by miles. The thing is, we waste it. Take goodness. Goodness is this…phenomenal resource that we haven't mastered yet. I mean, think about it. Just imagine if all those good people made a simple decision. To engage in construction. Refuse to get talked into destruction–good lord, especially in the name of peace and freedom. With all that energy, all that time, and money, and effort. Imagine what this planet would look like."

"I hope we get there, Willow. I do. But in the meantime–

Kai pointed to the rising water. I paid no attention. I was drowning in my own flood of pent up thoughts and emotions.

"Just tell me why good people continue to buy into the idea that war is a natural part of our existence? You know that's where the problem starts. They can't conceive of a world without war just because there's never been one. A lot of people say that it's human nature. What was will always be. But that's just not true. The truth is things change. Everything is subject to change. Even human nature. Look how far we've come already. We've channeled our energy enough to go from horses to space shuttles, from fire to lightbulbs. Just a mere seventy years ago, there were no televisions, computers or cell phones. People say war is in our nature. What's really in our nature is to achieve the things we believe in. Believe in war, concentrate on war, and that's what you achieve. The same goes for peace." I sucked in a weary breath.

"You know, Kai, I once interviewed a Tibetan Monk who had never been to America. Here was this brilliant, spiritual being who had all kinds of talent and self-control. More than I could ever imagine possessing. But the thing that surprised him the most about America? The thing he was filled with wonder about? It was the traffic. The monks were driven in a van from Philadelphia International to the campus of Bucks County Community College and this monk he couldn't get over all of the cars. Long lines of traffic sometimes four lanes across on the Boulevard, going fifty, sixty miles an hour. Weaving in and out of streets, stopping, starting up again, turning left and right–all those drivers in all those cars in agreement. The monk was amazed. Here? We turn sixteen and take a few Drivers Ed classes. No big deal. *We* take the flow of traffic for granted. Trust me Kai, when it decides to, the human race will eradicate war. The question is; how many more people, how much more of the goodness we possess has to be shredded to hell—before we figure that out?"

I looked up at Kai and the compassion I saw in his eyes made me swallow hard to keep down the cold lump of tears I'd frozen after coming home from Iraq. Not a scrap of judgment. Just compassion. I couldn't help wondering if that look would still be there a few minutes from now. After I told him the rest of the story."

"You can't shred goodness. Look at what you did for that kid and his sister. It's yours Willow, you own it."

"Yeah. Hold that thought. You haven't heard the rest of what happened. So Matt—he's got 18 days to go, right? So we're having coffee, and he's telling me all about Bonnie Jean and then all of a sudden he holds out his hand and points to this gold band on his pinky finger. He twists it around and shows it to me. One perfect little round diamond about half a carat. Says he's feeling superstitious. So he takes it off and presses it into my palm. Asks me to keep it safe for him. Tells me he's been writing letters to Bonnie Jean and when he gets out he's going back to Michigan and he's going to ask her to marry him again. Only now, he's pressing this ring into my palm and asking me to keep it safe until he's discharged. Wants me to promise that if something happens to him I'll make sure it gets to Bonnie Jean."

"And?"

"And I tell him no. I put the ring back on his pinky finger and tell him that he doesn't need me to hold anything. I tell him that he's one of the finest human beings I've ever met and that in 18 days he's going home. That's the promise I make."

"But?"

"But the next day we head back to the hospital. We load up some extras for the medics and more stuff for the kids. For safety we tag along with another company headed into Fallujah. Only we didn't make it. The tank in front of us drives over an IED and explodes. Ahead of us, balls of fire are flying in every direction, shards of glass and metal and fire crash down on our truck. Matt must have heard the trip—or he sensed it. Anyway, he knew what was coming way before I did. Out of nowhere, he grabs me in a bear hug and he's covering my body. We were knocked clear of the truck. We rolled together off the side of the road and down an embankment. Well me—and most of Matt. His left foot was gone, the rest of his leg crushed beyond recognition, and his left arm…."

My voice trailed off as I struggled to contain the blaring images. I'd spent so much time trying to squeeze myself out of them, snipping away at them as soon as the unwanted memories appeared, that it felt surreal to be consciously recalling the horror.

"His arm…" Kai gently prodded.

I felt the weight of Kai's hands on my shoulders and closed my eyes.

"His left arm was sheered off just below the shoulder. I…we…Matt and I could see it. Lying up there in the middle of the road. Between the truck and the tank. That god-awful tank…it was ripped open, burning. Men were screaming in pain. At first I couldn't process it, couldn't conceive of a thing that would cause such ungodly sounds. Until the smell of burning flesh worked its way into the cloud of dirt just above the ground where we were curled up. The screams, they didn't last long, probably less than twenty seconds. But that twenty second soundtrack, Kai…it's part of me now. As hard as I try, I can't always reach the off button. God I can still hear those poor men screaming, moaning, and me lying motionless on the ground, Matt practically on top of me; the two of us staring at his arm…resting up there in the middle of the road—still gripping his machine gun. I… we…could see Bonnie Jean's ring on Matt's finger. It was glinting in the sun."

"Then I heard Matt's voice, his lips, they were right on my ear, yelling at me…get it, go get it, go get it. Please, oh God, Willow, please you have to go get my arm. I…can't…move. My legs I can't move my legs. He tried though, he pushed himself off of me, but his other arm wasn't so good either…his fingers were…

I stopped for a second, my voice choking at the image of Matt's fingers, burnt and curled.

"Anyway, I should have done something. Should have done more. He was losing so much blood from his left shoulder. I took my belt and wrapped it around his shoulder to make a tourniquet. But it was awkward. Leaking. I just couldn't seem to process what was happening. Matt, he was screaming in my ear. I can still hear him screaming. Get it. Get it now. Hurry, please! Hurry Willow! My arm…the ring…you promised. You promised!

I started to crawl towards the road. I didn't get far. There were more sounds. People. We could hear them somewhere in the ditch on the other side of the road. We could hear men shouting. It wasn't English. Then quiet thuds. Almost like raindrops hitting the dry dirt near my arms and ears. Again, Matt knew before me that it was gunfire. He flung himself on top of me, threw his good arm over my head. By the time I realized what the sound was, the gunfire had stopped. 'Quick, Willygirl, get the grenades.' Matt was screaming at me. 'In my backpack…bleeding…can't reach. You have to do it.' His voice was a forceful growl in my ear. 'Snap out of it Willygirl, get the goddamn grenades now!' He rolled away from me so I could reach the grenades. I pulled one out and tucked it beneath me. But the gunfire stopped.

When I lifted my head he was there. Up on the road. Del. My little Del. Wearing one of the tee shirts we gave him. Only now, he's got Matt's gun in one hand. And he's holding Matt's arm up in the air with his other hand. Bizarre. By now Del, he was shouting something. I can't understand a word he's shouting but he's shouting and he's pumping Matt's bloody arm up in the air like it's the Stanley Cup and his team just won the championship.

Finally Del sees us. He cocks his head and looks at us—Matt and me—down there in the ditch. This nine year-old kid, wearing my tee shirt, carrying Matt's arm in one hand and his machine gun in the other. Then, I don't know why, because I'm scared shitless at this point, but I smile at him. For a second he smiles back. All the while, Matt's voice is in my ear. Real quiet. He's whispering, he's telling me to get the grenade ready. Get it now, he whispers. Del is moving toward us. He's about thirty feet away from me now, and this time I see it. This time I know what Matt knows.

My hand clenches around the grenade. Del raises the gun and points it at Matt. I know what's coming. This is what haunts me, Kai. I have the seconds I need. Enough time to pull the grenade and throw it. But I don't. Instead, I watch this kid point the gun at Matt's chest and pull the trigger. I can still feel the bullets jerking Matt's body near mine. I don't know Kai—I just don't know why I didn't do it. I knew it…I knew it was coming…but maybe I just didn't want to believe it. I've thought about it a million times. But I still don't know. I mean I loved Matt, right? He was like a brother to me. But then there's Del. This distraught, ruined, kid–and he's got Matt's gun. Maybe…I don't know…Matt's wounds…they were so bad. But it doesn't matter because I should have done something, right? Matt, he looks at me with this ugly, wounded look and he whispers at me, 'you promised'. You promised. Then he died. With his eyes, looking at me like that, he died.

The kid? Del pauses. He stares down at Matt and a noise escapes him. Something between giggling and hysteria. Then he turns and looks at me. The gun is at his side now. I see his hand. It twitches. He didn't raise the gun. His hand just twitched. That's all it took. I pulled the pin I threw the grenade. It hit him in the chest. He looked so surprised. Then it fell to the ground between his feet and exploded.

These days, I see it in slow motion. Like looking through a kaleidoscope. Eyebrows, earlobes, fingers, blood and teeth and patches of tee shirt, Bonnie Jean's ring, and a thousand pieces of bone. Soaring upward, fanning out against that blue, blue sky. Against the hot Iraqi sun.

Do you know where it landed? Bonnie Jean's ring?" I whispered into Kai's chest. He was hugging me so tight I could hardly breathe. Somehow the water in the cave had crept up to my shoulders.

"Where?" He responded his voice a ragged whisper.

"It hit me in the ear. I thought it was a bullet." Standing in the cave now, I giggled. It sounded an awful lot like poor Del did after he shot Matt.

"Yep," I told Kai. "I thought it was a bullet. I screamed bloody murder and rolled away from Matt, shaking my head like a loon. Only it wasn't a bullet. Just Bonnie Jean's ring, all shiny and full of promise. I picked it up out of the dirt. Across the road there were more guns discharging, people screaming. Next thing I knew, soldiers from other trucks in the convoy were there, picking me up, loading me onto a stretcher, tending my wounds."

"I'm sorry Willow. I'm so sorry you had to go through that."

"Had to? That's the thing Kai. I didn't have to be there. I threw a grenade at a nine year-old kid. Blew his life to bits. And I only did it when my own life was on the line."

"It's instinct Willow. The human will to live is strong. I guess you just couldn't harm that kid until you had no choice."

"But I did Kai. I had choices. I never should have been there in the first place. Neither should Matt. People say what he did was brave. That war has brought us to where we are. And you know, they're right. He defended me. Defended our Country. But can we really keep living with that solution? Doesn't the human race have an obligation to go below the surface, beyond the bravery and to change the circumstances that bring a nine year old kid into the road carrying a severed limb and a machine gun?"

"So do it."

"What if I'm too...damaged?"

"What kind of crap is that? You make a decision—you go after it. Go after what you believe in Willow."

I took a deep breath. "Before I met you...actually, until just a few weeks before I met you, I was in an ahhhhm...mental facility. I barely said a word for months when I came back from Iraq."

"So?"

That's all he said—so. Like I just told him I had eggs for breakfast.

"That's just it Kai. The flashbacks...I can't."

"It's like you said, all that time, all that energy we human beings possess. Use it. Use yours. The flashbacks, they don't own all of your time. Do they? I didn't see any signs when you were spouting off that big speech. By the way, kinda preachy."

He was teasing me. I couldn't believe he was teasing me. But it felt good.

"So. Answer me. The flashbacks...do they own you?"

"No." The answer fell out of me. Fast. As if it might be true. I could almost feel the weight being lifted. Kai was right. The flashbacks were...I couldn't come up with a word. But they didn't own *every* minute of my time. Not even most of it. The question I couldn't answer was, did they own my soul?

"You just need to believe in the best version of yourself," Kai said. "Then act on it. One day, one minute at a time. You'll get there, Willow. I promise."

"Small problem with that," I said, finally focusing on the rising water.

"What? This?" Kai chided. "It's a cakewalk compared to what you've been through. I'll get you out Willow. I promise."

"Don't make promises, Kai. It can do awful things to your insides when you don't keep them."

Kai leaned his head on mine and hugged me tight.

"Or they can save you," he challenged. "Isn't that what brought you to Hawaii, to me, in the first place? A promise to a friend?"

I didn't answer. Tiny waves of salt water lapped at the hollow of my neck.

"In about four minutes, we'll go," said Kai. "Relax and take some deep bre–

It felt like rubber shimmying up my thigh. I grabbed Kai's arm and squeezed it tight. Something was brushing against my leg. Something cold and…there it was again. Brrrrrng, brrrrrnging against the side of my leg.

"Kai! My cell phone. It's ringing!"

I was wearing a pair of Capri jeans with a wide pocket on the side. When I got changed after the charity auction I threw the cell phone in my pocket. It was still encased in the zippered pouch I used for the beach. The pouch was meant to keep out sand not water. Yet here it was, ringing like mad. Sending tiny ripples of sound through the water. I reached down and unbuttoned my pocket.

The shark, with its dorsal fin barely breaking the surface, was on its way out of the cave. There was no great sigh of relief since we had no clue the shark was there in the first place. No sense of panic either when the sound waves from the phone disturbed his journey. The fin did a complete one eighty and slipped beneath the surface.

It was tough to get the pouch high enough to keep it out of the water since there were only about six or seven inches of airspace left in the cave. But the phone was still ringing when I unzipped it and Kai took it out. It was Mak. Kai tried to tell him what happened but it was hard to hear Mak in the cave and they got cut off before Kai was able to give our exact location.

"Oh God! Is it dead? Turn it back on. Text him! If the phone's still working just text him!"

Kai's fingers flew across the keypad. Suddenly he jerked forward and up, banging his head on the roof of the cave and then plowing in to me. The phone fell out of his hand. Don't ask me how, but I caught it just above the water.

"What the hell?" I yelled.

His hand shot up out of the water and clamped over my mouth before I could say another word.

"Shark," he whispered. "Tuck your knees up to your chest. Now."

He was calm but serious. His tone was as collected as usual. Once I heard the word shark there wasn't enough calm on the planet for me. I moved his hand.

"Shark?! Did you say shark?!"

Hahahahaha…this is good stuff Willygirl. Not exactly Iraq…but ya gotta admit…beats that mellow garden in Angie's nuthouse, huh?

The phone rang. The sudden vibration against my hand startled me and I threw it in the air. It hit the roof of the cave with a nasty thud and plunged into the water. We didn't realize it but the phone hit the shark dead on the nose. It dove downward and skimmed the bottom of the cave.

Kai grabbed me by the hand.

"Come on, we've got to get out of here. Deep breath! Let's go!"

"You don't seriously think we can out-swim a shark. Do you?" I asked hopefully.

"Nope."

He took a deep breath and went under. He was still holding my wrist. I gulped and followed. It was about twenty yards to the mouth of the cave. Kai was right about the shark. There was no way we could outrun it. But we did make it out of the cave. Shark must've ditched us on purpose.

I popped through the surface and was able to grab a decent breath of air before Kai tugged violently on my wrist and dragged us to the left, toward the rocks. The tides washing in and out were brutal. It probably took us the better part of a half an hour to make it to the rocks but we did. Almost immediately the worst of the undertow subsided. I was so grateful, all I wanted to do was wrap my arms around that first giant rock and fall asleep. I was tired. But after a few minutes of rest Kai made us keep on going.

"It's not safe, Willow. We need to keep moving until we get to the cliff. The sooner we make it back up, the better."

We were almost there when the wave hit. It wasn't like the others. It felt more like God had dumped a giant bucket of water right over the rocks and down onto our heads. The pressure of it was fierce. My hand flew out of Kai's. Then, like a bug squirming in a puddle, I was *buoyed* to the top of the water pile and whooshed over the rocks. Out into the ocean.

Kai had little choice. I was gone. He made his way up the cliff. I know he felt bad. That he let me down or something. But in all fairness I never would have made it up that cliff anyway.

CHAPTER TWENTY THREE

Melanie went the wrong way. Instinct drove her away from the brick wall at the end of the row and toward the narrowing opening. There just wasn't enough time for her to process the idea that someone she considered a friend, would close the aisle on purpose. As luck would have it most of Melanie actually did make it out of the aisle before the steel walls slammed shut against each other.

Everything but her right wrist—which of course the heavy steel file walls then separated, in a rather messy fashion, from the rest of her arm. Poor Melanie didn't know what to do. She opened her mouth to scream. What she was looking for was a good, blood-curdling howl. Obviously what the situation warranted. What came out were those muffled grunts. You know, the kind that people make when trying to wake themselves up out of a nightmare.

Still, the rest of Melanie's body was free of the steel files, and her left hand was still working. She reached out and clawed at her killer. With a few good scrapes she gathered some valuable evidence under her fingernails and even managed to knock the small diamond out of the killer's hand. The thing is, Melanie wasn't trying to do either. She was looking for support, trying to hold herself up while wrapping her brain around her predicament. The smooth black stone rippled across her fingers and for a brief moment she curled it in her palm. Soon after though, shock and death caused her to drop it into the pool of blood oozing onto the floor from her lost hand.

Annoyed at the growing mess, the killer gingerly picked up the diamond, left the hospital unnoticed, and went to meet friends.

CHAPTER TWENTY FOUR

I didn't fight it this time. I just sped out into the ocean. It wasn't so bad. When the current finally shifted and settled into a nice lull I flipped onto my back and started drifting. After awhile the sun came up and in the beginning, the sky, it was spectacular, all slow and glowy. Later on there was nothing to look at but miles and miles of blue.

At first, I was worried about that shark. Not to mention his possible entourage. At first, but then not so much. Actually it was something Kai said in the cave that calmed me down. Be the best version of yourself. Be the best version. Seriously though, what does that mean?

Be the best terrorist? Stockbroker? Murderer?

Then I just decided. For right now, it meant that the best me didn't have to worry about the shark.

I should have gotten tired. But as time wore on and I stared at that empty blue sky I just got mad. Sure, it was vast and beautiful, blah, blah, blah. It was empty. I figured that if this was it—if my number was up, well, I kind of wanted to see the guy in charge of it all. It's not like there was a crowd out there. Just me.

Well, maybe not a crowd…but definitely not just yo

I wanted answers. Clarity. About all things big and small. War and famine. Disease and greed and natural disasters. Sanity and free choice. Not to mention all the personal stuff. Why didn't Shane and I last? Why Matt? He had so much good to offer. Did he really have to leave this world gun in hand? Okay, scratch that. Just tell me about the boy. Tell me about Del and his sister? Because I can't fathom any of that. Why God? Why did I throw that grenade?!

"Too much?" I yelled out loud. "Too many questions? Well I got more. Speaking of the grenade, why the flashbacks? Seriously. Being there in person…once wasn't bad enough? If you're gonna supply flashbacks, then why not let me in on some other important details. Like Angela. Please…what really happened at Angela's house? Did I do it? There's that voice sometimes…and the anger. With every flashback I feel the rage. Did I use it on Angie? On Bill? Why won't you let me remember? Oh and hey…let's not forget about those four days I lost. Might as well clue me in on those too," I shouted.

I waited. Drifted and waited. Nothing. No answers. Just blue blue skies.

"Fine. Be like that," I yelled. Then after a long dejected sigh I added, "If you don't want to chat then why am I still here? Why not just man-up and put me out of my misery? And skip the shark–that's too easy. How about a giant thumb? Yeah. Yeah! That sounds good. No conversation? No problem. But a thumb now that's something. I'm not even asking for the whole hand of God thing. Just a nice giant thumb down from on high so I can see it coming. We both know I have clarity issues. Big thumb, right amount of pressure and boom, I'm skimming the bottom of the ocean. Done. Smite and mercy. No more worries about war. Or dead friends. Or what I've done with my capable hands."

The skies remained clear, blue, and quiet. Except for the pelican that flew by and left some ass-juice on my cheek and forehead. Nice touch. I would have laughed. Really I would have. But all of a sudden I *was* tired. I just wanted to close my eyes and roll over. I prayed. But only bits and pieces that kept looping through my Catholic head. "Our Father who art in heaven, thy will be…Hail Mary full of grace. Pray for us sinners now and at the hour…now and at the hour…now

And then it came. Just before I drifted into a deep sleep. "Inside the waves," came the whisper. "It takes faith inside the waves. Clarity comes in the silences after."

CHAPTER TWENTY FIVE

Kai scaled the cliff like a man possessed. It took him thirty-five minutes, plus another fifteen to make it back to the house. He let go. One second his hand was full and in the next it was empty. Kai was still in shock over it.

The look of devastation on his mother's face, the guttural cry she let loose when she saw him, battered, but alive made everything worse. The last thing Kai's mother needed was more pain.

He was glad at least to see a police officer standing next to his mother. He found out that the text message had gotten through to Makani. Mak immediately phoned Kai's brothers, and his brothers called the Coast Guard. But it was after three in the morning when I went over that giant black rock. There wasn't much they could do.

Kai gave his mother a bear hug. He apologized for scaring her so badly. Then he gathered his brothers and went in search of a boat. He wasn't about to wait for daylight.

"Kai, no," his mother cried, trying to stop him at the door. He hugged her a second time. He whispered something Hawaiian in her ear, something kind and soothing. Then headed for the water's edge.

Seven hours later they dragged me from the ocean. Seven hours. A drop in the bucket of search time when you consider how vast the Pacific Ocean is. They called it a miracle. Had to be...right? Maybe it meant that God wasn't done with me just yet.

God...righhhht...couldn't be someone slightly less heaven bound now could it?

Miracle or not, they found me. My arms and legs were straddled over a long piece of 'ohia tree, my face strewn with seaweed and wet splinters. I didn't remember finding the wood. Let alone climbing onto it. In fact, I didn't remember much. But the look of love, the pure joy on Kai's face when they pulled me into the boat, well, it'll take a bad case of Alzheimer's to erase that memory.

I was sun burnt and thirsty but that was all. Well, and sort of tired. But not the kind of bone weary you'd expect after floating in the ocean all night. Instead I felt kind of slow and warm. It was a good feeling. But since I was about to break another promise, well, I didn't exactly expect it to last.

"What are you guys all doing here?"

"After a text like that, what do you think we're doing here?" Mak asked. We came to start a search party for you and Kai. Hell, do you two have any idea how lucky you are?"

"Don't think hell—or luck—had anything to do with it," I blurted. The room got quiet. Except for Kai, they all stared at me and waited. Like I had something to follow that up with some big nugget of wisdom after my night in the deep dark ocean. I didn't. I stared back, just as blankly, until my eyes lit on the woman standing next to Nick. She was standing so close, her blonde hair actually drifted across his elbow. I was genuinely surprised to see her.

"January. I'm glad you came."

"Don't be. I'm here because of Kai. Because I have an airplane and some friends here," her eyes lit on Nick, "who needed a lift."

"Doesn't matter. You're here. And we," I motioned to the rest of us, "have a few secrets to fill you in on."

"No!" Mak and Liat responded simultaneously.

Jan raised an eyebrow. Then she turned and flashed me a grin. The first genuine smile she'd shone me since I'd met her.

"Go ahead. I love secrets."

I looked at Mak. He gave his head the slightest shake, warning me silent, and pressed his lips together. The room got quiet. Apparently no one else was ready to share.

"Okay. So, Jan, you know that I came to Hawaii to bring you your mother's ring. Well it wasn't the only reason. Before she died your mother gave me something else. An old fashioned surfboard carved by Liat's father. It's the match to the one your father has in his study. Your mother? She made me promise to bring it here so I could find the Maui Snow. She also made me promise to keep you as far away from the whole situation as possible. She was afraid. I don't know why, but she didn't want you involved. The problem is, I can't keep both promises. We need your input to find the Maui Snow."

"Gee, your concern for me is touching. I feel all warm and fuzzy inside." Jan turned to the others. "Okay so that's the reporter's story. What are the rest of you keeping from me?"

Liat stole a glance at Mak and then stepped forward.

"Let's fly back to Oahu. Jan, there's some artwork you need to see. I'll explain it to you when we get there. In fact we really should get moving. Remember, the second leg of the Triple Crown starts tomorrow." Then to me she added, "Are you sure you're up for it Willow? Maybe you should stay behind. Kai's mom's the best. She'll have you back to normal in no time."

"Tempting offer," I responded, remembering the homemade soup she'd made for me earlier. "But that's okay, I'm good enough to go."

I wobbled a bit as Kai helped me to my feet. Then I reached out and touched Jan on the arm.

"The other surfboard, the one in your father's study. Can you get us in to see it? Without getting him involved? I've sort of been avoiding him since I got here because, well, the situation is complicated enough. Actually, what are the chances you could bring the board to us?"

January rolled her eyes and let out a sigh, as if she were dealing with morons. For a second I thought she was going to reach out and pet me on the head.

"You haven't been avoiding my father. If he wanted to find you he would. He doesn't want to find you anymore because I took care of it. I convinced him that the surfboard you have is a fake. A really bad fake.

She saw the look on my face.

"Yes, I knew about the surfboard. Vince told me. By the way, where is it?"

Something about the way Jan asked made the hairs on the back of my neck stand up. It wasn't a question born out of basic curiosity. I could tell by her tone. She *knew* the surfboard wasn't at the hotel.

"Safe," I replied. "What makes you so sure that your father thinks it's a fake?"

"Because I told him you were just a bloodsucking reporter after a story. I told him that you knew about *his* surfboard and that you faked another one so you could use it as an angle to get an interview with him. You know, so you could grill him about my mother and the rest of his ex-wives. It wasn't a tough sell. All I had to do was send him the article you wrote about my mother's death."

"Ease up Jan," Kai warned, as he laid a protective hand on my shoulder." Then his cell phone buzzed. He was about to say more but was distracted by the text message. When he closed the phone his face was serious.

"Unbelievable. What next?" He uttered almost to himself. Then to the rest of us, "You know that girl Melanie? The one who hangs out at the beach all the time and watches us surf? Well, she's dead. They found her this morning. Apparently she got stuck between some steel file walls while working at the hospital. And get this," he looked hard at Liat. "Her hand was cut off at the wrist. The police are investigating. Seems they found a bloody footprint at the scene."

Nick, Mak, and I, whipped our heads in Liat's direction too. Liat didn't say a word. Her face went pale and she gripped the edge of the windowsill. Nick stepped in. He dropped his shoulder underneath her arm for support and helped her to the couch. I watched, as Liat fell back against the pillows and for a second I was distracted by them, distracted from the awful news about Melanie. I didn't want to think about it. Didin't want to think about her. So I focused on the pillows. I couldn't help noticing how beautiful they were. Soft and plump, they were the color of lemon drops. Kai's mother had probably sewn them herself. It was a nice thought, a nice idea. After it passed though Melanie floated front and center into my brain once again. And so did another nice idea.

"Melanie? That's the girl we tried to call last night. Right? She's the one who found the olive after Mason choked on it."

Then I pointed at January. "You were there. You saw her too. In fact, you tried to get Melanie to give you the olive. But she didn't. She put it in her purse."

"What are you talking about?" Jan scoffed, shooting me the familiar 'you're crazy' look. "I don't stalk people for used olives." Then she looked at Kai and rolled her eyes. As if I were crazy. As if I'd dreamt the idea up out of thin air just to make her look bad. It worked. Kai shot me a brief but questioning look. Satisfied, Jan ubruptly changed the conversation.

"What's wrong with Liat. Why were you all just staring at her like that?"

I was frustrated. Jan was lying. Changing the subject and lying. I saw her with Melanie. Other people must have seen her too. Why weren't they saying so?

"Nick? You were there with me. You saw Jan and Melanie arguing. Right?"

Nick shrugged. "Sorry Willow. I was freaked out about Mason. And worried about Liat."

I was furious. Part of me wanted to shake the truth out of Jan right then and there.

Shake the truth out of...Jan?

The urge was surprisingly strong, stupid, but strong. For starters my body was still soft and wobbly from the ocean. That, and Jan was the only one who had access to the other surfboard. Upsetting her probably wasn't the best move.

"What's wrong with Liat," Jan asked again. "Why were you all staring at her like that?"

"You wouldn't believe us if we told you," I responded. "But if you get the surfboard from your father's study and bring it with you we'll show you Liat's art. There's a sculpture of Melanie that you have to see to believe. Well, part of Melanie, anyway."

Again Jan raised an eyebrow. But she didn't bite so fast at the dangled carrot. Instead, she picked up her keys and headed for the door.

"We'll see. Right now I'm going back to Oahu. To surf. I plan to crush the competition in the next round. Including you, Liat. After that," she said to me, with a wicked grin curling at the corner of her lips, "if you want to show me your surfboard. I'll show you mine."

"She's right," Nick agreed. "I need to get into some waves. The men's competition is coming up fast and I do not plan to lose."

"Nobody plans to lose," Mak laughed. "Someone better just makes it happen." He reached over to ruffle Nick's blonde hair. Nick ducked out of the way before he could but it was a small win. It was evident that Makani's self-assured confidence bugged him in places he didn't want to look at. Nick ignored the Hawaiian and stretched out his hand.

"You coming Liat?"

CHAPTER TWENTY SIX

Sunset Beach

It was eighty-one degrees and hazy. Not hazy enough, though, to disguise the massive waves exploding offshore. Forecasters were predicting near perfect conditions for round two of the Women's Triple Crown. By the time Kai and I got there, cars and bicycles were jammed up along the highway and reached well into the back of the parking lot across the street at the elementary school. Smart locals looking to make a buck were selling everything from cut pineapples to sandals with beer openers built into the bottom. Thousands of fans spread out across the wide stretch of sand. They played football and threw discs. Plugged themselves into music and texted. Ate, drank, and laughed, as they waited for the surfers to arrive. It was barely eight in the morning but that didn't matter. Sunset Beach was alive.

As I stared out at those waves it occurred to me that maybe I wasn't the crazy one after all. Heat after heat I watched them paddle into swells that were the size of sheer madness. Watching them, I felt like an outsider. Like I'd barely scratched the surface. I shouldn't have been surprised, because surfers, well, they immerse themselves. They'll be the first to tell you that surfing's a lifestyle not a sport. Maybe. If you ask me it's an energy thing. It hangs around them. They live and breathe it until it becomes this seamless thing, part of who they are. Sure, they have their individual personalities, their reasons for venturing into the ocean that are distinct to each of them but that thing—that whatever it is thing they all share—well it separates them from the rest of us.

January had mad skills. Relentless and precise she worked her way through the heats catching the maximum amount of waves possible, racking up the points and annihilating every surfer girl in every heat. As expected she made it into the final heat. So did Liat.

Wave after wave the two women squared off in the final heat. Jan was fast. With her longer leaner frame she made it to the lineup first and always had her pick of the waves. She made the most out of every one of them too, riding the walls down a bit too far, as far as she dared go before wrenching her surfboard upward again and shooting for the lip, executing carefully orchestrated moves as she sped across the water. She stacked three, four, five waves in a row with clean professional moves. The points flowed in, more than enough to take most heats. Most competitions. But she was losing. After three bad waves at the beginning, Liat suddenly ignited, painting the waves with effortless and intricate moves that made the crowd go wild. Flat on her board and frustrated, Jan skimmed the top of an unbroken wave, flowed over it, and paddled toward the line-up. Toward Liat.

"Careful. Might want to take the next set from the other side," Jan suggested. "There's a nasty tug over here and I almost didn't make it up after the last wave." There was indeed a growing undertow. But it was on the other side.

Liat ignored Jan. It was time to banish every distraction. Time to start winning again. She paddled toward the next wave and once again she let go of everything. Her mother had been right. Ignoring her skills, any of them, including her ability to surf, was no longer an option. The stakes were too high. Liat couldn't stop the men's competition. She couldn't prevent a winner from being crowned. But she could take the women's title. If the wave in her final sculpture was inevitable, then Liat planned to be the one riding it. For the next fourteen minutes Liat surfed with every fiber of her being. She weaved in and out of the waves like a fish, treating her surfboard as if it were just one more, slightly less, fluid layer of the ocean. She wowed the crowd and the judges. At the end of the day she walked away the winner.

Jan was furious. She'd told every surf magazine that had interviewed her in the last two months that this was her year. That she expected to sweep all three events and take the title unchallenged. The fans believed her too. Everyone could see that Jan was in top form, while Liat, well, Liat had been distracted all season long. They all knew. They saw Jan's efforts, her skills, paying off. Then, what, mid competition Liat makes a comeback, puts out on a few decent waves and suddenly all is forgiven. Forgotten? All of Jan's hard work is forgotten? At the end of the day that's what infuriated Jan the most. The fans. The crowd was suddenly behind Liat as if she hadn't suffered a bad moment, as if she'd been the favorite all year. Jan was flabbergasted. Once again she would have to fight for approval. Fight for the crown. The final event would be held at Honolua Bay on the island of Maui.

The women's event was interesting. The men's event at Sunset Beach was life changing. For all of us.

The sea was in a bad mood, almost from the start that day. Weather from the Aluetion Islands was pushing in much faster than expected and by mid morning the waves were gaining weight if not height. Fish, large and small, felt the changes and were imperceptibly agitated. Away from Sunset Beach, twenty miles out into the ocean, clouds gathered and clung. Waiting.

Mak had a rough start. He put up some points with his first wave but not enough to hold the heat. His second wave looked good but then it bent early. Mak did his best to make it down the wall and into the barrel but three quarters of the way down his feet parted ways with his board. He dropped through the bottom of the wave, crouched into a fetal tuck, and waited out the fury. It was nearly two minutes before his head popped through the raging foam and he was towed to safety. Determined not to go down in the first heat, Mak of course, paddled out again. He caught some better waves after that and squeeked through to the next round.

Despite the cranky waves, Kai's day was going much better. Somehow he surfed through one flawless heat after another. From the beach I watched him paddling into mountains of water, his feet maneuvering that thin board into death curdling actions. I sat, mesmerized, as Kai disappeared under heavy collapsing lips. It felt surreal. I was scared to death and proud all at the same time. I found myself shouting, cheering at the top of my lungs as Kai worked his way into the final heat. It was better than watching A.I. drag the 76ers out of a thirty point fourth quarter deficit into a one-point overtime win. Better than waiting for Shane to cross the finish line at the Boston Marathon. Wait. Better than waiting at the finish line for Shane? The thought caught me off guard. After all I'd been through over Shane, I never expected to feel this much for someone else.

As Mak predicted Nick was in over his head. He went down hard in the first heat. It wasn't pretty. Crushed by a thick wave, his board broke into three pieces. He limped to shore with a small gash on his left calf. It looked as if his big wave quest had come to an end. Nick did his best to hide the complete and utter relief flooding through his veins as he sloshed toward the sand. The cut on his leg was a respectable excuse. After weeks of pure terror since winning that first contest which gained him entry into the wild card contest, the massive blue walls rising at his back were now, finally, someone else's problem.

Well, they would've been someone else's problem. Should have been. But then Nick looked up the beach and spotted Liat. When he first caught sight of her his lips parted in a huge smile. Then Mak came up behind her and Nick's smile went south as Mak settled his chin on top of Liat's head and casually threw an arm around her waist. Nick held his breath. Liat broke away. But the moment was long. Way too long.

Nick brushed the blood off his leg before anyone had a chance to see that it was bleeding. Then he grabbed the first board he could reach, ran back to the ocean, and paddled out to find another wave. He chose the smallest one he could find. Then another. And another. As he rode the waves, struggling for balance, struggling for points, his ankle leaked blood into the ocean. Nearly a mile away, a young Great White twitched at the metallic scent.

The last wave in the heat was thirteen feet high and messy. Nick caught it any way. He worked it hard, harder than the other waves, willing his body to stay upright for the entire ride. There was no clean barrel but he did manage to score points. Enough points to put Nick ahead of Jay Darrow, and even enough points to squeak him into the next heat. Against Makani.

Triumphant, Nick lifted his surfboard out of the water and then reached down to brush the blood from his ankle one last time before stepping out of the ocean. The first thing he did when he hit the beach was look for Liat. It took a second to spot her in the growing crowd.

When he finally did, Nick waved. But Liat was busy signing autographs. He waved again and waited but she didn't see him. Something trickled down his leg. Blood. Nick reached down for a handful of dry sand and rubbed it over his aching wound.

Thirty minutes later, Mak and Nick stood shoulder to shoulder near the edge of the water for the second heat. The tension was palpable. The waves were higher, heavier now than during the first heat and there was no sign of them losing steam. The crowd hushed itself and leaned forward…waiting. A moment later the horn blasted and the two men took off.

Nick shot into the ocean like a bullet from a gun. He tossed his blue and white board in front of him, flew on top of it and began slicing through the water, taking an early lead toward catching the first wave of the heat.

Mak ducked under the breakers just like he had a thousand times before. He let the water drain over his body, then cleared the surface and came up paddling–right next to Nick.

Nick caught sight of him and his jaw dropped.

"Awwww come on brah," Mak chided. "You didn't think I was gonna let you get all lonely out in front here now did ya?"

Without waiting for an answer Mak cut swiftly to the left and paddled. Fast. Again Nick was caught off guard. The set he was eyeing was still rising in the distance. He watched as Mak rolled into an almost impossible wave and splashed across it with his best moves. It would never even have occurred to Nick to try for that wave. Not from the position they were in. Mak collected solid sevens and eights from the judges.

Nick turned back and paddled hard. He took the second wave in the next set and negotiated his way down the wall, keeping his feet in place, and managing a decent ride. Not as pretty as Mak's but enough to earn some points. Nick pushed his surfboard back into the ocean and paddled out for more. Of course by now the dry sand that he'd packed onto his cut had dissolved. Once again the wound began to ooze blood into the ocean.

The shark was only half a mile away this time, feeding on a small school of fish. It picked up the scent and turned fast.

Nick maneuvered into his second wave but his timing was all wrong. Almost as soon as he stood up the lip flooded in over the back of his board and down he went. It was a nasty wave but Nick got lucky. He got tossed over the back of it and popped through the surface right away. Then he dragged himself back onto his board and searched for another wave.

By now Mak had claimed three stellar waves and the chances of Nick catching up were slim. There were only eight minutes left in the heat. Once again Mak paddled up next to Nick and the two men sliced through the water, side by side, toward the next set of waves. There was barely four inches of space between them. So the shark zeroed in on both surfers. Neither one of them saw it coming.

All at once Mak cut away, heading for the third wave in the set. Nick continued on, paddling straight, hoping to get there in time to catch the fourth wave. Although the stream of blood was leaking into the ocean from Nick's leg, for some reason, when the two surfers parted ways the shark headed straight for Mak.

Mak's arms rotated through the water as he prepared to meet up with the gathering wave. Twenty feet below, the shark glided in beneath Mak's white and orange board. Finding his sweet spot, Mak raised his arms toward the sides of his board and prepared to pop his feet into place. His left foot padded onto the front of the board. A nanosecond later his right foot locked into place behind it. Whaaaaammm! Nose first, the shark smacked the bottom of the surfboard dead center and sent it spinning, spiraling, up and out of the water. Mak's body went flying off to the right of his board. He clutched hard at the sides of his surfboard and instinctively tried to reign his body back in over top of it. He swung his weight to the left and held on for dear life, all the while trying to fathom what was happening. One second he was in the water preparing to take a wave and the next he was airborn. Spinning upward. Then staring down at the ocean below and wondering what the hell happened. And that's when he saw it.

Mak caught a glimpse of the arching Great White just before it slid back into the ocean, jaws wide open, waiting patiently in the water for its stunned prey to return. Mak hung up there in the air like that for just the briefest second just long enough for the scene below to begin seeping through his skin. Then all at once he came spiraling down out of the sky, screaming right toward that open throat. His whole body jerked as he slid his hands forward, near the front end of his surfboard, which was slanting downward. Mak let out a fierce grunt and yanked the tip of the board up, yanked the board as straight as he could manage it and then waaaaaaaackkk!! He smacked the ocean flat, inches to the left of the shark and went skimming across the water. The shark closed its jaws, and ducked its head beneath the surface after Mak slid by. Forty feet later Mak's board slowed to a halt and there it was again, the long gray back of the shark. Mak let out a loud guttural yell, put a bare foot on the Great White's back and shoved at it. He followed it with his fists, pummeling the creature like a newborn beating against its mother's shoulder. Fat lot of good that did. The shark dropped down a few feet and swung around, prepping itself for the kill. Mak swung his head around and tried to catch sight of it, tried to catch sight of his bearings. Before he could form another thought Mak found himself once again rising atop the ocean.

A wave! Mak had skidded to a halt right in the middle of a rising wave. He was at a lousy angle, way off center, and too low for comfort. Not exactly his sweet spot but the swell was jacking up with a vengeance and Mak needed to move. Fast. But it was an ugly wave. More like a wave and a cross-wave rolling toward each other, with both waves, fighting for dominance. Mak could see that he was on the shorter wave, rolling toward the right and he immediately steered the board upward, toward the lip. He skimmed across it, toward the wave rolling left, and prayed for the two waves to merge, to break as fast and as heavy as possible. Sharks had a knack for avoiding the kind of heavy waves that might wash them too close to shore. Mak stole a glance down at the bottom of the wave he was riding. There it was. He caught sight of the shark, its thick body, its tail, fanning through the ocean, propelling itself upward now, toward the top of the wave. It was coming right at him. Mak hunkered down and gripped both sides of his surfboard. He could see its nose now, its bottom jaw dropping open, rows and rows of jagged teeth...three, two, ...aaaaaahhhhhhh...

Mak strained his body upward and lept the board toward the lip of the left crashing wave. He skidded up onto it and immediately spun the board around, speeding now in a safer direction. Mak let out a primal yell as the two waves crashed together, praying for the left to stay its course, praying that his feet stay locked in place so he could skim over the menacing shark, praying for the fluid thoughtful movements it would take to stand, to achieve such an act as the two waves fought and merged and heaved over themselves. Mak sped forward, looking down, as the much heavier more powerful wave went screaming on toward shallower water. The shark was still there, still gunning for Mak's board, rising up now toward the lip of the newly merged, newly crashing wave, a mere ten inches away. But as the wave rolled hard, the instinct to survive overcame its hunger, and at the last second the shark sliced through the back of the rolling wave and swam once again toward deeper waters.

Mak fell off the wave about thirty seconds later. He recovered his board and then slid on top of it, hugging it tight, pressing his cheek against it, and finally breathing a sigh of relief. A few seconds later, he bolted upright. Then started searching the ocean for Nick.

Nick actually caught the wave he'd set out to catch, the third wave of the set, without any trouble from the shark. In fact when he caught the wave, he still had no clue the shark was even there. He didn't see Mak fly out of the water. Or smack back into the ocean. Or scramble into the wave to get away from it. He didn't see Mak screaming and trying to get his attention afterwards either. He was busy chasing points. It wasn't pretty. He didn't make it all the way through the wave and he took a beating trying to surf it but at least he scored. Twos and threes. But he did score. Once again Nick paddled out. Determined to put Mak in his rightful place.

Try as he might, Mak couldn't get Nick's attention. He searched for one of the jet skis. But Mak was way out of position. The rescue teams were on the other side of the heavy waves. Closer to Nick. And Nick was paddling back out for another wave. Mak sighed. He knew the shark had gone back into deeper water. Nick was a sitting duck out there. Mak turned his board around and headed back out. It took him almost three minutes to catch up to Nick. He paddled in close, waved his arms, and shouted.

"Nick! Shark!"

Nick shot Mak a look that said 'nice try' and paddled toward the next set. Mak followed, moving in as close to Nick as he could get this time.

"Jeezus Nick, I'm not kidding. The damn thing tossed me in the air. I got lucky, caught a wave, and then I beat it the hell outta there. Come on, we gotta go."

But Nick kept paddling. Farther out. Once again the shark scented blood. By now it was eight hundred yards away. It hesitated for a second, sloshing peacefully in the deeper water. It sniffed again. Then it turned and once again headed toward the breaking waves.

"Nick, this is stupid. You've been getting crushed all day. Now let's go."

Nick ignored him again.

"Suit yourself," Mak declared. Then he turned his surfboard toward the rescue team, warned them, and caught a ride back to shore.

Nick paddled into his wave. It wasn't the biggest or the thickest but Nick made it work. He didn't break through the lip, but he did ride down the face of the wave and somehow kept his feet on the board. After a few cutbacks he managed his way into the barrel. An underwater photographer who had also ignored the warning was waiting there for him. Waiting to capture that perfect shot. With Nick's sunny good looks and his unusual mid-western bio, the surf magazines and sponsors would be lined up, ready to pounce all over a story like that. But Nick wasn't quite out of the tube yet. He wasn't quite there. You see, the skills that are mandatory to survive on the pro circuit take time and dedication to acquire. They take passion. Truth be told, Nick's real passion was the newsroom. The newsroom and Liat.

Nick was still in the tube when his feet separated from the board. It really wasn't that big of a wave by Triple Crown standards. Just a few tons of rushing water. The lip curled down over Nick and followed him to the bottom of the ocean. It tucked in tight around his body this time and sent him rolling with the wave. Once again, the shark powered through the back of the wave and headed out to sea. Nick rolled and rolled and rolled. Rescue units plowed into the foamy aftermath when he failed to surface. Then the next wave hit. Again, they zoomed in afterwards to search. They found him after the third wave receded and sped him to shore breathing air into his lungs and pounding him on the chest as they went. He was loaded into an ambulance and rushed to the hospital. Eleven minutes later a young ER doctor took over.

"CLEAR!!!" He shouted. Then he laid the paddles against Nick's silent chest, again, and again, and again.

CHAPTER TWENTY SEVEN

The news was not good. Nick was still alive when Liat, Jan, and I arrived at the hospital but much of his body was not functioning properly. A team of grave looking doctors approached Liat and began throwing around phrases like, touch and go. Swelling. Paralysis. Doing all we can.

Mak and Kai stayed behind. The competiton was delayed. While the surfers sat on the beach and waited, the waves grew higher and testier. Around mid-day the contest officials took a vote and made a unanimous decision to continue the contest. It all came down to one last heat with Makani and Kai. Both men caught a record number of waves that afternoon and the final was really close. At the end of the day it was Kai who squeeked past Mak for the win. When it was over Makani and Kai jumped into the same car and rushed over to the hospital.

Liat lost it. They wouldn't let us in to see Nick for hours. When they finally did, he was strapped to the bed and turned upside down in order to relieve the pressure on his back. His whole body was hooked up to monitors and his eyes were drugged shut. Liat tried to talk to him but he was just so groggy. It didn't matter anyway because after about two minutes the nurses shooed us back to the waiting room. That's when Liat bolted. We searched the entire hospital for her, starting with the chapel and ending with the parking lot but we came up empty. After that we tried Kai's place on the North Shore and then Liat's apartment. Nothing.

We found her at the University an hour later. She was in the basement of the art barn with a chisel in her hand and there were a bunch of nasty dents hacked into the back of her wave sculpture. Mak grabbed her in a bear hug while Kai wrestled the chisel away from her.

January was with us too. She followed us down the steps, took one look at the sculptures assembled in the center of the room, and let out a swift little swear.

"What the **** is all this?"

"My fault," Liat cried. "Please, lemme go! Give back the chisel…I have to stop it! Somebody has to stop it…please…somebody help me!" Her voice was bordering on hysteria. Mak cradled her in his arms.

"Shhhhhh…Liat…stop. It's ok, it's ok," Mak whispered over and over to calm her down.

"I never thought…God I never thought it would be Nick. I didn't want him to compete because I didn't think he was ready. But…but," she sobbed, "I never thought he was the surfer in my sculpture. I just…I thought it was Mak…or maybe me."

"Gee thanks a lot," Mak whispered jokingly. It didn't work. He took a stronger tone.

"Calm down Liat. Nick isn't the surfer in your sculpture. That wave today…it wasn't even that big. You, me, Kai, Jan, we've all surfed waves way bigger than that one. You had absolutely nothing to do with what happened to Nick today. That was Mother Nature and a dose of stupidity. Don't forget," he added, pointing to the surfer in the sculpture. "That's a Pipe Master's crown."

Mak looked at Kai for support. Kai looked at Liat and nodded his agreement.

Liat reached out and kicked the surfing sculpture. "So what? If you're right, if it wasn't Nick, that just means this wave, this monstrosity, is still coming."

She grabbed for the chisel again. "I will stop this."

"I repeat," said Jan, flinging both hands out at the sculptures, "what the hell?"

Kai caught hold of Liat and threw Mak a look. In turn, Mak motioned to January, took her aside, and tried to explain what was going on.

"You're kidding me, right?" I heard Jan say as I moved toward Kai and Liat.

"Look, if you want to end this," I told Liat, "then use your brain."

"So far all you've been doing is playing catch up. Let's face it kiddo, beating up on the artwork is hardly a solution. Maybe it's time that we got ahead of the events in your uhmm...collection."

"Come on," I added, coaxing her from Kai's embrace. "All for one and one for all."

Funny thing about that...in the end we all held something back from each other.

Of course it didn't start out that way. The plan was to put the two surfboards together, look at Liat's sculptures, and unravel the clues. And at first, that's exactly how it went. All of us jumping in with ideas and talking over each other in an effort to figure out what Sam Kawa's words meant.

We started with the first board. At the top was a fiery volcano with the inscription Pele's house. Underneath were eight Hawaiian Islands.

Molokai, Lanai, and Oahu were etched in blue.

Kahoolawe, Niihau, and Maui in green.

Hawaii and Kuai in red.

Then came the inscription. Some of the words were in red, some in green, and the rest in black.

By heaven's breath came a hail of black snow
some say within Pele's domain.
Pried from the ground by kahole,
Pele's patience is now wearing thin.
Maui Snow must be found and soon returned home
for the kahole are at it again!
Poliahu's house bears the final secret
But do not seek out of order.
Go first to Pele's volcano
And reach deep inside my daughter.
There you'll discover what Poliahu knows:
Where great treasure lies with destiny
And Pele's patience is Pilikia

"Let's separate the words by color," suggested Mak. "Maybe that will make a separate clue."

"Don't bother," Jan said as she wandered away from the rest of us to go get a better look at Liat's sculptures. "My father tried that. He even paid a cryptologist to look at it once but the guy said there was no discernable pattern. Just random word choices. He's right. I should know. I've been trying to figure it out since I was twelve. If the color of the words means something, then there must be a clue missing."

"Hhmmm," she added sarcastically, "maybe we should check the Poliahu board and see if it's there?"

We ignored her and did it anyway. In the red column was:

By
Pele's patience is now wearing thin
Are at it again!
Where treasure, destiny and Pele's patience is

In the green column was:

Heaven's breath
Black snow
Maui snow found home
Poliahu's house
Pele's volcano
Deep inside
Great pilikia

Everything else was in black.

We tried a ton of word combinations by color to see if there were any hidden clues. Nothing made any sense.

"Okay, let's start at the beginning of the poem. Take it line by line," Kai suggested next.

"Won't get anywhere with that either," Jan predicted. "Liat, your work, I have to admit, it's good. Really good. Way better than those boring canvases you did for the charity auction. You know if you had entered one of these in the Manoa competition a few months ago there's a slight chance you might've beaten me. Why didn't you?" She asked,

215

twirling strands of long blonde hair between her fingers as she continued to peruse the figures.

"You're kidding, right?" Liat answered.

"I would have," retorted Jan.

"Well I'm not you. In fact, I'm kind of amazed at your reaction. Don't you think it's the least bit creepy that these are sculptures of people dying? People we know. I mean, seriously, Jan, that's our art professor choking to death. And that? Apparently that's Melanie's arm."

"So? The sculptures themselves are exquisite. What's creepy is that you knew about this stuff and didn't bother to warn the poor slobs involved. Now that's creepy."

"I…how could I?" Liat stammered, her tone defensive. "I didn't know whose arm that was under the table. We still don't know whose hand that is," she said pointing to the one holding up the martini glass toward the professor. I mean maybe it's Melanie's but we don't know that for sure."

"Maybe," Jan mused. "But that's a pretty good likeness of Mason choking. Not to mention how obvious the ballroom at the Outrigger is. Who knows? If you had opened your mouth and said something you might've saved his life."

"I see it now," Liat admitted. "But I didn't know it before. I swear."

Kai and Mak looked at each other. Jan was obviously trying to get inside Liat's head. Hoping to throw Liat off her game before the final round of competition.

"Focus people," Kai interjected. "Maybe we should go line by line and keep the colors in—

"Looooook. Jan was right!" I shouted, dragging the Poliahu surfboard across the room and dropping it next to Pele's."

"What?" Everybody gathered around.

"Look. The first line of the inscription on Pele's board goes: By heaven's breath came a hail of black snow some say within Pele's domain. So, the word 'by' is in red and the words 'heaven's breath' are in green."

"So?"

"So check out the first board, Pele's Board. The islands are lined up just like they are on the second board. Both have the same colors, same names, right? Except that on the Poliahu board, inside The Big Island, Hawaii, there's a green dot."

"So?"

"So what if the green dot is a place on the island? The word in red 'by' could indicate the island of Hawaii and the green phrase 'heaven's breath' could be the place on the island. There's that place Hama-something or other—anyway it means 'breath of god'. Think about it—by heaven's breath—that could translate to near the breath of god.

"You mean Hamakua?" Asked Mak.

"Yeah, that's it. Hamakua. I read about it when I was researching Poliahu. Hamakua, it's on the big island right? It's on Hawaii."

"She's right," said Kai, comparing the two boards.

"So you think the Maui Snow is somewhere near Hamakua," stated Liat.

"You're gonna need to narrow that down a bit," added Mak. "Hamakua is at least fifty miles long on the North Coast of the island."

"Well let's look at the rest of the poem on the first board. Maybe some of that matches up to the second board too," I suggested.

"Don't get ahead of yourself," Jan cautioned. "Go back to the text of the poem first. Even if Heaven's Breath does indicate Hamakua, and even if we assume that 'hail of black snow' is supposed to mean black diamonds, the next part of the poem basically says that they were pried from the ground in Pele's domain and that the Maui Snow has to be found and returned there. That shoots a big hole in your Hamakua theory. It doesn't make sense because we know that the diamonds, that the Maui Snow, was dug from the ground on Maui. Not Hamakua, not on Hawaii—on Maui."

"Not necessarily true," I countered. "The theory is that black diamonds were formed during the explosion caused by a dying star, right?" Scientists found trace elements of hydrogen and nitrogen inside which is where they get the star theory. So they could have stormed out of the sky and—

"What makes them black?" Mak interrupted.

"Intense pressure from the explosion crushes the carbon into diamonds. They get crushed so fast and hard that dense aggregations of carbon are crushed together. White diamonds have single crystals.

Plus black diamonds have trace elements of hydrogen and nitrogen in them. Diamonds formed on earth don't have that," I explained.

"Who are you, Alex Trebek? What's your point?" Jan grumbled.

"My point is that the poem says, 'a hail of black snow'. When a star explodes the hailstorm that follows would be widespread. Just because they only found diamonds on Maui doesn't mean some weren't imbedded on the island of Hawaii."

Jan pressed her lips together. It was a slight movement, barely perceptible, but it was enough to catch my attention. When she tilted her head and threw a sharp, knowing, glance to someone behind me, I turned around. It was Kai. I felt a thud in my chest. The look he tossed back at her was clouded, unreadable.

"What?" I asked.

"Nothing," Kai answered, averting his gaze. "You make a good point."

"I have a question," Mak said. "Liat, your father, Sam, he was Hawaiian, right?"

"Yes."

"Then how come the only two Hawaiian words on the board, aside from the island names, are kahole and pilikia?"

"How should I know? I was seven when he did this."

But there was something about the expression on her face, something about her words that didn't quite ring true.

"What does kahole mean?" I asked.

"Kahole means rascal," answered Mak.

For a second, Liat's bottom lip edged up towards a smile. Then she noticed that we were staring and self-consciously bit down on it.

I didn't bother asking what pilikia meant because I already knew. Angela used the word repeatedly when she was dying. It's Hawaiian for trouble.

"Okay, so what we know so far is that black diamonds fell in the islands. Definitely on Maui and maybe in Hamakua. We also know that they were pried from the ground by rascals and that they are at it again. Not much to go on. So, let's skip to the next part. Maybe we'll have better luck there."

Pele's patience is now wearing thin.

"I don't know what we're supposed to make of that line since it's doubtful that your father had any control over Pele."

"Control? No," Mak agreed. "But in the legend, when Pele became frustrated at losing the sled race with Poliahu, Pele erupted lava flows in front of Poliahu to try and stop her from winning."

"I say we couch that line and move on," suggested Jan. "Besides, it's the next half of the poem that always intrigued me."

Poliahu's house bears the final secret
But do not seek out of order.
Go first to Pele's volcano
And reach deep inside my daughter.
There you'll discover what Poliahu knows:
Where great treasure lies with destiny
And Pele's patience is Pilikia

"Especially the part that says 'go first to Pele's volcano and reach deep inside my daughter'. The volcano part seems somewhat obvious. Pele is said to rule over Kilauea and Mauna Loa. But what's with the daughter part? Reach deep inside where great treasure lies with destiny. It makes me think of that whole throw a virgin into the volcano to appease the gods, kind of thing. You know, that maybe 'the daughter' was supposed to be a sacrifice. The thing is, aside from suggesting that she reach deep inside, there doesn't seem to be a whole lot of direction as to where she might actually find the diamond. Let's face it, Mauna Loa is big and Kilauea is big and still fiery."

"That's not it," said Mak. "You're too caught up in the legend. It's a lot simpler than that, isn't it Liat? This wasn't a treasure hunt for just anyone. This is a personal note. From a father to his daughter."

"What? No." The thought made Liat uncomfortable and she dismissed it. Fast. But Mak just went ahead and voiced a second thought, one that made her even more uncomfortable.

"Maybe that's what the trances and the artwork are about too," Mak added. "Maybe your father's been trying to tell you something."

"My father's dead," Liat answered. But what Mak said got under her skin.

"So what?" Mak argued. "You didn't just dream this stuff up. It is happening. It's gotta be coming from somewhere."

219

"Come on Liat, quick, off the cuff," Mak snapped his fingers, " Kilauea or Mauna Loa?"

"No! I don't know!"

"Kilauea or Mauna Loa, Kilauea or Mauna Loa," he snapped.

"Mauna Loa!!" Liat responded, her eyes wide as her hand flew to her mouth.

"Well, isn't that interesting," stated Jan.

She looked at Kai again, her gaze a little more discreet this time. I caught it anyway and felt the hairs on the back of my neck go up.

"Just because you used a stupid trick to get me to answer doesn't prove a thing," Liat scoffed. "You have both surfboards. Stop looking at me for answers and concentrate on that."

"She has a point," Jan argued. "Look, if the colors are important then we're still missing something. The words 'Pele's volcano' and 'deep inside' are in green. When you match it up to the islands colored in green, the only choices we have are Kaho'olawe, Ni'ihau, or Maui. Kilauea and Mauna Loa are both on the island of Hawaii. It doesn't make sense."

Jan stretched her arms over her head and let out a yawn. "Let's take a break. I don't know about the rest of you but it's been a long day and I need some rest before the next leg of the competition. I'm gonna head home."

No one answered. Liat was staring hard at Pele's board, alternately running her fingers over the words Pele's volcano and the island of Maui. Her look was more thoughtful than confused though. As if she were seeing something the rest of us couldn't.

Jan stopped yawning and paid attention. After a moment she looked away from Liat's hand and her attention was drawn to Poliahu's board. Suddenly Jan's eyes went wide with recognition. She looked at the rest of us for a second and opened her mouth to say something. Then, just like that, she clamped it shut.

"What?" I wanted to know.

"Nothing," Jan peeped, but her lips had curved into the slightest of smiles.

Liat saw the look on Jan's face too. She stared down at the board again but this time when she raised her head, Liat seemed confused, perplexed. She looked back at Jan again and tried to figure out what it was that Jan thought she saw. But Jan was already half way up the steps by then.

"Did you see her face?" I exclaimed. "Come on people. Jan figured it out. She knows where Pele's volcano is. We should follow her. Fast."

"You'd be wasting your time." Liat's voice was quiet but sure as she continued to study the poem on Pele's board.

Kai threw an anxious glance toward the steps and then made his way over to me.

"I'll take my chances," I responded, meeting Kai half way, thinking that we were on the same wavelength, that we were about to go chase January down and actually go find the Maui Snow. Instead Kai bent his head and caught my lips in a warm kiss. I was surprised. I kissed him back, but I was surprised. After a moment though I came to my senses.

"We should go," I murmured. "Jan...she's getting away."

"Liat doesn't think so," he responded. "Besides, I need to leave. I have to go check in on my dad."

His words were calm but I could feel his agitation.

"And you," he added, dropping another quick kiss on my lips before breaking away. "You should get some rest." Then he turned to Mak. "Can you give Willow a lift back to the hotel?"

"No problem."

"Get some rest. I'll call you later," he promised, dropping one last kiss on the top of my head before taking the stairs, three at a time. An instant later he was gone.

Yeah, that whole rest thing? Not happening. I was waaay too wired for sleep. I looked at Poliahu's board. The islands lined up the same as they did on Pele's board. Again, I read the inscription.

If you've searched the volcano and can't find the gem
Here's one final clue to your hand I will lend.
Search inside the sand and glass of life's tales
Aligned by time these connected secrets unveil
The island first shaped true by Poliahu's board
Her tipped wave now sings the Maui Snow restored.

I read it three more times in quick succession. Frustrated, I turned back to Liat.

"You said it was a waste of time to follow Jan. Why? You saw the way she ran out of here, with that cat-that-swallowed-the-canary grin on her face. Seriously, I half expected to see feathers stuck to her lips. Come on people," I shouted, pacing the floor in front of Mak. "January knows something!"

"Doesn't matter," Liat answered with quiet confidence. "Whatever it is Jan's thinking, she's wrong. Pele's volcano? The one my father is talking about? It's on Maui. At least that's where it was, when I was seven. It's a replica of Haleakala. My Dad sculpted it for a friend of his. We dubbed it Pele's volcano and scratched our initials in it. It was a really fun day," she told us. She paused then quietly added, "It was one of the last things we did together before he died."

I grinned at Liat and raced half way up the steps.

"Come on," I urged, turning back, motioning at Mak and Liat to join me.

"Let's go!"

They looked at each other, then back at me.

"Where?"

"Maui. Where else?"

"What about Kai? He thinks I'm taking you back to the hotel."

"Kai has his dad to deal with. If we find something we'll call him later."

"I don't know," Liat hesitated. "What about Nick? I should get back to the hospital."

I pointed to the sculpture of the surfer Liat had tried to smash.

"One step ahead," I warned. "The Pipeline Masters is just around the corner."

Liat sprinted across the room and by the time her foot hit the bottom step, I knew. She looked up at me with those magnetic brown eyes and right away I knew something had changed.

"It's time to get ahead of this thing," she called over her shoulder to Mak. "Willow's right. So was my mother."

CHAPTER TWENTY EIGHT

January was two minutes from the private hangar when her phone rang. She debated with herself for a second but then hit the end button. A minute later her phone buzzed with a text. Jan sighed. She pulled up to the airport and read it.

Where r u going? Don't even think about lying ...I'm right behind you.

"Damn," she spat. It was Kai. He had figured out where she was headed. Jan was afraid that might happen. It was unfortunate. She hadn't meant to throw him that look back at the Art Barn. It's just that she was so surprised when they saw that green dot on the Poliahu surfboard and zeroed in on the Big Island. It caught her off guard at first and she knew Kai must have been thinking the same thing. The Observatory. Then a few minutes later, she was watching Liat run her fingers over Maui on the other board and all at once it hit her. The poem. The clues. Suddenly she knew something that Kai and the others didn't know. Suddenly Jan knew exactly where to find the Maui Snow. In an hour it would be in her hand. But first she would have to ditch Kai.

Chill. My Pops called. Mtg. him for dinnr on Maui. Call u later.

Jan was lying. Kai knew that the second he read her text. Jan's father didn't call. He never called. The pair rarely ate meals together. Everyone knew that. She wasn't going to Maui either. Kai knew that too. The instant he saw that look on her face Kai knew right where Jan was going.

To the Big Island, to the Observatory up on Mauna Kea. Where he used to take his students to gaze at the stars and planets.

Kai slammed on his breaks and got out of the car. He was too late. With his engine still running, Kai watched from the parking lot as January's plane exited the hangar and sped down the tarmac.

CHAPTER TWENTY NINE

Maui

I handed my credit card to the ticket agent and winced as she rang up three tickets to Maui. After twenty minutes of sitting on the tarmac and about twelve more in the air we landed at the airport. Then we rented a blue VW Jetta, and set out for Lahaina. Lahaina is a neat little fishing town near the water's edge on Maui. In the center of the town there's a three-tiered outdoor shopping square lined with quaint little shops. Pretty, I thought as we raced across the parking lot.

Not so much, I decided a few minutes later as we rounded the third set of concrete stairs. My lungs were struggling. Kai was right. I should have gone back to the hotel. I needed rest. But then there it was, in the middle of the square, sitting atop a three-foot marble base. One perfectly sculptured five-foot miniature of the massive volcano that resides on Maui. Haleakala. Made out of plaster. And sand. And glass. All three of us saw it and thought the same thing. Sam's old artwork bore an amazing resemblance to Liat's current sculptures.

It was after ten by now and the shops were closed. Still it was a beautiful night in paradise; a million stars arched across a black sky, twinkling down on at least a dozen or so tourists who were still milling about the square. Some people had cones, dripping with pineapple ice cream, and they were chatting contentedly as they glanced in the windows of the closed shops. Others leaned on the railing and gazed up, tossing their silent wishes to the stars.

PEGGY FARRELL

Liat focused on the sculpture. She grabbed a white plastic chair from a nearby table and dragged it toward the volcano. Standing on tiptoes she jammed her right arm down the opening at the top. She combed the inside of the volcano with her hand but couldn't reach the bottom.

People were starting to stare. An old security guard sitting on the second tier near the southwest corner of the square crushed out his cigarette, coughed a few times, and then moseyed toward the stairs. He waved up at us, then bellowed a rather stern "Hey!" hoping it might shoo us from the sculpture before he actually had to climb the steps and walk half way across the square just to stop us.

"Hurry up," whispered Mak.

"I can't reach," Liat complained.

"Grab a leg," I told Mak.

Standing on either side of her Mak and I took Liat by the thighs and lifting her off the chair, we tilted her body head first toward the opening.

CHAPTER THIRTY

Big Island, Hawaii

Kai landed in Hilo and rented a car. He looked at his watch. It was nine-thirty. He estimated that it would be eleven o'clock before he reached the Onizuka Center for International Astronomy. Kai was headed for the visitor's center that sits 9000 feet high up on Mauna Kea, where the air is thin and on an average December night it hovers around 25 degrees. At least he wasn't headed up to the main telescopes. Visitors who are permitted access to the main telescopes up near 14,000 feet are required to stop at the lower levels first just to acclimate themselves to the thinning air. Still, by the time he turned down Saddle, which is the narrow winding road that runs between the looming peaks of Mauna Loa and Mauna Kea, it was dark and growing colder by the minute. Kai looked at his watch again and let out a sigh. Jan's plane was small enough to land at the visitor's center rather than the airport. She had a solid hour and fifteen-minute lead.

Dwarfed by thoughts of his astronomy class from two years ago, Kai barely noticed the massive volcanoes as he navigated his way up the slope. Every year he took a small group of his top students for an overnight trip to the Observatory. They couldn't use the main telescopes. Those were all in use. Scientists, even well known scientists had to wait years for a chunk of time on them. But he wanted his students to see the telescopes just the same. To get a feel, first hand, for the kinds of strides being made in understanding the Universe. He wanted them to hear the ideas to see the projects being tested because of the equipment that's based on Mauna Kea. There was a great deal of controversy in Hawaii over having the telescopes on the volcano. Kai understood why people were resistant. Further development, more telescopes, the envelope was always being pushed. At some point enough is enough. Hawaii is such a rare and wonderful gift and he had no wish to see it destroyed. Striking a balance between nature and knowledge isn't always easy but Kai believed it was worth it on both sides of the argument to negotiate some kind of balance. In the meantime he wanted his best students to check it out for themselves so they could make an informed decision about where they fell on the issues. Two years ago that group included five students. Of the five only January was still alive.

That night at the Observatory began like all the others. They ascended to the visitor's center, dropped off their sleeping bags and backpacks, and had dinner. No one ate much. They never did. Excitement and a lack of oxygen can kill any appetite.

After the tour of the large telescopes, after they made their way back down to 9,000 feet, Kai set the students up at the visitor telescopes and left them alone. As Head of Astronomy at the University, Kai was lucky enough to snag a small office at the OCIA two floors up from the cafeteria. Thinking the students were settled, he went to check his e-mails and make a few calls. An hour and a half later Melanie was standing in his doorway.

"They're gone," she cried, "They told me not to worry. Said they'd be back in ten minutes. Ten minutes. Professor it's been forty-five."

"Woah, slow down, Melanie. Who is gone and where did they go?"

"Everybody. They all went. Except for me. It looked…creepy down there and I…I didn't want to go. I told them I would stay back and watch the door," she paused for a second. "In case you came back," she added sheepishly. "But you didn't. Nobody did. And then they never came back either. Kenny, Jan, Alex, and Rachel…they're still down there, Professor. At least I think they are."

Kai got up from his desk.

"Start at the beginning," he told Melanie as he led her into the hallway and down toward the stairwell.

"We were looking through the telescopes outside the cafeteria like you told us to but then Kenny and Jan got bored. They went back to the cafeteria to get something to eat."

"The food stands are closed."

"Exactly," said Melanie. "So right away, Alex follows them in because he has a thing for Jan. Then Rachel drags me with her 'cause she has a thing for Alex."

Kai rolled his eyes.

"I know, right," Mel agreed. "Anyway, by the time me and Rachel get there Kenny is trying to get a pack of mallo cups out of the snack machine for Jan. But they got stuck. Kenny bangs on the glass a couple of times but it doesn't do any good. And then, well, you know Alex. He has to be BMOC, so he shoves Kenny out of the way and starts rocking the candy machine. No luck on setting the mallo cups free but then we hear this loud pop and some sparks from the back of the machine. Turns out Alex managed to unplug it. So next thing you know we're all trying to move the candy machine so Alex can get back there and plug it back in. He figured maybe he could mess with the switches back there and set a bunch of candy free too. We were only able to budge it a few inches from the wall though because there wasn't enough room for all of us to get at it. You see there was this ice-cream freezer smacked right up next to the candy machine. But the freezer was a whole lot smaller than the candy machine so Alex and Kenny decided to move it."

Kai opened the door to the stairwell and stepped aside for Mel to get by. The cafeteria was two flights down.

"Riveting story Melanie but where did everybody go?"

"Well that's when it happened. Kenny's got his back against the freezer and he's shoving it out of the way and the hem of his jeans gets snagged on this rusty nail. Actually, it was pretty funny. Kenny's so skinny and his jeans are always hanging half off his butt and he's shoving the freezer out of the way and all of a sudden he's still moving but his jeans aren't exactly goin' with the flow," Mel giggled. "They were down past his knees before he tripped on them and couldn't go any further."

Kai gave her a look and she continued.

"Okay, so they unhook his jeans but they find out that it's not just a rusty nail. The linoleum around it is peeled up a bit and Kenny's standing on it trying to yank the leg of his jeans free and it feels sort of hollow under his feet. Turns out, the rusty nail is attached to some sort of narrow trap door hidden beneath the linoleum. So Kenny and Alex start peeling up the linoleum. Only they still can't get the trap door open because the candy machine is on the other half of it."

"Mel, what happened after they moved the candy machine out of the way?"

"They opened the trap door and climbed down these steep, narrow steps. It was dark and scary and they must be really way far down Professor because when they didn't come back I started calling their names and nothing, zero—just my own voice echoing back. Wait 'til you see it Professor. I'm not kidding you, it's eerie."

Melanie was right. It was eerie. Kai descended into the dark hole and went in search of his students. After about ten discernable steps that led away from the cafeteria, the dirt flattened into a steep and uneven path that led nearly straight down. Kai followed the path to the bottom and found that it led into a large cave. It was so dark he nearly stepped off the path and into a pool of stagnant water. After that he opened his cell phone to light the way and kept it pointed just a few feet ahead. As he walked, Kai could hear things. Flapping things, high above his head. Probably bats. Still, he had no desire to point the light up there and find out. Kai kept moving. A few minutes later he heard voices.

"What do you people think you're doing?"

Rachel let out a deafening scream as the light from Kai's phone suddenly cast his shadow on the wall of the cave, advancing toward her.

"Jesus, Rachel, shut the hell up," Alex warned. "One scream like that could bring the whole place down."

"One of the many good reasons you have no business being down here," Kai confirmed. "Now move," he demanded, pointing the way back to the surface. "We'll sort this out in the cafeteria."

"We can't go yet Prof. Come here, look at what we found." Alex turned around and headed away from the light of Kai's cell phone and further into the cave.

Jan held a hand up to Kai and then ran after Alex. "It's okay, Prof. Stay here, I'll go get him. It's no big deal," she added. "Really. Just some big stupid bugs."

Once they climbed out of the hole and back into the cafeteria Kai laid into them big time, reminding them that the facility was built atop and along side of volcanoes. Active volcanoes. Messing around underground, no matter how tempting, was just a bad idea. He made them put back the linoleum flooring, as well as the candy machine and the ice-cream freezer.

After they cleaned up, Kai's curiosity got the better of him. He approached Alex to see what they found down there. He was still trying to wrap his brain around the idea that the cave existed so close to such an important facility. Not to mention the idea that someone had installed the trapdoor, and then covered it with linoleum, a candy machine, and a freezer.

"What did you find down there?"

Alex scrunched his shoulders in an overly deep shrug and then ran a hand through his shaggy brown hair.

"Nuthin' much Prof. Just some giant bugs. Roaches I think."

Kai didn't say a word. He just looked sideways at the twenty year old and after a moment, held out his hand. With a guilty grin Alex dug his hands in his pocket and pulled something out. Before showing it to Kai he stole a glance over the Prof's shoulder. Jan was back at the candy machines with Kenny, still trying to shake something loose.

Alex opened his palm and showed Kai three small and very jagged black stones. Despite being caked in mud, their luster was apparent.

"Jan thinks we hit the motherload, that these are black diamonds. Just like the ones they found near the pools on Maui back in the 1800's. We found them in a small cup on top of a workbench that's down there. Jan thinks there's more. She could be right Prof. But I doubt it. We found a bunch of tools and it looks like whoever owned these," he said holding up the stones, "had quite a party chiseling away at those cave walls. Nothing but a bunch of mud and holes left if you ask me."

Kai motioned for Alex to hand over the stones. "Is this it?"

"That's it," Alex lied. Kenny had two and so did Jan. But he wasn't about to rat them out. Kai stared a little harder trying to discern the truth. "Kinda makes you wonder who left those behind. And why," Alex added with a nervous laugh.

"Left what?" Jan came up behind Kai and asked in an innocent voice. Although the look she threw at Alex was anything but innocent.

"These," Kai turned and answered, holding up the stones before stuffing them into his pocket.

"Where are the ones you took?"

Kenny, Jan, and Rachel all denied having any.

"Alright," Kai responded. "This is how it's going to be. You will forget that cave exists. Understand? Don't even think about telling your friends or trying to arrange another expedition. I don't care what you think is down there."

Kai took one look at Jan and Kenny and realized that he might as well be spouting nursery rhymes to a couple of goldfish.

"Besides," he added in an effort to push his point home. "If you try to get down there again, you'll need a jackhammer. It'll be cemented shut tomorrow."

After that Kai went back to his office and made a phone call. Thirty minutes later he returned to the cafeteria and spent the rest of the night with his students. The next night, the entire cafeteria floor was refinished with plain but rather expensive blue Italian tiles, with an extra helping of concrete and new technology tucked discreetly beneath the tiles under the candy machine and freezer.

Kai never discussed the subject with his students again. That is until Kenny, Rachel, and Alex all died during the hiking incident on Mauna Kea and the authorities found two small black diamonds under a pile of clothes.

Kai went straight to January. When he confronted her about the diamonds Jan admitted that they were probably Kenny's but that she had no idea he was carrying them in the pocket of his jeans that day. If she had known Kenny had them, that they were on the ground by the pile of clothes, Jan told Kai that the police would never have gotten hold of them. There was truth and more than a little bitterness in her tone. Kai believed her. Just to be sure though, he went to the cafeteria. The floor was intact. Once again, he let the matter drop.

It was a mistake. With both hands on the wheel of his rental car as he turned into the parking lot at the Onizuka Center, it now occurred to Kai that he should have asked a lot more questions.

Kai put the rental in park and turned off the ignition. On a grassy stretch of ground about three hundred yards past the southwest corner of the parking lot, he spotted January's airplane.

CHAPTER THIRTY ONE

"Well?" Mak asked as he tightened up his grip on Liat's thigh and eyed the slow moving security guard now puffing his way up the concrete steps.

"Find anything yet?"

"About five wads of gum, a pack's worth of used cigarettes, and something latex and sticky that I have no wish to identify." Liat shuddered as she patted the bottom of the volcano with one hand and directed Mak's hand down closer to her knee with the other.

"Hurry up," I warned. "That security guard might be slow but he isn't dead.

As Liat felt around the bottom of the volcano she thought about the last time she'd been to the square. The day Sam had brought her to see his version of the volcano. She remembered how they'd scratched their names into it. She could see him kneeling down next to her, helping her hold the knife as she carved her name under his. Afterwards, he took something out of his pocket and showed it to her. He looked so sad. Liat remembered that look now and the way it made her feel when she was seven. Scared. She'd never seen him look at her like that and she remembered wanting that sad look in his eyes to go away. Just minutes before Liat and her dad had been having so much fun, carving their names. Suddenly Liat's heart began to race. The envelope! Her father was holding an envelope in his hand that day. It was blue and it had Liat's name on it. Again, she remembered the look in his eyes. He showed her the letter. He told her some day it might be important. Then he slid it inside the volcano, in a special place. Just above their names.

"Quick," Liat whispered down to us. "Look for the spot where my name is carved into the side of the sculpture and move me over it."

Mak and I strained our necks in opposite directions.

"This way!" I whispered. We scooted Liat about five inches to my left.

Liat ran her hands along the inside wall and down towards the bottom of the volcano until she felt an open niche. It was tight but she wedged two fingers down into. Sure enough, she felt something and wiggled it out.

"Got it! Quick, put me down!"

The security guard was up on the third tier by now and crossing the square but he was still a good sixty yards away. We dropped Liat to the ground, grinned at each other, and took off.

Back at the car Liat stared at the blue envelope from her father for a moment. Then she ripped it open.

CHAPTER THIRTY TWO

The cafeteria was undisturbed. Even in the dark, Kai could tell that no one had been there. Just to be sure though he turned on the lights and made his way to the candy machines. Not that January would ever have been able to move them. Not by herself. Still he had to check. He went to the ice cream freezer and moved it out of the way. The blue tile floor was completely intact. He checked the hallway, the bathrooms, and then his office. January was nowhere to be found. Kai made his way back outside.

The plane was empty but the cockpit door had been left open. There was a line of flattened grass in front of it. Something heavy had been dragged away from the plane. Kai followed the indentation into a densely wooded area.

Despite the few feet of vision afforded by his flashlight Kai was walking so fast he nearly fell straight down into the cave. His left foot buckled as the grass underneath it began to give way. Jumping back, he shone the light at the ground by his foot. Just in front of him was a perfect hole, nearly four feet in diameter. On the other side of it was a thick, perfectly round clump of grass nearly the same size. It looked like an exact fit to cover the hole. Kai went around and kicked it. Something hard but lightweight was tucked inside the grassy lid. Titanium. He dropped to his knees and held the flashlight into the hole. Steps. Neatly made steps. As far down as the light could show.

A few minutes later the steps ended and the narrow path ahead of him opened up into a spacious cave. The same one Melanie had alerted him to several years ago. From his starting position in the woods and judging by the shape of the cave, Kai figured he was still a good three or four hundred yards from the part that lay underneath the cafeteria. He stopped for a second to listen.

Every few seconds there came a rhythmic thwap reverberating off the cavern walls.

"January," Kai whispered to himself. "What in god's name are you up to?" He wondered out loud. Kai pulled the flashlight in close to create a tighter circle of light. With a grimace he forged ahead.

CHAPTER THIRTY THREE

Liat ripped open the envelope with shaking fingers. Mak and I read over her shoulder.

Dear Liat,

I love you with all of my heart and hope this letter finds you well. Unfortunately, if you are reading this note I can only assume that the latest visions I've had are coming to pass. It means that I've failed. That the task rests now with you and your friends.

Let me explain what I can. A year before I wrote this letter I began having visions of a terrible wave that would wash over the islands, leaving water as high as the peaks of Haleakala. I saw you Liat, my beautiful girl, on the beach building sandcastles. Near your hand was the great black diamond, the Maui Snow. Off in the distance I could see a tsunami rolling toward you.

At night in my dreams the snow goddess Poliahu would come to me. She said that Pele was very angry because the Maui Snow had been stolen from her. Then Poliahu flew me to a cave on Mauna Kea. Hidden inside were more black diamonds, one even greater in size than the Maui Snow. Poliahu was crying. I remember the tears, frozen to her cheeks, like tiny gems. Someone was in the cave tearing away at the walls, trying to take the diamonds. I recognized him. Poliahu begged me to stop him before Pele got wind of the diamonds and the thief. Poliahu warned that in her anger, Pele would devastate Hawaii. To appease Pele, she insisted that I take the Maui Snow as fast as possible and return it to the ocean near Maui.

I was haunted by these dreams but did not know what to do. Then one night Poliahu came to me and warned that time was running out. In the dream she had me shape two surfboards from koa wood and inscribe them. The very next day the curator of the museum approached me and asked me if I could shape some old fashioned surfboards made of koa wood for him. He looked as though he hadn't slept in weeks. He handed me two large planks of koa wood. Frightened by the connection to my dreams I decided to make them and see what happened. I made them exactly as Poliahu had directed.

The next night I went to the observatory on Mauna Kea. The cave was real. Even worse, I found someone inside digging for those diamonds. I tried to get him to stop. I told him of my dreams. I warned him of Pele's wrath and of Poliahu's dire predictions. He laughed. Nothing I did could make him stop. Dejected, I climbed out of the cave. As I walked away, I could feel the ground beneath my feet shake. The dreams got stronger after that. They always ended with you Liat. Always you. Standing on the beach with that awful wave speeding toward you.

I can't let that happen. Tomorrow I will take the Maui Snow from the museum and at Poliahu's direction will return it to its rightful place in the Pacific. After making this decision I fell asleep and had a different dream. You were grown. It gave me such joy to see you, and to know that that awful wave did not claim you as a child. For that reason alone I will follow through with my plan. Liat, in the dream you had good friends close by but enemies too close for comfort. I saw you reading this letter from me. If I am not successful, if time runs out before I can find a way to return the Maui Snow to its rightful position, then Poliahu has shown me the safest place to hide it until you are grown. If that has come to pass, if you are reading this letter, then heed what I tell you next.

First you must go to the observatory on Mauna Kea to the Onizuka Center. Leave the parking lot at the Southwest corner and enter the woods. The ground will be disturbed. About three hundred feet in you will find a man made opening to the cave. Inside, the kolohe will once again be destroying the cave and risking Pele's wrath. Stop them. Stop them or Pele will. The task will not be easy. But much life will be lost if you don't try.

Once you have stopped the kolohe then you must find and return the Maui Snow. Put the surfboards together. Compare the shapes and colors. Poliahu's shape is true. But Pele's color matters too. Liat, the answer is within your reach. Clear your mind and allow your work to connect. Put yourself inside of it. The surfer within will guide you to the Maui Snow.

Go now and Godspeed.

Love,

Daddy

Liat lowered the letter to her lap and stared through the windshield of the car for a moment. Then she looked down at the letter again but didn't say a word.

"You okay?"

Liat nodded yes but she looked a bit shell shocked. Mak and I looked at each other, wondering what to say next.

"You know," Liat finally whispered, as she slid a hand through her straight dark hair and let out a weary sigh. "I grew up thinking my dad was a jewel thief. It hurt. It just never really fit. Not with the dad I remembered. Still, it's weird to finally know what he was thinking all those years ago."

Mak gave her shoulder a comforting squeeze. "It's late. Let's see if we can catch a flight back to Oahu. We'll show this to Kai tomorrow. See if we can make more sense of it then."

Mak rubbed his eyes. "Besides," he added, "Pipe is coming up fast. I don't know about you Liat, but I plan on winning the title. When the contest is over we can all go back to the University and take another look at your artwork. I'm sure we can shake something loose."

"No way!" I argued, suddenly feeling an odd sense of momentum brewing inside. Things were starting to fall into place. Events were beginning to unravel. Backing off now was not an option.

"We should go to the Big Island. Now. That's what Sam said in the letter. We need to go check out that cave."

Hmmmmmm…a dark cave. Dark caves do come in handy.

"Willow's right," Liat chimed in. "The letter says to find the cave first."

I pressed a palm to my forehead and squeezed. That voice. That awful voice.

"Headache?" Liat guessed.

"I'm fine," I answered, brushing off her concerns. Too bad I couldn't brush off my own.

"Let's go." I put the keys in the ignition and started the rental. But before I could put the blue VW into reverse Mak reached over from the back seat and shut off the engine.

"Wait a sec."

"Liat you can't be serious about traipsing up Mauna Kea at this hour. Your father wrote this letter years ago. What exactly do you think you're going to find tonight? Kolohe?" He snickered.

Liat's eyes narrowed. "Actually, Mak, there's only one family I remember my father calling kolohe...rascals...pretty much on a regular basis. Jan Pokani's."

With that, Liat reached across to the driver's seat and turned over the ignition.

"To the airport," she demanded.

In the backseat Makani put a palm to his own forehead. As we sped out of the parking lot, he flipped open his cell phone and sent a text. To Alfred Pokani.

CHAPTER THIRTY FOUR

Years ago, near the center of the cave and somewhere up along the north side, a long panel of heavy linen had been nailed to the wall. On the left of the material someone had created a chart of the cave. It was marked off into thirteen sections. The number of diamonds that had been found in each section was marked next to it. There were eleven in all. Places where the search had been completed were x-ed out. All thirteen sections had been x-ed out. Twice.

On the right side of the panel was a large hand drawn map of Maui. Inside the map someone had doodled an amusing version of Haleakala complete with what appeared to be a plank of virgins being tossed one by one into the volcano.

Directly underneath the chart was a makeshift workstation. Someone had put a long metal table there and then piled tools, rags, and an old Coleman cooler up on top of it.

Thwap…thwap…thwap.

Kai followed the rhythmic sounds. They were coming from the middle of the cave, up along the north side.

Thwap…thwap…thwap.

As he moved closer to the sound, Kai kicked something. He pointed the flashlight toward his right foot and found an old bottle of Pabst Blue Ribbon. He panned the light farther out and spotted the open cooler turned on its side. Bottles of beer were strewn all across the damp cave floor. Ten steps later he saw the table. It was yanked away from the wall and overturned. The chart was ripped from the wall too. It was hanging now from the top left corner by a single nail. Behind the spot where the chart used to hang, there was a large, gaping, hole in the cave wall. From what Kai could tell, a good ten feet deep and eight feet high of the original wall had been hacked away.

Jan stood inside the hole, nine feet in, all the way toward the back of the hole. She had an axe raised over her right shoulder. With a tiny grunt she let loose a mad power swing and crashed the weapon into the back wall of the hole. Thwap... With the smooth motions of an expert she disengaged the axe, thrust it over her shoulder, and swung again.

"January! Stop!!"

Kai came up behind her in an effort to snag hold of the axe. All he got was a woosh of dank cave air up his nose as Jan finished her swing. Kai backed out of the way. Thwap...another cut fell deep into the wall.

"Stop!"

Jan lifted the axe from the wall and turned.

"Crap. I thought I ditched you at the airport. I knew you'd come here eventually, but I figured you'd wait until morning." She sighed. "I was hoping to be long gone. Whatever. Doesn't matter," she suddenly grinned. "It's here Kai."

"Woah. Take it easy Jan. Let me give you a hand with that." Kai moved forward, motioning for her to hand over the axe.

Jan turned and swung it between them instead.

"Back up, Kai. I found it. It's mine."

Kai inched away.

"Okay. Alright. But tell me," he said, trying to distract her from the axe, "What made you come here? You knew I had the cafeteria entrance blocked solid two years ago. How did you even know about the one in the woods?"

"I could ask you the same thing Professor."

"Come on, Jan," he cajoled. "You saw something back at the University and bolted. What was it?"

Jan lowered the axe, resting the metal tip on the floor of the cave and leaned both hands on the wood.

"Okay, but you first. Does anybody else know where we are?"

"No. Not yet. Now give."

"Alright. So we figured out that 'breath of God' probably means Hamakua, right? Hamakua is on Mauna Kea. So right away I thought about the cave. I know you did to Kai 'cause I saw the look on your face. But then I dismissed it because the colors didn't link up. 'Breath of god' was in green, remember? So if the color was a link to the location that meant it had to be either on the island of Kaho'olawe, Ni'ihau, or Maui. Not here on the Big Island. Besides, Alex, Kenny, and I, mined this place two years ago," she admitted. "Turns out, the chart was accurate. The only diamonds we ever discovered were those couple of little ones sitting in the bottom of that coffee mug we found on the first night, just before you dragged us out of here."

"Still, you must've seen something tonight that changed your mind. And what do you mean you and Alex, and Kenny mined this place two years ago? I had the entrance to the cafeteria blocked the next day."

"Come on Kai," Jan snorted. "You didn't think that was going to stop us did you? We found diamonds down there, puny ones but still. Besides, it's a natural cave. We knew there had to be another entrance. Found a good one too. The thing is someone put a lot of effort into those steps before we got there. Not to mention the grass covered lid. I always wondered about that. Figured some night we might even run into the previous diggers."

Kai hadn't known about the entrance from the woods. Still, he had a pretty good idea who was responsible. But that didn't answer the question he really wanted answered.

"You said you mined the cave for two years, but there were no diamonds down here. What changed your mind tonight?"

Jan smiled.

"Okay, so when we were back at the University staring at the poem trying to make sense out of it I noticed that Liat kept fingering the island of Maui. All of a sudden it hits me. I remembered the chart on the wall, the one with the map of Maui next to it and the crazy volcano with the plank of virgins drawn on it. Suddenly the clue fit. The colors link up. The island *is* Maui. It's just the map of Maui stashed neatly inside the Big Island. And the beauty of it is no one except me, and well, now you, will ever figure that out."

"Look." Jan leaned the axe against the wall and pulled the linen panel taut across the hole so she could show it to Kai.

"You know," she said, letting the old chart fall loose again, "we dug at this cave from one end to the other. Night after night we sat right here eating sooty burgers and fries and never once did it occur to any of us to move the table and take down the chart to look behind it. It was just a workstation. Today, when all the clues lined up, it hit me. I just knew. I couldn't wait to get out here and see what I could find. When I saw the hole I got all excited. I thought finally, I found the place where Sam Kawa had hidden the Maui Snow.

"So where is it?"

Jan let out a laugh. "I have no idea."

"What?"

"I was so excited when I pulled away the chart and found the hole. It was like I'd found Sam Kawa's secret chamber. Only it was just an empty hole. No Maui Snow. I couldn't believe it. I was miserable when I realized it was empty. I thought somebody else had gotten here ahead of me and taken the diamond. I kicked the walls a few times and then kind of collapsed on the floor. That's when I saw it. At the back of the crater."

She pointed to the spot at the back of the crater where someone else, long before Jan, had methodically hacked away at a big chunk of the wall. Kai looked closer and saw that there was a giant rock sticking out, at least a good twenty inches, both around and away, from the rest of the wall. Someone had smeared a layer of mud over it but with the flashlight Kai could still see glints of smooth brilliant black.

"Look at it Kai. It's waaaay bigger than the Maui Snow." Jan flashed him an ear-to-ear grin. Then she picked up the axe and swung it at the back of the crater once again. Thwap...

"Jan stop! This is crazy. We're in a cave. On a volcano!"

"Don't be so melodramatic Kai. There's no danger on Mauna Kea."

"How can you say there's no danger? Kilauea is only about thirty miles from here and still dumping lava into the ocean every day. The caves, the volcanoes, don't you get it Jan? Everything's connected. Think about the lava pipes. They're all over the place, and they're fragile. Bang too hard on the wrong part of this cave and God knows what you might disturb."

Jan shot him a dark look. Then took another swing.

"I'm not stopping Kai. This is big. I've been trying to figure out that damned poem, to find the Maui Snow, since I was twelve. My father? He caught me in his office once trying to copy it down. Man, he got so mad. He was ranting like a lunatic and then he tore it up. All I wanted to do was find it for him. It was so important to him. More important than...anything."

"Jan—

"I was only trying to help," she said, emotions getting the better of her as she took another swing. "I wanted to find the treasure so that I could give it to him for his birthday. But he was so angry. Told me to stay out of his business. Called me a stupid little girl who needed to learn her place."

"I'm so sorry. But Jan—

Thwap...thwap...

"Don't be." She frowned. I don't take that crap from anybody. I told the old man right then and there that I was smarter than he was and that I would find the Maui Snow first. I told him that if he wasn't nicer to me that I would keep it for my own birthday present. I swear the old man aged ten years right there on the spot."

thwap...

"I wouldn't though. I always intended to give it to my dad. The Maui Snow is the only thing I was ever sure he really wanted."

...thwunk.

"Jan, come..." Kai tried to stop her again but then halted mid sentence. Jan wasn't paying attention to him anyway. They both heard that funny sound. The one the axe made when it hit the wall.

Jan was already pulling out the axe. She laid it on the ground and brushed dirt away from the back of the rock. It was looser, but the back of it was still encased in the cave wall. The rock was dark, and big. A lot bigger than it first looked. Jan brushed away some of the mud along the wall and new bits of luster shone through. From what they could see it was about twenty times the size of the Maui Snow. From what they could see. There was no telling how much deeper this gem was imbedded into the cave.

Jan grabbed onto the diamond with both hands and tried to pry it loose. No luck. She cleared away more dirt with her hands and tried again. The rock wouldn't budge.

Jan sighed. Then reached for the axe.

Kai was close enough to stop her this time. He grabbed her by the waist and backed her away from the axe. January didn't take that too well. She knocked the breath out of him with an elbow to the stomach and then ground her heel into the top of his right foot. Kai was winded but he held on. Annoyed, Jan twisted her body as far around as Kai's grip would allow and gifted him with a left knee to the groin. In the space of a nanosecond, Kai's hands dropped from her waist, to his junk. It was a nasty shot, but Jan was fueled with adrenalin. She had invested too much of herself in this search over the years. Stopping was not an option. Kai groaned in pain. Jan ducked away and clutched at the axe.

She got in three more swings before Kai recovered enough to stop her. This time he threw the axe to the ground and stepped on it. Grabbing Jan by the forearms he backed her into the wall and held her in place, trying to reason with her.

"Get away from her!"

January's face lit up as she looked over Kai's shoulder.

"Daddy? Daddy you're here!"

"Come out of there," he told January. "Where's the Pele board? I know you took it from my office."

"But I did it Daddy. I finally found it!"

"You found the Maui Snow! Down here?" The old man sounded surprised but there was also a note of pure relief in his voice.

"Not the Maui Snow. Not yet. But I found another diamond, Daddy. This one is so big you won't believe it."

Alfred Pokani looked past his daughter and into the crater. He saw the myriad of fresh cuts axed into the wall around the old black rock and blanched. His daughter had made a great deal of progress on the diamond since he had left it all those years ago.

Pokani had been as determined as January to free the diamond from the wall back then. In fact, when Sam Kawa showed up and tried to convince him to stop, Pokani had laughed at him. But then Kawa left and the cave shook. Hard. When Pokani went home that night, the dreams began. Pokani looked around the cave now and shuddered. He looked in at the loose chunk of diamond, then back at his daughter, and nearly crumpled in on himself.

"You stupid, willful, child." Pokani railed.

"Why did you come here? I told you this was none of your business…I told you," he crooned.

Kai loosened his grip on Jan.

"But daddy, it's for you. I did it for you." January ran toward her father. "So you can be happy."

Pokani stiffened when she touched his shoulder.

"Daddy?" "Please," she choked.

Pokani wasn't listening. He stared past her at the crater. Then he turned away and staggered toward one of the chairs. January traipsed after him like a puppy in search of a treat. Kai watched the display dumbfounded. He was still trying to grasp Alfred Pokani's sudden appearance when he noticed the rest of us standing nearby watching the pair as well. January's meltdown into toddler-hood was hard to fathom. Angela's daughter had always seemed so tough minded.

"Mak, Willow, Liat. What are you doing here? Who brought Alfred Pokani?"

"That would be me," Mak answered. "We needed a fast ride to the Big Island. Me and Pokani? Well, we don't advertise it, but we go way back. I knew he could arrange it. He went ballistic though when he heard about the letter from Liat's father and found out where we were going. He insisted on flying us himself."

"Nevermind. I guess it's good he's here. For a second there I thought Jan was going to bring the whole place down."

Nobody said a word. We were all staring at the hole.

"How did you find us?" Kai asked.

"Better question. What are you doing here? I thought you went to check up on your dad. Instead you're here. With Jan." I tried to cover the edge in my tone with a joke. "You got some 'splainin to do Lucy." Okay, so I didn't say it was a good joke.

"Start with that," Mak suggested, pointing at the axe.

"Or that," added Liat, pointing to the twenty or so inches of rock sticking out of the hacked up wall.

Mak and I both moved into the crater for a closer look.

"Look at this thing," Mak exclaimed. "It's a monster."

"It's a black diamond, right?" I called to Liat as I dug away at the dirt surrounding it. "Just like the one your father described in his letter."

Mak dug his hands in next to mine and tried to help me tug it loose. We were both curious to see how much more of it there was.

All of a sudden Alfred Pokani ran past Kai and entered the crater.

"Stop! Don't touch that!" He wailed at us.

"What letter?" Kai wanted to know.

No one answered. Because the cave, it was shaking…and shaking… and shaking. Several miles below our feet a low-pitched rumbling snaked its way through the earth.

"Ruuuuuuuuun!!!" Pokani yelled.

CHAPTER THIRTY FIVE

Old man Pokani didn't have to bellow twice. Like lightning bugs caught in the jar of a four year old, we scattered, clinging to the shaking walls, we flipped on our flashlights, and crawled our way toward the exit.

We moved as fast as possible toward the steps that led back up into the woods. The entire time, old man Pokani was trying to yell over the noise. "The key, the key! The lunchroom! Stop. The lunchroom... we're going the wrong way...The key! Underneath the freezer...I have a key!!!"

He tried to break loose, tried to run the other way, but Jan and Mak stopped him. Grabbing him by the arms they led the old man through the cave and up the narrow steps with the rest of us. They shouldn't have. Turns out the old man knew what he was babbling about.

Kai tore up the steps and unhinged the lid. With a hand on either side of the opening he hoisted himself onto the forest floor then rolled onto his belly and reached back inside the hole for Alfred Pokani. But the old man wasn't having it. He snatched his arm away and shrank into his daughter.

The rumbling grew stronger. Dirt flew off the steps and walls. Kai reached in and grabbed at Pokani again. Again he broke away.

Mak squeezed past them and climbed out.

"Hold him still!" He ordered January. Then he lay on the ground opposite Kai and stretched his arm down the opening.

"On three," he yelled to Kai. "Grab an arm and pull!"

"One, two, three!"

Pokani's head and shoulders cleared the opening. The old man was still screaming bloody murder, his hands and legs flailing wildly, when the rumbling beneath the cave suddenly morphed to the surface in a violent growl. The ground next to Mak seized, then split apart, leaving a steaming gap nearly three feet wide and a quarter of a mile long. Trees wobbled. Their roots broke free of the earth and trunks crashed into one another like drunken tailgaters.

Both men let go of Pokani's arms as the ground shook. Mak rolled toward the smoldering crack. Grabbing him by the shirt and jeans Kai yanked Mak away from the edge and onto more solid shaky ground. Splayed flat now, feet and fingertips digging into the ground for support, both men watched helplessly as pressure from the quake shoved a steady stream of dirt, rocks, branches, and bugs down into the cave.

By the time the debris started pouring in we were already running. We could hear the walls and those first couple of steps collapsing in and we ran like hell back into the cave. The only thing louder and faster than the earth crunching closed above us, was when Mak and Kai first let go of Alfred Pokani. That old man came screaming down on us like a bowling ball headed for a strike. We all ducked out of the way. Then we gathered him up and took off.

Trapped in a cave. Again. At least there were no sharks. Still, I was trapped in a cave and this time Kai couldn't jump in after me. God must really be trying to tell me something I thought as I ran screaming through the cave like a banshee. Apparently though I was too dense to get the message. I had no clue what God or anyone else expected of me. No clue what had become of my soul or my hands since I threw that grenade at Del. All I had were questions. Then I remembered the Pelican, and smiled. I would ask no questions today.

The bats were going crazy trying to find some place to cling to in the shaking cave. I ducked my head and kept moving until we reached the center, the spot where we first found Kai and Jan. A few seconds later, everything stopped. Alfred Pokani was unconscious, and bleeding pretty badly. The rest of us were banged and bruised. But at least the cave was still.

Jan and Liat propped Pokani up against the wall to check out his injuries. Before they had the chance, an aftershock rolled in and Pokani slid to the ground. When the aftershock subsided Jan freaked. She leaned down over her father and started slapping him in the face.

"Daddy please! Come on daddy. Wake up!"

I pulled her away. Liat did her best to assess his wounds. A broken leg for sure. No x-ray needed considering the unnatural way it was twisted. His face was cut from his forehead to his chin and at the very least we figured he had a concussion.

"You're not helping. You are bleeding, but you're not helping," I told Jan, pointing at the gash on her left arm. "Give Liat a minute. Maybe she can get him to come to. In the meantime let's look for some water. Didn't I see a cooler down here somewhere?"

"Over there," she answered, pointing past the table.

I found the cooler then hunted around on the cave floor nearby but couldn't find anything but beer.

"It'll have to do," I mumbled but Jan wasn't listening. She had wandered toward the open crater and was staring in at the black diamond. It hadn't budged, despite all of the shaking. Jan began pacing in front of the crater. Then she spotted the axe and stopped.

I dropped the can of beer.

"Are you kidding me?" I shouted, body checking Jan and swiping the axe about a heartbeat before she could reach it.

"Hey. Give me that." She charged at me. I pushed back.

"Not on your life. Have you lost your mind?"

Hahahaha…a lot of that going around, Willygirl huh?

"We're trapped in a cave. We just had an earthquake. And you think what? There's nothing better to do so I might as well hack away at that stupid diamond?"

She reached for the axe again. Jan's blue eyes were dead cold as we locked gazes.

"Do not get in my way. You have no idea what I've been through over this diamond."

Something about Jan's words seemed familiar. I could actually feel the sound of her voice tweaking a buried memory. Angela's house! I tried to grasp it, to form a picture but the full memory wouldn't come.

Liat came up behind me and took the axe. She stopped Jan cold.

"Your father's in trouble. You want that diamond so bad?" With a flip of her wrist she threw the axe at Jan's feet. "Go for it. But you'll never make it out of here alive and neither will he."

Liat took a step toward Jan and stared hard at the tall blonde. There was something about her eyes something about the way she was looking at Jan that made the hairs on the back of my neck stand up. Jan must've felt it too. She backed away. She blinked a few times then looked down at the axe. She made no move to pick it up again.

Liat turned and walked away. "I don't know about you two," she added, "but I'm gonna find a way out of here. With or without your help."

"The quake is over. Kai and Mak are probably up there trying to dig us out. Somebody should go check." I turned to head back through the cave. Back the way we came.

"No!"

Old man Pokani's voice was weak but adamant. His eyes fluttered open. With both palms on the cave floor he tried to push himself up to stand. He grimaced in pain and only got about an inch off the ground before flopping back into place.

"Stupid people...should've listened to me. I have a key. The entrance," he huffed, trying to get some oxygen into his lungs, "There's a trap door in the lunchroom. That's the way out. The key...it's in my pocket."

Jan led the way while Liat and I scooped her father up and carried him between us.

The two-story slope that led up into the cafeteria was steep but still intact. I could see the metal panel Pokani spoke of at the top and it looked to be okay. The only way to tell for sure was to climb up and try it.

I held out my hand.

"Give me the key."

About eight steps up I lost my grip and slid to the bottom. The second time I fell in five.

"Oh please, this is pathetic." Jan huffed. "Wait here." She pointed her flashlight off to the right and disappeared into the dark. A few minutes later she came back with an extension ladder.

"Move out of the way," she ordered, dropping the ladder next to the slope.

"Impressive. Got anything else stuffed in your Bat belt?"

"How did you...where did you?" Liat stammered.

"Not me. Kenny. He was such a girl scout. He brought all kinds of crap down here."

At the mention of his name Liat was reminded of the sculpture depicting his death at the hot spring. She felt a rush of guilt at not having warned him.

"Poor Kenny."

A morose giggle escaped Jan's lips. "You have to admit Liat, it is kind of funny. I mean, come on. Kenny? The guy who is prepared for everything ends up dead over a little skinny-dipping."

Liat's jaw dropped. She was about to say something when Alfred Pokani let out a loud groan. His face was pale and sweaty, blood still dripping from the open wound on his cheek. Jan's misplaced laughter squealed to a halt at the sound of her father's pain.

The cave shook with another round of aftershocks. Jan screamed. Liat held onto Mr. Pokani. As the vibrations rolled through the cave I heard a whisper in the back of my head and suddenly I felt a sense of calm. Faith in the waves.

When the cave stopped shaking I went back and found another beer. Between us Liat and I did our best to clean up Jan's and her father's wounds. Aside from clearing away the blood though there wasn't much we could do. Alfred Pokani needed a hospital. Soon. Physically Jan was fine. But she was getting antsy. As soon as we were finished, Jan grabbed the ladder and stuck it back in the ground beneath the cafeteria.

She was half way up when I heard it: the sound of her shoe pressing into the rung. The creaking. Jan took the next step and again...it creaked. I looked up and glanced at her leg, at the back of her shoe. When she stepped toward the next rung the nerve endings in the back of my head exploded. I flashed back to the night Angela and Bill were shot. With rapid-fire precision the images fell into place.

"It was you!" I shouted, suddenly taking the ladder two rungs at a time. "That night at your mother's house. That was you on the stairs January." The pictures in my head continued to flash. "Oh my God! You did it. You shot Bill Priest!"

January let go of the ladder with one hand and turned to see me furiously climbing in her direction.

"You're shaking the ladder. Stop…what are you doing…get off the ladder!"

But I kept on coming.

"Get away from me! Somebody…stop her!" Jan shouted down to Liat and her father. "She's crazy! "Flat out crazy!"

Liat stood up.

Jan glanced up at the panel in the ceiling. There was no way she could get to it and open it before I reached her. So she came at me instead. She stepped down the rungs and the second she was close enough she hauled off and kicked me in the head. It was a nasty whack. She followed up with more of the same. I held onto the rung with both hands, swinging from side to side, ducking my head out of the way. Then she aimed the blows at my arms and shoulders. It didn't hurt nearly as much as the shot to my head but her plan was effective. I lost my balance. But Jan, bless her vicious little heart, was still kicking. I latched onto her ankle and gravity did the rest. Pulling, kicking, screaming, we dropped to the floor of the cave.

Liat was on us in a second.

"Shuuuut up! Do not move!" Before we could argue she gripped us each by the hair and had a foot pressed into our backs. Not that it mattered. The fall had taken most of the fight out of both of us.

Most of

"Listen!" Liat commanded. "Can't you hear that? Someone's up there."

The pounding was loud and clear above us. The voices more muffled. But it had to be Mak and Kai. I let out a sigh of relief, despite Liat's foot on my lungs. They were okay. And they were up there trying to get us out.

Liat let go of Jan's hair and snapped her fingers next to the girl's cheek.

"Give me the key."

"You two idiots—stay here—and don't even think about touching each other."

Liat went straight to the top. It took her a few moments to figure out where to put the key. Once she turned it though, the panel slid right open.

Kai and Mak were dumbfounded. They'd already dislodged the freezer, placed it sideways on the floor next to them, and had moved away the candy machine. Most of the tiles were cracked from the earthquake, and they were getting ready to take a sledgehammer to the cement when the panel slid open and Liat appeared.

"Liat! Thank God," Mak breathed.

"You're alright?" Kai asked as he leaned in over Mak. "What about the others?"

"We're all okay. Except for Mr. Pokani. He's in bad shape. He needs a hospital. Fast."

Liat put a foot up into the cafeteria. Mak stretched a hand down to help her up. It wasn't far or fast enough to beat the next aftershock. The initial quake clocked in at 5.6 on the Richter scale. The latest aftershock was a 5.3. Liat lost her footing and tumbled backwards into the cave. She tried to grab at the ladder for support but her body was moving too fast. All she managed to do was rip her hands against the middle rungs of the ladder before crashing to the ground and smacking the back of her head. Hard.

Up in the cafeteria, the freezer shimmied toward the opening then rolled over and was wedged in tight against the dirt and tiles. The lid fell open. Choco tacos, Creamsicles, ice-cream sandwiches, and one frozen mouse, showered into the cave.

Liat was knocked unconscious from the fall. Alfred Pokani's eyes fluttered open for a second but then slammed shut again as his battered body absorbed the vibrations of yet another aftershock. Thirty eight seconds later everything stopped.

Jan and I sat up and looked at each other. Neither of us said a word at first. We were both too busy listening. But there was total silence from above.

"Kai! Mak! Can you hear me? Are you up there?" January shouted at the top of her lungs.

Nothing.

"Kai! Mak!!!" She shouted again. Again, there was no answer.

I steadied myself against the cave floor and got to my feet. I went to Liat first. She was still breathing. Nothing seemed to be broken and it didn't look like she was bleeding. But there was a big fat bump on the back of her head. I tapped her on the cheek and tried to wake her. No response. Liat was out cold. I felt a pulse but didn't know how to gage its strength. Not knowing what else to do for her, I went and grabbed a couple of Popsicles and laid them under her head to stop the swelling. While I was tending to Liat January picked up the ladder and turned it upright. It was useless. She turned in my direction and shook her head.

"I'm going to die down here."

I didn't answer. I turned back to Liat and brushed the hair from her silent eyes. That's when January really freaked out. As if it had suddenly dawned on her that yes, we really were in trouble down here.

"Oh my God. I am. I'm going to die down here." Then she started jumping up and down, yelling and screaming.

"Mak! Kai! Help! Help me!" She wailed. "Maaaaak!! Kaiiiiii!!! Hurry! Oh God. Get me out of here!"

"Holy shit stop shouting. You'll bring the whole place down."

Someone had to calm her down

"Shhhhh....come on it's okay. It's okay, don't worry...sshhhhh," I crooned. Just like I did that night with her mother.

"Sshhhh...we'll be fine...we'll be fine...we'll be fine. There's nothing to worry about."

Nothing?

"You're crazy," she shouted, breaking away from me.

"Oh god, Liat's dead. My father's dying. Mak and Kai–they're probably dead now too. I need to get out of heeeeeeeere!" She shouted, continuing to back away from me.

I have to admit I never expected January to get so hysterical. I let out a deep sigh. Then bent down and picked a few ice cream bars up off the cave floor.

"Look on the bright side," I said, stepping toward her, tossing her a choco taco. "At least you won't starve to death." I unwrapped one for myself and took a nice big bite.

"Mmmmm. Melty, but delicious."

She held the ice cream in her hands and stared at me with that look. I didn't care. Because for the first time since Angela's death I knew for certain that I was not crazy.

Really? Hellllo, 'cause there's a second opinion in here. Hellllo! Knock, knock, knock, Willygirl, are you listening? Can anyone hear me?

256

I knew it for sure.

"Liat isn't dead," I said, taking another bite. "Neither are Mak and Kai. We're still alive. So are they. The aftershocks are bound to stop soon. They'll dig us out. And when they do," I promised in an upbeat tone as I took another step toward her. "You're going to pay. For what you did to Bill. For what you did to your mother. For what you did to me. I'm going to make sure of that."

Jan was pacing back and forth in front of the broken ladder. I took a few steps closer. Jan stopped dead and spun around to face me.

"You see Jan, I remember everything now."

She looked at me, her head bent sideways. As if I weren't making any sense.

"That night at your mother's house. I was coming up the walkway and I heard arguing. I looked in the window and saw you standing in the living room. You had a gun. Pointed at your mother."

"I don't know what you're talking about," Jan stammered. "You really have gone off the deep end. Back up...leave me alone," she cried, throwing the ice cream in my direction. "Mak!! Kai!"

"Bill saw you too," I went on, ducking to the right of the flying choco taco. "He came in from the dining room. Saw you shouting at Angela. Waving that gun in her face. Right away he pulled open the drawer to the hutch and took out the matching pistol. He screamed at you to to drop it. Screamed at you to get out. To get away from Angela. But you didn't listen. You just wouldn't listen. Why January?" I asked, putting a hand up to my throbbing temple.

"Why didn't you just put down that stupid pistol and go? Everything...everything could be so different."

Everything?

"Instead you had to go and cock it."

I swallowed hard at the memory. Fought back the lump in my throat.

"Bill had a clean shot. You were just far enough away from Angela to give him a clean shot," I said, moving a step closer.

"But I saw that look on Angela's face when Bill aimed the pistol. I was standing outside the window and I saw it. Right away I knew what she was going to do."

"No!" January cried as I took another step toward her. "You're wrong. I was never there. I never left Hawaii!"

I let out a bitter laugh. "That's what did me in you know. Probably why I had the flashback. Why I blocked the whole thing out in the first place. Seeing that familiar protect-at-all-costs scowl on Angela's face. I saw it every time she went to bat for me. Every day that she brought coffee and sat by my bed in that hospital. As soon as Bill pulled the trigger I knew what was coming. But I couldn't get there. Not fast enough. The thing is, Bill should have known it to."

I heard the accusation in my tone and was surprised. I couldn't really blame Bill, could I? He was just in the wrong place at the wrong time. With a gun in his hand...

"That stupid, stupid man," Jan said, her tone oddly quiet. The vehement denials of a moment before seemed to have physically drained from her body.

"He ruined everything," she said, squaring her shoulders and staring me in the eye as she spoke. "I wasn't going to shoot her you know. I just wanted the surfboard. I wanted to find the Maui Snow. My father's birthday was coming up and that woman owed me!"

"How did you even know she had it?"

Jan flashed a half-hearted grin. "What? You think you're the only one with a memory?"

She took a step back.

"About a month ago I was sitting in my father's office, staring at Pele's board and getting frustrated. My mind wandered and I started thinking about my mother. About the day she left me. Then something about the edge of Pele's board, the cut, the color, I don't know, but something clicked. I remembered the day my mother left. How she was pushing me toward the car. I didn't want to go to my father's so I sat on the curb and cried. She ignored me. She put her suitcase in the trunk. She tied her surfboards to the top of the car. One fell off. So did the cover. My mother let out a stream of curses and picked it up. Then she slid the cover back on, and tied it on top of the others."

Jan looked at me and in a bitter voice said, "I've thought about that day, the day my Mom left, about a million times since I was a kid. But I never thought twice about that surfboard. Everybody has surfboards

258

in Hawaii. It just never occurred to me before a month ago that my mother might have Sam Kawa's other board."

"So, what? No phone calls? You just hop a plane to Philly and go get it?"

"Pretty much. Besides, everybody else was soooo busy searching for Liat that night." She shrugged. "I got bored. I dropped a couple of people off on Maui to look for her and since I was already at the airport, I don't know...I just decided to go. At first I was just going to fly to San Francisco. Try and stir up some fun. But on the ride over I got to thinking about my dad and about the Maui Snow...and I don't know. I just decided to fly to Philadelphia and find out if I was right about my Mother having that surfboard. Funny thing is, I never expected a fight. I honestly thought she would give me the surfboard. She owed me. I thought she would give me the board and I would have a great birthday present for my dad. But she freaked out when she realized that I knew about the surfboard. She warned me to stay out of it, to stay away from the Maui Snow. She even opened the end table to get out the pistol but I reached in and got to it first. I told her she was crazy and that there was no way I was leaving Philadelphia without that surfboard. Honestly though I had everything under control. It all would've worked out fine if that idiot Bill hadn't gotten in the way."

"You invaded his home. Waved a gun at his wife. When he told you to get out you pointed it at her and cocked it. Bill was trying to protect his wife. He just didn't count on Angela stepping in front of a bullet to protect you."

"She was the worst kind of mother." There were traces of disdain along with great sadness in January's voice but no remorse. "She owed me."

"So why shoot Bill? Your mother was bleeding all over the floor. The man was devastated. The gun was down. He wasn't going to harm you."

"Wasn't going to harm me? He took my mother when I was a kid. Besides, let's not forget...Bill shot at me first. Afterwards," she added, in a rather matter of fact tone, "I wiped off the gun, put it in mother's hand and shot it again."

Jan smiled. "She helped me you know. Mother did her best to grip it even though she knew I was making sure that she was the one who would get blamed. Afterwards, all I wanted to do was get the surfboard and get the hell out of there. But then you came barreling through the door, screaming mother's name."

"I remember your foot on the steps," I said, the image coming into focus, "disappearing onto the second floor. You killed that poor sweet man in cold blood and then took off."

"Cold blood? Self defense?" Jan held her palms open and pretended to weigh the two.

"Yeah, well the police won't see it that way. You broke into Bill's house. Pulled a gun on your mother and then shot him dead. They have a witness who can testify now. I remember everything."

"Oh please," January laughed. "The police think you're involved. Don't bother denying it," she said, gauging the look on my face. "I checked the text messages on your phone. That Harry of yours is a real hoot. Smart too. I do have to agree with him about the ex-hubby. By the way does Kai know you're still carrying a torch for the ex? Does he know that if—what was it Harry called her? Pink and Preggers, that's it. Does Kai know that if Pink and Preggers hadn't come along and spoiled things for you and Shane that—

"Shut up. That's none of your business," I warned.

"Oh and for the record? I didn't break in. Mother opened the door. We even had a nice little chat before Bill came in and things went south. It was all about you, come to think of it. It seems she wanted me to calm down, stop all the loud fussing. She said you were on your way over. Yep, she told me all about her poor little war boggled friend. Said you were fragile and that she didn't want any arguing in front of you. Later on, when you showed up in Hawaii, I did some checking. Turns out that Mommy dearest was right to be concerned. Mmmm mm mmm," Jan shook her head. "I hear those flashbacks are a real bitch. Nothing a few months at Mother's garden spa won't fix though, right? So you go ahead, Willow. Call the police. Change your story. Tell them what you 'suddenly' remembered. I'll take my chances."

Shame rushed through me. My face and chest flamed with it, my knees buckled. I was mortified because she was right. I would not be believed. January had murdered Bill. And yet I was mortified. I knew there was something inherently wrong with the way I felt and yet my reaction stood solid. I was filled with shame and at that moment I wanted nothing more than to hide somewhere and scream it out of me.

January laughed. Now that she had the upper hand she couldn't help herself. She was right about the police. She was right about me. And she knew it. I sighed and then out of nowhere the thought brushed past my ears once again…faith inside the waves.

"The flight. There has to be a record of your flight to Philadelphia," I said, even though I knew I'd already checked.

"Daddy took care of that," she smirked. "You see he does love me. I'm his daughter," she said proudly. "He takes care of me. No matter what."

"So that's it? You get away with shooting Bill. And God knows what else."

"That's right," she agreed with a knowing grin. "Even if God knows what else, Daddy takes care of me."

There was something about her smug reaction. As if there was more to it than shooting Bill.

"January? What else—

Then it hit me. The ballroom. The argument she had with Melanie over the olive.

"Oh man…Melanie? The olive with the diamond in it! You went to get it from her. You did it, didn't you? You're the one who killed Melanie."

Suddenly my thoughts were tumbling all over themselves.

"Holy shit—the Art Professor? Eeeewww and those poor kids in the hot spring? You moved the warning sign! You killed all of them."

"Jeez, I can see why they put you in the loony bin." Jan rolled her eyes. "No, I did not kill Mason. Alcoholism killed Mason. I owed him money and I was trying to pay him back. I stuffed the diamond in the olive as a joke but the stupid twit sucked down his martini so fast I never had the chance to tell him it was in there."

It sounded like she was telling the truth. But Jan never denied moving the sign at the hot spring. Or…

"Melanie," I said with conviction. "You killed her. Why?"

Jan glanced around the cave. Her father was curled up against the wall. Liat was unconscious. The two of us were still trapped.

"Because she knew I put the diamond in the olive. She knew about the cave." Jan sighed with annoyance. "Because Melanie could do what you can't. Prove that I went to Philadelphia."

"Really? How?" I was genuinely surprised at this development.

Jan smiled. "If I told you that then I'd have to kill you."

For the first time since our conversation started, I smiled back.

"That's okay. You're right about the Philly police. Once they find out about my stay in the nuthouse there's no way they'll take my word against yours. But the Honolulu authorities? I doubt they'll turn their noses up at a fresh new DNA sample to test against the stuff they dug out of Melanie's fingertips. So far they've come up empty but I'm guessing you'll be a perfect match. By the way I don't see a mark on you. Where exactly did Mel scratch you?"

Right Willygirl...can't forget the scratches...

All of a sudden January lunged at me. I tried to side step her but she caught me nearly full in the chest. We fell to the ground and before I knew it she had me straddled and was squeezing my throat with both of her hands. I grabbed at her wrists and kicked hard with both my legs but I couldn't get her hands off my neck. She held on. Held me down. Seconds ticked by and I could feel the air melting from my lungs. My body started working overtime as fear steadily replaced the oxygen coursing through my bloodstream. Then all at once I felt a burst of adrenaline and kicked hard at her right side. I kept at it until finally... finally she buckled just the slightest bit. When I felt Jan's body give, I threw my weight in that same direction. Suddenly the two of us were rolling with a vengeance.

Once on top I let go of her wrists even though she was still choking me. I thought I could make her let go but she just wouldn't...she would not let go. So I did what I had to. I leaned in and grabbed at her throat too. I squeezed so hard my fingertips disappeared inside the folds of her skin. But Jan was relentless. She threw her weight and again we started to roll. It went like that, the two of us rolling over each other, flipping back and forth, clutching hard at each other's throats until one of us finally, mercifully, let go.

"Relax. I won't strangle you to death. I just want you to pass out. Then I can hit you with a rock. No one will ever be the wiser. You'll just be one more victim of the earthqua–

Above us a high-pitched sing-y-screechy kind of noise pierced the air. It lasted all of about six seconds. My eyes were closed but it's the kind of sound you can hear real well when an object is getting closer to you. It was kind of a loud shhwwwiiiiiiiiiiiiiiiiing. Followed by a thundering crash.

The ice-cream freezer that was wedged into the ceiling came slamming down onto the cave floor. It bounced a couple of times, spewing dirt and screws and other broken pieces of metal. Then it landed with a thud about an inch from our war locked bodies. Instinct made us both react. The death grip was loosened.

"Watch out!" Kai and Mak shouted down to us.

Gee thanks for the timely warning, I thought. Then I shoved Jan as hard as I could and jumped to my feet.

"Willow? It's Kai. I'm coming down. Is everybody alright?"

Seconds later he dropped a thick rope with a loop tied at the end of it, down through the cafeteria floor. Then he stepped into the loop, grabbed onto the rope, and yelled for Mak to lower him into the cave.

Jan stood just a few feet away, with the broken freezer now between us. I glanced in her direction. She stared back at me. Neither of us spoke a word. That is, until Kai reached the bottom. Right away he ran over to me and tucked me into a warm and comforting bear hug. Jan let out an awful yell and took off. She grabbed onto the rope, stuck her foot into the loop, and shouted up at Mak.

"Get me out of here! Hurry! Mak, Please. Get me out of here now!"

Alarmed, Kai let go of me for a second and stepped toward Jan. Mak poked his head through the floor. "Hurry," she stammered, yanking at the rope.

"Jan, are you okay? Are you hurt? Bleeding?"

January looked down at Kai as Mak pulled her to safety.

"No I'm not okay," she shouted down to him. "Your girlfriend just tried to strangle me. She's certifiable Kai. That psycho needs a straightjacket and another trip to the hospital."

Alarmed, Kai turned back to me. The barest smile was all I could manage. I was spent. Completely exhausted. But for once I wasn't worried. DNA was on my side. At least it would be soon enough. For now though Kai was staring at me. Staring at the nasty bruises on my neck.

"I'll explain later," I promised. My voice was weak and it cracked against my swelling throat. "Right now we need to get Liat and Mr. Pokani to a hospital. Liat hit her head. She has a pulse but she's been unconscious since the last tremor hit.

"I'm fine," Liat said groggily. To prove the point she sat up put a hand to the back of her head and scowled.

The sound of her voice was as much of a surprise to me as the falling freezer was a few minutes ago.

"Liat...you're awake. Are you okay?"

"We better get you to a hospital," Kai said as he bent down to take a look at her head. Liat waved him off.

"Better take Mr. Pokani first. I think he's in pretty bad shape."

There was one more aftershock. So light it was barely noticeable. Still, mud and steaming rock deep below the Kilauea Volcano shifted. Not much, one maybe two quarters of an inch. But it was enough. The extra pressure caused a rift along the bottom of a heavy lava tube. A slow leak of fiery orange earth began to spill into a narrower but much more densely flowing tube. It went from Mauna Kea to Mauna Loa and then on to Kilauea where it stretched for miles out into the Pacific Ocean.

January was gone. By the time Mak pulled the rest of us out of the cave she was long gone. We stumbled out to the edge of the grass because Mak and Kai and Liat were all convinced Jan would be there with the engines running. They had no *real* reason to think otherwise. By the time we got there though there was only one airplane sitting in the grass. I felt pretty bad about it then but as it turns out that was probably the biggest favor January did for me. She left room for doubt. Anyway, to make matters worse, Pokani was the only pilot. Poor guy was barely conscious and in no condition to fly. So Kai put in a call to the small group of staff and scientists working the telescopes up at 14,000 feet. They had three wounded of their own but promised to pick us up when the rescue unit arrived. We waited. Liat, Pokani, and Mak left with the first rescue flight.

Standing in the parking lot of the Observatory I looked out over Mauna Kea and watched the helicopter fly away. The view was nothing short of spectacular. More snow falling on the covered peaks above us.

Clouds loomed over Kilauea to my left. Looking down you could see peaks and slopes leading all the way out toward an expansive ocean. I stood still for a moment and inhaled it. I focused on the compelling beauty and let everything else drift away—the rage the fear the shame the sadness—all of it. Like mist on grass, it settled down and melted from sight.

Eventually, I told Kai about my confrontation with Jan. I started with the flashback of memories. I told him how Bill shot at Jan because he believed it was the only way to protect his wife. How Angela then stepped in front of that bullet to protect her daughter. I told Kai how afterwards January deliberately raised the gun and shot a completely defeated man point blank in the forehead.

After that I told Kai about Melanie. That January was the one who murdered her. When he asked me why, I did my best to explain that Melanie had some sort of evidence that would prove Jan had been at the Priests' house in Philadelphia the night of the murders. When he asked me what, I shrugged. I had no answer. I know how it sounded. Crazy. And it was, all of it. But it was true. It had to be. So then I showed him the bruises on my neck and told Kai how Jan had tried to strangle me. I patiently explained that if the freezer hadn't dropped from the ceiling of the cave when it did, that Jan would most certainly have strangled me until I was dead.

At first, Kai didn't say a word. Then he wrapped me in his arms, rested his chin on my head, and whispered my name over and over again until the helicopter came back for the two of us. His voice sounded so sad, so lonely. Kai loved me. Deeply. I could feel it emanating from every pore in his body. He just didn't quite believe me.

Once aboard the helicopter I pressed my cheek to the window and looked down. Past the icy slopes in search of the ocean and its constant waves. Faith.

CHAPTER THIRTY SIX

North Shore of Oahu

Nick's eyes were closed, his arms taut, his face locked in a sweaty grimace as he lurched forward.

"Come on. One more step. You can do it!" Liat commanded.

He let out a groan, pressed one foot at a time across the last few inches of floor mat, and then fell into his physical therapist's arms. It was his fourth trip across the bars. Nick was making progress. He seemed in a hurry to get his life back.

"Not bad," Mak joked, pointing at Nick's feet. "You know, if we throw a decent board under you and then tape those mangled puppies on tight, you could be back in the waves tomorrow. Really," he teased, "I'm sure nobody will spot the difference in your technique."

Nick wiped his face on a towel and threw it at Mak. It was a good-natured exchange. The animosity brewing between them had all but faded. Separately, and for whatever reasons, each man seemed to have made his peace with the other.

"Speaking of which don't you people have someplace to be?" Nick asked. "Pipe starts in an hour and a half."

"We're going," said Kai. "Heard you were up and moving and just wanted to see the good news for ourselves. You scared us maika`i`ole (bad)."

"Me too," he admitted, blushing under Kai's stern gaze.

We smothered Nick in a round of cautious hugs and headed for the door. Liat held back.

"Nick…" her voice choked up. He took her hand and squeezed it. 'Liat, it's okay. I'm fine baby. I'm fine."

"I'm so sorry." Tears streamed down her cheeks. "They said you were going to be paralyzed."

"Well I'm not. You have nothing to be sorry for. This isn't your fault Liat."

She let go of his hand and brushed at her eyes.

"I'm the one who picked up the surfboard, Liat. I threw it in the ocean. No one forced me. Mak was right. I had no business being in those waves. Truth is I'm lucky as hell to be sitting in this chair. And I know it."

Liat leaned down and brushed his lips with a kiss. In return Nick grasped both of her hands and drew her down next to him on the arm of the chair.

"Mak was right about my surfing. But there's one more thing I need to know, Liat. Was he right about the two of you? I'm in love with you Liat. Mortgage, minivan, ten kids in love with you," he admitted, tugging absently at the ends of her long dark hair. "But I need to know. Are you still in love with Mak? Did you only break up with him because you thought it would keep him from dying?"

"No! No. Maybe. I don't know!" Liat got up from the chair and paced in front of the window. Then she turned back to face Nick.

"Maybe I did break up with Mak because I was afraid for him. But that's not why I fell for you. Mak likes to talk about how connected we are and he's right…sort of. We do share—a connection. Only the thing is, I don't know if it's about love anymore, if there's even a chance we could be together. Mak's meant for someone else. I can't explain it. But that feeling…it gets stronger every day. The same way my feelings for you have…" Liat hesitated, then added "grown."

She let out a small sigh. But to Nick it was huge.

"It's okay Liat. I want you to be honest. I don't want to be with you unless it's real. I want the kind of love you shared with Mak. I deserve that."

Liat tried to say something but the lump in her throat was too big. It didn't matter. The expression on her face said it all.

"It's okay." Nick promised. "I'm okay." He meant it too. Nick looked down at his legs. Then he took Liat's hand in his and squeezed it tight. "I've had time to face some hard truths. I'm a reporter. Surfing is great but it'll always be second for me. That's one truth. Life's too short. That's another. Look, Liat, I want to be happy. I want the same for you."

Nick paused for a second but when he spoke again his voice was strong. Certain.

"I think it's time to call it quits. At least for now." Then rolling his eyes he added, "I can't believe I'm saying this but…what the hell… let's try just being friends. Who knows?" Nick grinned up at her, then pointed down at his body. "A few months without this and you'll come crawling back."

Liat smiled at him but it was laced with sadness. Nick let go of her hand and it fell across his ribs. He winced in pain.

"I'm sorry Nick," she sighed. "I hate those stupid sculptures."

Nick pulled her back onto the arm of the chair. When he looked into her eyes he saw that they were still swimming in doubt. He picked up her hand. He locked his fingers through hers and then reaching up, tapped lightly at her temples. "Get it through your head. You didn't hurt me. You're sculpture had nothing to do with this."

"Maybe," she conceded. "But the men's competition is about to start. When it's over a new Pipe Master will be crowned. I know Pipe is unpredictable and anyone can win it. But let's face it. The odds are pretty good that either Mak or Kai or both will make it to the final. One of them could take a wave and die. How do I stop that before it happens?"

"Maybe you're not supposed to," Nick suggested. "You tried to stop me. Look how well that went." He offered her a lopsided grin. "Liat, people make their own decisions. Sometimes stupid ones like me. But Mak and Kai belong at Pipe. You can't stop them."

"Then why the visions? Why the sculptures in the first place?" She complained. "If I can't warn my friends then what's the point?"

"I don't know." Nick's voice sobered. He thought for a moment, then asked, "what about the Maui Snow? Are you any closer to finding it?"

CHAPTER THIRTY SEVEN

There were tsunami warnings immediately after the earthquake but none materialized. Forty people died and hundreds more were injured. Homes and buildings were damaged too. In the aftermath of it all, Islanders gathered together to share what they had, help where they could, and comfort those in despair. When the earthquake made the news, people from the mainland, and farther, joined in the effort to help. Everyone was grateful. They all agreed. It could have been so much worse.

Underground at Kilauea the heavy lava tube that had been slowly leaking eventually split in half. The front half, suddenly relieved of its source of flowing fire, spun left a good ninety degrees and then smacked into a perpendicular tube, fused with it, and began emptying the tons of lava it still had left, into the newly formed tube. Meanwhile the back half of the broken tube, which originated inland and was the source of the lava flow in the first place, fell smack down on top of the narrower tube it had been leaking into since the quake. The thin top layer of the narrower tube was incinerated and what was once a slow leak branched into a massive flow of lava. The sides of the narrower tube swelled and flowed.

Pressure from the smack down of the tubes also had its effect on a solid wall of earth directly to their right. It cracked for nearly a quarter of a mile and then shifted. Slowly, methodically, the walls on either side of the crack began rubbing against one another. What was once a solid and tranquil mass just a moment in time before were now two competing forces bent on reclaiming the previously shared space. Still comprised of the same basic materials, the two separate walls were infinitesimally close and yet unwilling to peacefully sync movements without the intervention of a greater power. In the absence of such, the earth continued to press in on itself. Meanwhile the two newly altered lava tubes met paths in the shape of a cross about ten miles out into the Pacific.

CHAPTER THIRTY EIGHT

Ehukai Beach on the North Shore of Oahu,
The Pipeline

The swells were thick and nearing four stories by the first heat of the day. Both Pipe and Backdoor were accessible. Kai and Mak were expected to be in separate heats for most of the competition but still the anticipation was palpable. For the overall world championship title, Kai was ahead of Mak by eight points. For the Triple Crown event, each man had already claimed one leg, with Mak winning the first event at Haleiwa's Ali`l Beach and Kai taking the second at Sunset Beach. Everyone, officials and fans alike, were hoping for a spectacular finale. At Pipe anything is possible.

I sat down in the sand next to Liat and handed her a cup of coffee. "Kai's mother sent it from home." I breathed in the warm aroma and let myself relax. "It's so good."

She took the cup and placed it in the sand between us.

"Heard anything from January?" I asked casually.

"Mak saw her for about two minutes at the hospital. She went to see her father. She took off afterwards though and no one has seen her since." Liat hesitated for a second. "Willow, do you really believe that she killed your friend? And Melanie too?"

I looked out at the ocean and didn't answer.

"Kai told me," Liat admitted. "He wanted to know what happened down in the cave between you and January."

271

I shouldn't have been surprised. Kai was fair, and very logical. Gathering as much information as possible made sense. Too bad he was asking others instead of me.

"What did you tell him?"

"The truth. I told him you pulled Jan off the ladder and accused her of killing your friends and that the two of you fought until I made you stop. After that I fell off the ladder and don't remember much."

I sighed. "I guess he went to old man Pokani, too?"

"We both did," Liat answered. "I had some more questions about my father's letter. I thought that since Mr. Pokani really was in the cave all those years ago, that well, he might be able to tell me more. About my father."

"Was he able to tell you anything?"

"You know, all this time I thought Alfred Pokani was searching for treasure. Hunting for the Maui Snow, just like everybody else. A rich old man trying to get richer. It made me sick. But that wasn't it. Well, not in the end, anyway. He *was* mining for diamonds when my father first found him in that cave. In fact, those are the diamonds that he used to build his hotels. But after that night when my father found him there, after the cave shook, he never dug again. Mr. Pokani told me that he started having dreams about his own death right after my father died. He dreamt that if he didn't stop mining the diamonds that he would be trapped in that cave during an earthquake and then dropped down a hole when he tried to escape. That's when he decided to finish what my father started. He thought the only way to prevent it was to find the Maui Snow and return it to the ocean."

"No wonder the old man freaked out when Kai and Mak tried to pull him out," I said.

"Yeah. He was scared to death of that place. Apparently Kai called him a few years ago after Jan and her friends found the cave. Kai knew it was trouble and well, Pokani, is on the board at the Observatory. When Kai called though, Pokani knew that January would be back. That she wouldn't let it go. He told Kai not to worry, that he would take care of it. The next day the floor was redone."

"It's so strange," Liat mused. "I mean, think about it. What if Pokani hadn't been so scared? Maybe if he hadn't resisted so much, Kai and Mak might've gotten him out in time. Who knows? If he hadn't had the dreams if he hadn't fought them so hard we might've all gotten out."

"How is he?" I asked, somewhat distracted. I was thinking about what she'd said. If we hadn't run back into the cave and if we hadn't tried to climb out through the cafeteria I wouldn't have seen January climbing up that ladder. I wouldn't have heard the creaking noise it made. I might have lived the rest of my life without ever flashing back to the night Angela and Bill died.

"He's weak," Liat answered. "He broke his leg and most of his ribs. There were some internal injuries too."

"If he was so scared," I asked, "then why did he come with us in the first place? Mak was looking for a fast lift. It's not like he expected Pokani to fly us out there himself."

Liat took a sip of her coffee. "Atonement, I think."

I lifted an eyebrow. She put the coffee down and explained.

"There was a look in his eyes after he read my father's letter. He didn't say a word. He just took the keys from the pilot and climbed into the cockpit. I didn't realize it then but I think he felt responsible. Plus I think he half expected to find Jan down there."

Liat shuddered for a second and then absently rubbed away the goosebumps on her arms. It was catchy. I looked down and found myself rubbing the chill out of my own arms too.

Liat looked over at me and grinned.

"For years, I felt so alone. Like no one could ever understand… about the sculptures, really about everything. But the deeper in we get the more connected things…people seem to be. You know," she sighed, "I have no clue what's next, what I'm supposed to do. But at least now people know about it. At least now I'm not alone."

"That's good, considering that you and Nick are, well," I hesitated, then added, "anyway, I was sorry to hear about you two. I really like Nick. But I like Mak too." I stopped right there, knowing anything else that was likely to fall out of my mouth would only make it worse.

"It's okay Willow. Nick and I, we're fine. As for Mak, well," she let the thought drop.

After that we sat there for a few moments and didn't say anything. I was thinking about January. About Angela. I was wondering about how much of life happens because of impulse…how much is real choice… how much is fate? Liat must've been mulling things over too.

She reached out and touched my arm. "Willow, about Kai asking me questions and talking to Pokani. He's just looking to do what's right. You should know," she added, "that he went to the University yesterday, to Jan's office. He took a hairbrush from her desk and gave it to a friend of his on the Honolulu police force. He told them your story, all of it, including the post-traumatic stress you've been suffering since Iraq." She hesitated, waiting for my reaction, then added, "Look, Kai's got an honest streak a mile wide. He needs the truth. That's just how he operates."

I nodded but didn't say a word. So now Liat knew about the flashbacks. Slowly but surely the secret Angela had worked so hard to keep under wraps was making its way into the general population. Part of me was relieved. Part of me.

"Anyway, he convinced his friend to check the DNA from the hairbrush against evidence they have from Melanie."

I couldn't help grinning. "He did that? For me?"

Wait…he did what?!

"It'll be weeks before they know anything," Liat cautioned.

It didn't matter. I knew what the results would be. Besides, January was missing. Aside from a few minutes with her father no one had seen her since our fight in the cave. Fair or not I thought that her absence made her look guilty and gave me at least some credibility. I turned back to the ocean and stared out at the massive waves making their way toward the sand. I picked up my coffee, took a deep sip, and thought about how much I'd changed in the last few weeks. My strength and confidence were returning. Even my fair Irish skin was developing what some might call a healthy glow. A loud horn blasted across the beach. Then a man came over the loudspeaker and announced the first heat.

When the semi-finals were over Kai and Mak were indeed the last two standing. Everything was riding on that final heat. Both the Pipe Masters title and the World Championship were at stake. The excitement made me…hungry. For some reason all I could think about was food. Hot dogs. Actually, a good Philly street vendor hot dog with some ketchup, mustard, and a slew of fried onions, I thought, as I trudged through the sand in search of satisfaction. I came back with fish tacos and papaya juice. A few bites later, my hunger and all thoughts of Philadelphia slipped away.

"Here," I said, handing one to Liat as I settled back in. She took a half-hearted bite.

"Willow?"

"Yeah?"

"The last sculpture. What if it's today? Kai and Mak are in the finals now and...well, I was just thinking...we stopped January. Right? The letter from my father told us we had to stop the kolohe and we did that. That massive diamond is still in the cave wall. So maybe nothing bad will happen today."

I took another bite of the fish taco and mulled it over.

"Well, it's not like this final is a fluke. Mak and Kai belong here. Even if you had never sculpted that piece, they would be here."

"So you're not worried."

"Are you kidding," I quipped, "I get itchy every time I look at one of those things," I said pointing to the waves. "I mean I love surfing. But that?"

Liat smiled. "I've always felt so at home out there."

"Good. Then lighten up. This is supposed to be exciting, right?"

Once again Liat's face sobered.

"Do you think we should keep looking for the Maui Snow? I mean you got what you came for. Right? Or at least you will once those test results come in. Is that enough? Can you let it go?"

"Sometimes I think that I could head home tomorrow and be fine without ever setting eyes on another diamond. For me the Maui Snow was a path to answers. I never really needed the gem. Just answers," I told Liat. I believed it too. It felt good...I felt good. Except for that slight headache that I just couldn't seem to ditch.

"As far as the Maui Snow goes, Liat, well, to put it bluntly, my dad is home in Philly. Probably sitting in front of the T.V. watching a ballgame with my brothers. Finding that diamond has always been about you Liat. About you and your Dad. But if you really want to keep looking you can count on me. I'll help you find it."

At the end of the day, the Pipe Masters came down to one final wave. It was gorgeous. Liat saw it coming and bolted straight up out of her chair. She said it was the kind of wave you hope for at Pipe during the winter months. Kai was there. Waiting at Backdoor when it rolled in clean.

Through binoculars I watched him play with the glassy wall like it was an old friend. He did barrels and rolls and all kinds of loops and turns that I hadn't learned the proper lingo for yet. Then he hunkered down. The lip heaved over him and he disappeared. I held my breath and waited. Faith I thought. Such an easy thought…such a hard thing to hold onto. Later, what felt like hours later, Kai surfed back into view, standing straight, head high, with the wave thundering down near the back of his speeding board.

The crowd on the beach went wild. Liat dropped the surf magazine she was autographing and picked up the little girl who was waiting for it, twirling her in a happy dance. I raised an arm and cheered with the crowd as Kai picked up his board and made his way into the sand. It was a spectacular moment.

I could feel myself getting separated from Liat amidst the crush of fans and didn't bother to fight it. **Give Kai a hug for me. Tell him b hppy n I'll find him later** I texted her. I watched from the back of the beach as Kai was crowned and a thousand pictures were snapped. I gathered stats and quotes from some fans for my story then headed back to the hotel. This was Kai's time. An interview with the winner could wait until later.

Parties were thrown by several of the sponsors but in the end most of the local surfers straggled back to the beach house on the North Shore. The bonfire was bigger than last time and even the edges of the ocean were bathed in a soft glow. It was a warm celebration full of love. Well, that and alcohol. Everybody was happy for Kai. Including Makani. They were big wave surfers. Their friendship was rooted in mutual respect.

"Enjoy it old man," Mak teased without a hint of resentment. "The next one is all mine."

CHAPTER THIRTY NINE

Sandy Beach b there at 8. I read the text through bleary Grey Goosed eyes. For three days I had tagged along with Kai to sponsored beach parties and endless photo ops. **No thnks** I texted back. Then rolled over and snuggled into Kai's warm body. Thirty seconds later both of our phones buzzed. I tossed mine aside and groaned. Kai picked it up. **C'mon. Sandy Beach. U r ready.** But I wasn't. I felt disoriented. Had to be the vodka I convinced myself. I wasn't much of a drinker and since Iraq I'd barely had any. I should have abstained, like Kai. But Liat makes a killer Cosmopolitan. The night before I had at least three. I closed my eyes and Kai's voice filled my ears.

"Might as well get moving." With a gossamer touch he brushed aside my curls and planted a kiss on the back of my neck.

"They're not gonna give up."

"Can't you guys take a few days off? Have a little fun?" I groaned.

Kai laughed. Competition is over. Just surfing? That is the fun."

"Okay, I agreed, "but let's drive separately. I want to go back to the hotel afterwards and fax some stuff to Harry for my story on the women's competition. I know I still have another day but I want to stay on top of it."

Kai kissed my neck again. "About that," he said. "We should talk."

"What? You want me to interview you for the article on the women's competition too? Man, a few days as Pipe Master and whoooosh there goes the head, swelling like a–

He cut me off with a warm kiss.

"Don't go back to Philadelphia. Stay here. You can write in Hawaii. If you need ideas I'll give you some," he promised.

"Then I guess we should…talk." I grinned at Kai.

"Tonight," he said, changing his mind. "We'll talk about it tonight."

We never got the chance.

Later on…afterwards…I tried to reconstruct the details. But there were gaps. Blank spots I could not fill in. I must have had another flashback. A really bad one this time because I couldn't remember anything. When the morning started, when the text to go surfing came in, Kai and I were happy. We were together. After that it gets fuzzy. Then Kai, he was just…gone.

I remember the shower. I was in the shower scrubbing hard at… the long red strands of my hair. Kai might have opened the bathroom door while I was in the shower. Actually, he must have. I strained hard at the edges of my brain to bring the memory back.

And there it was…Kai's voice through the open bathroom door. He sounded…I could feel…how upset he was. He was talking. At least I think he was. Okay, yeah, I'm sure of it. He was definitely…talking. But there was something about his throat, his voice. It sounded wrong. It sounded all…clogged…all hollow and far away.

Talking? Right, okay, he was…talking.

Yeah it was Kai. Definitely. Okay, now what was it he said? Something about meeting a friend…yeah that's it…meeting a friend on the way to the beach. I grasped at that concept and held onto it. That was it. Had to be. Sure. Kai went to see a friend. Yep, and then afterwards he was going to meet me at the beach. Just like we decided after the texts came in. Before I had the flashback. Before I took that shower. Kai loved me. He was coming back.

My hair was a mess. Oh it was clean alrighty but the curls, well, somehow, they had morphed into a big, poofy, unruly, mess again. Under the circumstances I decided the best I could do now was twist it into two tight braids at the back of my head. Afterwards, I went back into the bedroom. Kai was definitely gone. The place was a mess too. I ignored it and got dressed for the beach. I tried not to worry. About the flashback, I mean. It was just one. So I had another flashback. So I lost some time with this one. Twenty, thirty minutes, tops. So what. It didn't mean anything. Come to think of it, it was a big improvement when you consider those four lost days I still couldn't account for. Kai was right about the flashbacks. They were one small part of my life. They didn't have to own me.

It's just that I felt so bad. I thought that after January, after I remembered so clearly what happened at Angela's house that night, well, I thought I was cured. No more problems no more lost time. Okay, so I was wrong. Big deal. It was one, out of the blue, flashback. Nothing had changed. Nothing at all.

Once outside I noticed that there were two surfboards tied to the roof of my rented Jeep. Kai must've tied them before he left. How thoughtful. That was Kai alrighty, kind to a fault.

I turned away from the surfboards and something on the ground caught my eye. It was a cell phone. I bent down and picked it up. It was Kai's. Hmmmmmm...he must have dropped it on his way out, I thought. Funny thing is, I knew he wouldn't miss it. Most people go crazy without their cell phones. I would for sure. Not Kai. Stuff was such a minor part of Kai's existence. That's why he had so much room for the people in his life–people like me. Still, it was a good thing I saw his phone when I did. Otherwise, I might've crushed it when I tried to back out.

CHAPTER FORTY

Forty minutes later I pulled up to the beach. Except for a dozen or so surfers the place was nearly empty. It was hot but it was still early. The sun hadn't obliterated the morning haze. Yet.

I stood at the water's edge, holding onto the green surfboard Kai had given me, fingering the sticker of the half full coffee mug he'd put there. I glanced through the waves for Mak and Liat. Nothing. Just strangers. A few feet to my right a young couple tossed their boards into the ocean and paddled out. I couldn't help thinking about Kai. About the day we met. The day he rescued me. All of a sudden I felt a slight tug on my left braid.

"Where's Kai? What took you so long to get here?"

It was Liat. My stomach tightened. I opened my mouth to form an answer but before I could say anything, Mak flashed me a wicked grin and threw my surfboard into the ocean.

"Surf now. Talk later," he demanded.

The waves at Sandy Beach are rough. At first I had Mak and Liat flanking me on either side, carefully picking out the right swells, but it still took everything in me to concentrate on those waves. It was such a blast. Standing up on water walls that scared me half to death. Falling. Way more than I wanted to but not on every wave. I was determined though so I kept at it and actually managed to ride some of them start to finish. Talk about wild. Of course, it wasn't nearly as dangerous as Pipe but when it's your own personal easy to crush body at risk, wild is sort of relative. Anyhow, we were two hours into it before it dawned on me that I still hadn't seen Kai. My phone was on the beach. Then I remembered. I couldn't call him anyway. I had Kai's cell phone in the car. There was no way for me to reach him.

Liat paddled toward me and tugged on one of my braids again. Only this time she cocked her head and stared at me kind of funny. At first I thought it was because of the nasty scratches on the back of my neck. Without thinking, I slid a hand up to cover them. Turns out it was my hair she couldn't stop looking at.

"What you never saw braids before?"

"Ahh, no...I mean yeah, just never on you." She shook her head then and dropped the braid. It fell down my back and smacked the top of the ocean.

"So what, am I too old? Or are redheads banned from wearing braids in Hawaii?" I teased.

"No, it's weird, it's just that..." she stammered, then finished the thought. "Something about your braids reminded me of that first sculpture. The one of the shark and my doll and Benny...I mean Mak," she corrected.

"Anyhow, forget about that. I need to ask you something."

"Sure," I answered. But I was already distracted. By now I was scanning the ocean looking for Kai.

"I went to read my dad's letter again last night but I couldn't find it. The hospital doesn't have it. I checked. Neither does Mak or Kai. Have you seen it? I had it in my pocket when we went down into that cave."

"Nope. Haven't seen it," I responded half-heartedly. Kai wasn't in the ocean. I scanned the beach.

"Have you seen Kai?"

"Not yet. But Willow, I am anxious to take a fresh look at the sculptures. I was hoping you'd come with me. You know, add an extra pair of eyes."

"Yeah, sure," I answered. "In fact," I decided, digging my hands through the water so I could turn my surfboard toward the beach. "Let's head in."

I flipped open my phone with one hand and toweled off with the other. I was hoping Kai would have borrowed his friend's phone to call me. Nothing. No calls. No texts. It wasn't like Kai to just not show up. I asked Liat if she'd heard from him. I scanned the ocean again while she checked her phone. Nothing. Then I looked back at my car. Kai's surfboard was still tied to the roof.

Actually, seeing his surfboard made me feel better. At least he wasn't lost in the ocean somewhere. After all, Kai was the reigning Pipe Master. I hadn't realized it but Liat's surfer sculpture must've jacked itself up in my subconscious and was now wreaking havoc. Never mind what I'd said to Liat on the beach a few days ago during the competition. That was before Kai had actually won the crown.

"Twenty minutes," I called to Liat as I headed for my car. "Let me grab a shower and then we can head straight to the University."

Liat agreed. "I'll pick up sandwiches and meet you in the lobby."

We should have told Mak where we were going. We tried to wave at him from the beach but he never saw us. By then he was busy paddling for much deeper waves.

One hour later Liat opened the basement door to the Art Barn. Right away we heard something. It sounded like a creak near the bottom of the steps. After that I could swear I heard *something* skittering away.

"What was that? Did you hear it, Liat?"

"I don't know. Rats maybe?"

"Angry gods?" I joked.

"I'll take the rats," Liat quipped.

The room was quiet by the time we reached the bottom step. Liat went right to the sculptures and started pulling at them.

"Grab the surfboards," she directed.

I leaned them against the wall by the stairs. Liat stopped what she was doing for a second and stood back, looking hard at the sculptures.

"Something's different," I stated. "They've been moved. And where's the tarp we threw over them?"

The tarp was across the room. Liat and I looked at each other then gave the room a hasty scan. Empty we decided. It was a quick decision. More underground drama was the last thing either one of us really wanted to find.

"Okay, what now?"

Liat took hold of the ballroom sculpture and scooted it closer to the giant wave. The last sculpture.

"Help me move these. Make sure they all connect."

That's when I noticed it. The bell. Floating in the bottom of the wave next to some flip-flops. It wasn't just a bell. It was the liberty bell. Somehow I had missed that before. Too busy checking out the figure of me in Angela's living room I suppose. Maybe that wasn't the piece of artwork I should've been concerned about. After all, the bell was floating at the bottom of Liat's giant wave. A replica of the liberty bell, like the one located in Philadelphia. And since I was the only one from Philly—

It was an uncomfortable thought to say the least. But as I brushed my fingers over the bell I saw something else. A name. And a date. The liberty bell was inscribed with Bill Priest's name and it was dated for the night of the Juvenile Diabetes event. Bill was supposed to be honored at the event and Angela was going to present him with the award. In fact, I was talking to her on the phone when it arrived at the house by courier. She couldn't stop babbling about the darned thing. How heavy it was and how it was one of a kind and how the artist had molded it out of some new state of the art material, blah, blah, blah. I remembered the conversation vividly now because the award arrived at around ten in the morning—the same day that she and Bill died. The bell was at the house the day they died. It was at the house the day they—

"This is it!" I exclaimed. "I bet this is what Melanie had on January!"

"What are you talking about?"

"Before the knock-down drag out between me and Jan I asked her why she killed Melanie. She told me that Melanie could prove she was in Philadelphia that night. I asked her how and Jan actually laughed. She said that if she told me what it was then she would have to kill me too."

"She did try to kill you. Well, and you tried to…I saw the bruises on both of your necks," Liat finished.

"Yeah well at that point Jan still thought she could talk her way out of it. She didn't go for my throat until I let it slip that all we really needed to do was get some DNA from her to match against the stuff under Melanie's fingertips."

"It'll be weeks before those results come in," Liat reminded.

There was still a note of caution in Liat's tone. She hadn't made up her mind just yet which way things were likely to go. I felt bad but I understood. Trust is such a funny thing. Like children, we sometimes hand it out too freely, with nothing more than an introduction and a smile as collateral. The thing is, once that first crack appears, the right words, the right expression to restore trust can be nearly as impossible to find as, well, a rare gem like the Maui Snow.

"This must be weird for you. You and Jan—you've been surfing against each other since you were like five, right?"

"Yeah its weird. I mean, its not like we're bff's but Jan—

Liat hesitated.

"She belongs," I finished the thought for her.

Liat nodded. Then she pointed to the sculptures. Pointed to the wave.

"Right now I'm more interested in figuring out where the Maui Snow is. Help me push these together."

"Why are we pushing these together?"

"The last paragraph of my dad's letter. He said something about the colors and shapes on the surfboards. He also told me to connect my work. It got me thinking. You know those connect the dot books you play with when you're little? Well my dad used to bring them home for me all the time. We used to sit at the kitchen table and race each other to see which of us could figure out their picture first. So I figured what if he means it literally? It's worth a shot, right?"

"Which piece do you want me to move?"

"They're already in date order. Just push them together, sort of in a circle, until they all touch."

"Now what?" I asked when we were finished.

Liat stretched her leg, up and over the side of one of the sculptures, and then stepped into the center. She stood there for a moment and looked around.

"Well?"

"I don't know."

"Your dad's letter—didn't it say something about the surfboards? Something about shapes and colors."

Liat thought for a second. "Poliahu's shape is true."

"And Pele's color matters too," I finished.

Liat wandered the inside of the sculpture. The shape was vaguely familiar but she couldn't quite put her finger on it. Then all of a sudden it clicked.

"The diamonds in each of the sculptures, that's it! Paper. Quick get me paper! I need big pieces."

"Back there," Liat pointed past the stairway. By now she was snapping her fingers and talking fast. "To your right. There's a large closet. It's full of supplies; sheet metal, wood, paint; all kinds of crap. When you open the door, look at the shelves on your left. There should be some sketch pads."

I opened the closet and started rummaging around. I should have noticed the foot sticking out from the row of paint cans lined up along the floor on the right side of the closet. Clearly it didn't belong there. I should have noticed. But I didn't. I never saw it.

But what if I had? What if I had caught just a glimpse of that *other* person, the one hiding in the closet? If only I had been more…aware. Maybe I could have done something. Who knows? If I had turned real fast–slammed that door closed–locked it tight. Then maybe I could've gone for help…right there and then…before anything else bad happened. But I didn't know. I just didn't know.

"Got em," I called out. I picked up three of the tablets and ran back to Liat.

As soon as I reached the sculptures Liat grabbed one of the pads and started tearing.

"Quick, start ripping," she directed. By now she was throwing pages on the ground covering the area inside the sculptures.

"What are you doing?"

"I need a pen. Better yet, get me a marker."

Once again, I went back into the closet.

"Here," I said handing her a brush and a can of paint when I came out. "That's the best I could do."

For some reason, this time, I left the closet door wide open.

"Close enough," she replied, the excitement in her voice growing as she ripped the lid off the can and dipped the brush into a lively green. Then she stood in front of each work of art, located the small black diamonds she had sculpted, and then painted dots on the paper directly beneath those locations. When she was finished, Liat dipped the brush again and connected the outline.

"Ahhh, I get it…the diamonds…connect the dots." I watched as she rounded the paint toward the last dot.

"What is it?"

Liat stood back and looked. Then her face broke into a smile.

"Not what. Where," she answered. "It's Maui."

"Are you sure?"

"Quick, get the surfboards. The islands are on the surfboards. Poliahu's first. Let me see it." She took the board and traced the outline of Maui with her finger. Then she pointed to the makeshift map she'd just painted. The outlines were the same.

"Check this out," Liat said. "Look at the second to last line of the poem."

Search inside the sand and glass of life's tales
Aligned by time these connected secrets unveil
The island first shaped true by Poliahu's board
Her tipped wave now sings the Maui Snow restored.

"It says, the island first shaped true by Poliahu's board."

"Yeah, so, all of the islands are etched into both boards," I said.

"Look at them," Liat directed. She stood the Pele board and the Poliahu board up next to each other.

"If you look at the islands on both boards you can see that the order of the color lines up. The islands that are green are green on both boards. The islands that are red are red on both boards."

"And?"

"Well look at the shapes. I can't believe I missed it. On Pele's board Oahu and Maui are transposed. It says Maui inside the island and the color is green but the shape of the island is wrong, it's Oahu. On Poliahu's board everything lines up. The shape, the name, the color."

I brushed a hand over Poliahu's board. She was right.

"None of us saw it. Without putting the boards together you just don't notice it. But it has to be Maui. The diamond has to be on Maui somewhere." Liat made her way toward the sculpture of the surfer.

"Now for the last part." She stood beneath the tip of the wave and looked down. Then she looked over at me and scratched her head.

"What?"

"I need a real map. With names on it. The general direction of the coast is obvious but I can't pinpoint a real location without a map of Maui. Even then I'm not sure if I'll be able to line it up right."

"Yes you can. And I know right where to get one."

I sprinted toward the steps.

"Hey, wait for me," Liat demanded as she climbed her way out of the sculptures. "Where are we going?"

"All we need is a computer. We're at the University. January has an office on campus, right?"

"Oh no. We are not breaking into Jan's office. There're plenty of computers in the library. We can use one of those."

"Relax. Kai probably left the door unlocked when he took her hairbrush. We won't be breaking in we'll just be...visiting."

"Bullshit," Liat exclaimed. "You just want to look for that liberty bell. You think it will prove she was in Philadelphia the night your friends died."

"Woohoo—give the girl a Clondike Bar!"

"Oh just shut up and let's go," Liat groaned as she brushed past me and ran up the steps. "But if it's locked or there's police tape covering the door we're using the library."

Police tape was the last thing on my mind. Finding tangible evidence that Jan had been in Philadelphia was crucial. My sanity, my happiness with Kai depended on it.

I didn't know it at the time but as we climbed the steps someone floated from the shadows. Past Liat's connect the dots map of Maui, and followed me silently to the upper campus.

There was no police tape across Jan's office. And yes, Kai had left the door unlocked. Liat was still edgy. She really was a goody two shoes and the idea of using someone's computer without asking went against her grain. I sat down at the desk and typed 'Maps of Maui' into the Google bar.

"Here's a list of sites," I said to Liat as I got up from the chair. "Pick one and print a map while I look for the liberty bell."

It was an art teacher's office at a university so of course it was cramped. There was a desk. Behind Jan's chair there was about a foot and a half of space leading to a credenza that was nestled under a small window. Adjacent to the credenza and next to the open door was a narrow closet for supplies. I rifled through the credenza. Student files. Plus some sketches and an assortment of self-portraits.

"Shhhhhh. You're making too much noise," Liat complained.

The printer beeped and she nearly jumped out of her skin.

"Look through the desk," I suggested. Liat was uncomfortable with the idea but complied.

"There's nothing here Willow. No liberty bell. Just a bunch of student files."

She stood in front of the printer and waited. When the map was finished she grabbed it and went for the door. I was on the floor of the closet rifling through a box with more sketches. Then I saw the beach bag.

"Hurry up!"

I looked at Liat and made a quick decision. I tossed her the keys to my rental.

"Bring the car around. I'll meet you at the doors to the lobby."

Liat caught the keys then hesitated.

"Go. I'm almost finished."

Liat took off. A few minutes later I jumped into the passenger seat with Jan's beach bag.

"What's that?"

I unzipped the bag and held it open. "Look underneath."

Liat lifted the towel. At the bottom of the bag was the liberty bell. Just like the one she'd crafted inside her sculpture of the wave.

"It's real," I heard her say.

"It's real, alright," I grinned. "And I bet Jan's real fingerprints are all over it. Melanie's too."

"What about the police? Don't they need to find that kind of evidence themselves, you know, actually in Jan's office? Maybe you should put it back," Liat advised.

"No!" I answered defensively. "I'm lucky I found it. Jan is still out there somewhere. It's obvious that the police aren't watching her office.

What if she comes back? Seriously," I continued to press my point, "I'm surprised she didn't get rid of it already."

I zipped up the bag and tossed it over my shoulder. Funny thing. It hit the back windshield and then landed on the tarp that completely covered the back floor of the Jeep. I tossed it pretty hard. The bag should've sunk right to the hard flat bottom with a decent clunk. That liberty bell was oddly heavy. But something fleshy muffled it. The thing is I should have noticed that fleshy sound when I threw the gym bag. In all fairness to Liat, she really should have noticed it too. I guess we were both…distracted.

We drove back down to the Art Barn and parked the car.

"Let's do it. Let's go," I said, opening the car door.

"Wait a sec," Liat responded. She already had the map spread across the steering wheel and she was busy running her forefinger over the outline of Maui. "This map is kind of small but once we line it up with the one downstai-

"Holy cow!" She interrupted herself. "That's it! Honolua Bay. It's Honolua Bay!"

"Great," I answered, stepping *one* foot on the ground. "Let's go. We really should go back downstairs. We'll put the map inside the sculptures and then you can show me exactly where the diamond is."

But Liat wasn't listening to me. In fact she started the car. Her movements were so fast, so damned unexpected. *I* was startled. I slid my foot back in the car and gave the door a weak tug.

"What are you doing?" I started to ask Liat. But my voice sounded hollow. Far away. I could feel the blood rushing through my veins. Could sense the oncoming panic. I did have that fleeting moment. The one I get sometimes just before an oncoming flashback. It's more of an inkling really. The kind of inkling that if you're lucky enough to get it, and you're strong enough, well, it helps you put on the breaks. It gives you that split second to breathe, to back down the demons. Sometimes. Other times it just gives the panic a little extra room to ramp up.

Liat threw the car in reverse and sped out of the parking lot. I gripped the dashboard with both hands barely noticing the door as it slammed shut so close to my foot.

"We're going to the airport," she replied. "To Honolua Bay."

Liat turned and looked at me. I must've looked pale as shit.

"Don't worry. I'll pay this time," she grinned. "I finally caved in and got a credit card."

I didn't answer. The smell of dirt and Matt's blood coated the inside of my nose. Bright sunlight and body bits exploded in the windshield in front of me. Bonnie Jean's diamond landed on my ear with a tiny thud.

"Relax Willow," Liat's voice echoed from somewhere off in the distance. "I know where the Maui Snow is."

CHAPTER FORTY ONE

I stared out the window of the airplane, grateful to see the steady dark cone of Haleakala poking through the white clouds. The bullets. Matt. The thousand tiny fragments of blood and bone were gone. I knew that my rental Jeep was parked in the garage at the airport on Oahu. What I couldn't remember was most of the ride to the airport. Before I knew it, we were touching down in Maui.

"You okay?" Liat asked. "You haven't said a word since we left the University."

"I'm fine," I lied. Truth is, I was anything but fine. Two flashbacks? Two in one day? Something was wrong. Something big.

"Where are we going, again?"

"Honolua Bay," Liat answered. "There's a house that my dad used to take me to when I was little. Actually though, it's not the house I'm interested in."

"Honolua Bay. That's where the final leg of the women's competition is being held tomorrow, right?"

"Yeah, but we're not going to the beach."

I didn't ask any more questions. I couldn't. Eventually Liat pulled onto a wide dirt road lined with houses. She parked in front of one that looked as though it'd been built circa WWII.

"Whose house is this?"

"I think it's your friend Angela's."

That caught my attention.

"Come on." Liat opened the car door and took off.

The one story house was old but well maintained. Angela must have paid someone on the island to take care of it after she moved to Philadelphia. I followed Liat across the grass but was surprised when she didn't head for the front door. Instead she moved across the sparse lawn and went around the back. Fifty or sixty yards behind the house sat the entrance to a grove of fruit trees. Liat entered the grove and turned right, winding her way through rows and rows of trees. I followed.

The smell was amazing. Fresh papaya scented the air. I was so taken in by our surroundings that I failed to notice the second house.

"Come on."

I looked around. I could hear Liat but she was nowhere in sight.

"Come on!" She yelled again, this time from above.

By the time I found her, Liat was halfway up the tree. There was no ladder and only thin lower branches to hold onto.

"How the heck are you doing that?"

"Look close," she advised. "There are impressions worn into the trunk. They might not look it but they're deep enough to support your weight–if you let them. Go ahead, lean into them. Once you've got a decent leg up on the tree you can reach for a good strong branch and go from there."

I had nothing to lose. I searched for a foothold and climbed. It was hard. Somehow I managed to scratch every visible inch of skin on my arms and legs. But I kept my neck tilted up and my eyes peeled to the rising bark. Before I knew it a large limb brushed against the top of my head. I reached for the branch and kept on climbing. Eventually, Liat stretched down a hand and lifted me the rest of the way up.

The tree house was made of Koa wood. The same wood Liat's father had used to shape the surfboards. The hut-like roof was covered in thick branches from the tree so that the house was barely visible from the ground. The inside of the tree house was standard fare, one room with a table and some chairs. Knickknacks were nailed to the wall, among them a pink baseball glove and some of her father's old surfing ribbons. There was even a photo of Liat with her mother and father. Under the table was a box filled with toys and old junk. On top of it sat a radio. There were three windows built into the tree house. One faced the main house and two adjacent windows offered spectacular views of the Pacific Ocean.

I leaned out one of the windows and sucked in a deep breath of sea and fresh fruit. Then I leaned out a little farther and let the sun settle on my face as the warm scents seeped into my skin.

"This must be what heaven smells like."

"Mmm hhhmmm," Liat agreed.

"That's Honolua Bay," she added, pointing out the window to my left.

"It's beautiful."

"Isn't it? And listen to this," Liat tilted her head and cupped a hand around her ear. I followed suit. We stood there in silence for a moment listening to the ocean swell and crash, to the leaves rustling throughout the orchard. It was so peaceful, a real moment. Funny how it was empty of so much that we consider essential to our modern lives and yet it was fuller, more abundant, than a lot of the years we spend living with all that crap.

"Your dad built this tree house?"

"Yeah. When I was about five."

"Did you live here?"

Liat hesitated for a second. "I used to come here with my Dad on weekends, sometimes longer when he had the time. He was helping Angela fix the place up. She had him build the tree house out here for her kids. I remember because I was jealous. But the thing is they never actually used it. By then Jan's mother was spending all of her time on Oahu. So it sort of became mine. Mine and my dad's. Until I was seven. I haven't thought about this place in years."

"Why now?"

"The map. And the poem. The last line of the poem had been nagging at me. 'Her tipped wave now sings the Maui Snow restored.' I couldn't figure out what my dad was trying to tell me. I could feel something vaguely familiar but I just couldn't put my finger on it. When I looked at the map and saw that Honolua Bay was in the area where the tip of the wave was pointing to, it finally clicked. My dad used to bring me up here at night, sit me in his lap, and tell me great stories about the ocean, the islands. He used to sing to me."

"Stories about Pele and Poliahu?" I asked.

"Yeah, come to think of it. But it was more than that. Hawaii is full of legends. Full of history. Anyway, when he was finished, he would get

293

very quiet and he would put his hand to my ear. He would say, listen Liat...listen to the waves. Can you hear them sing? We would listen to the waves and then we would sing with them. We used to sing Ke Aloha O Ka Haku. It's a prayer that Queen Liliuokalani wrote as she faced the loss of her kingdom. In it she prays for peace in the islands and peace for the people of Hawaii.

Liat sang the queen's song, and a tear escaped the corner of her eye. I could see how bittersweet the memories were. How much Liat missed her father. When she finished, I reached across and gave her hand a gentle squeeze. Then we sat for a moment, staring out the window of the tree house, content to breathe in the peaceful winds of paradise.

"It must be here," Liat said, brushing away a final tear. "This is the perfect hiding place."

She scanned the room. Her eyes settled on the box of toys under the table. We rummaged through it together and found coloring books, connect the dots, jacks, a Mrs. Potato head—and one toy surfboard. It was about a foot and a half long and a good five inches thick. Way thicker than a surfboard should be. Liat pulled it out of the box. On the surface there was a blue wave carved into the wood. A small fin, about an inch in height, jutted from the bottom of the wave.

Liat and I looked at each other.

"You think?"

Liat shook the surfboard. Something rattled inside. She turned it around in her hands looking for an opening but the wood looked seamless. She shook it again. There was definitely something inside. Liat eyed the edge of the table.

"Smash it?" She suggested reluctantly. Her father had made it. Destroying it was the last thing she wanted.

"No. Try the fin. You know, like a jack in the box," I suggested.

Liat twisted the fin and the entire blue wave began inching upward. It was a lid. When the fin wouldn't twist anymore, Liat turned the box over and shook it. The Maui Snow fell into her palm. Liat held it up between us, up into the sunlight. For a brief second we stared at it, then at each other, and grinned. The diamond was magnificent.

"Finally."

We jumped at the sound of the voice, and then jerked our heads toward the entrance to the treehouse. January was standing on the trunk of the tree and she was leaning into the house. With a rather large gun pointed in our direction.

"Hand it over," she demanded, motioning with her free hand.

"What are you doing here," I snapped back, my tone more than a little harsh. I couldn't help it. This day was not going at all the way I intended.

"How did you find us?"

"I've been following you two all day. Well, actually, I was at the University before you got there. I was down in the basement of the Art Barn with your father's letter trying to make sense of everything. I ducked into the closet when I heard you coming."

"What are you talking about? I was in that closet. Twice. I didn't see you."

"Yeah, I almost shot you when you opened the door the first time," January admitted casually. "But then I heard the excitement in Liat's voice and I could tell you were onto something. So I decided to wait it out. When you bolted, I followed, and while the two of you were snooping around my office, I decided to sneak into the back of your car so I could hear you better. Tracking you on the ground in Maui was a bit trickier. But well, here we all are," she said with smile. "Now hand it over."

"Come on Jan. Put the gun down," Liat cajoled. "Let's not get stupid about this."

But all of sudden there were new sounds. Branches breaking.

"Oh crap," Jan swore, as the branch below her feet wobbled.

I looked out the window. Kai was climbing up the tree after her.

"Unbelievable," Jan shook her head and grumbled. "Every time I turn around there he is."

"Kai stop!" She yelled down at him. Then she shifted back to us and straightened her aim.

"Get off this tree right now Kai or I swear, I will shoot." Her tone was clear. She meant what she said.

"Willow first."

She never got the chance. Kai shook the tree hard. Jan's right foot slipped. Lucky for us the rest of her body followed it so fast that Jan never had time to pull the trigger. Kai put an arm up and swerved out of the way when the gun fell at his head. Jan came flailing down so fast after it that Kai had no choice. He let go of the branch he was holding onto, dove toward the ground, and rolled out of the way. Jan was screaming and groping for branches but none of them were strong enough to hold her. Liat and I stared out the window in shock as she landed on the ground with a nasty thud.

The lump above Jan's right eye reached past her forehead and into her scalp. She was dazed and mumbling when we carried her back to the house and laid her in Angela's bed. Kai assessed the rest of her wounds. Talk about luck. She had no broken bones, just a bunch of cuts and scrapes and that wicked bump.

Liat went to the medicine cabinet in search of first aid supplies. I went to the kitchen for some ice. There was none. The refrigerator was empty. I found a dishtowel and ran some cold water on it. It would have to do. Kai walked into the kitchen as I was wringing it out, and laid the gun on the countertop. Then he crossed the kitchen and sat down at the breakfast nook, facing me, with his back against the window bay.

"Shouldn't you be in the bedroom keeping an eye on Jan? She's dangerous Kai. I don't think we should leave her alone."

"I took the gun away," he said, "and Liat is with her. The fall shook her up pretty bad. There's nothing to worry about Willow. I know Jan. I'm sure she's more scared than anything."

"Don't underestimate her Kai. She is scared. Of us. We know what she did."

Kai sighed. He turned and looked out over at the bay.

He still had doubts about me. Why? Jan was the one toting the gun. Kai wasn't saying it, but I could tell that he did. I came over to the breakfast nook and sat down next to him. New subject, I thought.

"What happened to you this morning? I went to take a shower and when I came back you weren't there." I left out the part about the flashback I had. I told Kai the flashbacks were gone.

"When you didn't show up at the beach I got worried. Not to mention," I added, "you dropped your cell phone."

"You have my phone? Okay good. I thought I lost it."

"When I couldn't find you at the beach all I could think about was Liat's sculpture. You are the reigning Pipe Master, Kai. After awhile I started thinking the worst. That Liat's wave...that you were lost in the ocean somewhere. I don't understand why you didn't just borrow your friend's cell phone and call?"

Kai ran a hand through his dark hair and rubbed at the back of his head before answering.

"Because the friend I met this morning was January. She called while you were in the shower. She apologized for leaving us back at the Observatory. She was really upset. Said she freaked out after the earthquake, after being stuck in that cave, and that she didn't mean to take off without us. She just needed space. Fresh air. Then she asked me to meet up with her. She said it was important. That she had a lot to tell me."

"Let me guess. She let out a round of boohoos and tried to convince you that I was crazy. That it was me who tried to strangle her down in that cave."

"January's not exactly the crybaby type, Willow."

"Oh," I responded, letting the air out of my lungs slowly. Not exactly the response I was hoping for.

"She did warn me about you Willow. She said that the Philadelphia police were looking into your involvement in her mother's death. She said that you were just trying to throw suspicion off of yourself and onto her."

"What did you say?" I tried not to sound vulnerable. It was impossible.

"I told her that the Honolulu police were testing her DNA and that it would all be cleared up in a few weeks. She got up from the table. Started ranting that there were a lot of other things I didn't know about you. She told me that I should be very careful. The next thing I knew she took off."

"So?" I wasn't sure what Kai expected me to say. I was hurt. I wanted him to believe in me, one hundred percent. Before the DNA test results came back.

"So, I followed her," Kai continued. "She was out of the parking lot fast. I spotted her car pretty quick on the highway but it wasn't easy tracking her. The girl drives like she surfs, in fast, tight moves. Anyhow, she took the exit for the University from two lanes over. I missed it and had to double back. I combed every parking lot on campus looking for her car. It took forever but eventually I found it. That's when I saw you,

Willow. I was leaning on Jan's car, waiting for her, when I saw you come out of the building. I called out to you but you didn't hear me. Before I could cross the parking lot I see Liat flying out of nowhere, in your rental, and then the two of you drove off. So I ran back to my car. Next thing I know, I'm on the highway trailing you to the airport. I grabbed the first parking spot I could find. By the time I spotted your car, you and Liat were gone but then I saw Jan, climbing out of the back of your car and running toward the terminal. I was stunned. Wondering what the devil was going on. I figured I better follow and find out."

"She's dangerous Kai. I'm telling you."

"You should listen to your girlfriend."

Our heads jerked around at the sound of January's voice. She had an arm wrapped around Liat's waist and a Swiss Army knife against her neck. She edged her way to the kitchen counter and grabbed at the gun. Then she shoved Liat in our direction, lifted the weapon, and pointed it at the three of us.

"January put the gun down," Kai demanded. Your head's a mess," he added, picking up the dishcloth and holding it out to her.

"I'm fine," Jan spat. "You on the other hand," she said, pointing the gun at my head, "not so much."

She took a few steps closer.

"Most of this mess is your fault. If you hadn't shown up at my mother's house I could have taken the surfboard and it would have ended there. I would have found the diamond on my own. And no one in Hawaii would have given my mother's death a second thought."

"Not true," Liat stated evenly. "You never would have found the Maui Snow. Not without Willow. Not without me." Jan shifted the gun slightly.

"Sure I would." Jan answered, raising her eyes to Liat's.

Liat stared back. For a moment the gun in Jan's hand wavered.

Standing next to Liat, I felt a small wave of static electricity. There was something, some sort of energy, emanating from her body and pushing forward, toward January. I stood there, staring, not sure what to make of it, or Liat. Whatever it was though it didn't last. Liat was either too weak or too far away.

Slowly. Very slowly, Kai began inching toward the left, closer to the door.

"Move! Over there!" Jan swerved, pointing the gun directly at Kai's chest.

Kai raised a conciliatory hand and then stepped gingerly toward us once again.

"What now?" Kai asked.

"I take the Maui Snow and disappear. The question is what to do with you three. I don't care about you," she said focusing the gun on me again. "You should have stayed in Philadelphia. Kai, Liat, don't you see? This is all her fault. You should have let her drown Kai."

"Okay. You have the diamond. Take it and go. No one knows we actually found it. But if you kill us—

"You shut up!" She shouted at me.

"She has a point," Kai offered. "Think about it, the competition is tomorrow. People will be looking for us. They'll be looking for Liat. Even more important," he said, stoking her ego, "they'll be looking for you."

"You don't want to do this Jan," he cajoled. "Just give me the gun."

Jan shook her head no and gripped the gun tighter.

"You're too smart for this," Kai tried to convince her. "Look, we can fix everything. About Melanie. There's no real investigation yet. That DNA sample I told you about? It's not like it's official. I gave it to Kerry Anders down at the police lab. That's all. A quiet favor for a friend. A very quiet favor. Jan, you have plenty of time to take the diamond and go. You don't have to hurt anyone else."

Jan put a hand over the lump above her eye. "I can't just leave. If I do you'll tell. They'll believe you Kai. People trust you. I can't let you tell them. I just...I'm sorry. I don't have a choice." She pointed the gun with purpose again.

"Yes you do," argued Liat. "I've got an option for you. How about winner takes all?"

"What?" The three of us looked at Liat.

"You heard me. Winner takes all. You and me Jan. We go to the competition tomorrow. Whoever takes the crown wins. If I win you give me the Maui Snow, admit what you did, and turn yourself in. If you win, you walk away. Kai will call his friend and get him to cancel the test. You said it yourself. People listen to Kai. He can make it work."

Jan laughed. "What if somebody else wins? It's not like you and I have a lock on it."

"Highest points then. Personal competition. Whichever one of us out-surfs the other. Not that you stand a chance. That crown is mine."

"Do I look stupid to you?" Asked Jan. "The second I let you out of here you'll call the police. I have the diamond. That's enough."

"Liar," Liat goaded. "You want that crown. You want it in the worst way. You think you're better than me. You always have. At least that's what you tell yourself and everybody else. But deep down you're afraid to go for it. Afraid you'll lose again. Truth is I am a better surfer than you. A better artist too. Hell, even the men you want prefer me. You couldn't get Nick if you tried. Oh that's right. You have tried."

Jan's face fumed red. Quiet little Liat–who would've guessed? I brushed away the goosebumps on my arm with a small unconscious stroke. Liat was full of surprises.

"Oh and let's not forget about Mak," she added. Liat was trying to fuel the fire. But that jab backfired. Jan smirked at the mention of Mak's name.

"I never wanted to date Mak. He's my brother."

"You knew?" I gasped.

"Again, do I look that stupid to you? Of course I knew. He's my brother."

Liat was caught completely off guard. "But the flirting. I've seen you flirt with Mak. In fact there were times when you were all over him. Why?"

"Because it was fun. I was curious to see how uncomfortable I could make him before he gave up the big secret. Kind of interesting that he never did. Don't you think?" Then she shrugged. "He had his reasons I guess. I had mine. I didn't want my father to find out. He was way too fond of Mak as a kid. The last thing I needed was the return of the prodigal son."

"Like I said, just afraid of a little competition." Once again Liat's voice was all steel. "Mak? Me? It doesn't matter. Deep down, you know you're not good enough Jan."

"Keep it up Liat. I might just shoot you first." Jan shifted slightly.

"No you won't," said Kai. "You're not going to shoot Liat. You're going to shut her up. Tomorrow. At Honolua Bay. When you take the crown."

"Ahhhhh, no." But Jan's tone didn't match her words. Her voice wavered.

"Yes you will. You'll do it because it's the smart thing to do." Kai's voice was calm, confident. Jan turned toward him to listen.

"You can't leave three more dead bodies, including mine, and expect to walk away. I'm the current Pipe Master," He reminded.

North Shore surfers were a tight community. If Kai and Liat turned up dead and Jan disappeared, they would not let up until they had answers. Even I knew that.

"Besides, I'll make you a better deal than Liat. She is right. I can fix the DNA inquiry. You know Kerry Anders, Jan. You know he owes me. I can do it."

"So?"

"So if you win I'll make a phone call. Get the whole thing dropped. You walk away, no questions asked. If you lose? Well, you've already got the diamond. Keep it. Go ahead and take off after the competition. We'll give you a head start. No phone calls. No police. We'll give you a week to disappear. That's more time and less heat than you'll get with bloodshed. I give you my word."

He kept his eyes on January. "Liat? You good with that?"

Liat sighed. "Personally, I think you should man-up and turn yourself in after I beat you. But yeah, if you wanna run I'll respect Kai's timeline."

"Come on Jan. You've got nothing to lose here now and everything to gain. You cannot outrun three more dead bodies."

My mouth dropped open.

"Have you lost your minds?!"

"She killed Melanie. She shot Bill Priest. I'm not just gonna let her walk away like it never happened. Hell, I nearly went crazy thinking I might have done it. I woke up from a flashback with a gun in my hand and Angela bleeding on my lap. All because of you," I said, pointing at Jan.

Part of me couldn't believe I'd just said that out loud. But it was true. From the moment I peeled off those jeans covered in blood, the fear that I'd harmed Angela had seeped into my skin and stuck there. When I came back from Iraq, I was full of rage and despair. After what happened at Angela's, I was terrified of what might happen, what I was capable of during a flashback.

Oddly enough, having Jan standing there pointing a gun at me now was actually a relief. Even if I didn't make it out alive, at least I knew for sure that I was innocent. Maybe Kai knew that now too.

Okay, so 'relief' was probably going a bit far. In fact, the second Jan raised the gun and shot at me, relief disintegrated pretty fast. The bullet whizzed past my curls and splintered the kitchen wall behind us. I jumped and let a few choice words fly. When I turned to look back at Jan, at the gun, I couldn't see her. Kai had stepped in front of me.

"No!" He shouted at Jan.

"Too bad Kai. I was just about to take you up on your offer." There was disappointment in Jan's voice. She sounded tired. Truth is her head must've been pounding something awful.

Still, Jan straightened the gun and steadied her aim.

"Get out of the way Kai. There's no way I can let Willow go. I believe you and Liat. I trust your word. But Willow will never agree."

"Yes she will," said Kai. "She'll do it for me."

"No I won't."

Kai held a conciliatory hand up to Jan again and then slowly turned his back to the gun. He took me by the shoulders and stared me in the eyes.

"The past or the future Willow. Which is it? You can only live in one of them. Nothing changes in the past Willow. There's no room for improvement. Take a chance. Please Willow. Give me your word. I need your word. And you need to mean it."

"I can't do it, Kai. I can't know what I know and just let her walk. I can't believe you're asking me to."

"You don't just walk from this kind of stuff Willow. Jan will live with what she's done for the rest of her life."

"Yeah. In a jail cell," I replied.

"There are all kinds of prisons Willow—and more than a few flavors of fair, in life. You know that better than most. You just have to trust in it. Trust me. He eased his grip on my shoulders. "Please. Let go of the controls on this one."

I looked at Liat. She was as calm as a lake, not a ripple of conflict in her demeanor. Past Kai's shoulder I saw the gun pointed at me, and it made me mad. Then I looked at Kai. At his strong body and his warm brown eyes. I stepped aside to face January.

"You have my word."

Jan stared me down. She looked at Kai then back at me to make sure that I understood the stakes clearly. I did. If I went back on my word, I would lose Kai's love. I would lose Kai. He wouldn't be able to help it. She smiled and took two steps back.

"I keep the diamond. I get my life back tomorrow. If by some unimaginable fluke you win, Liat, then you all back off for a week while I disappear."

"Done," said Liat. "Let's order some pizza. I'm starving."

"On it," said Kai. He crossed the kitchen and began opening drawers in search of the standard household stash of take out menus.

Jan put the gun in her back pocket. She turned on the sink, ran the dishcloth under some cold water, and pressed it to the bump on her forehead.

"Hey Liat, why don't you call and check the forecast," Jan called over her shoulder. "See what kind of swells we're looking at for tomorrow."

I sank into a kitchen chair and shook my head, watching the three of them. It was like the twilight zone. Then I thought of the newsroom. I stopped to consider all of its quirks, the shorthand that exists between reporters and editors when a big story is breaking. The camaraderie. I belonged to it heart and soul. With only a few weeks of surfing under my belt I was getting the hang of the mechanics of it. But in that world I was still just a tolerated guest. I watched the three of them interact with an ease that most people rarely attain with their own families. Kai, Liat, and Jan were as different as three people could be. But they understood each other in a way I couldn't fathom. The deal was made. They'd given their words and that was that. I watched Kai phone in the pizza order and realized that I had barely scratched the surface.

CHAPTER FORTY TWO

The slightly muddy water of Honolua Bay shimmered, offering the day a sunny illusion of normalcy. Hardcore fans arrived early to secure a spot on the small crescent of beach that was made more of rocks than sand. Because of the space constraints most fans kept their possessions to a minimum. Binoculars, some sandwiches, and a few hidden beers were standard fare for the day. Above the bay, up on the cliffs, there was a decent view and room for even more fans. By seven thirty in the morning both areas were packed. The distance from beach to water is short at Honolua Bay but the waves that break there are a different matter. They are far out into the water. Once a surfer picks a swell, the ride back toward shore can be as long as six hundred yards. A lot can happen in six hundred yards.

Much farther out into the bay where the water was a more pleasing blue, two lava pipes, flowing in cross directions, reached their pressure point at the intersection and blew a small hole up and into the ocean floor.

Perched in the rocky sand near Kai, I watched the surfers throw their boards into the ocean and paddle into the lineup. I wanted to talk to him but there was no real time for conversation. Kai's fans were keeping him occupied with autograph books and an assortment of sharpie ready body parts. Adding to the distraction was a set of twins directly in front of me. The girls looked to be about ten or so and they were fighting over everything. Gummi bears, a bucket and shovel, even a broken seashell. Three different times their mother picked up the offending object, told them to stop bickering, and then handed it to the kid closest to her. Eventually the short-changed twin had had enough. She stood in front of her mother and stomped her foot in the sand. With great conviction she declared, "You always give her everything. You love her better than me." I tried to block the kids out. Tried to think.

Mak came up next to me and dropped an arm around my shoulders. He blew in from Oahu around eleven the night before. Liat sent him a text knowing that he would be flying over for the competition and asked him to bring all of the boards and equipment. Mak was surprised when he found out the rest of us were already in Honolua Bay but they brought him up to speed pretty quickly. Like the rest of them he took the deal in stride. I don't know why I was surprised.

"You okay?"

"Are you talking about the ample fans or last night?"

Mak grinned. "Take your pick."

Before I could answer, Kai's fans spotted Mak and spread out to include him in their squealing circle of hugs. I threw him an, 'I'm good' smile as they enveloped him, and then made my way closer to the ocean.

Truth is, I wasn't good yet. But I would be soon. Like the rest of them I had given my word. Jan could take the diamond. She could even have a head start if it came to that. But no one, including Jan, had said a word about the liberty bell. Aside from DNA from Jan, it was the perfect piece of evidence. Jan's fingerprints were on it for sure. If it still had Melanie's prints on it then not only would the bell connect Jan to the deaths in Philadelphia but it would give the police in Honolulu a motive for Mel's death as well.

I remembered about the bell just before we left for the beach. The problem was I couldn't find it. The gym bag it was in yesterday was empty. January must have taken it and put it somewhere else. As I sat watching Kai autograph paper and people, the thought ate away at me. There was a ready look in Jan's eyes this morning. She would disappear fast, with all of her stuff, if things didn't go her way. Think, I told myself. She must have packed the bell in a different bag. There's no way she would have left it behind.

A loud horn blasted, signaling the start of the competition. I crowded in with the rest of the fans to watch the first pair of surfers take to the waves. It wasn't long before I spotted Jan up on a wave. I checked the clock on my cell phone. Damn. I should have moved sooner. Not enough time now to weave through the crowd, find her things, and discreetly remove the evidence before Jan was out of the water. I held up my binoculars just in time to catch Jan's competitor, Reenie Sawyer, taking off on her first wave. It was a beauty. Long and clean. Reenie made the most of it too but the lip was heavy and she wasn't fast enough to escape it. She lost her board and went under. A disappointed awwwwwe rippled through the crowd. By now Jan was paddling into the next wave. She caught it, popping to her feet just as the swell jacked up to its full height. As she rode the wall I found myself willing her feet to stay with the board. Jan had to win this heat. The more rounds she was in the ocean the more time I had to find that bell.

There wasn't much time but I decided to make my way up the beach anyhow. I had to try. The waiting area for the competing surfers was roped off and the crowd nearby was thick. Somewhere overhead I heard the horn blasting the end of the heat. I moved faster, groping my way to the front and eventually I caught sight of Liat. She was kneeling in the sand, waxing her board. I wanted to call out to her. To tell her what needed to be done. But she was deep in thought, engrossed in her task, and the last thing I wanted to do was break her concentration before she entered the water. Besides, there wasn't enough time anyway. All of a sudden, a few feet from where I was standing the crowd parted. January and Reenie trudged through the fans, dripping wet, graciously signing autographs. I lowered my head and stood back as they moved toward the waiting area and ducked under the rope. A few seconds later, the announcement came. Jan had won the heat. I breathed a sigh of relief. There was nothing more I could do but wait for Jan to go back in the ocean. Wait and watch.

None of us felt it. Not the surfers. Not the judges. Not the crowd. Maybe a couple of bugs in the sand but no one paid attention when they scurried off. The rest of us continued our day as if nothing had happened. But it had. One of the lava pipes shifted slightly and started to collapse. The other, heavier, pipe continued to run strong, spewing lava through the small hole that had erupted in the ocean floor earlier, making it bigger.

Tucked inside the crowd I watched as Jan made her way to the back of the waiting area. To a row of benches adjacent to where the surfers kept their boards. A pile of gym bags had been strewn on and under the benches. Jan dug through the pile and came away with a sleek green and yellow bag with the Billabong logo on the side. It wasn't the only Billabong bag in the group. She toweled herself off and threw on a dry t-shirt. Then she took out sunblock and smattered some on her nose and shoulders. After that she zipped the bag closed and tucked it back under the pile, just beneath a black Quicksilver bag and next to a blue and white Roxy one. Green and yellow Billabong I repeated to myself. Billabong. I was satisfied that I could find it. Getting to it without being noticed? That was another matter.

I tried. Slipping under the rope was no problem. Looking like I belonged there was something else. I asked questions. Interviewing the surfers was the best reason I could think of for being behind the ropes even though reporters weren't allowed back there during the competition. It didn't help. Just being back there wasn't enough. I couldn't rifle through the bags without being seen. There were too many people milling around. Before I could figure out what to do next, security spotted me and escorted me outside the ropes. I slipped back into the crowd and tried to form a new plan. Meanwhile Jan and Liat fought it out in the ocean whittling down their opponents in separate heats and steadily advancing toward the final.

"Liat!" I waved my arms and yelled to her, jumping up and down from the crowd outside the ropes.

"Liat!"

She didn't see me. Frustrated, I made my way to the front again and slipped under, careful to keep an eye out for security.

"Liat." I called again.

She turned this time, a look of surprise on her face.

"What are you doing here?"

There was no room for private conversation.

"Look," I whispered. "I need you to do something for me. I've been trying all day to get at Jan's bag but I can't. It's a green and yellow Billabong and it's near the end on the right side. There's a blue Roxy bag next to it and a black Quicksilver bag on top. Liat you have to go get it for me."

"Let it be Willow. I gave my word. You gave yours too."

"Not about this. Remember the liberty bell? The one I took from Jan's office? That was never part of the deal. Come on Liat. That bell is the perfect piece of evidence. Please. She'll be back any minute."

I waited by the edge of the rope. Four minutes later Liat came back. Empty handed.

"All she had in there was sun block, a towel, and some clothes," Liat whispered.

"What about the diamond?" I whispered back, confused.

"Knowing Jan she probably taped it to her body."

I shook my head. "She wouldn't do that. Would she? I mean, what if it falls out?"

Liat thought of Nick and it made her grin. "So what if it does? There's nothing we can do to change things now."

"You mean let her get away with it. No way." I paced around for a second and then stared at Liat.

"There has to be another bag. Even if she kept the diamond with her, she had to put the gun and the liberty bell somewhere else."

The horn went off again. The crowd hushed itself as the final heat of the day was announced. January Pokani and Liat Kanunu.

"Gotta go," Liat shouted over the noise. She turned and headed toward the stack of surfboards. January was already there, choosing her board for the final heat.

I crossed the beach in search of Kai. He wasn't hard to find. All I had to do was follow the trail of giggling bikinis. Kai was patient as always, signing autographs and chatting with the fans. I was determined to get that liberty bell and yet I found myself standing back a minute to watch him. It wasn't jealousy. My heart swelled. I was happy for him. Surprising, and maybe a little stupid considering the bouquet of bodies arranged at his fingertips. It didn't matter. I could feel his kindness. It radiated through the crowd and warmed a part of me I thought had been dead and buried along that dirt road in Iraq. He looked up. Saw me and flashed a brilliant smile. Then he motioned for me to join him. When I hesitated he came and drew me near.

"Where've you been all day?" Then he added. "Never mind. You're here now." He raised his binoculars and floated his arm around my shoulders.

"Unbelievable, right? Both of them making it to the last heat. Man, this morning I thought Reenie was gonna take Jan down in the first heat. It must've scared the daylights out of Jan though because she's been on fire ever since. Look at those swells. This is gonna be something else."

Kai's enthusiasm was infectious. We stared out at the ocean watching Jan and Liat fight their way toward the biggest waves. Jan edged into the first wave and rose with the swell. She sped down the wall, plied it with some quick, snappy moves and then somehow broke through the lip. I don't know how her ride went after that though because all I could think about was the bell. I had to find that bell before Jan came out of the ocean.

The car. If it wasn't in her gym bag it had to be in one of the cars. Between us we had four rental cars. Liat and I drove to Angela's house in one. Jan followed us in another. Kai rented a third and Mak came in a fourth after flying to Maui last night. Four cars. We'd driven only two of them to the beach. Kai and I in one. Jan, Liat, and Mak in the other. I seriously doubted that Jan had plans to go back to the house so that let out two of the cars. Kai and I packed the Firebird, so that was probably out. The Toyota. The liberty bell was in the red Toyota Camry. It had to be. There was no time to be wrong.

"Kai where's Mak?"

"What?"

"Mak. Where is he? I need to talk to him."

"Uhhm..." Kai dropped his arm from my shoulder and scanned the crowd.

"Over there," he pointed.

I followed his finger to the water's edge. Mak was chatting with some photographers and—was that Nick? It looked like Nick. Perched on crutches, standing next to Mak. I didn't have time to wonder what he was doing at the contest. I started toward them.

"Hey wait!" Kai tugged at my hand. I turned and gave him a quick hug. Too quick. I should have tried to make it last.

"I'll explain later. Promise," I said, breaking away and moving toward Mak as fast as the thick crowd would let me. I made it to his side just in time to see Jan pick up her fourth wave.

"Hey Wil," Mak grinned. "Man what a contest! Liat's as fluid as ever but you gotta give Jan credit."

"She's really going after every wave," Nick agreed.

"I don't know," Mak said. "This thing could go either way."

I grabbed at Mak's hand and started tugging him toward the cliffs, toward the parking lot.

"Mak let's go. The keys to the Toyota—where are they?"

"I don't have them."

"What?!" I stopped dead in my tracks and turned to stare at him. Nick was staring at both of us.

"What do you mean you don't have them? You drove the car to the beach, right?"

"Jan took them. Right after we got to the beach. I guess trust only runs so deep, huh," he quipped, throwing a sideways glance at Nick. Nick had no clue what he was talking about. In some ways he was as much of an outsider as me. Nick never would have agreed to the deal we made.

"No...no friggin' way." I stood in the rocky sand and shook my head. Then I grabbed Mak's hand again and tugged harder.

"Come on let's go. We don't have a second to waste."

I had no idea how true that was.

Behind us Liat and Jan lay flat on their boards churning their way through the ocean, fighting for position on the next good wave. There was a decent chance it would be the last one before the horn blasted the end of the heat. Winner takes all.

Jan's stroke was forceful. She was a good bit taller than Liat and absolutely relentless. Liat was unconcerned. She synced her board and body to the powerful rhythms swaying beneath her. When she was ahead by a few feet, Liat turned her board into the rising swell and edged Jan out. The wave was hers.

Then something made Liat stop. Some deep-seated instinct lit every nerve ending she had. Liat stopped stroking. She sat up on her board and let the wave get away.

Jan saw it and stroked liked mad to pass Liat and make it into the wave. On the beach the crowd groaned at Liat's lost opportunity, then howled triumphantly as Jan stole the moment back. It was a good wave and she rode it well to the crowd's delight. It was enough to put her ahead of Liat.

Liat paid no attention to Jan or the crowd. She'd already turned her board back to the ocean. She sat and waited for the last wave in the set. It was barely visible. On the beach an official picked the horn up off the table. He checked his stopwatch and counted down the seconds.

Liat felt the ocean rising. It rolled toward her with sloppy movements but by the time Liat paddled in and popped into place, the wave had fixed itself into a long even wall. The late day sun glared across it as the white lip hung ever so briefly before curling down perfectly over the glassy beauty. Liat danced up and down the wall with expert precision. Then she sped through the tube riding every nuance of the wave as if she'd carved the watery bumps herself.

Everyone saw how magnificent the wave was. No one knew why. No one noticed the sand shift ever so slightly either. But it did. All because the broken pipe of lava that had been forcing tons of pressure against one side of the cracked stretch of earth that ran below the Kilauea volcano and out into the Pacific Ocean was now empty. Weightless. No one felt it. No one noticed. After all, the earthquake was days ago. But all at once, the two walls that were cracked for miles and had been fighting for days to occupy the same space, groaned out an agreement. One side remained stationary. The other side slid upwards, a good five inches. Liat's wave was already headed for the beach and it did get a slight boost from the upward slide, just enough to make it spectacular. But it was barely an inkling of what was to come.

"Where are we going?" Mak wanted to know.

I didn't answer until I was under the rope.

"Wait here," I told him. Then I went straight to the benches. It was faster than trying to explain things to Mak. Kneeling on the ground I unzipped Jan's bag and ran my hands along the bottom. Thirty seconds later I felt metal hit my palm and breathed a sigh of relief. I pulled out the keys and headed back to the rope.

"Hey! What do you think you're doing?!"

A muscular woman with wet blonde hair and a tattoo of an owl in a tree, splayed on her right calf, grabbed me by the hair and yanked me backwards.

"Jeeze. Let go of me!" I barked, squeezing my fingers over the fistful of hair she was holding.

"It's okay Grace. You can let her go," Makani advised as he ducked under the rope. "She's with me."

The tattooed blonde turned toward Mak, taking her chunk of my hair along for the ride.

"Oh, hi Mak," she smiled. He motioned for her to let go of me.

"Yeah, I don't think so," she replied. "I just watched this chick rip something off outta somebody's bag."

Just then we heard the final horn blasting across the beach. The competition was over.

With her free hand Grace pried open my fist.

"See?"

Mak leaned in and took the keys.

"Yeah. These are mine. Well, actually they're Jan Pokani's. We came together and I really need to get something out of the rental car. Don't worry. I'll bring 'em right back. Fast. I Promise."

Grace eyed Mak for a second. He flashed her a winning smile.

"Alright," She relented, unwinding her hand from my hair.

"Nice meeting you to," I quipped, rubbing my head and ducking back under the rope before she could change her mind and snag another chunk.

Nick hobbled up behind Mak. "What's up?" He wanted to know.

Mak and I looked at each other. The beach at Honolua Bay is located on a Marine Preserve and it's anything but easy to access. After climbing the steps to the cliff, you have to go through a small forest just to get to the parking lot. Nick would never make it. Not fast enough.

"Stay here. We're just going to the car to get something. We'll be right back."

Mak and I didn't wait for an answer. We took off at a rapid sprint.

"You going after the diamond?" Mak asked, incredulous, as he ran next to me.

"Something better," I responded. I didn't want to elaborate. Mak was Jan's brother. In hindsight, taking Mak with me wasn't completely necessary. I could have left Mak at the water's edge as soon as I realized he didn't have the car keys. If I had, Nick might have stayed behind too.

What if? What if? What if? But I don't do what ifs these days. Not me. Not anymore. Done with that.

The announcement for the crowning ceremony came a few moments later. Just about the same time that data from the rising wall in the ocean hit the computers at the Pacific Tsunami Warning System based in Honolulu. It's a good system. If a tsunami forms way out in the middle of the ocean, then countries with shore points most likely to be affected can get advanced warning. If it forms way out in the ocean. Closer to shore? Not so much.

We heard the twang of the bullhorn being turned on as the announcer stepped up to the podium to proclaim the winner. Mak and I both stopped at the top of the cliffs to listen.

"Liat Kawa!" He shouted. The crowd went wild.

All I could think was—January lost.

"Mak, come on, let's go!"

But Mak just grinned at me like a proud papa.

"Go Liatttt!!!" He shouted down over the cliffs. People nearby joined right in. "Liat! Liat! Liat!" They chanted. The crowd on the beach picked up the chant and swelled with it, right back up to the crowd on the cliffs. Liat! Liat! Liat!"

I was happy for Liat. Really. I wished I could join in, be in the moment with them. But all I could think about was Jan. The crowning ceremony wouldn't take long. She would be on her way to the car in minutes. Anxious, I glanced toward the steps. Jan wasn't coming yet but Nick was. Great, what next, I wondered as I watched him hobbling his way to the top of the cliffs. I tapped Mak on the shoulder and pointed in Nick's direction. Mak shook his head.

"Go ahead," he said, tossing me the keys. "I'll catch up."

I found the car pretty quickly. It was the first thing that went right all day. But the back of the red Camry was packed full. Go figure, finally something Jan and I had in common—too much baggage. I dumped out everything that wasn't nailed down and started sifting through it. When I unzipped one of Jan's bags and the liberty bell tumbled into the parking lot, I nearly cried.

"What's that?" Nick asked as Mak leaned him up against the car and released him with a grunt.

"Sweet freedom," I replied kissing the crack on the bell.

Makani let out a long whistle. Then he hunkered down next to the back right tire and lifted something out of the dirt.

"If that's freedom then what do you call this?"

Nick and I turned to look.

In the palm of his hand was the Maui Snow. The 43-carat black diamond glinted in the sunlight. With all hell breaking loose after we found it in the tree house, I never did get a good look at it. It really was a beautiful diamond. Rare and precious, right? Looking at it now though I couldn't help thinking how absurd that was considering what January had done, was willing to do, over a rock. It was sad really. To take something genuinely rare and beautiful and apply *so much* value to it that we corrupt ourselves over it and in the end warp its natural value—warp its place in the universe. Because at the end of the day the Maui Snow is just a rock. One rock in a vast universe of rocks and dirt and stardust. As I stood there, staring at the gem that fit so neatly into the palm of Mak's hand, thoughts of Iraq popped into my head. Not a flashback this time—just a stream of clarity and some incredibly sad thoughts concerning the middle east in general. It was, after all, dirt and stardust. A rock deemed extraordinarily valuable. All in the name of, what, religion? Oil? Instead of finding a way to appreciate its beauty, to share it, to use it productively, we resort to wasting an even greater resource, the best resource we have at our disposal. Our humanity. After all of the death and destruction, the centuries of people willing to kill each other's children, sisters and brothers, aunts, uncles, friends, after reducing their precious lives to a cycle of kill or be killed, in the end what's been gained? The ability to fight the same battles over and over again? To reclaim the same weary patches of dirt? It makes no sense when we live on a planet still brimming with promise, in a universe vast with untapped opportunities. Why not use some common sense, some imagination? Figure out new ways for everyone to prosper. Recognize the true freedom, the absolute beauty and value in that. Then stick with it. If not, if no agreement can be struck then plant some pansies on the space and please, call it a day.

"Put the diamond down and let's go," the better part of me advised. Setting the bell aside, I started shoving the rest of the stuff I'd piled on the ground, back into the car. The last thing I wanted to do was run into Jan in the parking lot.

I headed through the small forest and back toward the steps that led down from the cliffs. I was in a hurry to get back to the beach. Back to Kai. That's when I heard it. The sucking sound. That's the only way I can think of to describe it. A loud, out of place, sucking sound. Something about it made me stop. I stared out over the edge of the cliffs. Down at the people who all seemed to be staring at the ocean.

Afterwards I looked over my shoulder for Mak. He was about thirty yards behind me. Helping Nick. When I turned around and looked over the cliffs again I noticed the birds. They were so quiet. For a moment there wasn't a single peep in the air. Just that loud, loud sucking sound. Then it came. The birds let out one long and disturbing screech. In a single movement they all fluttered and then sped across the sky. The hairs on the back of my neck stood up. Something about it must have bothered Mak too because he unhitched himself from Nick and sprinted toward the cliffs. He cocked his head sideways and listened. That's when I noticed the beach. It looked…bigger. Before I could say anything, Mak gripped my arm with a vicious tug. Then he shoved the car keys in my hand. His gray eyes were huge.

"Go! Willow! Get Nick to the car. Fast. Get Nick to the car and get the hell out of here!" Now!"

"What?! Why?" I turned back to the cliffs. The beach was growing. I raised the binoculars and saw fish flopping in the wet sand. And people. Some of them were playing with the fish. Others were running for the cliffs. It was still oddly quiet. Except for that sucking sound. Then, all at once you could feel it. The terror rising. Like fog steaming off a lake. Not much screaming. Just running. It seemed that in an instant the steps leading up to the cliffs were clogged. There was a glut of people near the back of the beach by now. They looked at the steps and they knew. So they latched onto the bottom of the cliffs and started climbing.

Mak smacked the binoculars out of my hand and shook me.

"Tsunami!!" He screamed at me, almost at the same time as the announcer on the beach blasted it over the bullhorn.

"The ocean is pulling back," Mak shouted. "It's pulling back and in minutes it's going to roll through here faster than a 747!"

"But the cliffs," I argued. "We're so high."

"No time!" Mak shouted. "Get Nick. Get out of here now!"

He turned me around and shoved me toward Nick. Toward the trees. Toward the parking lot. Most of the people who'd been watching the competition from the top of the cliffs were running by now. I ran toward Nick, stopping once to look over my shoulder at Mak. He was on his knees. Leaning over the cliff to help a young boy near the top. When he was done he leaned down and pulled up the next person. I turned back to Nick. He was hobbling awkwardly toward the trees with the rest of the crowd. I caught up to him, threw my arm around his waist, and together we sprinted as fast as we could manage. All I could think about was Kai. And Liat. Even Jan. I looked behind me again, hoping to see Mak. He should be coming by now. Where was he? Where was Kai? I kept on running, the sucking sound ringing in my ears.

"Car or the trees?" Nick wheezed.

He should have stayed in the hospital. We both knew he was in no condition to be running. Still, it was a good question. Car or trees? Speed or height? Once the wave hit there would be no outrunning it.

"Can you climb?"

"Probably not. But you can, Willow. Go, I'll be fine."

"Car then," I said, gripping him a little tighter and forcing us to pick up speed. We ran in sync. Like the perfect couple who always wins the three-legged race. I guess panic has an upside. In the end we reached the car faster than I thought possible. It took us three, maybe four minutes.

I unlocked the door and that's when I saw them. Five neatly stacked surfboards tied to the roof. I recognized two of them right away. Pele and Poliahu. Mak must have brought them. There was no time to wonder why.

"Nick you can drive, right?"

"Good," I added without waiting for his answer. I opened the car door, unhooked him from my shoulder, and leaned him inside. I put the keys in the ignition.

"The car!! Where's your mother?! Where's the friggin' car?!!" Shouted a slender man in his thirties, not more than five feet away. He was pushing two small children in a stroller, while a third stood petrified at his side, watching the crowd of people run past them in search of their own cars.

"Over here!!" Nick and I shouted at the same time. "Hurry!" I added. "You can look for her on the way out." The man didn't hesitate. In another minute, the parking lot would be jammed with drivers, all trying to exit at the same time.

"Give me twenty seconds to get these boards down," I told Nick as the man tossed his kids in the car. "Then back up and take off."

"Wait. Willow, what are you doing?" He shouted. But I was already up on the running board, unhooking the ropes. I threw three of them out into the grass. There were a lot of people trying to climb up those cliffs. A lot of people who would never make it to their cars. I picked up the Pele and Poliahu boards and then banged on the roof of the car.

"Go!"

Nick was shouting out the window at me to get in the car. With the surfboards locked under my arm, I took off for the cliffs. But the boards were too heavy. I dropped Pele's before I even got ten steps from the car. Afterwards I clutched Poliahu's close and forced myself to keep running with it. I strained my ears, listening for the odd sucking sound but it was so feint now I could hardly hear it. Not that it mattered. Nick was gone. The car was gone. There was no going back.

I actually found Mak. He was running hard in the crowd by now and well away from the cliffs. Plenty of people were still climbing, still hoping for a hand up and over the stiff incline. It wouldn't have mattered. It was too late.

Mak grabbed the board from me and we ran like hell through the trees. We picked the first empty one we could find. There was barely enough time to climb. We got as high as we could and then wedged ourselves in between two thick branches with Poliahu's surfboard tucked underneath of us. All around us people were running, climbling, clinging. Mak and I huddled together and stared out at the beach. It was a sight I'll never forget. So many people. Still running.

The wave had drawn itself back from Honolua Bay for nearly three quarters of a mile–shoving itself up hard against the full weight of the Pacific Ocean. With 232 quintillion gallons of water to work with, the Pacific grunted–and shoved back.

"Ohhhhhhhhhhhhhhhh...Holy mother of God!"

***

Kai was about three steps from the edge of the water when the ocean went all hinky. He was facing the podium, his gentle eyes locked with Jan's ruined blues, willing her to do the right thing. But then there was that starfish. It was glinting in the sun and it distracted him. Off to Kai's right, directly across from the podium, the starfish was sitting about three feet out into the ocean. Only it wasn't in the ocean. It was in the sand. Where the ocean was supposed to be. Kai looked away from the podium, craning his neck farther to the right to get a better view of the beach. Pure terror raced through his veins. There were visible strips of coral. Hermit crabs and seaweed, sea turtles and globefish were all strewn across the beach. Like leftovers waking up from a keg party, they were groggy, flopping, completely disoriented by their sudden change in circumstance. Kai stared in horror as a giggling toddler plucked the starfish from its perch in the wet sand and ran to show the prize to his mother. The beach was getting bigger by the second.

On the podium, Liat bent down toward the chubby, contest Official as he placed the lei around her neck and then a leafy crown upon her head. She was a vision, with her lengthy Polynesian hair wisping in the breeze as she waved to the throng of fans.

Kai cupped his hands around the edges of his mouth and shouted with every fiber of his being. "Tsunami!! Tsunami!!!"

The Official scowled at the interruption. Some in the crowd twittered, thinking it was a badly timed joke. But others had already begun to notice the same changes as Kai.

"Tsunami!" He shouted again.

This time the Official stole a quick glance at the ocean. His face went white. He picked up the bullhorn and blasted the tsunami warning across the beach. People stopped mid-laugh and ran for the cliffs.

Kai scanned the crowd, his stomach muscles clenching tighter with each passing second. Liat stepped down from the winner's perch and tugged at his hand. Jan stood on the podium behind them. She swept a glance out at the ocean and the growing beach. Then bolted, and immediately began clawing her way through the crowd of people all rushing toward the cliffs.

"Have you seen Willow?"

"No. Not since before the last heat. What about Mak and Nick?"

"Half hour ago at least. Down by the water." Kai stretched his neck and searched the crowd again. Liat tugged harder.

"Kai! Come on! We gotta get outta here!"

They took off for the cliffs. But the crowd ahead of them was already getting frantic. Liat stole another glance at the receding ocean. She'd never seen anything like it. They had a surging crowd in front of them and an unfathomable wall of seawater forming at their backs. They were screwed. Liat patted the crown on her head and squeezed Kai's hand a little tighter. Royally screwed.

Then an idea hit Kai. He looked down at Liat and before he could even say it, her eyes grew wide with acknowledgement.

"Fat Lucy!" They both shouted.

Without another word they turned toward the left and took off down the beach. They ran past the waiting area for the competitors. Past the stack of surfboards. Behind the judges' tent and toward the giant gray rocks that led from the ocean back up toward the cliffs.

Somewhere in the middle of those rocks was the entrance to a cave that resembled a giant elephant. Fat Lucy. Lucy's right ear flapped forward and curled away from the ocean. As kids they would climb in Lucy's ear and race their way up through her upturned trunk, which split into two separate caves that eventually led to Lucy's right and left nostrils. They would race through the tunnels and then up through openings which dumped them a few feet from the top of the cliffs. The first kid up would beat their chest and declare themselves king/queen of the cliffs. Any kid in Hawaii who had been dragged to an all day surfing event at Honolua Bay eventually discovered the wonders of Fat Lucy.

Clawing her way through the crowd January turned anxiously to check on the monster forming at her back. The ocean was still receding. As she turned back toward the cliffs she noticed Kai and Liat break away from the main crowd and cut down the beach toward the rocky cliffs to the left. It took her less than a second to figure out why. Once she did she turned back to the crowd of people still in front of her, assessed her chances, and then sprinted toward Fat Lucy.

They made it to the entrance pretty quickly but there were others already climbing over the rocks toward Lucy's ear. Kai hoisted Liat up onto a rock and then climbed up after her. Suddenly there was a tug on his right ankle and he nearly toppled backwards. Liat reached out and grabbed his hand. Kai caught his balance and looked down.

A sturdy woman of about thirty-five, wearing a sky blue baseball cap, held a toddler up toward Kai. With tears in her eyes, she begged Kai to save the child. Kai remembered him. It was the boy he'd seen clutching the starfish. Kai took the child in his arms. Then he dropped an arm down to the woman so that he could yank her up onto the rock with them. But she put both hands up and backed away.

"I can't," she protested, turning to look behind her.

Kai followed her line of sight and saw the wheelchair. Inside was another boy. He was about fourteen. He had bucked teeth and hands that curled in toward his elbows.

Three quarters of a mile away, the sucking sound stopped.

Kai shifted the toddler to Liat. Without another thought he jumped down and closed the short distance to the wheelchair. In one awkward movement he lifted the boy's stiff body out of the chair, threw him over his shoulder like an infant and ran back to Liat. Somehow he managed the boy and then himself up the rocks. He turned back to help the woman but she was already half way up, climbing the rocks on her own.

"Go. Take the boys." She waved him away. "I'm right behind you," she promised.

Kai, Liat, and the boys squeezed through Lucy's ear. There were at least forty people already in the cave ahead of them. Most were moving rapidly toward Lucy's trunk. The entrance to the cave was getting more clogged by the second. Kai leaned the boy against the cave wall, next to a balding man with a goatee and a beer gut so round it look like he was about to give birth. The man looked miserable. When the partially paralyzed boy toppled a bit and fell into him he shot Kai a dark look.

"Friggin' asshole! Can't ya see people are tryin' ta stay alive. Ya got no business draggin' a cripple in here. Dumbest thing ever."

That's when my lovable Zen-like Kai formed a rapid fist and sent it straight toward the man's jaw. Funny thing. It was the crippled boy who stopped him. He flew his mangled hand up at the air in front of the man's goatee and managed to stop Kai's punch just before it landed. Regaining himself, Kai pulled back and mouthed a silent thank you to the boy. The teenager flashed him a brilliant buck toothed grin.

Liat missed the entire exchange. She was staring at the entrance. "Where is she, Kai? The boys' mother. She should have made it in by now."

"Get them moving Liat. Fast. You," he shouted at the balding man. "You help her, help him." Then he deposited the crippled boy into the man's arms, leaving no room for argument. "Head as far into the trunk as you can get," Kai directed. "I'll go find her."

"Left!" The teenager wheezed at the balding man. "Left!"

Liat looked back at Kai for confirmation.

"It's easier to get up the cliffs from the right," Kai admitted.

"Left!" The teenager insisted. "Left!"

Kai shrugged.

"Okay, left." Liat repeated.

Kai weaved his way toward the entrance just in time to see January squeezing through Lucy's ear. He didn't realize who it was at first. Her head was bent and her ponytail was tucked up under a sky blue cap. Kai brushed past her to get to the entrance. She looked up and for a brief moment their eyes connected. Kai's stomach lurched. He climbed up and over the protective cover of Lucy's ear to search for the boys' mother. She was nowhere in sight. He looked to his right and saw that the cliffs were full of people clutching at dirt and roots, hair and tee shirts, arms and legs, anything they could use to shelter themselves from the ocean swelling at their backs. People were falling. Stragglers from the back of the beach, who had been confused at first, were now scrambling with a vengeance to get a foothold at the bottom of the cliffs. More people fell. Kai closed his eyes and turned his head away–his heart nearly stopping at the awful sight. When he opened them again he saw the newly formed mile of beach getting swallowed whole by the Pacific Ocean.

"Back! Get Baaaack! Go! Gogogogogogogo!!!!!

People inside the cave were moving fast. They huddled close and ran inwards like skittish zebras vying for the middle of the herd–hoping to keep as far from the encroaching lions as possible. Kai skimmed along the edge of the cave wall and did his best to catch up to Liat and the boys.

"Liat!!"

Liat shifted the toddler in her arms and turned just in time to see January push past a slender man in his sixties, running to Liat's left.

The man tripped and fell. In an instant he was gone. Trampled over by the crowd. Liat's stomach tightened. A burst of heat rushed through her veins. The crowd growled with anger at January's thoughtless action and then—reacted without thought. Despite the danger to themselves they shoved back at her. Hard. Two more people fell. The entire incident unfolded in less than eight seconds, and then the crowd pressed on. Just like that. Suddenly Liat found herself running shoulder to shoulder with January. It was an unexpected moment and the two women locked eyes. January opened her mouth to say something but then...nothing came out. She blinked. Liat's eyes were so big. So full and they were spilling so much thought into...January tried to close her lids again but they wouldn't budge. She didn't want to see. She didn't want to understand. Liat stared harder. Like her brother Benny, January would have to choose.

Kai found them just before Fat Lucy's trunk split.

"Left!!"

The crowd split and there was a steady stream in both directions. Kai put an arm across Liat's shoulder and steered left. The balding man holding the screaming teenager had other ideas. He turned to Kai and dumped the boy in his arms.

"You said right was faster, and I'm goin' right. The wave won't get as high as the cliffs but water is definitely gonna spill in through the lower entrance."

"Some maybe," Kai conceded. "But Lucy's ear flaps forward and curls under. It's pretty well covered."

"No! Mister no!" The boy reached over and pawed at the man's sleeve with his curled hand. "The water...too high too fast," he wheezed. "Left side...blocked tight...like puzzle pieces. Jammed it...myself. Safer back there."

The man snorted at the idea and pulled his arm free of the boy.

"After first wave...…recedes," the boy tried to convince him between labored breaths. "After...then we climb out...…run like...…the wind!"

But there was no convincing him. The man turned and ran the other way. So did a lot of others. Seconds later the entire cave shook with the impact as the tsunami slammed against it. Within moments, Kai, Liat and about a dozen others were up to their calves in water.

322

Nobody spoke a word. They just ran. Up, far up through the left side of the elephant's trunk—as fast as their feet would carry them.

They stopped about thirty feet from the top of the left nostril and scoped out a safe spot near an arch in the cave wall. There was a young man in his twenties, one of the underwater photographers from the surfing event, who volunteered to run ahead and check the opening. The nostril was blocked tight. Just like the teenager had told them. The boy hadn't had the breath or the time to explain that he used to hang out in the cave with his friends on a regular basis, before he slammed his neck against the bottom of a swimming pool. And that he knew from his friends that the rocks they had jammed into place five months ago where still intact.

They settled in and waited as the ocean flowed over the cave. It flowed and flowed and flowed. The screams came next, god-awful howls that started in the direction of the right nostril and echoed throughout the cave. Within minutes they faded into gurgles. Eventually they stopped altogether.

"What's your name?" Liat asked the teenager.

She was trying to distract the boys, as well as herself, from the floating bodies. The tsunami had rushed over Lucy's trunk, violently flushing the people down her right nostril, and back into her cheeks. They were then swept upward again by the rising water that was seeping in through Lucy's ear.

"Solomon," the boy answered as he watched the balding man with the beer gut float by.

"Solomon Frost."

Liat barely heard him. Another body brushed past her leg. Looking down at it, her knees began to shake. Her skin shivered. It was January. Face down with her arms and legs spread wide in the typical dead man's float. The toddler sitting in Liat's lap reached into the water and plucked the sky blue cap from January's head. He held it out to Liat with a smile and chirped, "Mommy hat. Mommy hat." Tears slid down Liat's cheeks. She pressed her chin to the boy's head and glanced over at his teenaged brother. Solomon's head was down, buried deep in the crook of his damaged elbow. Kai held him tight. There was little else he could do.

"What now?"

323

"We wait," Kai answered, the water rising toward his thighs. "Wait and pray."

Outside, the Pacific Ocean raged over Fat Lucy's trunk and sped hard at the cliffs.

***

One second Mak and I were climbing a tree. The next we were staring in awe and scared shitless as the beach at Honolua Bay got swallowed whole. You can't even fathom that much water. A mile of sand and blue sky, stacks of people, with heels, over heads over heels, at least fifteen layers high, all clawing up those cliffs. All engulfed in an instant. It was like watching water poured too fast into a fishbowl. The gravel and the goldfish, even the junk in the treasure chest, all of it, everything, goes flying in an instant swirling in lumpy circles waiting for the downpour to stop. But the water just kept rolling in.

The ocean roared over the cliffs and came straight at us flowing and flowing and flowing. Snapping branches, snapping trees. Mak and I held on, turning our heads as the Pacific rushed in about ten inches below our dangling feet. Then it spread across the parking lot and headed out toward the road. I let out a small breath of relief as I watched it go.

"Get ready!" Mak shouted.

"Ready? Ready for what?"

Mak didn't answer. He grabbed me by the shoulders and pushed me down flat over the surfboard. Then he pressed himself on top of me and gripped the edges.

"Oh no," I said trying to sit back up. "The surfboard was just in case. We made it," I cried. "We made it up the tree. We're safe."

"Hold on tight Willow. Do you hear me?" He shouted. "In a few minutes all that water is going to rush back through here. And it's going to be a helluva lot more violent on the way out. I know it's hard to imagine it can get any worse but trust me. It will."

Mak pressed me back into the surfboard. This time I stayed.

"Mak?"

"Yeah?"

"I'm glad I met you."

"Right back at ya little mermaid. You know, if Kai hadn't beaten me to it, I'd a been all over you."

"Mak? Tell him I love him."

"Tell him yourself."

"Mak, if I…and you don't…I'll tell Liat."

"She knows," Mak whispered against my ear. "She already knows."

We heard the trees. All around the small forest, snapping randomly. And then came the cars. They rolled in from the parking lot ramming into each other like bumper cars, twisting and turning, slamming into floating branches, into people, into trees.

A cool red and white vintage '66 Mustang crashed into the bottom of our tree, bounced off of it, then slammed into the one behind us and got wedged into that tree's trunk. It quickly started filling with water. Most of the cars that passed by us were empty. Cars, whose owners, never made it off the beach. But the Mustang had passengers. We watched, surprised, as a woman suddenly climbed out of it and threw herself up onto the roof. Then she leaned back in the window and pulled two kids up there with her. They looked familiar. It was the twins from the beach. I remembered the one girl stomping her foot in the sand as her mother gave the pack of Gummi bears to her sister. Mak and I looked at each other. The car was sinking fast.

Right then, our tree snapped with a loud pop and just like that we were in the speeding water too, rushing backwards through the forest. Mak tried to steer the surfboard. He did his best to keep us from getting annihilated by all the debris. When we banged into the top of the Mustang and stalled for a moment, the woman didn't hesitate. Without any warning she reached across and shoved one of her daughters at us. The poor kid was screaming at the top of her lungs. She was dangling half way between the surfboard and the Mustang. I latched onto the back of her shorts and slung her aboard. Afterwards, I crushed her face against my tee shirt, shielding her from view as best I could while her mother locked the other girl in a tight hug and sank with the Mustang below the rushing water. Earlier on the beach the girl in my arms had accused her mother of liking the other twin better. Judging by the expression on her Mom's face as she sank below the surface, I'd have to say the kid got it right.

Like I said, Mak did his best to steer us clear of the debris. But he couldn't do anything about the current. The wave was still receding, dragging us straight for the cliffs. We sped through the crumbling forest, hanging on for dear life.

The tree was huge. Mak and I both saw it coming at us at the same time. It was about six feet higher and a whole lot thicker than the one we snapped out of a few minutes before. It was the last defense in sight before the cliffs. Before the vast, raging Pacific Ocean.

"Go for it!" I shouted.

We were fifty yards and closing. The center of the tree was wide open with four big beautiful branches curling out of either side.

"Grab onto the right!" he shouted. "I'll take the left and try to wedge us in!"

We were twenty yards and closing. Mak steered the board straight for it. Then bam! We were blind-sided by something and went spinning out of control. I squeezed the little girl beneath me and held on tight as the surfboard spun like a blade in a blender. She was too scared to even scream. We all were. Suddenly I could feel Mak shifting above me. He was purposely throwing his weight in the opposite direction. Doing everything he could to slow us down. I looked up and tried to place the tree. Tried to see what hit us. As the spinning slowed to a twirl I saw it and screamed.

"Waaaaaaatch outttttttttt!!!"

Again we smacked right into it. I looked up and saw that it was three giant blocks of connected wood, with nearly a dozen people hanging onto it. It took me a second to figure out what it was. It was the winner's stand. Liat had been crowned there–what–like five minutes ago? We hit the blocks and bounced off again but the impact wasn't nearly as hard this time. They went screaming straight into the tree. People hanging off the blocks grabbed at the branches. A few made it. Others bobbed up and down in the raging water and then sped toward the cliffs.

We came screaming into the tree right behind them. Mak reached out but we were still spinning. He managed to clip an arm around one of the branches but couldn't hold the surfboard still and he had to let go. The branch snapped back and a thin little piece with a handful of leaves curled around it broke off and landed on the crown of Makani's head. I looked over at Mak and was struck by the sight. Even in the midst of all that chaos I couldn't help thinking about Liat's sculpture.

When Mak let go of the tree the board spun around and a slender woman of about fifty reached out and grabbed me by the arm. We managed to wedge my end of the surfboard in as best we could but the onslaught of rushing water was intense and the board kept bucking. Mak did everything he could to keep it straight. Just then, a man reached down from a higher branch, past the woman, and snagged onto my arm so he could pull me up. But the little girl was clinging to my waist. With my free arm I reached down and hoisted her up onto my hip. But the kid must've weighed a good fifty pounds and I couldn't get her any higher. I smiled up at the man and nodded. He understood and let go of my wrist. With both hands free now I shoved the little girl up and into his arms.

Once her weight was lifted from my end of the board, I slid right into Mak. The board bounced loose of the tree and the front end sprung straight up out of the water. Mak and I both fell off the back. I went under fast. Despite the shock of being in the water my eyes popped open and the first thing I saw were Mak's legs kicking furiously above my head. Mak launched himself at the surfboard and slammed it flat down on top of the water. I reached out and grabbed at his legs. With years of experience scrunched into a single heartbeat, he slid his chest over the board, and then hauled the rest of his body, including the extra hundred and ten pounds clinging to his legs, back above the surface of the raging water.

"Up here!" Mak shouted. "Hurry!" He grabbed onto me. I let go of his legs, reluctantly, and shimmied forward. As soon as I was close enough he slipped me under his chest. Seconds later, with Mak pressed flat against me, we washed over the edge of the cliff, and sped out into the ocean.

It was probably a full five minutes before I had the guts to look up again. Everything was gone. The parking lot. The forest. That last tree. The cliffs. The beach. All of it was completely out of sight.

That's when I felt it. Something sharp digging hard into the top of my thigh. It wouldn't let go. And it hurt. I couldn't turn my head to see what it was, but I pried my fingers from one edge of the board and squeezed a hand between my body and Mak's to get hold of whatever it was that had dug itself into my leg. I couldn't quite get at it. But it was razor sharp. When I pulled my hand back up to the front of the board there was blood on it. Alarmed, I tried again, rooting around this time until I could get a grip on whatever was poking at me. Then I yanked. Hard. I brought my hand up again and there was more blood.

"Stop it! You're gonna knock us off the surfbo–," Mak yelled, just before his voice went deathly quiet.

I couldn't help it. All of a sudden I could barely breathe. Something was digging so deep into my flesh it felt like my leg was breaking off. Once again my hand drifted down, as if in slow motion, to the space between Mak's body and mine. I shoved my hand beneath the fabric of his shorts and locked my hand around the object, pulling at it for all I was worth. With a grunt I wrenched hard, desperate to free it from my leg. When I brought my hand up I caught a glimpse, and then… total shock.

I tried to open my mouth, to shout something to Mak, but the surfboard bucked violently and went into a tailspin. My legs slipped over the side and fell into the ocean. Mak held onto me. He really tried. He was pressing his chest over my shoulders, determined to pull me back up.

I was in the water up to my waist by now and the pressure tugging on my legs was tremendous. I slid further into the ocean. Mak put a hand out to stop it, grabbing at my forearm, begging me to hold on. Instead I flashed him a rueful grin. Then I pressed the Maui Snow into his palm.

Mak must have had it still in hand just before the tsunami hit. The thought made me smile and as I loosened my fingers on the gem the ocean tugged hard at my hips and I let go. The last thing I remember was Mak crouching on the board, staring at the black diamond, disbelief etched into his face as I swirled away.

CHAPTER FORTY THREE

I came to in the coma ward. Well…came to is relative, I guess. I couldn't move. There were tubes and monitors attached to my limbs. I couldn't speak. But to say I was unconscious would be inaccurate. I was aware. More aware than I'd ever been when speech was part of the program. In fact, I was acutely aware of Kai sound asleep in the chair by my bed. He'd been there for weeks. Holding vigil. Waiting for me to wake up. I longed to give him his wish. More than anything I wanted to pick up his hand and run out of that dull gray ward so that once again I could feel the light of Hawaii burning on my skin.

"So do it," offered Makani. "Do it for both of us."

I threw an arm across Mak's shoulders. Granted, it was a lighter more ethereal version of the arm sprouting tubes and resting motionless beneath the sheets below us. I was in what I guess you would call another dimension. Only it's not what you think. It's not some far away separate place. It's much closer than that. More like a lighter brighter version of existence, as we know it. Textures, colors, scents, hearing, everything has less density but a whole lot more oooommpf to it. There's more speed, more knowledge, and much more clarity. It was amazing. Except that I couldn't talk to Kai.

Or rather he couldn't hear me. I could hear him just fine. I could hear Kai and everyone else for miles. It was as if I was plugged into a different frequency now and Kai's antenna couldn't tune in. I could see like that too. I could see the past and the present. All the good and awful deeds I was so desperate to remember just a short time ago were now clear as a bell. It was quite a realization. A bruising adjustment. Then again, having Mak around helped. Mak and all the other coma patients could hear me just fine.

That clarity, the ability to see and hear came almost immediately. For instance, even though I had no physical memory of what happened after I slipped off the surfboard, when I came to in the coma ward I could see it all happen. I knew.

I watched myself drop into the ocean, drifting downward, toward the shark's open mouth.

Mak pressed himself flat to the board. He let go of the Maui Snow and dropped it into the ocean. He reached down and actually caught hold of my hand but then he lost his balance and tumbled past me into the ocean. Mak drifted ahead of me, pushing me out of the way, saving me, as he fell toward the shark's open mouth. But our hands were locked. And I wouldn't let go.

The shark sped up and bit just above Mak's elbow, just below his old wound. It clamped down hard and then swam away, with me still holding Mak's hand, still trailing behind them. The shark dove toward the bottom of the ocean as the muscles in Mak's wounded arm went into a spasm and his blood splurted into the water. And then I saw it. The Maui Snow.

It floated past me, glinting strangely, as it drifted through Mak's blood. I don't know why but I let go of Mak's hand then and reached out for it. I came close. Really close, nearly bending my fingers closed around the rare gem. But a small rush of water brushed against my palm and somehow the diamond drifted out of reach. The Maui Snow floated downward.

I watched myself go in the opposite direction. Like a balloon cut from its string I bounced to the surface. Then I saw myself flailing. Fighting for oxygen. Going under and coming back up, under and up, under and up, working hard but knowing that the last up was on its way. Without warning I was plucked from the ocean. Two young men floating by on an orange Volkswagen Bug found me and pulled me up onto the roof.

We drifted for a while under the calm blue sky and then the second wave surged in.

Somehow we stayed afloat as it sped forward. We flowed back across the cliffs. Past the forest and the cars. Flowing all the way into town. Eventually we landed on top of a shoe store where the car smashed in tight between some pipes and an open door on the roof. When the water sped back out into the ocean, the Volkswagen stayed put. We hung on for dear life and that's when I hit my head. Banged it hard on one of the pipes and haven't spoken a word since. Medically induced coma the doctors called it. They told Kai that giving my swollen brain a ten-day break was the only thing they could do to save me.

That was three weeks ago. The coma was no longer medically induced. The doctors had begun avoiding Kai's eyes, and his daily questions. They had no explanation for why I hadn't come around.

I could see what happened to the others during the tsunami too. I watched Kai and Liat climb to safety after the first wave receded. I watched January float behind a rock in Lucy's right cheek and get stuck there. I saw her hand bounce, her fingers twitch in the fast streaming water before it landed on top of the rock and stopped. I wanted to stay. To hover above that rock a little longer—just to make sure. But a moment later the cave was gone and once again I was deep inside the ocean. Following the Maui Snow, following Mak.

The Maui Snow drifted out of my reach. It floated past Mak and struck the Great White in the eye. The shark balked. The diamond was a momentary distraction. But it was enough. The shark loosened its jaws and released Mak's arm. For a moment it nosed after the shiny object, gulping down gallons of the bloody water circling the gem. Meanwhile Mak shot to the surface. The shark eventually lost interest in the gem and swished its tail, raising its nose toward the surface as it considered circling around Mak for a second attempt. By now though the water was churning with easy prey.

I followed the Maui Snow as it spun through blood and water and drifted for miles through the turbulent currents. Then something else caught my eye and I felt all movement stop. It was the open hole where the two lava pipes had collided and first sprung a leak. The leak was growing, the gap getting bigger with each passing second. I felt a new jolt, a sense of catastrophic danger. So I reached out for help.

Suddenly Mak was with me—by my side in the coma ward—then drifting alongside of me in the ocean. He was pointing at something

331

in the swirling water just above the hole. It was the liberty bell. Slightly imperfect, slightly cracked, and yet fashioned to withstand great pressure.

The small bell tumbled to the ocean floor and was sucked upside down into the hole. It clanged once as the ocean floor fused around the bell's wide outer edges. It was a perfect fit. Once again, the lava pipe was intact and flowing along a relatively harmless route. It would not collapse. It would not cause a deep rift along the floor of the ocean. A tsunami much worse than the one that had just occurred, a wave that would have literally drowned the islands, had been avoided. Meanwhile the Maui Snow continued to drift within the heavy currents of the Pacific. As for me, I would never again drift in the ocean and question God.

"You have to go soon," Mak told me. "We both know that if you don't," he warned, pointing to the handsome young doctor who'd just entered the ward, "he won't let you."

I looked at Mak and suddenly felt heavier, tinged with grief. Our comas were different. I should have...could have come out of mine a week ago. Mak's was more long term...if not permanent. The thing is most of his doctors, his surgeons, didn't know why. Yes, he had lost a lot of blood when they found him. And yes, his organs had begun shutting down. But the surgeons did a good job of patching him up at the hospital. Everything was up and running–lungs, heart, kidneys, liver, even his brain. They didn't know why he was in a coma. Severe blood loss and shock...those were the only reasons the doctors at the hospital had been able to offer. So he'd been moved to the coma ward. Where things were not as they appeared. Not in Kai's dimension, or in mine.

"I won't be able to help you. I won't be able to keep you safe from him," I nodded at the handsome doctor. "If I go back I don't think I'll remember."

Mak smiled at me, his gray eyes full of light. "It's okay Willow. I have a purpose here."

"I'll miss you."

"I'll be right here," he grinned. Don't worry so much Willow." Mak could see things too. He knew exactly where I put that ticket to

Philadelphia and what I did during those four lost days. He knew about the pink suede pouch and what hard awful secret was tied up inside of it. He knew all about the flashbacks. He knew all about Iraq and the terrible voice that had followed me home. Mak could see the impact of war on the human soul. The effect it has, long after, on even the strongest of human beings. Mak understood about the ripples. How one act of violence…or kindness…moves forward in the world.

"You're free Willow. You bent way too far but you didn't break. The choice for the future is yours."

"Go." Mak nudged me toward my body in the hospital bed. "I have important things to do here." Mak moved away from me then, lighting himself between a young pregnant woman and an old timer from the coma ward.

I opened my eyes. My head hurt. My eyes hurt worse. I closed them again and reached across to touch Kai on the arm. I felt him move and forced my lids open again. I didn't want to miss the look on Kai's face. It was worth the pain. He yelled for the nurse. I was surprised at how far away his voice sounded. Then he picked up my hand and squeezed it in his own.

"Hey," he said softly. "Aloha."

***

Three days later they let me leave the hospital. Liat helped me get dressed while Kai took my things to the car. I stopped by Makani's bed on the way out to say good-bye. It was hard. Really hard. Makani was so full of life. Seeing him motionless, without the ocean at his back, well it just didn't feel right.

I kissed his forehead and turned away. In the next bed lay a woman in her late thirties. Sitting in a chair next to her was a pretty brunette of about nineteen or twenty. Something about them seemed so familiar. Images, sounds of them, floated in my head like fireflies. When they lit up I tried hard to catch hold of them but they wouldn't stay put. The doctor told me to expect that. That I would have moments of confusion but eventually they would lift and I would see more clearly. Funny thing is it felt like the opposite. Like I knew things coming out of the coma. Big things. Stuff about Liat and the way she could look straight through a person. Stuff about those four lost days. Only it felt like the fog was rolling in now—not out.

"What's his name?" It was the young brunette. She stood up and came toward us. I took a moment and studied her face.

"Makani," I finally answered, a smile on my lips. "It means wind." I motioned for her to come closer. When she came to the side of the bed I lifted Makani's hand and placed it in hers.

"Makani meet Zoey." Her eyes widened when I called her by name. I was almost as surprised as she was.

"Do I know you?"

"Not exactly," I replied. "But I think Mak is good friends with your mother."

Unsure what to make of that, she glanced down at Mak. In the end, I think the idea comforted her somehow and she gave his hand a gentle squeeze.

I smiled and headed for the door, absently giving a wide berth to the young doctor, who was reading the chart of a patient just across the aisle. A chill went up my spine as we passed by and I found myself walking a little bit faster. Something about the man bothered me.

Liat must have felt it too. Only she didn't move faster, she stopped. She turned around to face the doctor and stared. Waiting. When he looked up the two of them locked gazes. The doctor's eyes grew wide and he immediately took two steps back. His hands were trembling. Then he stopped dead in his tracks. Liat raised a hand of her own and I could swear she was about to touch his face. But then his chart dropped. It fell out of his hands and hit the floor with a clang. Liat blinked. The doctor stepped back fast and bent down to pick it up. The moment was over.

I don't know why, but I glanced back at Makani. Zoey was still by his side. Seeing them together made me feel better.

Liat came up next to me and I could feel the heat emanating from her body. I was about to ask her about it but Liat had her own questions.

"That's her isn't?" Liat asked, as she took my arm and led me out of the hospital.

"Who?"

"I told Mak there was someone else out there for him. Someone he needed to be with more than me." Liat sounded wistful but resigned. "That's her isn't?"

"Hey you're the one that's got the whole voodoo-vibe-thingy going on," I suggested. You tell me." I hadn't shared with Liat, or anyone else for that matter, the sort of mind-boggling experiences that occurred during my coma. One tweaked critter in the group was enough for now and I was more than happy to let it be Liat.

"That's her." Liat affirmed, giving my hand a squeeze as we headed for the car. "I get the feeling that with her around Mak will eventually wake up. He'll come out of this. Just wait and see."

There was a new air of confidence about Liat. I liked it. It felt almost…contagious. I thought it was because she had no more worries. Her sculptures, her work, had all come to fruition. It was over. Turns out I was wrong about that. In fact Liat was just getting started. The confidence I sensed was because Liat no longer feared the future. Apparently Liat had been busy while I was in the coma.

"Ewwww, what's that?" I asked, dropping Liat's hand. It was sticky, sandy.

"Art materials!" I blurted. Then, just like that, I had a flash. A memory from the coma of something I'd seen Liat working on. One sudden and perfect image etched into my head of…a cruise ship? It lasted for about five seconds and then slipped into oblivion. So, a cruise ship.

"Your work," I asked, suddenly very curious. "Canvas or sculpture?"

Liat didn't answer. She just flashed me one of her enigmatic smiles and opened up the passenger door of the car for me.

A few days later I returned to Angela's house on Maui. Something about the place had settled in on me. Maybe it was the tree house. Maybe it was just a good place to write. After talking to Kai, I spoke to Bill's relatives in Philadelphia and made arrangements to rent it. For the most part it was undamaged by the tsunami. The wave had surged in as far as the mango trees in the orchard but the force of the water had been greatly diminished by the cliffs before reaching Angela's house. Others in Honolua Bay and along the coastal areas of the islands that were hit were not as fortunate. The death toll from the tsunami was over a thousand and still rising. Nearly a month had passed by then but there was still a lot of work to be done in the community. Despite Kai's protests that I should rest, I was more than ready to join the effort. Hawaii felt like home to me now. I wanted to take good care of it.

In all the turmoil after the tsunami, Kai's friend at the police lab forgot to pull Jan's DNA sample. The test went through. It was a perfect match to the DNA they extracted from Melanie's fingernails. They searched her father's mansion. Apparently the liberty bell wasn't the only thing Jan brought back from Philly. Hanging in her closet was a denim jacket. Smudged along the edge of that jacket on the lower right hand side was a dried clump of blood along with several strands of fiber from Angela's shirt. Most of the blood was Angela's too. But further up, stuck to the right sleeve of the jacket, was a tiny piece of skin from Bill's forehead. Not that it mattered. January was dead. Kai's friend at the lab was kind enough to call the Philly detectives to explain. He even sent them a copy of the report.

One week after I left the hospital, we joined Kai's family on the Big Island to celebrate Christmas. It was mid January by now but no one cared. It was a great Christmas. Nick and Liat came. Solomon Frost and his brother came too. They were living with an Aunt now, and doing their best to cope. But I knew Kai. He was in their lives now. He would watch over them for a lifetime.

Most of my own family flew in for the celebration too. Even Harry. Everyone I loved was in that house. It was one of those rare celebrations where strangers become fast friends. The night was full of genuine warmth and laughter. It was the kind of Christmas that settles over you and sticks to your skin. I was grateful. It was one more protective layer against life's demons.

After the meal Kai and I slipped out the back for a long walk. We ended up on a hill facing the cliffs and the ocean. Kai dropped his jacket on the ground and we snuggled together to take in the view. Off to the North, Kilauea spewed orange sparks into the night while the ocean answered Pele's fire with endless patient waves. Kai held me close filling me with waves of his own. Afterwards, tucked in his arms I stared out up at the massive black sky all lit with stars. My eyes welled up at the sight. In my watery vision the stars swelled and swayed and raced through the sky like tiny snowflakes. Maui Snow.

***

FIVE MONTHS LATER
St. Martha's Church and grade school in Philadelphia, PA

Two fifth grade girls snuck gingerly out of the confession line at St. Martha's and made their way downstairs to the cafeteria.

"We're gonna get in trouble Frannie. Let's go back." Lizzie tugged on the rolled up sleeve of Frannie's school uniform but it did her no good.

"No way," the slight girl with the blonde pixie haircut answered.

"Sister Mary Katherine is lying on her stack of bibles and I am gonna prove it. She promised us ice cream if we helped her weed the garden. We stayed after school. We weeded. Every day this week I asked her about the ice cream. She keeps telling me they haven't gotten their shipment in yet. But I saw her, Lizzie. I saw her slip into the teacher's lounge this morning and she was eating ice cream. I went and peaked through the window to be sure and there she was, sitting in the air-conditioning, all by herself, licking the sides of an ice-cream sandwich. It wasn't even ten o'clock! I mean come on Lizzie—it's like eight hundred degrees out here. Where's our ice cream? Sister Mary Katherine lied to us. She's got a stash of ice cream hidden away and I'm gonna prove it."

Frannie grabbed her timid friend's hand and together they worked their way to the back of the cafeteria, then through the double doors, and down another dank smelling flight of steps.

"The kitchen's that way," Lizzie whispered. "Frannie? Where are you going?" Her stomach was doing flip-flops. Confession would be over in nine minutes and they would get caught if they weren't back in Science class the same time as everybody else. Frannie was her best friend but she was always getting the two of them into trouble. That. Plus Sister Mary Katherine was scary on a good day. Lizzie had no desire to provoke that particular beast.

"It's a shortcut to the annex. Billy Mateo showed it to me last year. They used to teach classes for the slow kids down here but nobody uses it anymore. There's just a bunch of old desks and blackboards and erasers down here now."

337

"So what are we doing here?"

"There's a freezer all the way in the back. I know because it makes an awful noise and I nearly jumped out of my skin when I heard it. Billy got a good laugh outta that."

"So?!"

"So I'm bettin' that's where Sister Mary Liar Liar Pants on Fire is hiding the ice-cream sandwiches that she says never came in. Look. There it is. Just like I told you."

The two girls crossed to the back of the annex and pulled open the freezer. There were no ice-cream sandwiches inside. Just old freezer pops and the body of Cathy Tanglewood. There she was, the pretty new wife of Willow's ex-husband, Shane Galveston, tucked inside and looking cool as well...cool as a freezer pop. She'd been missing for over five months and three days now.

Cathy was still wearing that lovely pink coat over her frozen baby bump. But there were a couple of things missing from her trendy ensemble, like most of the blood leading from her carotid artery. Oh, and the third finger on her left hand. You know, the finger that Cathy had used to flash that shiny pink heart-shaped diamond ring at...pretty much everybody. Yep, all gone. Still, Cathy did manage to hold onto *something*. Neatly tucked into the other fingers of Cathy's frozen hand, was a white bakery bag. With one cherry Hamentashen left inside.

"Holy shit," cried Frannie reaching past the freezer pops to poke the corpse.

Lizzie let out a blood-curdling scream. Rather impressive considering her timid nature. In fact she screamed all the way up the steps, through the cafeteria, up the next flight of steps, and into the back of the church. She ran screaming all the way up to the pew where Sister Mary Katherine was sitting, rosary beads in hand, and fainted at the nun's abundant knees.

YARDLEY, PENNSYLVANIA

In a trendy suburb of Philadelphia, Shane Galveston's mother, Harmony, picked up the remote and aimed it at CNN's Anderson Cooper, who was busy relaying the details of her daughter-in-law's tragic circumstance to the world. Over the journalist's right shoulder was a glossy picture of her son, Shane, after a swimming contest in Lake Placid. Harmony hit the mute button. She preferred the scenery over the sound and after a suitable snuffle (Shane *was* in the next room) she moved the pillow next to her on the sofa and drew a slightly frozen lemon hamentashen out of the plastic bag that was hidden behind it. Harmony downed the cookie in two large bites and with a satisfied smile crumpled the unnecessary bag.

NORTH SHORE, OAHU

Perched in the sand with a cup of coffee I watched Kai throw his board into the ocean and pick through the massive waves at Pipe just for fun. It was a glorious morning. Warm. Breezy. I settled back, lifting a copy of the *Philly Chronicle* up off my growing belly and absently twisted the pink heart-shaped diamond on my finger as I set the newspaper down in the sand next to me.

Ignoring the headlines about Shane and Cathy, I breathed in a sweet drift of air and concentrated instead on the baby's arrival. Just three and a half months from now. A brand new life, maybe with Kai's eyes. With Kai's beautiful heart. Those headlines, well, they were part of the past. A past *most* of which I had come to terms with here in Hawaii.

Since coming out of the coma, my time in that other dimension with Mak had grown fuzzy. I could no longer remember every day every *minuscule* detail about my past. What I had been left with though were a few certainties. Some about myself. Some about the human race in general.

I killed a boy. I could not take that back. Could not change the decisions I'd made that had brought me to those circumstances. Now, sitting in the sand, rubbing my belly, twisting my ring, I no longer questioned or feared what I was capable of. Or what I believed in. In the end, if pressed, would I defend the child growing inside of me against an oncoming attacker? Absolutely. As human beings though we need to question how far we dare go in that pursuit. For instance could I torture a captured human being? One that has been rendered completely defenseless? No. *Well, of course not, Willygirl.* No. The lines of humanity must be drawn. Otherwise humanity itself disintegrates... one decision at a time.

But I had discovered something else, something much more hopeful. A staunch belief that in time the human race will evolve beyond all acts of war. How? With one human being...one decision at a time. The good news is most people want peace. They know that societies that rely on war and torture eventually implode because war is force—not power. I was confident now that my anger and my own issues were part of the past and I felt hopeful that I could be a part of the solution. Part of that future.

I watched as Kai stepped from the ocean, surfboard under his arm, sun shining across his wet skin as he walked toward us. I felt the baby kick and a momentary wave of satisfaction washed over me. Happy, I lifted the cup of freshly brewed coffee to my lips and swallowed the last of it. But as I set it down on top of the *Philly Chronicle*, streaks of brown liquid dribbled down the side of the cup and over my knuckles. Some of it seeped deep into the crevices of my striking new wedding band (made of gold and sand and that lovely pink heart-shaped diamond that I felt compelled to have set at its center) then the rest of it spilled down onto the newspaper. Without thinking, I brushed the coffee off the headline, and for a second, couldn't stop myself from sneaking a peek: **Triathlon champ's wife found in freezer full of ice pops.** Not to worry though because I shut my eyes fast against it. Carefully blocking out all of those gory details in the news article...you know, with its school children and its missing ring finger. Then, with a healthy sigh, I turned the paper over and laid that story in the sand.

Hmmmmmmmmmmmmmmm

Aloha

ACKNOWLEDGMENTS

This is my first novel and getting it out of my head and into an actual book has been an interesting process that was sometimes fun and sometimes frustrating. Either way I never would have crossed the finish line without the patience and support of my family and friends. So thanks a bunch to my husband and sons, Pepsi, Danny, Chris and Tommy, and also to my mom and to my sisters, brothers and spouses, SallyMikeJohnnyMaryLeenieDonAnnieReidJoeyand Eileen. I especially want to thank my first readers, Michelle Farrell, Sally Conchewski, Mary Kay Behar, John Farrell, and Ann Leaness. I can't thank you enough for your honesty, your insights, and your suggestions. With each edit of the manuscript you helped me to produce a cleaner better story. I'd also like to thank the editing team at iUniverse, and especially Kathi Wittkamper for breaking down into a convenient, usable list, all the important details that contribute to a good story. Thanks also to Rachel Moore for helping me navigate the strange and wondrous world of publishing.

Hawaii is a magical place. But the spectacular landscape pales in comparison to its people. It is their warmth, their spirit of generosity that is Hawaii's real treasure. I hope they won't mind that in the interest of fiction I squished the men's and women's surfing competitions side by side to move the story along. When it comes to surfing I'm new at it and not very good yet, but I am an enthusiastic fan. I just hope that any surfers who read the novel will take it as it was intended—one novice's glimpse into a fascinating world.

I also want to acknowledge that the reference to the sled race between Pele and Poliahu came from Pele and the Snow Goddess by W.D.Westervelt, Paradise of the Pacific, January 1910. Also, there is a real scientific theory about how black diamonds are formed, although none have ever been found in Hawaii. The research actually did come from a study in the Astrophysical Journal in 2006 by Jozsef Garai and Stephen Haggerty, along with researchers Sandeep Rekhi and Mark Chance.

Breinigsville, PA USA
24 November 2010
249958BV00001B/9/P